P9-DEL-730

*You are cordially invited to attend
the most anticipated holiday party of the year!
Will very pregnant Julie Harrison give birth?
Will everybody's favorite marrieds,
Steve and Rebecca Wilson, reconcile?
Will most eligible CEO Lucas Harding
bring his secretary, Sarah Lewis, as his date?
Please join your Grand Springs neighbors and
friends for wine, food and conversation...
and perhaps some festive sparks will fly!
Where? Randolph's Restaurant
When? Monday, December 18
R.S.V.P.—to experience the Christmas season
that will change everything!*

Dear Reader,

Welcome to Grand Springs, Colorado! In this exciting anthology, featuring three brand-new stories by three beloved authors, you'll be an eyewitness to the dramatic night that changed everything for the folks of this quiet little town.

Just days before Christmas, a festive holiday party turns to turmoil when a storm hits, bringing the men and women of Grand Springs closer together. In the first story of the collection, Mary Lynn Baxter tells the tale of a pregnant beauty who rushes out into the stormy night and goes into labor, only to be rescued by the cowboy who has always loved her from afar. Next up, Marilyn Pappano reunites a doctor with his estranged wife—and shows that love can conquer all when put to the test. The collection wraps up with a story by Christine Flynn featuring a boss who offers a very convenient proposal to his pregnant-and-single secretary—and discovers a passion for his new wife he never bargained for!

And just in case you aren't ready to leave Grand Springs just yet, join us for more stories as 36 HOURS continues next month in Silhouette Intimate Moments with *A Very...Pregnant New Year's* by Doreen Roberts, followed in January 2001 by *My Secret Valentine* by Marilyn Pappano.

Happy reading!
The Editors at Silhouette Books

# MARY LYNN BAXTER
## MARILYN PAPPANO
### CHRISTINE FLYNN

**36**
HOURS

# THE CHRISTMAS
## THAT CHANGED
## EVERYTHING

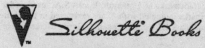

Published by Silhouette Books
**America's Publisher of Contemporary Romance**

If you purchased this book without a cover you should be aware
that this book is stolen property. It was reported as "unsold and
destroyed" to the publisher, and neither the author nor the
publisher has received any payment for this "stripped book."

Special thanks and acknowledgment are given to
Mary Lynn Baxter, Marilyn Pappano
and Christine Flynn for their contributions to
36 Hours: The Christmas That Changed Everything.

SILHOUETTE BOOKS

36 HOURS: THE CHRISTMAS THAT CHANGED EVERYTHING

Copyright © 2000 by Harlequin Books S.A.

ISBN 0-373-48412-7

The publisher acknowledges the copyright holders
of the individual works as follows:

A PREGNANT PAUSE
Copyright © 2000 by Harlequin Books S.A.

HOLIDAY REUNION
Copyright © 2000 by Harlequin Books S.A.

CHRISTMAS BONUS
Copyright © 2000 by Harlequin Books S.A.

All rights reserved. Except for use in any review, the reproduction
or utilization of this work in whole or in part in any form by any
electronic, mechanical or other means, now known or hereafter
invented, including xerography, photocopying and recording, or in
any information storage or retrieval system, is forbidden without
the written permission of the editorial office, Silhouette Books,
300 East 42nd Street, New York, NY 10017 U.S.A.

All characters in this book have no existence outside the imagination of
the author and have no relation whatsoever to anyone bearing the same
name or names. They are not even distantly inspired by any individual
known or unknown to the author, and all incidents are pure invention.

This edition published by arrangement with Harlequin Books S.A.

® and TM are trademarks of Harlequin Books S.A., used under
license. Trademarks indicated with ® are registered in the United States
Patent and Trademark Office, the Canadian Trade Marks Office and in
other countries.

Visit Silhouette at www.eHarlequin.com

**Printed in U.S.A.**

# CONTENTS

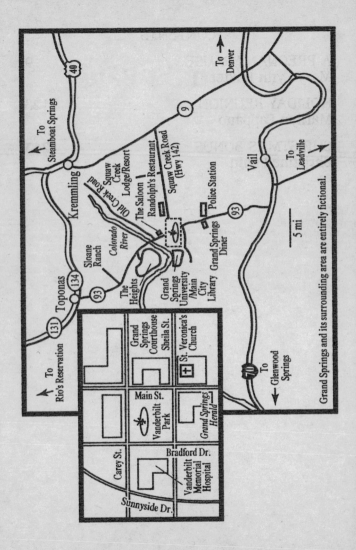

To Denver

To Steamboat Springs

40

To Leadville

9

Kremmling

Squaw Creek
Lodge/Resort

Squaw Creek Road
(Hwy 142)

The Saloon
Randolph's Restaurant

Police Station

Vail

Old Creek Road

Colorado River

93

Grand Springs Diner

Sloane Ranch

134

The Heights

93

Grand Springs
University/Main
City
Library

Toponas

131

To Rio's Reservation

To Glenwood Springs

70

5 mi

Grand Springs and its surrounding area are entirely fictional.

Grand Springs
Courthouse

Sheila St.

St. Veronica's Church

Main St.

Vanderbilt Park

Grand Springs
Herald

Carey St.

Bradford Dr.

Vanderbilt
Memorial
Hospital

Sunnyside Dr.

# A Pregnant Pause
## Mary Lynn Baxter

Dear Reader,

Christmas has always been a special time of the year for my family and me. I was therefore delighted when asked to do a short story with the holiday as a theme.

Because Christmas is often warm in my beloved state of Texas, it was fun to write about a state where the weather was definitely Christmas-like, cold and stormy, with the fireplace roaring.

Also significant to this particular story, *A Pregnant Pause,* is the fact that another baby was once born long ago, which is the real reason for celebrating Christmas.

Writing this story left me with a warm and cozy feeling of shared tears, laughter and love. But most of all, I came away with the promise of a new beginning.

I hope you, as a reader, will experience those same treasured emotions.

*Mary Lynn Baxter*

# *Chapter 1*

The party was a drag.

But then what had he expected? Shane McCoy peered down at his pointed-toed boots in order to hide his annoyance. He hadn't planned to attend this community-wide event; social functions of this nature weren't to his liking, especially on a Monday night before Christmas. But for some reason, he'd let his neighboring rancher cajole him into showing up.

Maybe he'd felt the need to reacquaint himself with Grand Springs and the people in it. He'd been back to his hometown in Colorado over a year now and for the most part, he'd kept to himself.

Or maybe his friend had been able to twist his arm because it was the Christmas season, a time not to be antisocial. More than that, it was a time not to be alone. And he was a loner, which didn't bother him in the least. Shane had learned long ago not to let people's opinions affect him, holding on to the old adage that what anyone else said about him wasn't *his* business.

Shane swallowed a sigh before turning his attention to what was going on around him. People were milling about with drinks in hand, talking and laughing. Some were even dancing as a band was belting out one of the latest pop songs.

He had to admit that as far as parties went, this one sponsored by the Grand Springs Chamber of Commerce held in Randolph's Restaurant, a popular eating place, was well done. A huge tree dominated one corner of the banquet hall that was located in the rear. The fir was decorated with what looked to be a million sparkling ornaments and ablaze with the same number of white lights. In addition, bright red poinsettias were arranged in clusters about the room.

A festive environment. A festive time. So again, why did he feel so disjointed, so out of place? Shane shifted from one foot to the other, wishing he were back at his ranch, in his homey living room, in his skivvies, slouched on his leather sofa, listening to the rain pound on his new metal roof.

Instead, here he was at a community shindig, feeling as irritated as a hornet in need of someone to sting. He downed the last of his beer, then tossed the can in the nearest garbage. His gaze once again perused the room, this time concentrating on the guests.

That was when he realized that he knew very few people in attendance; all the more reason to thank Jake Williams for the invite then get the hell out of Dodge. Still, Shane didn't move, knowing it wouldn't hurt him to hang around, to mix and mingle for a change.

But he doubted very seriously if he'd mix or mingle. That just wasn't him. Yet it wouldn't be wise to leave either, as the wind and rain had turned on a destructive course.

Swallowing another sigh, Shane refocused his attention on a couple whom he'd met once in his banker's office—Steve Wilson, a local doctor and his wife, Rebecca. They seemed to be arguing, though.

He also recognized another pair whom he'd been introduced to not long ago. Lucas Harding, vice president of a major public relations firm and his secretary, Sarah Lewis, were together at the bar getting drinks.

Close by was Jake Williams, his rancher friend, who was holding court in the midst of several other men. Shane could hear their laughter from where he stood.

The thought crossed his mind to join them when he heard a voice behind him say, "Well, well, I can't believe my eyes."

Shane swung around, cringing inwardly. The last person he wanted to hear or see was Wanda Russell, a woman he'd dated a few times.

"Why is that?" he asked in a neutral tone.

"I never expected you to be at this party."

She gave him a come-hither smile which turned his stomach. What had he ever seen in this woman? Oh, she was pretty enough, endowed with dark hair, dark eyes and a voluptuous figure. But underneath that surface beauty was someone with no ambition and no purpose in life. She was an airhead.

"Life's full of surprises," he said, his tone having turned cool.

"So, how are things going?"

"Can't complain." His tone was guarded.

"Me either," Wanda said, lowering her voice and moving closer. "Except that I miss you."

He knew better than to respond to that. He just wished she'd move on to her next victim and leave him be.

She smiled, showing her perfect white teeth. "Are you here with anyone?"

Shane was tempted to lie, but thought better of it. Hell, he didn't have to justify himself to her or anyone else. "No."

"I'm alone, too."

No way in hell was he going to get stuck with her. "Look, Wanda—"

As if she sensed his mood and where their conversation was heading, she said, "Hey, don't be such an old scrooge. How 'bout dancing with me?"

"I'll pass, but thanks."

Her full lips puckered and her voice turned whiny. "Aw, come on. It'll do you good."

He gave her a borderline smile. "I don't think so, but thanks again."

Her eyes narrowed in anger. "You can be a real jerk when you want to, Shane McCoy."

With that she whirled around and walked off. Shane instantly breathed a sigh of relief. After he'd stopped calling her, she started calling him. Before he'd gotten the message across to her that he wasn't interested in any type of relationship, things had turned rather nasty. Hence, he was surprised she'd even approached him.

Deciding he'd remained antisocial long enough, Shane pushed away from the wall and was about to make his way over to Jake when he pulled up short, both mentally and physically.

He blinked, then blinked again. Nah, it wasn't her. Even so, he couldn't look away. That was when he realized he hadn't made a mistake. It was her—Julie Harrison, a longtime friend. The bottom dropped out of his stomach when he noticed something else: she was pregnant.

It had been several years since their paths had crossed. He recalled that it was after Julie had married. He had run into her at a restaurant.

During that brief encounter, Julie had been her warm, cordial self, but the shadows in those exquisite dark blue eyes hadn't escaped him.

But then nothing about Julie had ever escaped him. He'd been in love with her all his life, or so it seemed. However, that was a secret he'd never shared with anyone, certainly not her.

They had grown up together as neighbors in Grand Springs. And because he was only two years older than she was, they had run in the same crowd at school and moved in the same social circles outside of school as well.

He'd had every intention of turning their friendship into something more when she started going out with his best friend. Much to Shane's chagrin, that relationship had endured until Julie left for college, where she met her husband.

Thinking of her husband forced Shane's thoughts

back to the present, back to Julie who was talking to a woman who appeared to be a close friend.

Shane's eyes greedily soaked up how lovely Julie looked, lovelier than ever now that she was pregnant. If only things had turned out differently, that would be his child growing inside her. If only he'd said something to her that night he'd kissed her...

"Damn," he muttered, refusing to dwell on the past and what might have been. Anyhow, it was too late for them. He'd had a full life, despite the loneliness that dogged him at times.

And it wasn't as though he were alone in the world. He wasn't. He had his mother and sister who lived in Denver. When the loneliness became unbearable, he either went to see them or invited them for a visit, especially his sister whose husband and twin boys loved to come to the ranch. It was just the season making him out of sorts.

As for Julie—well, she was probably in the best of holiday spirits. After all, she had a baby on the way to love and care for. And a husband lurking in the wings, Shane reminded himself harshly.

Still, he found himself unable to take his eyes off her. He muttered another curse and leaned back against the wall.

"Are we having a good time yet?"

Julie cut her friend, Millicent Everette, a scolding look. "Not yet, but then I haven't been here long enough."

Millie grinned, relaxing her pixielike features. "I know. What I can't believe is that you actually came."

"Why?" Julie asked in an innocent tone.

"This weather, for starters."

"I caught myself in a weak moment." Julie shuddered as she glanced out a window. "Can you believe all this rain? And it's getting colder, too."

Millie gave her a brief hug. "It's the pits, but I'm glad you braved the elements. It'll be worth it."

Julie shoved a strand of her straight, shoulder-length blond hair behind her ear and sighed. "Well, I have to admit I almost chickened out, but for more reasons than the weather."

"Don't go there," Mill said, giving Julie a stern look. "'Tis the season to be jolly, remember? Unhappy thoughts are taboo."

Julie smiled, though it never quite reached her eyes. "Whatever you say."

Millie was her best friend who had stood by her through the tough times as well as the good ones. Friends were priceless to Julie who'd been an only child of parents who were now deceased. She and Millie had taught school together for years and spent a lot of time with each other, especially as Millie had never married.

"Give me a smile," Millie demanded. "You, me and the baby are going to have fun."

Suddenly a loud clap of thunder rocked the room and for a moment, the lights flickered. Julie held her breath, thinking again she had just gotten there in the nick of time. The storm had come to a heaving downpour right before she'd gotten in her car. However, while she'd driven to the party, the rain had slacked off.

Now, the sky seemed to have erupted again.

"I wish this mess would stop," Millie was saying in a disgusted tone.

Julie frowned. "Me, too. I'm afraid we're going to flood if something doesn't give."

"Oh, Lordy, don't say that." Millie shivered. "This town's already been through hell thanks to Mother Nature."

They were both quiet for a moment, then Millie added, "Do you know that man over there?"

"What man?"

Millie angled her head. "The one in the corner. He's been staring at you for the longest time."

"How do you know?"

"I've been watching him out of the corner of my eye."

"Where is he?" Julie asked, figuring Millie's imagination was doing a number on her.

"Behind you, to your right. He's off to himself."

Julie eased around, not wanting to be too obvious but curious, nonetheless. At first, she didn't see any man alone. The ones she noticed were with other woman or other men. But then, he moved out of the shadows.

For some reason, she caught her breath and held it, especially as Millie was right. He was staring directly at her.

Millie nudged her. "So who is he?"

Julie didn't respond. She was too busy returning his intense stare.

"I can tell by the look on your face that you know him."

"That I do," Julie said without removing her gaze.

''Well, tell me. Don't keep me in suspense, especially as he's making a beeline toward you.''

''It's Shane McCoy, an old friend.''

''As in boyfriend, I'll bet.''

''No,'' Julie admitted. ''But he should've been.''

*Chapter 2*

"Well, all I can say is that your *old* friend is one fine-looking dude."

Julie couldn't argue with that as she watched Shane make his way toward her, a smile on his face. Had he always been that good-looking, that ruggedly virile? She didn't think so. But then someone who was now thirty-one, two years her senior, had to have changed over the years. Shane just happened to have been among the lucky, having age on his side.

Surely he was married. Someone with his assets couldn't have escaped the bonds of matrimony. Now why on earth had that thought popped to mind? Mortified, Julie wanted to turn away, but she couldn't. Something about that smile of his held her captive while another absurd thought hit her.

Just why hadn't she gone after *him* instead of his

best friend? That uninvited thought sent heat flooding to her cheeks.

"Should I get lost?" Millie asked, a knowing smile suddenly quirking her lips.

"Yeah, why don't you," Julie said, surprising herself.

"Well, some friend you are." Millie's tone was playfully huffed.

Julie ignored her. "See you later."

"Yeah, right," Millie countered drolly.

Julie merely smiled, a smile that remained on her face when she met Shane in the middle of the room and peered up into his light blue eyes. Good grief. Up close, he was even better looking.

His skin was tanned and leathered from the sun, adding to his rugged maturity. His hair hadn't changed much. It remained a light brown, though with more blond highlights than she remembered. It curled slightly at his collar, which for some crazy reason was a turn-on to her.

God, what was she thinking? Suddenly Julie felt her smile freeze on her lips.

"Long time no see," Shane finally said, after their eyes met and held for another long moment.

"It has been a while." Julie heard the breathless note in her voice and felt even more mortified.

"Don't I get a hug for old times' sake?"

"Sure."

Before she could make a move on her own, Shane placed an arm around her shoulders and pulled her close against his hard, muscled side, then let her go.

"You look great," he said, his eyes delving back

into hers, then seeming to wander over her body, lingering just slightly on her swelled breasts.

Julie flushed, then placed a hand on her protruding stomach. "You don't have to be nice, you know."

Some of the wattage went out of his smile. "Hey, I'm serious. You do look great."

Julie's mouth took a downward turn. "Well, thanks. I'll keep that in mind the next time I look in the mirror."

"You do that."

"So what's going on with you?" Julie asked, suddenly eager to know all there was to know about her old friend and neighbor. She certainly hoped his life had fared much better than hers.

Her gaze slipped unobtrusively to his ring finger and she saw that it was empty. She didn't know whether to be happy for him or sorry.

"Do you have a minute to chat?" he asked, giving her a thoughtful look.

"I have lots of minutes, actually." She figured he was probably wondering where her husband was. Thank goodness he hadn't asked. At least not yet.

Shane looked around, and her eyes followed his. The room had grown even more crowded, absolutely teeming with people. To add to the confusion, the music had grown louder, making rational conversation almost impossible.

"Let's get out of this madhouse. I don't know about you, but this racket's about to drive me nuts."

"Me, too."

"Come on, let's head for that deserted corner on the far side of the room."

Julie felt his hand gently touch her in the middle

of the back, nudging her in the right direction. Moments later they were seated, facing each other.

"I have to say this is much better." Julie shifted, trying to get comfortable in the metal chair.

"You okay?"

"I'm fine now. At this stage in the game, I have to find a position that suits both Elizabeth and me."

A confused look darkened his features for a second, then as if a lightbulb switched on inside his head, he grinned. "Ah, so it's a she, and her name is Elizabeth. I like that."

"Thanks." Again, Julie's hand went to her stomach. In that moment, the baby decided to kick her. Her tummy quivered.

This time Shane's eyes widened. "Well, I'll be damned."

"You noticed?"

"I noticed," he said in an awed tone.

"You don't have any children, do you?"

His features sobered. "No."

Following that succinct admission, an awkward silence fell between them. Then he stood. "How 'bout I get us something to drink?"

"I'll have some hot tea."

He grinned. "Hot tea coming up."

Julie watched him as he turned and ambled off, wondering what or who had put those shadows in his eyes.

Instead of one beer, he needed two in each hand. Damn, but his insides were scrambled. Only Julie could do that to him. Still, he wasn't about to give up the chance to be with her even if it was just for a short time.

It seemed like forever since the good old days when they were young and carefree with no concerns or worries except who was going to date whom and who was going to win the football game.

Would he go back? Hell, yes, but he'd do things differently. He wouldn't let his best friend get the one upmanship on him again. He would've shown more aggressiveness and asked her out himself.

Aw, to hell with that kind of thinking, McCoy, he told himself. Thoughts like that would only add to his discontentment and misery. Besides, the past was a done deal, and he couldn't change it. All he could do was enjoy her company, then hightail it back to the ranch where he belonged.

What about her? Why was she alone? *Where was her husband?*

That last question nagged at him while he got their drinks, and it was still nagging when he made his way back to her. She wasn't looking his way which gave him a chance to study her again.

God, she was lovely, though not in a flamboyant kind of way. Hers was a soft, gentle beauty that seemed to come from within. However, she could hold her own in a crowd of women, no doubt about that.

If nothing else, her dark blue eyes, surrounded by dark, thick lashes, were a magnet that pulled him toward her. And her blond hair that used to be short was now straight and shoulder-length and resembled the finest of silk.

He hoped Elizabeth looked just like her.

A deep sigh escaped him as he eased down into the chair next to her. She smiled her thanks, immediately taking a sip from the cup.

"Mmm, this hits the spot," she said.

"I'm glad." He took a swig of his beer then looked back at her.

But before he could ask all the questions that wanted to fly from his lips, she said, "So tell me what's going on with you. Are you living here now or just visiting?"

"I bought a ranch outside of town about a year ago and moved back." He shrugged. "So I guess you could say I'm a working cattle rancher. Along with my trusted foreman, of course."

She gave him a teasing smile. "Of course. But I bet you could run it just fine all by your lonesome."

He shrugged again. "Maybe."

"How's your mom and sister? It seems like forever since I've seen them."

"They're great, though I don't see them as much as I'd like. Mom moved to Denver to be near her grandchildren. My sister has twin boys."

"Oh, what fun."

His brows lifted in unison.

"On second thought, two at once would be mind-boggling."

"You got that right. Those two have nearly driven Kathy nuts. I don't know what she would've done had Mom not been close."

"Next time she comes, let me know. I'd love to see her."

"She would you, too, I know. She always considered you one of hers."

Julie turned pensive, and the shadows deepened in her eyes. He wished he knew the reason for them. No, he didn't. It would just upset him more because there wouldn't be anything he could do about it.

"Those were the good old days," she finally said.

"Yeah, they were."

"Do you remember the time we all got together and smoked those packs of cigarettes?"

A twinkle narrowed his eyes. "Boy, do I, especially you. You turned green as a gourd and puked your guts up."

"Okay, you don't have to rub it in."

"I bet you never smoked again, right?"

Julie rolled her eyes. "Never. Just the thought of it turns my stomach. But if I recall, you didn't fare much better."

"At least I didn't lose my cookies."

"Let's change the subject, shall we?" Her tone sounded prim even to her own ears.

He chuckled. "How 'bout the time I saved you from drowning in old man Fortenberry's pool?"

Julie lifted her chin. "You're exaggerating."

"I don't think so. You were floundering in that water, and I dove in in the nick of time and saved you."

Julie made a face. "I hardly think it was that dramatic."

"Damn straight it was. I had to give you mouth to mouth. I'll never forget that."

And he wouldn't. Later, after he'd gotten home and into bed, he'd remembered how soft her lips had felt under his and how much he'd enjoyed sucking the life back into them, back into her. He'd had to take a cold shower afterwards. He'd never forget that. Shortly thereafter was when his friend had made his move. He'd never forget that either, dammit.

Those renegade thoughts sent a shot of color to Shane's face. He covered it by taking a long draw on his beer.

"What I remember most about that incident," Julie said, "is the look on Mr. Fortenberry's face when he came flying out of the house and caught the bunch of us."

"I'll never forget that either," Shane added, "especially as his hair was standing on end."

"What little hair he had, you mean."

Shane laughed. "Thank goodness he didn't find us until after I'd revived you or he would've gone into cardiac arrest."

"Stop saying that," Julie demanded, though without much vigor.

"What? That I revived you?"

"Yes."

"All right," he teased, "but you know it's the truth."

"So, tell me, is there a Mrs. McCoy lurking in the wings?"

He should've expected that question, but somehow it caught him off guard. Maybe it was because he didn't want to return to the present where life was tainted and not nearly as simple as those good old days. But he couldn't ignore the question. "Nope," he admitted.

Julie's eyes widened, and for a moment, he wanted to dive into them and see what was lurking inside that lovely head of hers.

"Have you ever been married?"

"Nope."

She laughed. "Well, it's not too late, you know. You're still young."

"Too young to get married, that's for sure."

They both laughed.

"Speaking of marriage, where's your better half?"

Julie's face lost its animation, and he sensed he'd stepped on an exposed nerve. He cursed silently and waited.

"I'm divorced," she said simply.

"I'm sorry." His tone was gruff in spite of the fact that he tried to temper it. Pregnant and divorced. Now, that was a helluva note.

"Don't be. It's for the best."

He doubted that. However, he let that comment slide, knowing that if she wanted to confide further in him she would. Of course, he didn't expect her to.

Time had rendered them strangers. Too bad. He sensed she needed someone to hold her and assure her everything was going to be all right. But he wasn't that guy. No sir. That would be the equivalent of intentionally playing with a live wire.

"I'm much better off without Mike Harrison in my life."

That added comment stirred his anger. What kind of man would let Julie go? He must be sorry as they come. "Only you know best about that."

When she didn't answer, he went on, "So are you working?"

She visibly brightened at the change of subject. "I teach first grade, but I've already started my leave because I'm nearly full-term."

"That's smart."

She smiled, then said in a teasing voice, "I'm glad you approve."

For some crazy reason, another bout of color surged into his face. Careful, you're starting to play with that live wire again.

Suddenly a commotion at the front of the restaurant drew their attention. Shane turned and watched a couple walk on the stage and stand adjacent to the band. The man was tall while the woman beside him was short and clinging to his arm.

"Oh, my God," Julie whispered.

Shane whipped his head around and noticed that her face was now as pale as a ghost. He frowned. However, before he could voice his concern, the man on the podium spoke.

"Ladies and gentlemen, may I please have your attention."

The room fell silent.

"I'd like for all of you to join us in toasting our engagement."

Shane watched as Julie covered her mouth but not before a gasp escaped.

# Chapter 3

"What's wrong?" Shane demanded, his eyes narrowed to slits. Julie opened her mouth, but nothing came out. She placed her arms around her body and began to tremble.

"Dammit, Julie," Shane said for her ears alone, "talk to me. Is it the baby?"

"It's…him," she whispered in a disjointed voice.

Shane's frown deepened, peering once again at the stage where the couple who had just made the announcement were surrounded by well-wishers, seeming to bask in the glow of attention.

"Who's him?"

"My ex-husband, Mike Harrison."

"Where?"

"He's the one who just made the announcement."

"Son of a bitch," Shane muttered under his breath.

However, Julie heard him. Her answer confirmed that. "You got that right."

Her trembling had worsened, and Shane was growing more concerned by the second. He didn't know anything about women having babies, but it didn't take an Einstein to conclude that stress like Julie was experiencing couldn't be good for either her or the baby. He felt the need to do something. But what?

"Calm down," he urged gently. She looked as though she might faint any minute. He couldn't allow that. He knew her well enough to realize that she would be mortified if he called attention to her.

She didn't argue. He reached for her cup of tea. Even though it was now cold, he urged her to take a sip of it. Watching her quivering mouth and trembling hands, he felt so damn helpless.

"Want to talk about it?"

She handed him the cup. That was when he noticed her trembles had subsided somewhat. But her eyes would continue to haunt him. They were dull, like nothing was alive inside her.

Damn! He'd like to yank that jerk down from the podium and teach him a lesson in manners. But he knew that wasn't going to happen. Too bad.

"I didn't know he was here."

Julie's fragmented voice brought him back to reality with a start. "If you had, I'm assuming you wouldn't have come."

"No way."

"Do you still love him?" He hated asking that. Hadn't planned on it, either. The words just spewed from his lips.

She winced as if he'd visibly struck her. "God, no."

He knew the relief that shot through him was absurd. Whether Julie still loved her husband or not had no bearing on him. After tonight, he wouldn't see her again unless he made the effort to do so. And he wouldn't.

The last thing he needed was a woman in his life, especially one who was about to have a baby. And he had enough sense to know that the last thing she needed was another man.

It was obvious she was still terribly scared from what this bastard had done to her. Yet he wouldn't have walked off and left her if his life depended on it. As long as she needed him, he would stick by her.

"He did that on purpose."

Again, her softly spoken words jarred him out of his thoughts. "So you think he knew you were here?" he asked.

"Oh, yes," she said with bitterness. "Nothing ever gets by him."

Shane stretched his mouth into a thin line. "Why would he deliberately want to hurt you, for God's sake?"

"He's that kind of man."

"But that's his child you're carrying. Doesn't that count for something?"

"Not with him." Her bitterness had multiplied. "The woman he just became engaged to is the one he was having an affair with while married to me."

Shane cursed.

For a second, a shadow of a smile crossed Julie's lips, but it was so fleeting that Shane wasn't sure he hadn't imagined it. Sitting with her hands folded in her lap, she looked so fragile, so wounded that it was all he could do not to grab her and haul her into his arms.

Then what?

He didn't dare even think about answering that loaded question. Besides, he wasn't about to do anything to bring her further humiliation and pain. All he could do was stay with her and listen if she wanted to talk.

"I'm sorry, Julie. I wish there was something else I could say."

"There's nothing else to say."

"Do you want me to take you home?"

Julie didn't say anything for a long minute, her eyes going back to the stage where the couple remained. Suddenly, she stood. "Will you excuse me?"

Shane gave her a troubled look, a bad feeling tightening his gut. "Sure, but—"

He didn't have time to finish the sentence before she turned and took off. He watched her thread her way through the crowd, fighting the urge to follow her.

Hopefully she would seek out her friend with whom she'd been visiting a little earlier. Maybe she could be of more comfort to Julie than he could. For now, his hands were tied, a feeling that didn't sit well with him.

But what choice did he have? Julie was none of his business. And no matter how much he might want to change that, he couldn't. Some things were unchangeable. And their relationship was one of those things. Still...

"McCoy."

For some reason, the sound of Jake Williams's cigar-tainted voice irritated him. Yet he swung around and forced a smile. "Hey, Jake."

"Where's your beer, boy?" Jake shifted his unlighted cigar to the other side of his mouth. "Parties are made for drinking, especially on a night like this one."

"I've had plenty to drink."

"The hell you say." He turned and grabbed a waiter who was passing by. "Bring this man another beer, will you?"

The waiter nodded, then hurried on.

Shane hid his growing irritation with another plastic smile. But Jake wouldn't know the difference. The burly rancher was already three sheets in the wind.

"So are you having a good time?"

"Great," Shane said.

"That's good. That's real good." Jake paused and shoved his hat farther back on his head. "Whatcha doing for Christmas dinner?"

"I'm not sure. Why?"

"Angie wants you to eat with us. Afterward, I thought we might do some dickering over that livestock you're hankering to buy from me."

"I didn't think you were interested in selling." Shane forced his voice to remain calm even though he wanted to shout his excitement. He'd been trying to get his hands on some of Jake's prime beef for a long time without success.

"I wasn't, but things change."

"We'll certainly get together, then."

"For Christmas dinner?"

"I'll have to let you know. I may go to Denver to see my folks."

"Whatever. Meanwhile, find you a pretty filly and get out on that dance floor."

Shane snorted, then smiled. "See ya, Jake."

Once his friend had lumbered off, Shane's eyes immediately scanned the room for some sign of Julie. When he didn't see her anywhere, his uneasiness mounted.

Surely she hadn't done something stupid like leave. Of course she hadn't, not with it still storming. His gaze went to the nearest window where he watched the rain slam against the glass.

He was beginning to get really concerned. If this storm didn't give soon, it was going to be more dangerous than ever when the party was over and everyone tried to return home. He feared some of the bridges might already be impassable.

That helpless feeling washed over him again. He balled his fists more determined than ever to find her. He was worried about her. Again, he knew he had no right, but he couldn't help how he felt. And he damn well wasn't going to apologize for it.

He was heading toward the front when he came face to face with Julie's ex-husband. His fury almost got the better of him. He'd come across some cruel and heartless bastards in his time, but this one topped his list.

Afraid of what he might say or do, he was about to step out of the way when Harrison asked, "Have we met?"

"Nope," Shane said.

"I saw you with my wife."

"Don't you mean ex-wife?" Shane said harshly, holding on to his temper by a mere thread. Like Jake, Mike had had too much to drink. He reeked with the smell of whiskey. What could this creep possibly want with him?

"Yeah, right," Mike said after a second, an oily grin sliding across his lips. "So did she say anything?"

"About what?" Shane asked in disbelief.

"My announcement."

"You don't want to go there," Shane said, his voice as cold as his eyes. "Not with me, anyway."

Mike laughed, then placed a hand on Shane's shoulder. Big mistake.

"Take your hand off me."

Mike laughed again but did as he was told. "Are you sleeping with her?"

"Go to hell," Shane said in a cold, dismissive tone.

Mike's features twisted. "Why, you can't talk to me like that."

Mike had no more slurred those words when he pulled back and took a swing at Shane. Seeing the fist coming, Shane dodged, and the blow missed him.

Shane then grabbed Mike by the tie and jerked his face so close their breaths mingled. "I ought to beat the living stuffings out of you, but I'm not because you're too drunk to appreciate my efforts."

Shane let him go so quickly that Mike hit the floor. "Consider this your lucky day."

He strode off without so much as a backward glance.

# Chapter 4

"Julie, honey, are you all right?"

"I'm...fine," Julie lied, having just thrown up in the toilet. But she wasn't about to let Millie know that. She'd just worry, which would be all for naught.

There was nothing anyone could do to help her feelings except make Mike Harrison disappear from the face of the earth. And that wasn't going to happen.

She turned away from the mirror and looked at her friend whose face was lined with genuine concern.

"You look like the devil," Millie said. "I know that's not very comforting, but—" Her voice trailed off.

"It's okay," Julie said. "It's the truth."

"He's not worth it, you know."

Julie pushed a limp strand of hair out of her eyes.

"Oh, I know that, believe me. Still, why did he have to choose this party to make the announcement?"

"Because he's a bastard and always has been."

"It seems that everyone picked up on that but me. What does that say?"

"That you loved the guy and didn't see his faults until it was too late."

Julie blew out a long breath. "What a nightmare. I felt as though every eye in the room was staring at me with pity."

Millie gestured with her hand. "Who cares? But, I bet if I went out there right now and took a poll, you'd come out the winner, hands down."

"Well, like you said, it really doesn't matter. I guess my condition sent me into a tailspin because I honestly don't care a whit about Mike. He can marry whomever he pleases."

"You're just glad she's got him now instead of you, right?"

"More than you'll ever know."

"Then don't give him and his bubble-brained fiancée another thought. He's the loser here, not you. Just remember that."

"I know. It's just the way he handled it."

"So what about your friend Shane?"

"What about him?"

"Oh, come on, you know what I mean. Are you going to see him again?"

"No, Millie. I'm not in the hunt for male companionship."

"I wish I weren't," she countered, down in the mouth.

Julie couldn't help but smile. "Hey, you'll find someone worthy of you one day."

"I hope it's before I'm too old to give a damn."

Julie gave her a frustrated look. "Think positive. You're a good catch."

"We'll see."

"Thanks for caring," Julie said, changing the subject.

"Of course, I care, silly. When Mike marched his butt onto that stage and opened his big mouth, I wanted to walk up there and clobber him."

"I think Shane did, too."

"Well, he should've."

"Yeah."

"Let's head back to the party, shall we?"

Julie shook her head. "You go on. I still have some major repair work to do. I look like an old hag."

"Are you fishing for a compliment?"

"Get out of here."

Millie grinned. "See you later. And don't worry about what people are thinking. You just take care of yourself and Elizabeth."

Julie nodded, then smiled.

However, the second Millie disappeared so did her smile. No way was she going back to that party. Somehow, she was going home. No matter what Millie said, she couldn't face those people, many of whom were her friends. The Lord only knew what they were thinking after Mike had totally humiliated her.

Thank God, she didn't love him anymore. And thank God, he didn't want any part of their baby.

Still, she didn't want to remain, suddenly feeling exhausted to the bone. What she needed was a soak in the tub before crawling between the sheets.

With that thought uppermost in her mind, Julie left the rest room and wound her way toward the front door, passing only a few people that she knew. After getting her coat, she stepped outside and instantly the raw wind, mixed with a hint of ice, took her breath. But at least the rain had slacked off a bit which was definitely in her favor. Yet she was still wet and chilled to the bone when she made it to her car, got inside and slammed the door. None too soon either as the sky suddenly opened once again.

Shivering, she cranked the car and eased out of the parking lot, realizing the mixture of rain and ice was now coming down in sheets. She put her foot on the brake. Had she lost her mind pitting herself against this weather? Should she reconsider and go back to the restaurant?

No. She couldn't bear that. Even if she had to pull off onto the shoulder of the road, she'd rather do that than face her ex-husband and the bimbette whom he was going to marry. Nor did she want to see any of her friends and their looks of pity.

Suddenly, she thought about Shane, and her heart lurched with guilt. She should have told him she was leaving. He had been there for her, and she hadn't even thanked him, which was just as well, she guessed.

He was probably on the dance floor about now anyway, having a high old time. Dismissing him from her mind and how good it was to see him, Julie took her foot off the brake and inched forward. She had no idea how far she'd gone before she had to stop again, the rain hitting her windshield so hard she couldn't see.

Feeling tears of frustration further impede her vision, Julie groaned. The baby chose that moment to kick her as if she didn't approve of what her mother was doing.

*What was she doing?*

Something totally crazy and totally out of character for her, she told herself. However, it was too late to turn back now, especially when her engine suddenly choked down, then quit.

Great. Now what? Julie tried to see outside her window to get a sense of where she was, how far she'd gotten from the restaurant. Nothing doing. The only thing she could see was a black void.

Meanwhile, she had no choice but to wait. Tears saturated her cheeks while horrible thoughts ran like demons through her mind. What if she'd done something so stupid that she'd endangered her child's life?

"Oh, Elizabeth," she whispered, peering down at her stomach, "I'm so sorry."

Her tummy didn't move. Still, Julie rubbed it, drawing comfort from the life that was growing there.

Deciding she couldn't just sit idle, she decided to open the door and see how high the water was. It sounded like she was sitting in the middle of a raging river. She knew better, deciding her imagination was running away from her.

Still, it wouldn't hurt to check. Carefully, she eased the handle up, then barely cracked the door. Dark, rushing water instantly filled the floorboard.

"Oh, no!" she whimpered, then slammed the door shut.

Panic in the form of a lump in the back of her throat froze her to the spot. She had to get out of there. The high water would soon seep inside on its own. She turned the key. Nothing. The engine was dead.

She was stranded.

That thought hit her like a blow. What if no one missed her? What if she and the baby weren't found until they were...

No! She wouldn't think like that. Someone would find them. They would.

Hugging her stomach, Julie placed her head back against the seat and prayed.

Where the hell was she?

Shane had looked everywhere for her and hadn't found her yet. His agitation was mounting by the second. His altercation with Harrison hadn't helped his mood any. He could easily have bitten a tenpenny nail in two.

What would he say to her when he found her? What if she told him to get lost?

He didn't care. All he cared about was making sure she was okay. The weather had worsened, strengthening his resolve to take her home whether she wanted him to or not. As far as he was concerned, that was nonnegotiable.

Pregnant or not, Julie didn't need to be driving in this mess. Even with his four-wheel drive truck, he would have a difficult time, but he could at least drive.

When he walked to the front of the restaurant where the rest rooms were located, he saw her friend deep in conversation with a man he didn't know. But that didn't matter. He wasn't above interrupting.

"Uh, excuse me," Shane said, tapping the young woman on the shoulder.

She turned around, her face creased into a smile. "Hi, Shane."

He was taken aback and it showed. How did she know his name? Then it dawned on him. Julie. They must have discussed him. Mmm, interesting. Wonder what Julie had said. However, that wasn't important at the moment. His top priority was to find Julie and see for himself that she was all right.

"Sorry, I can't return the honors," he responded with an answering smile.

"No problem. I'm Millie Everette, Julie's best friend. We teach together."

"Nice to meet you." Shane paused, his features sobering. "Have you seen her? In the last few minutes, I mean."

Millie seemed to pick up on his anxious vibes for she frowned, then said, "As a matter of fact, I have."

Relief almost made him weak. "That's good."

"I left her in the rest room." Millie's frown deepened. "But I have to say, she wasn't in great shape."

"I know."

Millie was quiet for a long moment. "Maybe I'd better go see if she's still in there."

"I'd appreciate that."

A few minutes later, Millie returned, shaking her head. "No Julie."

"She wouldn't have left, would she?"

"Of course not. She wouldn't dare go out in this weather, not without telling me."

Shane raised his eyebrows. "I hope you're right."

"If you're talking about Julie, she did leave."

Both Shane and Millie stared at her companion as if he had suddenly sprouted another head.

"Surely you're mistaken," Millie cried.

"Nope," the young man said, his sharp chin even more jutted. "Saw her just walk out the door. I wondered what she was thinking."

"She wasn't, that's the problem," Millie muttered.

"I'm going after her," Shane said. "What kind of car does she drive?"

"A ninety-eight bronze Camry." Millie began ringing her hands, clearly disturbed. "Oh, God, I can't believe she pulled a stunt like this. I know she was upset, but—"

"Don't worry," Shane interrupted in a clipped tone. "I'll find her."

"Oh, thank you," Millie said. "And when you do, please throttle her for me."

Shane almost smiled. "Will do."

The second he walked out into the rain, he stopped and looked around. There was no sign of life anywhere. And checking the make of any vehicle was almost impossible as the rain peppered down.

How could this have happened? If she made it out of the parking lot, she'd be damn lucky. Visibility was zero. He tried not to let fear get the better of him. Just calm down, he told himself, keep a cool head.

Maybe she was still on the premises. Maybe she was stranded in her car. However, his gut instinct told him otherwise. Listening to it, Shane dashed to his truck, jumped in and cranked the engine.

Thank goodness, there was only one main road into this place. If she had stalled, she would still be somewhere on the main drag.

He hadn't been driving long, his windshield wipers going full blast, when he saw the car. Without identifying the range of emotions charging through him, he pulled up behind her, got out, and waded through the high water to her vehicle.

"Julie!" he shouted, beating on the window. "Let me in."

Seconds later, he was sitting beside her.

"I'm so glad to see you," she said in an unsteady tone.

He didn't have to look at her to know that she'd been crying, although the streetlight close by allowed him to see her face.

"I'm sure you are."

"I didn't think or I wouldn't have pulled this stunt."

Shane blew out a long breath. "You had me plenty worried. And Millie, too."

"I'm sorry. I just couldn't stay a second longer."

Shane didn't speak. He thought it better if he kept his mouth shut. Apparently, she had no idea how dangerous the situation was or what could've have happened to her.

"Will you take me home?" she asked, sliding her gaze to him.

"No."

She gave him an incredulous look. "No?"

"Even if I wanted to, I doubt if we could get there."

"What do you suggest, then?" Her voice cracked.

He didn't so much as hesitate. "That I take you to my ranch."

# Chapter 5

"I really should've gone home."

They were inside his house that would soon be cozy and warm. He had tossed more wood on the fireplace which was beginning to hiss and spew.

Shane gave Julie a strong look. "That wasn't possible, and you know it."

Once he'd said those words, Shane winced inwardly. Maybe he'd exaggerated a bit. Maybe he could have gotten her home. What then? After the emotional trauma she'd suffered, he couldn't have left her alone to fend for herself.

So he'd gone with his knee-jerk idea to bring her to the ranch, and he didn't regret it. So far.

Julie nodded wearily. "You're right, of course. But—"

"Hey, it's going to be all right. I'll have you home in no time. You'll see."

Even though he said that with as much confidence as he could muster, Shane had his doubts. The driving conditions there, even in his truck, had been scary as hell, and he lived on much higher ground. They had barely made it. The torrential rain, combined with the rising water, was a lethal twosome.

He'd kept such a tight grip on the steering wheel the whole time they had crept to his place that the bones in his hands were actually sore. But they had made it, and that was what counted. He wondered about all the other people at the party. It wouldn't surprise him if they'd have to spend the night at the restaurant.

As if she could read his thoughts, Julie said, "I hope Millie gets home okay."

"Me, too."

"I should try and call her."

"That's a good idea. I know she's worried, especially after we both tried to find you."

"Oh, Lord, she'll be having a conniption fit."

"As soon as you get warm," Shane said, "feel free to use the phone."

"Do you think it'll stop raining soon?"

Her question was so childlike and filled with such anxiety that his heart wrenched. "I'm sure it will," he lied.

The weather reports had given very little hope of this front moving through anytime soon. But there was no point in telling her. It would just make her worry more which wouldn't be good for her or the baby.

The baby.

Shane couldn't believe he was standing in the middle of his living room with a pregnant woman who was shaking all over. Suddenly, he felt terrible that he hadn't noticed her condition earlier.

"Hey, you're chilled to the bone."

She gave him another anxious look as she rubbed one shoulder, then the other as if trying to ward off the chill. "I hate to be so much trouble."

"Hey, will you stop that. What are friends for? And we've been friends for a long time despite the fact that we lost touch."

She almost smiled. "I know, but—"

"There you go with that 'but' again. Just relax and try to get warm."

She clamped down on her lower lip. "All right. You win for now."

"Good girl. How 'bout I nudge the fire, get it going full blast? Then I'll get you something dry to put on."

"Thanks," Julie muttered, her face white and her eyes appearing much too big for her face.

Shane knew she was terribly uncomfortable with this situation, becoming more so by the second. Hell, he was too. He didn't know the first thing about taking care of a pregnant woman whose baby was due anytime.

His stomach pitched suddenly, like he was on a ship in rough waters. What if... Nah, that wasn't going to happen. She and Elizabeth would remain attached until he could get her home. He just needed to control his imagination and get about the business at hand and everything would be A-okay.

"You're house is nice," she said.

That soft voice jerked him out of his thoughts and

into action, especially when he noticed that her teeth were banging together.

Nerves and fear. Another lethal combination.

"Move closer to the fire. That will help."

Once she did as she was told, Shane peered down at her. "You're not going to faint on me or anything like that, are you?" He forced a teasing note into his voice, trying desperately to put her at ease.

"No, I'm not going to keel over like a damsel in distress."

In spite of the awkwardness of the situation, there was a hint of teasing in her voice as well, though her teeth continued to chatter like a chipmunk's.

"I'll be right back."

Once he'd rummaged through his closet and located his thick robe, he charged back into the living room where he stopped abruptly. She was staring into the now-roaring fire as if mesmerized by it while her hand slowly moved over her stomach.

It was a touching sight, and for a moment, he had to swallow hard to find his voice. Then he still didn't say anything. His mind and body were going haywire. God, but she was lovely. If only—

She chose that moment to look up. Their eyes met and held for a precious minute, then she averted her gaze. But he didn't miss the color that rushed into her cheeks and knew that his staring at her had put it there. Damn, in another second, he would've been really turned on.

Wasn't that a helluva note? He had reached an all time low, lusting after a woman who was defenseless and pregnant.

"This should do the trick," he said, after clearing

his throat. "The bedroom and bath's in there." He nodded to his right.

"I refuse to take your bed."

"It's yours, and that's that."

Julie stood, only to suddenly sway on her feet.

Shane sprang forward just in time to grab her by an arm and steady her. Concern roughened his voice. "Hey, take it easy."

Julie slumped against him, her entire body trembling. He placed an arm around her and held her close. Shock? Had she gone into shock?

He forced himself to remain calm, to evaluate the situation with detachment. "Julie, look at me."

She raised her eyes. Although they appeared dull from fatigue, he saw no signs of shock. Yet she was in no shape to do for herself, which meant he had to take over.

He didn't hesitate. "Come on, young lady, it's bedtime for you."

When he led her into his room, she didn't protest. It was only after he eased her onto the side of the bed and began unbuttoning her blouse that her eyes widened in panic and a whimper erupted.

"It's okay," he assured her with as much composure as he was capable of. "I'm not going to hurt you or do anything you don't want me to."

"Shane—" Her voice broke and tears flooded her eyes.

He couldn't bear to look at her or he just might do something stupid, like haul her into his arms and crush those luscious, quivering lips against his. "Let me take care of you." His voice sounded strangled, and he cleared his throat again. "You can trust me."

She nodded, then sat silently while he removed her clothes, even her bra and panties since they were as wet as her outer clothing.

Once he had helped her into his terry cloth robe, he yanked back the sheet and bedspread. She lay down and once he'd covered her back up, he stood and stared down at her. "I'm going to bring you a cup of hot chocolate."

"Why are you being so good to me?" she asked.

"Why not?"

"I—" Her voice played out.

"Look, you've had a rough night. We both know that. I'm just sorry it happened, but I'm glad I was there to help."

She didn't say anything right off. But when she did, her words took him aback.

"I don't love him anymore."

"That's good."

"But he still has the power to hurt me. Why is that?"

Shane let out a pent-up breath. "I wish the hell I knew."

Julie seemed lost in her thoughts for a moment, then she said, "Thanks again for coming to my rescue. I owe you."

"Nah, you don't. I told you that's what friends are for."

With that, he turned and made his way into the kitchen. Shortly, he walked back into the bedroom with two cups of steaming liquid on a tray only to pull up short. Julie was sound asleep.

He simply looked at her then set the tray down before pulling the leather rocker closer to the bed. He figured she wouldn't appreciate him baby-sitting her, but he didn't care. For some unexplainable reason, he didn't want to leave her. She might need him, and he wanted to be there for her.

He eased his head back against the soft leather and closed his eyes. He was dog-tired, not physically so much as mentally. Still, he couldn't sleep.

Julie haunted him. He couldn't stop his mind from going berserk, from thinking about how she'd looked naked in the lamplight, how soft and creamy her skin had felt against his callused hands.

A deep sigh escaped him. And her breasts. Oh, how he'd wanted to touch their burgeoning fullness, first with his fingers, then with his lips. He groaned silently, shifting in his chair.

And her stomach. He'd wanted to touch it as well, run his hands over that distended flesh. He'd never felt a baby inside a woman's stomach. He'd never even thought about that until Julie had come back into his life. Now, he ached to touch her there, wishing again that he'd been the one who had spilled his seed into her and begun that new life.

Shane's eyes popped open, and he muttered an expletive. He had to keep a tighter rein on himself or he'd never last the night. He bunched his shoulders, then relaxed them, knowing he should get his rear up and go to the spare bedroom.

He didn't move. Instead, he simply stared at her, wondering what he was going to do when she walked out of his life again.

"Oh," Julie moaned.

What was that pinching feeling in the pit of her

stomach? She placed her hand over it, then forced her eyes open, gazing about her. Everything looked strange. She recognized nothing. Then suddenly everything fell into place, and her heart faltered. She was at Shane's ranch, trapped by high water.

That was when she noticed him sitting in the chair beside the bed. His head was back against the cushion, and he was asleep.

What time was it? She pulled her eyes off him and searched the dimly lighted room for a clock. She found one on the wall surrounded by several pictures. Five o'clock. What should she do? Should she wake him? For what?

She could hardly insist that he get in bed with her. Her face turned red at the thought. It was too early to do anything else. What a nightmare. Here she was nine months pregnant, sleeping in Shane's bed on a dark and stormy night.

She might have laughed at her crazy thought that had come straight off the page of a book if the situation hadn't been so serious. But it was serious, especially when she felt another pinch in her lower abdomen.

Julie forced herself to take several deep breaths which helped. The pain didn't come again. Hopefully, she could go back to sleep, then later she would be better equipped mentally to deal with her off-the-wall circumstances.

Bless Shane.

She couldn't believe what a good sport he'd been. Still, she hated that he'd had to be burdened with her. As for his removing her clothes—well, she dared not let herself think about that. Nor would she let herself dwell on how her ex-husband had humiliated her at the party.

Without warning another pain struck her belly. She winced, then ground her top teeth into her lower lip to keep from crying out. What in the world was going on? The baby wasn't due for another few weeks, yet she couldn't ignore the pain that penetrated her entire belly.

Just to be on the safe side, maybe she should wake up Shane. No, she told herself. The pain had to subside; it just had to. Stress. That was the culprit. Her sorry husband, the weather, the situation itself all factored into her feeling this way.

Another pain hit, and she bit harder, tasting blood.

"Oh, God," she whispered, only Shane didn't hear. He appeared dead to the world.

Tears stung her lashes as she moved her hand down to the lower part of her stomach which felt as if it were going to explode. That was when she experienced yet another pain, followed by a feeling that she had wet her pants.

Panic froze her.

Her water. It had broken. The baby *was* coming. Forcing herself to take more deep breaths, she tried to think logically. But the pain was too severe. She had to have help.

"Shane." Her voice came out so weak that he obviously didn't hear her.

He didn't so much as move a muscle.

"Shane," she cried at the same time another contraction ripped through her.

His eyes flew open and he lunged out of the chair. "Julie?"

She heard the uncertainty in his voice followed by a thread of panic that matched hers. "Are you okay?"

"No," she gasped.

"No? What does that mean?"

She blew her breath out in rapid segments, then cried out, "It means I'm having the baby!"

# Chapter 6

"**B**ut that's not possible!"

In spite of the pain, a brief smile relaxed her face as she saw the terrified look on Shane's. "Oh, yes it is."

"It's not time is it?"

"My water broke, Shane."

"Oh, brother."

"And the contractions are coming closer and closer."

Shane eased down on the side of the bed and grabbed her hand. She clung to it, squeezing, as another sharp pain pierced her belly. "Ohhh," she cried.

"Aren't you supposed to breathe a certain way?" Shane asked, leaning over and pushing a damp strand of hair off her forehead.

"Yes."

"Then do what you've learned in that class."

"That's easy for you to say!" Julie cried. "You're not the one in pain."

He smiled briefly himself, and Julie wanted to slug him. However, she took his advice and began to pant and blow, to try and slow down the contractions.

She expected there to be pain. Every book she'd read, every one she'd talked to had told her that. Although she'd believed them, she still wasn't prepared.

She cried out again. "I can't stand this!"

"Yes, you can. Breathe, Julie, breathe deeply."

She did as Shane told her, and for a moment the pain subsided enough that she asked, "What are we going to do?"

"We're...*you're* going to have this baby," Shane said, seeming to have completely regained control of himself and the situation. Cool under fire was the thought that came to her mind.

"Oh, Shane, I'm so frightened."

"Don't be," he said again, his voice low and confident. "I'm going to get you through this."

"But how?"

"I'm going to deliver Elizabeth."

He made that statement with such calm, blatant self-assurance that Julie was at a loss for a response. But it didn't matter as another pain chose that moment to rip through her again. She moaned, thinking this was going to kill her.

"I have to leave you for a second to go get some boiling water and rags."

"Shane, you can't deliver this baby. We have to call for help."

"Surely you know I'd have you at the hospital in

a heartbeat if that were possible. But it isn't. We're flooded in. None of the roads are passable.''

"Don't tell me that!''

"Look, you have to trust me. I can do this. *We* can do this.''

"How can you be so sure?'' If she hadn't been hurting so much, she knew her words would've come out a shout.

His expression never changed. "I've delivered about as many cattle as most doctors have babies.''

"Terrific. And you think that's the same?''

"No, but it's damn close.''

Julie squeezed his hand again. "I wish I weren't so scared, but I am.''

"I know you are, and I am, too. I'll admit that. But you have to know that I'm not going to let anything happen to you or the baby. Believing that is the only way we're going to get through this.''

Julie nodded while sweat mixed with tears streamed down her face.

Shane hesitated another long moment before he got up and strode out of the room. Julie hugged her stomach and gave in to the pain that pounded her with the same force the rain pounded the earth.

What if something went wrong? What if Shane couldn't come through? Stop it! she told herself. Women had babies in all kinds of bizarre places and under all kinds of crazy circumstances. Women in the olden days had often delivered their own babies, for heaven's sake, she told herself, feeling perspiration ooze out of every pore.

But they were tougher than rawhide and had no choice. Well, she wasn't tough; she would admit that.

She had made her doctor promise that when the time came to have Elizabeth that she wouldn't feel a thing or know a thing until her daughter was born.

Now, her worst nightmare was about to become a reality. She was going to feel and know everything that was happening. She couldn't handle it.

Oh, yes, you can. You have no choice.

Damn Mike. If he'd loved her and been the faithful and loving husband he should've been, none of this would have come about. She wouldn't be trapped in a ranch house with a man she hadn't seen in years to have her baby. Instead, she would be home where she could've gotten to the hospital or at least a professional could've gotten to her.

But what if she'd been in the same situation in her own house and Mike had had to deliver Elizabeth?

Julie shuddered at the thought. He would've lost it. He couldn't have handled the pressure. Mike was weak. If this had to happen, Shane was the type of man to have by her side. She didn't know how she knew that or why, but she did. With that assurance came an inner peace that heretofore had escaped her.

"How're we doing?" Shane asked, returning to the room, supplies in hand.

"While you've been gone the contractions seem to have let up."

"You want me to leave again?"

Her eyes widened. "No!"

"Just kidding."

Julie watched as he stood over her and pulled back the covers. For a moment, another wave of panic hit her as she realized the intimacy that they were about to share, an intimacy that only husbands and wives and lovers should share. They were neither.

But Shane was the man of the moment, and again, she didn't know what she would've done without him. Even so, she closed her eyes when she felt him open the robe and gently urge her legs apart.

"Julie," he said in a gruff, but soft voice, "I can see the baby's head."

"Oh," she said, then cried out as another pain ravaged her body.

"You're going to have to help me. You're going to have to concentrate on your breathing as well as pushing."

"I can't!"

"Yes, you can," he said with the patience of Job. "I have the baby's shoulders."

"You have no idea how much it hurts," she moaned, digging her fingers into the sheet and clutching it.

"No, I don't, but you know it'll be worth the pain when you hold her in your arms."

"I can't wait." Julie heard her voice rising with each word she spoke, but she couldn't help it. Something had to give and give soon.

"Push hard," Shane told her.

"Shane!"

"She's coming. You're doing just great. Give me one more big push."

Julie pushed, crying out as she did so. Shortly thereafter was when she heard another cry, that of her baby. She stared at Shane in awe and disbelief.

"You did it." Shane was grinning from ear to ear. "Miss Elizabeth Harrison just entered this world."

"Oh, Shane," she whispered, "I can't thank you enough."

"You don't owe me anything," he said thickly.

A short time later, he placed the baby in her arms. "Now, how are you?"

"Exhausted but okay."

He rubbed his bristled chin. "I wish I could get you to the hospital."

She smiled weakly. "Don't worry, I'm just fine, thanks to you."

"But I am worried." He almost smiled. "Now that it's all over."

She reached out and took his hand. "You did good."

With that, her eyes drifted shut and, cuddling the baby, she fell asleep.

He was beyond exhausted. Every muscle and bone in his body felt abused. Tension. He blamed it on that. He'd held himself so rigid and concentrated so hard on birthing Elizabeth that his body had taken the hard knocks.

But it had been worth it. He wouldn't take anything for what he'd just experienced. He was lucky, though. Damn lucky. Things could've gone the other way, terribly wrong. For starters, the birth could've been a breech. Then what would he have done? He didn't want to think about that or any of the other possibilities.

Sweat poured off him. His clothes were drenched even though the temperature inside was normal. He stared out the window at the rain that kept on coming. Would it ever stop? He wasn't worried about his place flooding or at least the house because it was on high ground. But there was his cattle. The livestock were a different matter altogether. However, right now, he couldn't do anything about his ranch.

Everyone in Grand Springs was suffering in one way or the other. He hoped to venture outdoors, look around and assess the situation. As to when, that depended on what was going on in his bedroom.

*A baby.*

He'd delivered a baby. God, what a miracle. And the fact that it was Julie's made the taste of that miracle even sweeter. Yet it was all mind-boggling, too.

So what now? he asked himself, rubbing his eyes that felt like someone had tossed sand into them. He suspected that bringing Elizabeth into this world had been the easy part. Julie was weak as a newborn kitten and would need help caring for the baby.

Could he do that? Of course, he could. Julie would tell him what to do. Thinking of her once again sent him away from the window in the kitchen and back into the bedroom.

He paused beside the bed and stared down at Julie and the baby, a smile on his face, only to have that smile fade into a frown.

Julie opened her eyes about that time and smiled at him.

"Hey," she said in a soft, dreamy voice.

"Julie, let me have the baby." He tried not to show how panic-stricken he was, but he must not have disguised his feelings very well for Julie's eyes widened when she looked down at Elizabeth.

"Oh, no, she's turning blue!" Julie cried. "Shane, do something!"

## Chapter 7

Shane grabbed the baby and placed his mouth over hers.

In those seconds while Shane was bending over Elizabeth, his lips almost covering her entire face, Julie thought she would die. Even if she didn't, she knew she wouldn't want to live if anything happened to her child.

"Her color's returning," Shane finally said, pulling back and letting out a shuddering breath.

Julie couldn't speak. Her throat was too full. Shane seemed to understand as he reached over and grazed one side of her cheek with a finger. She couldn't read the full range of emotions that played on his face, but she knew he'd been frightened, too.

"It's okay," he said softly. "*She's* okay."

Julie looked away from his mesmerizing eyes and

drew a shuddering breath of her own.

Shortly, Elizabeth pinked up again and was breathing like nothing had ever happened.

Once she was back in Julie's arms, Shane eased down on the side of the bed. Both were silent as they watched Elizabeth's chest move up and down in easy rhythm.

At last, Shane shook his head, then said, "Apparently, I didn't get all that stuff out of her throat when I delivered her." His eyes delved into Julie's. "I'm sorry."

That was when she realized again just how close he was to her. She could almost feel his breath on her lips. In fact, she had felt it.

She swallowed with difficulty, but didn't look away. "You're sorry. You don't have anything to be sorry for. I'm the one who should be apologizing for having put you through all this." Julie felt tears prick her eyes. "You brought my baby into this world, only to then save her life."

Shane's eyes kept on delving. "Wouldn't you say that makes her part mine?"

"I'd say so," Julie responded in a slightly breathless tone.

Elizabeth began to cry suddenly, breaking the spell.

"I bet that baby girl's hungry," Shane said on a husky note.

Without realizing it, her robe had come open, and the full breast next to Elizabeth was exposed. Without any direction, the baby latched on to the nipple and began sucking.

Julie felt her face flush when she looked up at Shane. However, Shane wasn't looking back at her. Instead, his eyes were concentrated on Elizabeth and what she was doing.

"Does that hurt?" he asked, awe in his voice.

Julie's flush deepened, but she answered him. "It doesn't hurt as much as it feels odd."

He raised his gaze to meet hers.

"Does that make sense?" she asked, forcing herself to make eye contact.

"Yeah, it does." His voice was low and slightly gruff as if he needed to clear something out of his throat.

Julie didn't say anything. Instead, she watched as he stood. "I'll go fix you something to eat." He paused. "Is there anything you need before I go?"

"No, thanks. Not right now, anyway."

He turned then and walked out the door. Julie sagged against the pillow like a rag doll who'd just had all its stuffing jerked out.

Why me? she wanted to cry out loud. Why did this have to happen to me? Why anyone? she immediately reminded herself. This was a situation that no one in their right mind would want to be in. She had no choice but to make the best of it.

But it was hard. Oh, God, it was hard. When she thought back on what had just transpired, she held Elizabeth even closer. She might have lost her if it hadn't been for Shane.

What would she have done without him?

If that had been Mike faced with the same situation, he wouldn't have had a clue what to do. All rational thinking would have deserted him. Under adverse circumstances, that was his mode of operation.

Shane, however, had come through like a champ. Again.

Julie closed her eyes and tried to breathe past the fear still lodged in her throat. The sound of the rain filled the silence. What was she going to do if it didn't stop soon?

The thought of imposing on Shane for much longer heightened her anxiety. Having been saddled with a woman and a newborn baby, what must he be thinking? She could imagine, and the thought was not a pretty one.

But had he complained? Not for one minute, at least not verbally. He'd been a rock, the perfect person to have around in a time of crisis. Still, he was a stranger in so many ways.

She didn't know which disturbed her the most: his delivering Elizabeth or watching Elizabeth suckle her breast. Julie squirmed in the bed, only to realize just how sore and uncomfortable she was.

However, she had a lot to be thankful for. The birth, while painful, had been an easy one. Except for the scare with Elizabeth, she hadn't missed being in the hospital. For that, she was more than grateful.

Suddenly, though, it hit her how utterly exhausted she was and how much she longed for a bath and some sleep. Her head turned toward the clock and she saw that it was nearly noon on Tuesday. Of course, it was impossible to gage time by looking outside. The entire sky was an ugly, milky gray.

She removed her gaze from the window and shifted positions. Elizabeth was through nursing and was sound asleep. With ease, Julie placed her on the bed beside her.

Shane walked in about that time. She looked up and gave him a brief smile.

"How is she?" he asked, sitting the tray filled with food on a nearby chair.

"As you can see, she's sleeping."

"Like a newborn babe that I brought into this world," he said with humor in his voice.

"My, but you're awfully proud of yourself, aren't you?"

"Any reason why I shouldn't be?"

She grinned, though a bit self-consciously, realizing how awful she much look. "Now that you mentioned it, none that I can think of."

"Are you in any pain?" he asked, his expression sobering.

"Just a little."

He frowned. "I hope you can eat something."

"I'm not really hungry. I'm too weary."

"Well, you need to eat, anyway." He paused, his eyes narrowing. "Especially after I've slaved over a hot stove."

"Really?"

"Really," he said with deadpan seriousness. "I heated up a big can of soup and opened a package of crackers."

"Ah, a gourmet cook."

"Woman, are you making fun of me?"

"Now, why would I do that?"

They both laughed then, which did little to relieve the heightened tension in the room. Julie's laughter faded first, as she watched him reach for one cup of the soup and hand it to her.

"This will help replenish your strength," he said, not looking at her.

She took it and for the next few minutes, they ate in silence. When they were both finished, she smiled at him. "Thanks. That was good."

"I'm sorry it wasn't more, but I have to admit cooking is not my forte."

"Who's complaining?" she said softly. "You've already gone above and beyond the call of duty."

"Hey, stop that. I only did what I had to do."

"We both know better than that, but I'll give you a break and stop thanking you for the moment."

Shane rolled his eyes, then said, "How 'bout I watch Elizabeth and give *you* a break?"

"I would love to take a bath."

"Are you up to doing that alone?" he asked in what she thought was a gruffer than usual voice.

She couldn't meet his direct look. "I think so."

"If not, would you ask for help?"

Julie forced herself to make eye contact again, even though she knew her face was flushed. Would she ever get used to this forced intimacy? Somehow she doubted it. Yet she wasn't going to dwell on it. To do so would only add to the turmoil already raging inside her.

"Julie."

His raspy voice forced her back to the moment at hand. "Of course, I'd ask for help," she said in a halting voice.

"Good girl."

She paused. "First though, I should call Millie. I've put that off as long as I dare."

"That'll work, that is, if the phones are still operational."

"Oh my, I hadn't thought of that."

Shane uncoiled his large frame and stood. "With this storm anything's possible."

However, when he walked over to the cordless phone that was now working and handed it to her, the dial tone sounded loud and clear in her ear.

"It's okay now," she said, "which means we're not totally marooned."

He headed for the door. "Call me when you're off the phone."

"Where are you going?" She sounded panicked which was crazy. Where could he go? Under the circumstances, not far.

As if he could read her thoughts, he gave her a reassuring smile. "I'm only a holler away."

Once he was out of the room, she punched out Millie's number and waited. When her friend answered, she said without preamble, "Are you okay?"

"Thank God, you turkey. I'm fine but you've had me worried out of my gourd."

"I know, but you won't believe what's happened."

"Oh, Lordy."

"I've had Elizabeth."

"No."

"Yes."

"Where and when, for crying out loud?" Millie demanded, a note of disbelief still tampering with her voice.

Julie told her what had happened.

Millie gasped. "Are you all right? I mean—" Her voice faded on a note of hysteria.

"Calm down. I'm fine and so is the baby, thanks to Shane."

"My God, Julie, I can't believe this."

"When I let myself rehash it, I can't either."

"Weren't you scared out of your mind?"

"I hurt worse than I was scared."

"And you had nothing for pain." Millie's words were a flat statement of fact.

"That's right."

"Well, you're a better woman than me."

"When you have no options, you do what you have to."

"So what are you going to do?"

"What do you mean?"

"Well, you can't stay there."

"I have no choice, Millie, unless you know something I don't."

"Like what?"

"Like the high water's receding and we're no longer at the mercy of the weather."

"I can't tell you that. Pretty much everyone's in the same boat." Millie paused, interjecting some humor. "No pun intended, of course."

"Of course."

They both chuckled.

"Geez, this is unreal," Millie finally said.

"If I hadn't let my emotions get the best of me, perhaps I wouldn't have gone into labor so soon."

"Well, you can thank your scumbag ex for that."

"I hope he's happy."

"I hope he's miserable."

Julie sighed. "Me, too."

"I wish there was something I could do for you."

"Well, there's not."

"Except keep me posted on what's going on."

"I will as long as the phones are still working."

"I'll talk to you later, then. Oh, and give Shane my thanks for taking care of you and Elizabeth."

"I'll do it."

Julie put the phone back on its hook, only suddenly to freeze. She opened her mouth to scream, but nothing came out. All she could do was stare at the big snake that lay curled in the far corner of the room.

## Chapter 8

"Are you ready to eat?"

Though she'd lost her appetite earlier, thanks to that snake, she kind of liked Shane taking care of her along with the baby. It was quite a change from what she was used to. Once Mike left, she'd had to fend for herself.

However, she couldn't get used to being pampered, she cautioned herself. She needn't worry; this situation was only temporary.

"I'll be out shortly," she said through the closed door.

"That's not what I asked."

"I'm okay."

"You don't feel faint or anything?" he pressed.

Julie knew he was alluding to the snake incident, which sent another shudder through her. "No," she called back. "Actually, I'm putting on my clothes."

"Perfect. Dinner's just about ready." He paused. "So work on your appetite."

When she didn't hear anything else, she assumed he'd gone back into the kitchen, leaving *her* with thoughts of that vile-looking creature that continued to work on her psyche.

Julie tried to concentrate on something else. However, her mind refused to cooperate. That reptile flashed in vivid color before her eyes. She had the same reaction she'd had then—she couldn't move.

She recalled how she hadn't been able to get her voice to work either. It was like its mechanism had broken down.

Finally, though, her throat had come back to life, and she'd let out a bloodcurdling scream while grabbing Elizabeth and scrambling as far against the headboard as possible. Too bad she couldn't get up on the chair. But a woman who'd just had a baby wasn't meant to climb.

Wild-eyed, Shane had dashed into the room. "What the hell?"

She opened her mouth only to have nothing come out.

The fear was stark on his face. "Is it Elizabeth?" His gaze then went to the child in her arms.

"No," Julie managed to say between trembling lips, her limbs still frozen so that she couldn't move anything except her mouth and her eyes.

"Dammit, Julie! What's wrong?"

His voice hadn't risen a decibel, yet there was fear mixed with the steel that jolted her into action.

"There." She angled her head. "It's…it's over there."

"What's over there?" Shane demanded, his eyes roaming around the room.

"Down. Look down." Julie's teeth once again began to bang together so hard that she had trouble getting the words out. In addition, her heart was hammering at such a fast pace that she thought she might black out.

"I don't see anything."

Shane sounded exasperated now, which made her furious.

"It's a snake!"

"Don't move," he demanded in his steel-coated voice.

"Do you think I'm crazy?"

She saw his lips twitch, and she wanted to hit him. But then, his features sobered as he made his way cautiously toward the snake that remained coiled in the corner of the room.

"Ohmygodohmygod," Julie whispered.

"It's going to be all right."

"No, it isn't!" Her voice had reached the upper range of hysteria.

"Julie, look at me."

She did as she was told.

"The snake's not going to hurt you or the baby. Now, turn your head."

"Oh, Shane—"

"Just do it, okay?"

Julie nodded, then laid a still-sleeping Elizabeth down beside her. She closed her eyes and shuddered.

Moments later, Shane walked back into the room.

"You can open your eyes now. The snake's history."

"How…how do you know it won't happen again?"

"Trust me. I took care of the problem."

He was standing beside her with his hand extended. Wordlessly, she took it and let him help her up. Then before she realized what was happening, she was buried against his chest, his arms tightly around her.

She didn't know whose heart was beating the hardest—his or hers.

After a few minutes, she pulled back, embarrassment washing through her. "I'm sorry, I didn't mean to get your shirt all wet."

"It'll dry," he said in an odd voice.

When she looked at him closely, she realized his face was strained and that his lips were tight. Apparently, he hadn't been as cool and calm as he'd let on. Or maybe he'd hadn't liked her behaving like an idiot and clinging to him like a frightened child.

"I guess you think I'm awful," she said, sniffling.

He brushed the tears off one cheek, his lips beginning to twitch. "Now why would I think that?"

That twitch seemed to release the tension, and she smiled back. "I hate snakes."

"Aw, really?"

She gave him a look. "What did you do with it?"

"Do you honestly want to know?" His smile and voice were indulgent.

A chill darted through her. "No."

He chuckled, then he turned serious. "You were right to be frightened."

"I didn't know if it was poisonous, but it sure looked deadly."

"It is, or rather was."

Julie blew out a breath, bypassing him to stare at her daughter. His eyes followed her. "Can you believe she didn't so much as move a muscle?"

"Doesn't surprise me. She knows when she's got it made."

Their eyes met and Julie saw the glitter in his. She looked away, disturbed. And for some unexplained reason that disturbed feeling had remained with her.

"Julie."

The sound of Shane's voice forced her back to reality, back to safety. Having dredged up memories of that snake again made her clutch her stomach. Surely, she wasn't going to be sick. She took several deep breaths and the nausea passed. She buttoned her jeans, then slipped into a pair of Kathy's slippers. Thank the Lord, he had a sister. Otherwise, she would've been in trouble.

Had she really been marooned at Shane's ranch house for three days now? She had, yet it didn't seem possible. So much had been crammed into those days that it seemed like she'd been living there so much longer.

And the most unsettling part was that she felt at home. She knew that was crazy, but the feeling was there nonetheless. Hormones. That was the reason for that craziness. Hers were definitely out of whack. But then wasn't that expected of someone who had just had a baby?

No matter, her mood swings from crying to laughter didn't seem to faze Shane. He took it all in stride and hadn't seemed to miss a beat. He was the same way with the baby.

Amazing.

When she wasn't nursing Elizabeth, Shane was taking care of her. Thank goodness, his sister had twins and came to visit him often. In the spare bedroom where he slept, the closet had been full of miscellaneous baby stuff, such as diapers, cradle, clothing and baby blankets.

If something didn't happen soon, she knew the items would all be used up. But she wasn't worried. Knowing Shane, he'd find a way to make sure Elizabeth was provided for.

What a man.

The woman who landed him would be one lucky soul. For a second, Julie frowned, feeling a pang around her heart. Was she jealous? Was that what that pang was all about? Of course not, she told herself, her mouth tightening. That was absurd. The last thing she wanted was another man. She still hadn't changed her mind about that.

She had traveled down that road and wasn't the least interested in doing so again. From now on, it would be her and Elizabeth. She intended to be both mother and father to her child.

What about Shane? her conscience asked. Somehow she knew he'd want to continue to see Elizabeth. After all, he'd done more for her than most birth fathers. With she, Julie, being so listless and tired, Shane had diapered and bathed Elizabeth. It had been a sight to behold, his big hands, handling that tiny body.

Most men would have shunned that duty. Again,

her ex jumped to mind. No way would he have done what Shane had. He was too self-absorbed, mean-tempered and arrogant.

Shane was more of a man than Mike would ever be. Shane was both sensitive and rugged—a man's man who seemed to know what he wanted and went after it.

Sometimes she thought he wanted her. Her heart faltered at that thought. Yet she couldn't deny that look she'd seen in his eyes. Still, at times, he had a tendency to treat her more like a child than a woman he was interested in.

"Julie," Shane called.

"Coming!" she responded, rushing out of the bathroom.

When she walked into the kitchen, she pulled up short. Shane was holding Elizabeth who was beginning to fret.

"What's the matter, darlin'?" he asked, peering down at the baby, an anxious look on his face.

Julie's breath caught while an emotion she couldn't identify tugged at her heartstrings. But there was something so touching, so incredibly sweet about that big, strong man holding that weak, tiny baby in his arms, that she wanted to cry.

Shane looked up and saw her then. For a moment, their eyes met and held. He was the first to turn away, back to the baby. "I was hoping to quiet her." His voice was uncertain.

"I suspect she's hungry."

"Oh, right."

Julie smiled. "You want me to take her?"

Elizabeth was crying outright now.

He sighed. "I guess you'd better. Whatever I'm doing, she's not liking it."

Once Julie had Elizabeth against her chest, her greedy little mouth started moving.

Shane laughed. "Why, that little beggar thinks she's starving. Imagine that."

Julie hesitated. "I'll go back to the room and feed her."

His eyes darkened. "Why?"

"Why what?" Her words came out sounding strangled.

"Why would you want to do that?"

"You don't mind if she nurses while we eat?"

"Of course not," he said thickly.

He held out the chair for her to sit down. Once he seemed satisfied that she and the baby were situated comfortably, he served their plates with pasta and salad, then sat down.

Suddenly hesitant to look at him, she peered at Elizabeth who was busy suckling her breast. When she finally lifted her face, Shane was watching her.

"Sorry," he said roughly.

"For what?"

"For staring."

"That's all right," she said, feeling her face suffuse with color.

Would she ever stop doing that? Not when those blue eyes of his had that glint in them, she told herself, a glint that she still couldn't identify and didn't want to.

"It's just that I find the whole process a fascinating miracle."

"It is that, for sure."

A silence fell between them during which neither touched their food. Elizabeth nursing was the only sound in the room. Even the rain seemed to have stopped.

Suddenly, Shane coughed, then lifted his fork. However, he didn't take a bite of anything. He just kept looking at her.

"Go ahead and eat," Julie said, her stomach moving in waves.

"Uh, I'm waiting on you," he said huskily.

Suddenly, the thought of food made her sick. She stood abruptly. "Perhaps I'll eat later. I'm going to get ready for bed."

He stood. "Julie—"

She kept on walking, his muttered curses following her all the way to the bedroom.

## Chapter 9

He should not have stared at her. He should've known better. What had come over him? Lust. He'd admit that, though it wasn't an admirable admission. When he'd watched Elizabeth attach her mouth to Julie's breast and begin to suck, it had turned him inside out.

He'd ached to take the baby's place.

Lord amercy, he thought, tossing back the covers and lunging out of bed. His body was drenched in a cold sweat, despite the warmth of the house. He walked to the window where he closed his eyes and rubbed his forehead.

Still, he couldn't get the image of her beautiful, creamy breasts out of his mind. The first time he'd seen the baby nurse had affected him as well, but not like last evening. He'd been so turned on that if he'd been forced to move, he would've been in big trouble.

He shuddered to think of what she would've thought of him then. Water or no water, she would have probably insisted on leaving. But thank heavens, she hadn't noticed as she'd been too busy bolting like a frightened kitten, which hadn't surprised him.

A man, much less one with a lusty gleam in his eye, wasn't on her agenda right now. More than likely one never would be again, not after what she'd been through.

How could a man in his right mind let her go? For the life of him, he couldn't figure that out. Mike Harrison had to be the biggest idiot in the world to throw away his relationship with a woman like Julie for the bimbette who was attached to his side at that party.

Shane would've given anything to have Julie as his wife. He squeezed his tired eyes harder together and took several deep breaths. He had to get a handle on his emotions. He couldn't keep on letting them have free rein or she'd figure out how he felt. He could never allow that.

At this point, his pride was about all he had left.

His eyes sought the clock. Seven. He never slept this late, but then he hadn't gone to sleep until the wee hours of the morning. He'd lain awake thinking about Julie and the baby, how dramatically they had changed his life in just thirty-six hours.

It would never be the same again. *He* would never be the same again. But when the time came to let them go, to take them home, he wouldn't have any choice. They didn't belong to him and never would.

He winced, feeling like someone had taken a knife and plunged it into his heart.

Maybe it was time he got himself off this ranch and started dating for real. Maybe he would find another Julie.

"Yeah, right," he muttered into the silence.

Well, something had to give. If he was in this kind of shape now, he shuddered to think how miserable he would be when they did go.

Opening his eyes, he peered outside. Although the rain had stopped, the water was still too high to make any kind of move. Yet if it didn't rain anymore, which according to the latest weather report it wasn't predicted to do, the water would finally begin to recede. But then they would have to contend with ice.

Suddenly the phone rang. He grabbed it quickly, hoping that it hadn't awakened Julie and the baby. She needed all the rest she could get.

It was his foreman, Jeb Carson.

"Are you and your family okay?" Shane asked right off, feeling a twinge of guilt because he hadn't checked on them. But then, he'd been otherwise occupied.

"We're fine," Jeb responded in his crusty voice. "How 'bout yourself?"

"Same here."

"So how are things around the place?"

"Don't know. I haven't been out."

There was a long moment of silence during which Shane could envision Jeb's strong features darkening in disbelief. However, before he could offer an explanation, Jeb asked, "Are you sick?"

Shane almost laughed. "No."

"Then what the hell's going on?"

If they hadn't been good friends, Shane might have taken offense at Jeb's bluntness. But they were friends, and he knew that if the roles were reversed, he'd be asking Jeb the same question.

His ranch was his life and Jeb knew that. Hence, Jeb couldn't understand why he hadn't checked on things, especially his livestock.

"A baby is what's going on."

"A baby? Have you been drinking?"

Shane finally laughed, and it felt good. A few moments ago, he'd felt like he would never laugh again. "Nope. I'm stone-cold sober."

"Then suppose you explain."

Shane did.

"Well, I'll be damned."

"So now you know why I haven't checked the damages."

Jeb chuckled. "That's an understatement."

"But since it's stopped raining and all seems to be quiet in the other room, I'm going to take a look-see."

"Give me a call back."

Once the phone was back in its place, Shane didn't waste any time scrambling into his clothes. A few minutes later, he stood at Julie's door and listened. When he heard nothing, he knew they were still asleep. With luck, he'd be back inside before they ever stirred.

Still, he didn't move. Instead, Shane eased open the door and peered inside. The night light and the beginning of daylight allowed him access to both Julie and Elizabeth.

His chest tightened at the sight. Julie's hair, looking like the finest of silk, was spread over the pillow while her lips looked as if they were smiling.

The baby lay in the crook of her arm, its tiny face pressed against an exposed breast.

When he closed the door and walked away, he didn't know which ached the worst, his heart or his loins.

Julie stretched, then her eyes went to Elizabeth who hadn't moved so much as a muscle. She stared at her daughter for a long moment, marveling at her perfection.

Then she scooped Elizabeth into her arms and transferred her to the cradle close beside the bed. She was on her way to the bathroom to shower when she realized she didn't hear any noise on the roof.

She stopped in her tracks. The rain had stopped. Did that mean she would be going home today? Not likely, she told herself, knowing that the rising water would be a deterrent, especially where she lived.

Would her home be flooded?

If so, then she would deal with that trauma when she had to. Thanks to Shane, she and Elizabeth were safe and well. For the time being, that was all that counted.

Soon enough, she would return to the real world. Julie smiled to herself when she thought about how isolated, how cut off she felt from everything and everyone. It was as if she were in a surreal setting.

For the most part, her life had been lived in the fast lane as she'd made ready for the baby to come.

She had thought she'd had everything planned down to the last detail.

Ha!

Boy, had fate had a field day with her. Shane was definitely her hero, and Elizabeth would grow up knowing who he was, if he were agreeable.

By the time she'd be able to leave here, he might not ever want to see them again. Deep down, she knew that wasn't true, recalling that certain glint she'd seen in his eyes. Too, he seemed to genuinely enjoy their presence. Maybe that was because he was lonely and needed companionship.

Hell's bells, who was she to say what he needed? She certainly couldn't take over his life and presume to manage it. Under the circumstances, she was going to have trouble keeping her own together.

Rearing a child as a single parent, teaching it to be a good citizen, was an awesome responsibility. She prayed she was up to the task.

Thrusting those thoughts aside for the moment, Julie took a quick shower and dressed. As she made her way out of the bedroom, it hit her again how quiet the house was. No sign of Shane. He was usually up long before her.

In fact, she didn't think he ever slept. Maybe this morning was different, and he was making up for lost time. Since she was feeling more like her old self, she'd just surprise him and prepare breakfast.

Julie had the bacon frying and the pancake mix stirred when her intuition told her something was wrong. If nothing else, the smell of bacon frying would've awakened Shane. Also, she'd been making more than her share of noise, opening drawers and cabinets, as she hadn't known where the cooking utensils were. Surely he was okay, she told herself, feeling her anxiety mount. Hormones again. They were still out of whack or she wouldn't be so skittish.

By the time she'd made and poured the orange juice, Julie decided to tap on his door. Even if he was asleep, he wouldn't mind, or at least she didn't think so.

They were almost strangers who were living together.

Squelching that disquieting thought, she made her way down the hall toward the smaller bedroom. On the way, she peeped in on Elizabeth who continued to sleep peacefully.

A smile touched Julie's lips before moving on to Shane's door where she pulled up short. The door was open, and the room was empty. The bathroom across the hall, the one that he'd been using, was also empty.

Frowning, she walked back in the kitchen. He was outside. That was the only possible explanation. He wouldn't have gone somewhere in the truck without having told her. Or would he? Again, she didn't know Shane McCoy, not the grown-up one anyway.

She knew it was downright stupid to worry about him and his whereabouts. Yet she couldn't seem to stop her anxiety from building.

She didn't have to be told that he was worried about his ranch and his livestock. After all, that was how he made his living. But what if he'd slipped down and fallen? What if he was lying unconscious somewhere?

Stop it!

Her imagination was going haywire. Correction. Her hormones had really kicked in. Suddenly, she felt the urge to sit down and cry her eyes out.

Dammit, she'd better get a grip or she'd be sitting in the middle of the room bawling like an idiot. However, the thought of him finding her doing just that did nothing to deter the tears. They began streaming down her face while she stirred the pancake batter harder and faster.

Finally, she put the bowl down and walked to the window and peered out. Even though it wasn't raining, the sky remained a nasty-looking gray. And ice was everywhere.

She longed to open the front door, walk out on the porch and call him. But it was so wet and frigid, she feared she might get chilled. She couldn't afford to get sick. She had more than herself to think about now. She had Elizabeth.

Still, she couldn't concentrate on anything. Momentarily, she knew the baby would awaken and want to be fed. Where was he? She wiped the tears off her face and began walking the floor in the living room.

As usual a fire was burning in the fireplace, which made the rustic room homey and cozy. So why did she feel so alone, so frightened?

She was blowing his absence way out of proportion, she told herself again, fighting back a new onslaught of tears. When he did come back, he'd think she had lost her mind.

*If he came back.*

She placed her hands over her ears as if to shut

out those tormenting thoughts. God, she was losing it. She'd never been this way about Mike.

She had just removed her hands when she heard footsteps. She stopped, whirled around and faced the door just as it opened.

He took one look at her tear-drenched face and said, "Julie, what's wrong?"

She sniffed and hurried toward him. "Are you all right?" Her eyes scanned his body and saw nothing out of the ordinary.

"Of course, I'm all right." His voice was gruff with concern. "What about you?"

Suddenly she felt her insides crumple, and she began to shake all over.

"Hey," he responded, closing the distance between them in nothing flat. "Is it Elizabeth?"

"No," she sobbed, "it's me."

"God, Julie," he whispered, reaching for her and pulling her against his chest. "You're scaring me half to death."

"You scared me, too." She pulled back and gazed up at him.

"How?"

"When I got up and couldn't find you, I thought—" Tears damned her throat.

"You thought what?" he asked, his voice thickening.

"That something had happened to you."

"Oh, honey, I just went out to assess the damages, to check on the livestock."

Now that he was back, she could smile. "You think I've lost it, don't you?" she asked, suddenly embarrassed, especially when she realized she was still in his arms. Surprisingly, she made no effort to leave them.

"No," he said, delving deeply into her eyes. "I don't think any such thing. It's nice to know that you were concerned." His hand began to rub her back.

She stiffened, suddenly feeling something strange and unwanted flutter inside her. "I'm…sorry," she whispered.

"Don't say that. You have nothing to be sorry for."

She gave him a watery smile. "I practically threw myself at you."

For the longest time, his eyes held hers. Then he said in a low, raspy tone, "Who's complaining?"

# Chapter 10

"So how are things going in your world?"

"Rain and more rain," Millie said in an exasperated tone.

"It had stopped here for a little while, but it's raining again."

Millie sighed. "This weather depresses the hell out of me."

"What do you think about me?"

Millie chuckled. "Ah, it's just your bod. It's still out of whack."

"I'll get you for that," Julie responded in an indignant tone.

Millie seemed always to know when she needed cheering. Today was no exception. After blubbering in Shane's arms the day before, she'd been in a state. She had tried to keep herself as busy as possible, which really wasn't possible at all.

Although the house was rather large, it seemed small, especially when three people were marooned in it.

"When do you think you'll come home?"

"Your guess is as good as mine."

"How are you and Elizabeth really doing?" Millie's question was pointed.

Julie sighed. "What you're asking is about Shane, right?"

"You read me like a book."

"Actually, he's been wonderful."

"Mmm, that's interesting."

"What does that mean?" Julie snapped.

Millie laughed. "Nothing, unless there's something going on that you're not telling me."

"I don't think so." Despite the note of sarcasm, Julie felt her face turn red. The fact that she'd had physical contact with Shane was none of Millie's business. Besides, it hadn't meant anything. Like her friend had said, her body hadn't settled back to normal, and she was supersensitive.

"But I bet it's been awkward," Millie said.

"He's been wonderful, actually."

"He's got my vote, that's for sure. Any man who would do what he did has to be special." Millie paused, then added a teasing note to her voice, "Hey, do you think he might be in the market for a wife?"

Julie teased right back. "Are you interested?"

"I just might be," Millie said, laughing.

Julie suddenly didn't share the humor. The thought of Shane with a woman seemed odd. In fact, the thought didn't set too well with her at all, which was

*A Pregnant Pause*

crazy. What did it matter to her if Shane had an entire harem at his disposal?

"I can't wait to get my hands on Elizabeth."

"Even if she is mine, she's absolutely adorable."

"Of course, she is, even if she's part of Mike, too."

"You could've talked all day without mentioning his name," Julie said, her tone hardening.

"Just remember he's the loser, not you."

"Don't worry, I know that."

"Purposely changing the subject, do you realize what today is?"

Julie thought for a moment, then said in amazement, "Christmas Eve. I can't believe it. These last few days have whizzed past."

"It's hard for me to grasp, too, especially with the weather playing such havoc with everything."

"At least you're in your own home."

"Well, don't be too hard on yourself. Maybe Shane could've taken you home, but considering your condition after your ex pulled his stunt, things worked out for the best."

Julie blew out her breath. "I guess."

"I'm just thankful nothing went wrong and you didn't need the hospital."

Julie shuddered inwardly. "I can't bear to think about that, especially when it comes to Elizabeth."

"Again, I can't wait to get my hands on her. So the minute you two hit civilization again, give me a buzz."

Julie chuckled. "Count on it. Meanwhile, Merry Christmas Eve, dear friend."

"Same back."

The second she got off the phone, Elizabeth began to fret. Julie walked over and lifted her out of the cradle, and smiled down at her.

"Hey, Mommy hadn't forgotten you, darling. I know you're hungry, and I'm going to take care of that."

Once she was seated, Elizabeth began nursing like she'd never had anything to eat. Julie shook her head and smiled down at her.

"Starving her again, I see."

Startled, Julie looked up at Shane who stood in the door, dressed like he was heading to the North Pole.

"Oops, didn't mean to scare you," he said, smiling. "I knocked."

"I didn't hear you, but that's all right."

They looked at each other for a long moment, then Shane shifted his feet, but not his eyes. Julie couldn't help but notice that they were locked on her breast again. But now, for some unexplainable reason, his obsession no longer embarrassed her.

"Uh, I'm headed outside to try and move some cattle."

Julie frowned. "By yourself?"

He shrugged. "My foreman can't get here to help, so it's up to me."

"I don't see how you can do anything in this mess."

"I have to try," he said patiently.

"You'll be careful, won't you?"

His features softened. "Don't worry. I'll be fine. I just didn't want to leave without letting you know."

Her mouth turned down. "I guess not, after the stunt I pulled."

"You've just had a baby, so cut yourself some slack."

"That's no excuse."

"Hey, like I told you, there's no complaints from this corner."

This time her face did flame with embarrassment. He laughed, then said, "You two behave."

Her eyes trailed him to the door. "Merry Christmas."

He swung around, a kind of disconcerted look on his face. "Merry Christmas to you, too."

The afternoon passed fast. Maybe that was because she stayed busy. First, she straightened the house. She would've loved to have done more, but she wasn't physically able. After all, it hadn't been quite a week since she'd had Elizabeth.

Still, each day she felt stronger, less tired and sore. In no time at all, she'd be back to full steam ahead. Once she was done with the chores, she made a big pot of chili. Thank goodness, Shane believed in stocking his pantry and his freezer, even though he wasn't a cook.

The chili smelled up the house, making it seem more cozy and warm. For a second, it was almost as if she were married again, only this time happily.

Forget that.

But Shane was different. He should be married with a family. If anyone was ever husband material, it was him.

Thrusting those disturbing thoughts of marriage aside, Julie glanced at the clock. To her way of thinking, Shane should've already been back. But she promised him she wouldn't worry, and she would stick to that promise. Still, she'd feel much better when she saw him walk through that door.

Meanwhile, it was Elizabeth's bath time. That would occupy both her hands and her mind. "Come on, sweetheart," she said to her daughter, "let's do our thing."

Julie had just placed the baby in the sink filled with warm water when she heard the front door open, then shut. She breathed an inner sigh of relief and suddenly all was right with the world again.

Shocked at her thoughts, Julie shut them off and concentrated on the task at hand.

"Julie?"

"I'm in the kitchen."

A few minutes of silence followed, then Shane commented, "Something sure smells good."

She turned as he strode through the archway. He had shed his coat, leaving him dressed in a thick shirt, jeans and boots. His hair was the only thing that appeared damp about him.

"It's chili, which is supposedly one of my specialties."

"Works for me."

"How did it go?" she asked, turning back to Elizabeth.

He came to stand beside her. "Several cattle are dead."

"Oh, Shane, I'm sorry."

"Me, too."

"Is it still raining?"

"No, and the water's actually draining off."

What he didn't add, Julie realized, was that the roads would soon be passable if they weren't already.

"So, how's the little lump of sugar?" he said in his gruff, yet gentle voice.

"As you can see, she loves her bath."

Julie wished he wouldn't stand so close to her. She was aware of every inch of his big body and his smell. It surrounded her like a cocoon.

"Need any help?"

Her eyes sought his. "You can dry her off, if you want."

"You betcha."

Julie watched with a sudden mist in her eyes as he lifted Elizabeth and placed her on a big, fluffy towel, wrapping her tightly in it. Then lifting the bundle, he cradled it in his arms. Elizabeth merely gazed up him, a contented look on her face.

"You should marry and have kids, you know," Julie said without thinking.

He looked at her for the longest time, then asked, "Is that a proposal?"

She sucked in her breath and drew back.

"Just kidding," he said.

He might be kidding, but that unsettling glint was back in his eye, the one she couldn't identify. She shifted her gaze, trying to control the rapid beat of her heart. What was happening to her?

"She's fallen asleep," Julie said for lack of anything better to say as the tension between them grew by the second. The fact that he remained so close didn't help any. The memory of how it felt to be held tightly against his hard chest rose to the forefront of her mind.

"Let's put the cradle in the living room."

Julie raised her eyebrows. "Any particular reason why?"

"Yep, but it's a surprise."

She grinned. "Whatever."

A few minutes later, Shane carried the cradle into the living room, Julie following on his heels. She saw the surprise immediately and her eyes widened.

"Oh, Shane," she cried, fighting back the threat of additional tears.

"I went through hell cutting it down, but I made it."

"It's lovely just like it is."

And it was. Julie stared at the perfectly shaped tree that was mounted on a stand in the far corner of the room not far from the fireplace.

"Christmas isn't Christmas without a tree," Shane said, "especially when you have a baby."

"Oh, Shane," she whispered again, "I can't believe you did this."

"Me either." He chuckled. "But what the hell? It's Elizabeth's first Christmas in this world, and I couldn't stand the thought of her not having a tree."

"And she'll thank you for that one day," Julie said gently.

He shrugged. "That doesn't matter. But what does matter is that it looks a bit more like Christmas."

"We've had other things on our mind."

Shane rubbed his chin. "I know, but I bet you've thought about how festive your place is and that you're not there."

"It's no big deal. Elizabeth's my Christmas."

Light blue eyes delved into dark ones. "Mine, too." His voice sounded strained.

"Do you have any decorations?" Julie asked, desperate to relieve that suffocating feeling expanding inside her.

He rolled his eyes. "Tons."

"You're kidding?"

"Nope. My mother and sister saw to that."

"So what are you waiting for?"

"Food."

She laughed, and it felt so good that she laughed again. "First things first, I guess."

Two bowls of chili were consumed in record time. Once the kitchen was cleaned up, which they did together, they headed back to the living room. Elizabeth was still asleep.

"She's a little angel," Julie said, leaning over and kissing a rosy cheek.

"Nope, she's a lump of sugar."

Julie merely shook her head, then faced the tree. "Shall we get started on this monster?"

"Hell, woman, we'll have that whipped in no time."

She gave him a look. "Not the way I decorate."

"Oh, Lordy, I'm in trouble."

An hour later, Julie stepped back to get an overall view.

From atop the ladder, Shane asked, "So what's the verdict?"

"Perfection."

"Can I get down now?"

"Not until you straighten the star on top. It's still a little crooked.

"Women!" he muttered.

"I heard that."

"I hope so."

She grinned at him as he climbed down. They both stood back and gazed at the tree, ablaze with what appeared to be a million lights.

"It's lovely," she whispered, peering up at him.

"Not nearly as lovely as you."

Her breath caught as she met his greedy gaze. "I—"

"Shush." He pulled her to him, lowered his head, then sank his lips onto hers. At first, Julie didn't respond as she felt as if all the air had been let out of her body. She felt depleted of energy, too weak to move.

But when his mouth turned insistent, grinding against hers, her lips parted of their own volition. She met the force of his kiss with equal energy. He pulled back, only to groan, then kiss her again, this time sucking on her lips like Elizabeth sucked on her breasts.

Her head spun, and she clung to him. It must've been his whimper that brought him to his senses. He pulled back suddenly, forcing air through his lungs.

"Shane," she whispered through swollen, trembling lips.

He shook his head. "If you're about to ask for an apology, you can forget it."

# *Chapter 11*

"I wasn't going to ask for an apology."

Shane blinked in astonishment. "You weren't?"

Julie took a deep breath. He could feel her heart beating like a runaway train before she stepped back as if to remove herself from harm's way.

Smart move. The way he felt right now, she wasn't safe.

"No," she said with a ring of honest sincerity, "but I don't want you to…kiss me again."

Shane sighed, then thrust his hand though his thick hair. Still, he didn't take his eyes off her. "It wasn't knee-jerk. Kissing you is something I've wanted to do for a long time."

She averted her gaze toward the sleeping child, but not before he saw color invade her cheeks. Then she turned back around, her eyes troubled. "Look—"

He held up his hand, cutting her off while kicking

his backside. "Enough said. Want some hot chocolate?"

This time an astonished expression crossed her face and then she smiled. "Uh, sounds good."

At least he'd relieved the tension that was as murky as the water outside, he told himself. It hadn't helped his situation any, but then he was a fool if he'd expected her to invite him into her bed. That wouldn't have been possible even if she'd been receptive. Hell, she'd just had a baby. Where was his brain, for God's sake?

When he returned with the cups of hot chocolate several minutes later, she was sitting by the fire, staring into it. He wondered what she was thinking about. Him, and those hot, stolen kisses, most likely.

Was that the kind of stunt her ex-husband would have pulled? Shane winced at that thought, almost dropping the tray.

Julie turned and when she saw him, she smiled. Shane released his pent-up breath. In that second, her smile meant more to him than a million dollars would have.

"Smells good."

"It's out of a package," he said with a lopsided smile.

"Is there any other kind?"

His smile broadened, as he was again relieved that things seemed back on an even keel. Still, he had no intention of apologizing. With the slightest encouragement, he would ravage her lips again. The only problem was, he wanted more, so damn much more that he actually hurt.

Yet the memory of her moist lips and her full

breasts poking into his chest would warm many cold, lonely nights for him.

"Mmm, this is good," Julie said into the silence. "Just what the doctor ordered."

He dragged another chair closer to the fire and sat down. Without drinking any chocolate, he set his cup on the hearth.

"Speaking of doctor, have you spoken to yours?" he asked.

"No, believe it or not. Anyhow, the office has probably been closed several days."

"Right. Somehow, I forget it's Christmas."

"That and the weather."

"He'll be shocked."

"*She* will be shocked," Julie corrected.

"Ah, so your doc's a female."

"And she's wonderful, too."

He reached for his cup. "Man, I'm so thankful you haven't needed her."

"Thanks to you," she said softly, angling her head to one side and giving him a deep look.

Shane frowned. "I thought we'd gotten past all that gratitude stuff."

"I rest my case."

"Good."

She was quiet for a moment, then she said, "I feel like I know you." She paused with a flush. "But then again, I don't. I mean I don't even know where you lived or what you did before you came back here."

"I was in the oil and cattle business in Houston." He gave a nonchalant shrug. "Now, it's just cattle."

"Speaking of that, I'm sorry about your livestock. Will you recover?"

"Yep, but it'll take a while."

"Some people won't ever recover," she responded in a small voice.

"When I got the tree, I checked the bridge. It's no longer under water."

Her eyes widened. "But is it safe?"

"Safer."

"As in passable?"

Lie. Tell her it's still too dangerous to cross. She won't know the difference. "Yes."

"So we're no longer trapped?"

He couldn't ignore her pointed question, though he wanted to. The thought of her leaving was unbearable. "I didn't say that."

"You're not making sense."

"It's Christmas Eve," he said lamely. "Need I say more?"

"Absolutely not," she said with a lilt in her voice.

He reached for his cup and held it up. "Cheers."

Julie put hers against his, then took a sip, staring at him over the rim of her cup. "Why haven't you ever married?"

His features changed. "You don't want to know."

Her chin jutted. "Yes, I do."

"Trust me, you don't."

She gave him a compassionate look. "That bad, huh?"

"Not really," he admitted, though with extreme caution. "Oh, I've had women. I won't deny that, but—" His voice trailed off.

"But what?" she pressed.

"Nothing." Hell, he couldn't tell her that he loved her, that he'd always loved her. She'd think he'd lost his ever-loving mind. "Hey, I know I'm being an ass," he added, "but that's just something I'd rather not talk about."

"I'd say you were smart."

Shane didn't miss the bitterness in her tone, and knew exactly what she was talking about. It made him want to snatch up that son of a bitch, rip his heart out then stomp it.

"Not all men are like him."

"God, I hope not."

"The two of us had a run-in."

Her jaw dropped. "You and Mike?"

"Yep."

"What happened?"

He told her. When he finished, she said, "Damn. I wish you'd knocked his block off."

Shane threw back his head and laughed. "I was just thinking the same thing, more or less."

"Aren't I awful?" she said, though her lips twitched.

"What happened?" He asked that before he thought. He hadn't wanted to share his heart. What made him think she did?

"You mean with Mike?"

He nodded.

"I didn't realize it at the time, but our marriage was doomed from the get-go. He didn't want me to teach, but he didn't want any children either."

"What did he want?"

"Me to cater to him. Be at his beck and call twenty-four hours a day."

"But you went to work."

"Right, and that's the only thing that kept me sane."

"So when did you know about the other woman?"

"Women," she corrected, her bitterness deepening. "From what I was told, Nelda, his fiancée, wasn't his first."

"But you never knew?"

"No, which doesn't speak well for me. But I trusted him."

"That's the way it's supposed to be." He paused. "How long before you found out about her?"

"Not until after I was pregnant."

"Did you want a baby?" Another loaded question, but one that had to be asked.

"Yes, I did. I wanted a child so badly that I buried my head in the sand."

She turned toward the cradle then, her face lighting up with a smile so sweet that it took his breath. "And if I had it to do all over again, I wouldn't change that. Elizabeth is now my life, my reason for living."

Shane wished the hell she was saying that about him, especially when he ached to jerk her in his arms and kiss her until those luscious lips were as full and swollen as her breasts. But his need wouldn't stop there. He wanted to bury himself high and hard in her. Make another baby. *His baby.*

Shane cleared his throat and shifted uncomfortably in the chair. "Well, I agree, Miss Elizabeth is the cat's meow."

In the intervening silence, they both faced the cradle. When they finally looked back at each other, both started to speak at the same time.

Laughing, Julie said, "You first."

"I was just wondering how a tree that lacks presents can be so beautiful."

"Because Christmas is not about presents."

"You're right."

"It's about love."

For a heartbeat, their gazes held. He clenched and unclenched his hands, itching to haul her into his arms. In fact, it took all of his willpower to keep his distance. He wanted her so desperately.

That desperation must've shown because she stood abruptly and said, "I think it's time I went to bed."

He rose to his feet. "You're right, it is getting late."

It was on the tip of his tongue to blurt out that he loved her. But if he did, he knew it would spook her, and he'd lose her for sure.

Once Julie had Elizabeth in her arms, she faced him again and whispered, "Merry Christmas, Shane."

He could only nod. His throat was suddenly too full of sadness to speak.

Sleep eluded her. She tried every trick in the book to drift off into never-never land. Nothing worked. Her eyes remained open and her brain active.

Shane.

She couldn't block him out of her mind. She couldn't stop thinking about his kisses, either, how breathless and tingly they had made her feel.

If she felt this way now when she couldn't have sex, how would she feel later? Would she be dying of lust for him? That thought made her face flame with color.

But in defense of herself, Shane was one fine-looking man, sexy as hell. Shane's bed could be kept as busy as he wanted it to be. She had no doubt about that.

Big deal.

His sex life, active or inactive, should make no difference to her. But it did, especially as he was so secretive about it. Had someone hurt him deeply? She didn't know nor should she care.

"Grrrrh," Julie muttered in frustration, turning over and punching the pillow.

She didn't want to become involved with another man. It was too soon. However, Shane wasn't just "another" man. He was special, and she knew that. He was a prize catch. And she knew he cared about her.

Suddenly her torrid thoughts were interrupted by a tap on the door. Frowning, she sat up in bed, drawing the covers with her.

"Yes."

Shane opened the door. Still dressed, he stood in the doorway. A light from behind in the hall, allowed her to see him.

"I'm sorry if I woke you up."

"You didn't," she said, a catch in her voice.

"I've been thinking."

"About what?"

"Us." When she would've intervened, he went on, "Hear me out, okay?"

Julie nodded, clutching the sheet tightly in her hand.

"I don't want you and Elizabeth to ever leave."

Her heart almost stopped beating. "Ever?"

"That's right."

"But we have to."

"No, you don't. Not if you marry me." He paused, then added, "For the baby's sake, if for no other reason."

# Chapter 12

*Marry him.*

Every time those words hit her brain with hammerlike force, her heart almost stopped beating. Of course, she couldn't marry him. Had he lost his mind? More to the point, had she lost hers for even thinking about it?

When he'd thrown out his off-the-cuff proposal, she'd been too stunned to do anything but stare at him with her mouth open.

He hadn't said anything either. He'd just stood there and calmly stared back at her.

But when the silence become deafening, he said thickly, "Julie, I asked you a question."

"Surely, you're not serious," she responded, blinking at him several times.

"I've never been more serious in my life. About anything."

"But that's not possible."

"Why isn't it?"

"Because you don't know me." She knew that sounded about as inane as anything she could've said, but at the moment that was the best she could do. She was shaken to the core and it showed.

In fact, the world seemed to have stood still while she tried to regain what little composure she had left. He'd taken a lot of it when he'd set her on fire with his hot kisses. She had enjoyed them far too much.

He smile briefly. "How can you say that after all we've been through?"

Even though his words sounded clichéd, right off the pages of a poorly written romance novel, they were the unvarnished truth. He had delivered her baby. He had seen her at her best and at her worst. Still...

"Why on earth would you want to marry me and take on the responsibility of someone's else's child?"

"That's a good enough reason right there. Elizabeth. She needs a father. It's just that simple."

"But do you need a wife?"

He hesitated and his eyes narrowed. "As a matter of fact, I do. I've needed one for a long time only I didn't realize how much until you and Elizabeth came into my life."

"But that's no reason to get married. I mean—" She couldn't say anymore. She wanted to ask him about love, about being in love, but the rest of the words seemed to have dried up in her throat.

"I think Elizabeth's a solid reason for getting married."

Julie placed a hand on her forehead and rubbed it.

"You realize this conversation is ludicrous, don't you?"

"Stop being so practical minded. Go to bed and think about it, okay? Promise you'll do that."

She swallowed hard, then nodded.

"Just go with your heart," he added on a thicker note. "Then in the morning, Christmas Day, we'll talk about it some more."

Now, as Julie lay in bed with Elizabeth in the cradle beside her, she fixed her gaze on the ceiling. But all she could see was Shane's face. It haunted her as did his words.

Go with her heart, he'd said.

At the moment, her heart was in such a chaotic state she couldn't depend on it to help her out. Her head was her only safety net. But it was also failing her, telling her that maybe she should accept his proposal.

Love?

How did it fit into this bizarre equation? How did she feel about Shane? Physical attraction certainly wasn't a problem; she was more than attracted to him. But was that enough? No. Maybe in the beginning, but not for the long haul.

So why couldn't she just say no with a clear conscience and go on about her life? She cared about him, that was why. But after Mike, how could she ever trust another man?

What if Shane was all hot for her now and the responsibility she brought with her only then to grow tired of both? After all, he would be rearing another man's child. What if he grew tired of being married, period?

Granted, Shane was different from her ex-husband. He had proved himself beyond a shadow of doubt. At the onset of her relationship with Mike, she had thought the same thing about him, that he was an okay kind of guy. She didn't find out who the real Mike was until she'd lived with him.

Well, she'd lived with Shane and had no complaints. So did that mean she should throw caution to the wind and marry him? It would be wonderful to have a strong, loving man to lean on, to take care of her and Elizabeth.

But could she take the risk?

With no immediate answers to her hard-hitting questions, Julie felt herself panic. Soon it would be daylight and she'd have to face Shane.

She couldn't do that. She needed more time to sort through her thoughts. Her only choice was to leave. The rain had stopped, and Shane had said the bridge was passable.

But how? She had no car. She couldn't drive Shane's truck. There would be no one to hold Elizabeth. Suddenly an idea struck her. But could she pull it off? She wouldn't know until she tried.

Millie. She was the key.

With her heart pounding in her ears, Julie picked up the phone and punched out her friend's number.

Shane could barely contain his excitement. Hell, he was like a kid waking up on Christmas morning with sugarplums dancing in his head.

What a crock, McCoy, he told himself.

Yet he couldn't stop grinning inside or out. He couldn't wait to see her and Elizabeth, though he didn't have any present to offer them but himself. Boy, was he ever in a smaltzy mood. If he kept on, he'd be wallowing in it.

With that unappetizing thought, he sat up on the side of the bed and looked at the clock. It was seven. Too early to go barging in Julie's room to see if she'd made up her mind, that was for sure.

He'd have to cool his heels. The thought that she might not accept his proposal made him physically ill. At least she hadn't said no, he reminded himself, getting up and making his way into the bathroom.

A short time later, he left the guest room and went to the kitchen. When he had to, he could make breakfast. Today, he wanted to. That would be the perfect icebreaker.

When he had prepared the best meal he could with his limited culinary skills, he poured himself another cup of coffee and frowned. She never slept late. Was she afraid to face him?

He sensed that was the case. Without torturing himself or her any longer, he made his way to her bedroom and tapped on the door.

No response. He tapped again. Still, no response.

"Julie," he said, tapping yet again.

When the room remained silent, fear twisted in his gut like a knife. Something was wrong. Without a second thought, he shoved open the door, only to stop dead in his tracks.

The room was empty.

All the air left his lungs, leaving him dizzy. He propped himself against the doorjamb, feeling a devastation like none he'd ever felt.

Had he frightened her that much? Or had his pro-

posal been so distasteful to her that she couldn't face
him? God, he couldn't believe she'd bolted—and in
the middle of the night.

How?

Turning he ran toward and out of the kitchen door,
his heart lodged in his throat. When he saw his truck,
he relaxed but only for a second. She hadn't driven
herself which meant someone drove her.

*Who* didn't matter. All that mattered was that she'd
left without saying a word. Maybe if he'd told her
that he loved her, that he'd always loved her, the
outcome might have been different.

Even so, he couldn't just let her disappear from his
life. He just couldn't. He eyed the truck while his gut
churned in turmoil.

Hell, he might as well go for it. What did he have
to lose?

Home.

She should've been ecstatic. Instead, Julie had
never been more miserable. It was Christmas Day
and she was staring at her lovely tree, all decorated
and lighted to the finest degree.

Her gaze dipped to the presents that littered the
space underneath. Their sparkling paper seemed to
wink back at her. She averted her eyes, having lost
all desire to open them.

She had thought when she returned to familiar territory she would be able to put things back in perspective, put Shane in perspective. So far, she hadn't
been able to do that.

Once Elizabeth was fed and bathed, then put down
for a nap, she had begun walking the floor. She

couldn't seem to stop, unable to believe what she'd done. What must Shane be thinking?

A pain shot through her heart. Everywhere she turned, even in her own house, she saw his big body. She couldn't stop thinking about how wonderful he was when he'd rescued her, then delivered Elizabeth, the look on his face when he'd first held the baby.

How could she have left him without any explanation after all he'd done for her?

Chicken. That was the word that came to mind, and it wasn't very flattering.

Even Millie had been exasperated with her and with good reason. After all, she'd awakened her in the middle of the night with a frantic cry for help.

But being the friend that she was, Millie had driven to the ranch and helped her and Elizabeth sneak out. It wasn't until they were at her house that Millie placed her hands on her hips and said, "What the hell is this all about?"

"You're mad at me, aren't you?"

"Oh, what gave you that idea? Hell's bells, I'm used to getting a frantic call in the middle of the night on Christmas Eve. Happens every year."

Julie shot her a look. "Some comfort you are."

"I was just teasing, and you know that. But seriously, I think you owe me an explanation."

"Of course I do."

"First, though," Millie said, rubbing her bleary-looking eyes, "let me fix us some coffee."

Julie didn't argue, too fractured to make sense of anything.

A few minutes later, they faced each other on the

couch while Elizabeth slept peacefully close by. They sipped in silence.

"So?"

"I panicked."

"Did he come in your room and jump your bones?"

"No," she snapped.

Millie cocked her head and said, "Well, something had to freak you out."

"He asked me to marry him."

"Ah, I see."

"Once I thought about having to face him this morning and give him an answer, I lost it."

"That you did, my friend." Millie softened her words with a lopsided smile.

"He probably hates me now," Julie said in a forlorn voice.

"I doubt that. Besides, he's probably still asleep and is none the wiser."

"Well, when he wakes up and finds me gone, he'll—" Julie stopped for a second. "I have no idea what his reaction will be."

"If he loves you, he'll be hurt."

"He never said that he did."

"How do you feel about him?" Millie asked. "Do you love him?"

"I honestly don't know," Julie cried. "I'm attracted to him, that's for sure."

"Well, that's a start."

"Millie, what am I going to do?"

"Nothing, at least not right now. You're home, out of harm's way, so to speak. Go to bed and get some sleep. In the daylight, things will look different. Then we'll talk some more when you and Elizabeth come for Christmas dinner.''

Now, with Millie having long gone and the sky bright with the dawn of morning, Julie hadn't closed her eyes. She'd been pacing the floor the entire night.

Suddenly, she heard Elizabeth fretting. She made her way into the bedroom and sat beside the cradle, rocking it.

Wide-eyed, Elizabeth stared up at her. "If you only knew the stunt your mommy pulled, sweetheart, you'd be so upset.''

Elizabeth merely looked at her.

"It's awful, what I did, especially when I love him.''

Julie froze. What had she said? The truth. She had admitted the truth, and it had come straight from her soul. Oh, God, what had she done? Had her selfish behavior ruined everything? Could she make it up to him?

There was only one way to find out. She reached for Elizabeth. That was when she heard the doorbell.

Not happy with the unexpected interruption, Julie dashed into the living room and jerked open the door.

Shane stood in front of her.

"Oh,'' she whispered in a breathless voice.

"May I come in?''

Once they were inside, both the warmth and the silence closed about them. Shane was the first to break the silence. "I just wanted to tell you that I loved you, that I've always loved you.''

"Oh, Shane,'' she whispered with an overflowing heart, "I love you, too.''

His eyes widened along with his arms. She leapt

into them, and he held her so tightly that she thought her bones would crack.

Finally, he pulled back, and she noticed his eyes were filled with tears that matched her own.

"I'm so sorry for being so stubborn," she whispered. "Can you ever forgive me?"

He kissed her, then, a long, wet kiss that conveyed his forgiveness like no words could. "Will you marry me?"

"Yes, yes, yes."

He kissed her again.

"Will you let me be Elizabeth's dad legally?"

"Yes, yes, yes."

He laughed out loud, then hugged her close again. "Come on, let's go tell Elizabeth."

Julie, overcome with love and joy, lifted her eyes heavenward. Miracles do happen, especially at Christmas.

\* \* \* \* \*

# Holiday Reunion
## Marilyn Pappano

Dear Reader,

Like Rebecca in *Holiday Reunion,* my favorite part of Christmas is unpacking the ornaments. My husband and I have built our collection over twenty-two years of marriage, starting with four boxes of brightly colored glass balls (with a twenty-two-year-old price tag still on them: two boxes for $1.50). We have everything from angels to reindeer, porcelain to tin, extravagant splurges to...well, two boxes for $1.50. There are ornaments with photos of our son, as well as our dogs; ornaments from places we've lived or visited; ones I've picked out myself and plenty that were gifts; plus our son's entire collection, started at birth twenty-one years ago.

Each year we put up the tree, then bring down the decorations from the attic. I take my sweet time unpacking them—and it *is* a sweet time. Virtually every one of them brings back memories, and I spend hours savoring them before putting them on the tree. Once they're in place, then it's official. The Christmas season has begun.

Wishing you the merriest—and most peaceful—of holidays.

Marilyn Pappano

# Chapter 1

Rebecca Wilson stood in front of the floor-length mirror in her bathroom and wrinkled her nose at her reflection. There was nothing wrong with the outfit she'd chosen—a sheath and jacket in a green so dark it was almost black, black hose, black heels and a simple diamond pendant. No, the clothes were great. The problem was her.

The last thing she wanted to do this rainy December Monday evening was go to a party. The annual Chamber of Commerce celebration had started at six o'clock, and most people she knew had gone straight from work. She had made the excuse that she needed to run home first, had promised that she would be there in no time. Now it was a few minutes after seven, and she hadn't yet managed to push herself out the door. Going to the party would force her to acknowledge that Christmas was only a week away,

and that would lead to the reminder that she would
be spending it alone.

Without Steve.

Her reflection's mouth tightened and sadness filled
her eyes. Rebecca ordered her own mouth to relax,
ordered the sadness back inside where it belonged.

In the six weeks since they'd separated, she and
Steve had done a pretty good job of avoiding each
other. It shouldn't have been an easy thing to do in
a town the size of Grand Springs, but they managed.
She stayed away from the hospital where he was on
staff, and he avoided City Hall where she worked.
She didn't go near the old house they'd bought upon
moving to Grand Springs and had spent the years
since in a constant state of renovation, and he stayed
away from her apartment…at least, since that first
week.

But he was likely to be at the party tonight. The
administrators of Vanderbilt Memorial were big on
community involvement. They encouraged the staff
to take part in every civic activity that came along,
and the Chamber's Christmas party was no exception. Barring a medical emergency, Steve would be
there.

So she would be careful to avoid him. It wouldn't
be difficult. The banquet hall at Randolph's was a
big room. There would be a lot of people there, and
Steve was obviously no more anxious to see her than
she was to see him. She would put in an appearance,
make certain her boss saw her, and then come home.
It would take an hour, tops, and then she could snug-
gle on the couch in her favorite pajamas and fall

asleep to the sounds of the television, as she did most nights.

It was a very short walk from the bathroom through the bedroom to the front door. The apartment was so tiny that it would fit into one corner of Steve's house. Of course, his house would fill less than one corner of one floor in the house where she grew up. The estate, her parents called it. Wentworth Mansion, according to most folks in Denver. Home, decreed her grandmother. A cold showplace filled with cold people and bad memories, as far as Rebecca was concerned.

She had so many bad memories.

But she wouldn't think of them right now. She would paste on such a smile that no one who saw it would ever guess how many times her heart had been broken. She would get through this evening the way she got through life these days—one hour at a time.

The party was in full swing when Rebecca arrived. The decorations were festive, the music Christmassy, the partygoers in a holiday mood. She got a cup of eggnog to occupy her hands, then worked her away around the perimeter of the room, keeping one eye out for her boss, so she could show she'd obeyed his directive, and the other for Steve, so she could stay at least a hundred feet away.

She located her boss sharing opinions over drinks with several of his cronies. With a smile, he drew her into the group. "Rebecca, you know everyone here, don't you?"

Of course she did. As assistant to the mayor, she made a point of knowing virtually everyone he knew. She reminded him of names and birthdays, kept him filled in on personal details as well as business. She said hellos all around, then touched the mayor's arm. "Sir, the senator and his wife just arrived."

He looked around, then spotted his target. "And her name is—?"

"Betsy. They have four children—three in college back east and Tyler, still at home."

He grinned at his friends. "Can you believe this girl? I couldn't get along without her. Excuse me, gentlemen."

Rebecca excused herself as well and continued her circuit around the room, smiling until she thought her face might freeze that way. She wondered if everyone else was as happy as they looked, or if some of them were just good actors, like her. Though it was said that misery loved company, she wouldn't wish this awful hurt and loneliness on anyone.

Except Steve.

When she spied Juliette Stuart sitting alone at a corner table, she gave a sigh of relief and headed that way. "Mind if I join you?"

"Not at all." With one foot, Juliette nudged a chair out from the table. "You look lovely tonight."

"Thanks. So do you." Though Juliette was always pretty in a delicate, almost ethereal way, when she was pregnant, she glowed like a Christmas tree. This was her second baby in the three years she and Colton had been married. The first had been an adorable boy with his daddy's eyes. In another month, they'd find out whether Marty was getting a brother or a sister.

In another month, Rebecca would simply be another month older, and sadder.

"Where's Colton?" she asked, determined to keep up the pretense that she wasn't slowly dying inside. "It's not often I see you without him."

"He's getting me some food—and it had better not be any of those delicate little finger foods, either. I'm famished. I keep reminding him that I'm eating for two, but the concept doesn't quite register. He's regularly amazed at how much food I can put away in one sitting." Looking past Rebecca, she smiled. "Ah, here he comes now and—"

She broke off so abruptly that Rebecca knew why immediately. She felt it in the goose bumps that raced down her arms and in the tightening in her stomach. If she turned around, she would see the police chief approaching, and he would be accompanied by the last person on earth she wanted to see.

"Hey, darlin'." Colton set two full plates in front of Juliette, then kissed her. "I see you didn't waste away from hunger while I was gone, in spite of your dire predictions. I made a point of telling everyone that all this food was for you. Hi, Rebec—" Like Juliette, he looked behind her and tensed.

Rebecca called on years of living with her parents and her grandmother to summon what she knew appeared to be a genuine smile. "Hello, Colton. I hope you're enjoying the party. It's not as if you don't attend more than your share of them. Juliette, it was good to see you. Take care of yourself."

She rose gracefully and started away without so much as a glance behind her, but she made it only a few feet before he spoke.

*He.* Steve.

"Can't you even say hello, Rebecca?" His words

were clipped, his voice strained, but still it sent a shiver down her spine. She steeled herself against it, replayed in her mind that same voice destroying her one cruel accusation at a time, then slowly turned to face him. He'd obviously come straight from work, evidenced by the tousled look of his hair, the faint shadow of beard on his jaw, and the slightly rumpled appearance of his dark suit and white shirt. Even so, he was still the handsomest man at the party, the handsomest man she'd ever known, and she loved him, wanted him, hated him and wished she'd never met him.

Praying her voice would be steady, she gave him a cool, phony smile. "Sorry, Steve. I didn't see you there."

He came closer, moving around the table to stop right in front of her. "I assume your plan was to get in and out without having to face me," he said bitterly.

"That presumes that I even thought about you enough to make plans. I generally don't."

"Damn it, Rebecca—"

"No, Steve." The chilly congeniality disappeared from her voice, leaving it low and ragged. "Damn *you.*" Spinning on her heel, she stalked away, heading for the door. Of course, escaping him couldn't be that easy. He followed her to the exit, catching up to her while she waited for the valet to deliver her car.

"How many times do I have to say I'm sorry?" he demanded furiously.

"Gee, you know, I remember hearing a lot of things from you, but 'I'm sorry' doesn't seem to be one of them." Unable to stand politely inside, she walked out, waiting under the porte cochere. It was freezing, and she could hear the proof of it on the roof overhead. In the short time she'd been inside, the rain that had started earlier in the evening in a downpour that threatened to flood low-lying areas had turned to sleet. Just what she needed to cap off a perfectly rotten night.

The valet who'd taken her ticket came hurrying back, shivering in spite of his parka. "It'll be just a minute, ma'am. Your car is blocked by another. We'll have to move it."

Of course. And to add insult to injury, as he returned with the keys necessary to do that, Steve came outside. "Okay, Rebecca," he said, his voice taut, his patience strained. "I'm sorry. I'm sorry I yelled at you. I'm sorry I didn't let you explain. I'm sorry I overreacted. I'm sorry for every damned thing I've ever done or might ever do. Are you satisfied now?"

She gave him a scornful look. "You're sorry, I'm sorry, we're all sorry. So live with it."

"Damn it... Don't be this way, please. It's been six weeks! You haven't talked to me, you won't return my calls, you won't read my letters. Please, Rebecca, you're killing me. Don't let it end like this. Give me a chance, please."

She turned so he was nothing more than a blur in her peripheral vision. "Do you think an apology can make everything right?" she demanded, her voice low and shaky. "Do you think you could possibly say anything to make me forget the things you've already said?"

If she released her control for one instant, the memories would come flooding back. His anger. His

accusations. His bitterness. She'd thought she had experienced the worst pain imaginable by the time she
was twenty, but she'd been wrong. The sorrow she'd
felt at her parents' betrayal, at Devin's and her grandmother's, had been nothing compared to the agony
of Steve's betrayal. She'd loved him more than life
itself, and he'd stood there in their kitchen and cut
out her heart one angry word at a time.

As the valet returned with her sedan, she glanced
in Steve's direction. She wanted to demand a divorce,
to tell him to go to hell, to beg permission to go back
to the way they'd been before. But they couldn't go
back. And she couldn't bear to go forward, and so
she said nothing. She simply looked for a moment
before trading the valet a tip for the keys.

And then she drove away.

Muttering a curse, Steve watched until her headlights disappeared from sight, then realized the valet
was watching him curiously. Shoving his hand in his
pocket, he found the ticket for his own car and
handed it over. He wanted to hit something really
hard—wanted just once for the pain he lived with to
have a real, easily fixed source. Broken fingers or a
broken hand, he could deal with—hell, he was a doctor—but he didn't have a damn idea what to do about
a broken heart. Especially Rebecca's.

Not an hour went by that he didn't regret their
fight. He never should have yelled at her, never
should have walked away from her or verbally attacked her. His only excuse was…hell, he didn't have
an excuse. His ego had been wounded. He'd thought
he was her best friend as well as her husband, thought

she'd confided everything important in her life to him. Discovering her secrets had stunned him. He'd been hurt and had struck out at her, and he'd lost the single best thing in his life.

And he didn't have a clue how to win her back, or how to survive without her.

He overtipped the kid who brought his truck, then climbed in and pulled out from under the shelter of the roof into the frozen rain. The sport-utility vehicle was big, heavy, and made for weather like this. It had cost a small fortune, but he'd talked Rebecca into the purchase last spring when they'd still been trying to have a family. He'd swayed her with facts about safety features and accident survivability, with images of a back seat filled with smiling, chubby-cheeked, *safe* babies. Back then, he'd refused to realize that he and Rebecca were a family in and of themselves. He'd insisted their lives would never be complete without children. Now he was alone, and he had no one to blame but himself.

But what was he supposed to do, damn it? When she wouldn't talk to him, when she'd just told him that nothing he could say could undo the damage he'd already caused, what the hell was he supposed to do? Live the rest of his life alone and miserable?

Or accept that the marriage was over?

The question, a whisper even in his mind, made his fingers tighten around the steering wheel and tied his gut in knots. He could never accept that it was over. That would mean his life was over. All his hopes, all his dreams, everything he'd worked for— gone. Lost in one moment of anger.

Feeling the ache as surely as if it were physical,

Steve forced his attention to his driving. There wasn't much traffic on the streets. Most people in town were at the Chamber party or hosting parties of their own. They were headed for Denver to finish their Christmas shopping or off to spend their holidays elsewhere. Still, if the rain didn't stop soon, there would surely be flooding, and the sleet coming down now made travel even more treacherous. Maybe he should go to the hospital instead of home. There were bound to be a few accidents tonight, and if he was there to help the duty staff, maybe it would save them from calling out someone else later. If he was wrong and the night remained trauma-free, he could sack out on the couch in his office. He'd done it plenty of times before. It was the only way he got a decent night's rest these days.

Cautiously he turned onto the street that ran past the park. A few blocks up, if he turned right, he'd be at the hospital. Going straight would take him to Grand Springs College, closed now for the semester break. Turning left would take him any number of places, including the apartment complex where Rebecca now lived. He'd been there a few times, standing on her tiny stoop, banging on her door, painfully aware that she was inside, listening and not caring. After his last visit had brought the neighbors out to stare sympathetically, he hadn't gone back.

He eased the truck to a stop at the intersection, then glanced left to make certain it was clear. The only lights he saw through the pouring sleet were taillights, heading in the opposite direction. After moving his foot from the brake to the gas, he hesitated and looked again. There was something about those taillights... Was the car moving at all? Had the driver gotten stuck on a particularly slick patch? Or was it—

Abruptly, he realized the problem—the taillights weren't on the road at all, and they were tilted at an odd angle. He checked traffic once more, then turned left, creeping along the icy wet roadway, wondering idly what December in Hawaii was like. As he drew closer, he saw that he'd been right. There were deep skid marks cutting across the lane and down the embankment, where the car that had made them was lying on its roof.

Steve stopped at the side of the road, traded his overcoat for the warmer parka on the back seat, then took out the nylon gym bag that held his emergency first-aid kit before slipping and sliding his way toward the vehicle. He was only a few yards away when something about the car registered in his mind—the fact that it was blue, or that it had a Vanderbilt Memorial parking decal on the back window, or maybe the peculiar ding in the left rear fender— and for an instant he stopped moving, stopped breathing.

It was Rebecca's car.

Forgetting caution, he tore across the ground, fumbling with the passenger door, losing precious seconds in opening it. Once it was open, he crawled inside, maneuvering awkwardly in the upside-down vehicle. Though the engine wasn't running, the key was still on, the wipers still scraping across the glass, the stereo still playing. There was no sound from the driver. "Rebecca? Rebecca, can you hear me?"

She'd been wearing her seat belt, thank God, and

now it held her dangling upside down, her hair swaying around her face. Her eyes were closed, but her pulse, he discovered when he ripped off one glove to check, was steady and strong.

He reached inside his jacket for his cell phone and dialed 911. First he got a recording, and then was placed on hold. It seemed an eternity before the dispatcher finally came on the line, though his watch said it had been less than three minutes. Rather than requesting the paramedics, he identified himself and asked the status of the county's ambulances. All of them were on emergency runs. The best estimate the dispatcher could give him was twenty minutes, maybe longer. With a curt thanks, he hung up, then removed a cervical collar from the first-aid kit.

Ordinarily he would never consider moving an accident victim, especially one who'd suffered head trauma, but the north wind that drove the rain made the temperature feel close to zero, and Rebecca's lips were already tinged pale blue. He could wait twenty minutes for an ambulance that might not show, or he could transport her to the hospital himself in under ten minutes. Under the circumstances, he didn't see a better choice.

Gingerly he fixed the collar in place, then did the best examination he could manage in the cramped space before unfastening the seat belt. She slumped into his arms, moaning softly as he caught her. "You're all right, darlin'. It's all right. I'm going to take you to the hospital just as soon as I get you out of here. Can you hear me, babe? You'll be all right."

He backed out of the car, half lifting, half dragging her, then scooped her into his arms. There was a knot on her left temple, most likely where she'd banged against the side glass when the car had rolled. It looked grotesque against the delicate curve of her forehead, and it made him feel helpless and guilty and angry. Other than that, she appeared uninjured, though she would surely have some seat belt bruises. He wouldn't stop praying, though, until he'd done a full examination, including X rays.

After opening the rear doors, he maneuvered her into the cargo area where she could lie flat, then spread his overcoat over her to warm her. Once inside himself, he turned the heat to high, then directed all the vents toward the back. "We'll be at the hospital in just a minute, babe," he said, carefully maneuvering into a tight U-turn. "Just hold on, darlin'. We'll get you taken care of."

Though she was unconscious, he continued to talk, as much for his own benefit as hers. "You should have taken the truck when you moved. I know you said it was too big and hard to park and drove like a tank, but, hell, in weather like this, you need something that drives like a tank." Unbidden, the corners of his mouth lifted in a tight smile. "The way you drive, you need a tank no matter what the weather's like. You've managed to dent that car in places that the body shop people haven't yet figured out how to fix. I remember the first time I ever rode with you, I said—"

"I gave bats out of hell a bad name."

Relief rushed through him as he risked a quick glance over his shoulder at her. She hadn't moved, but he could see that her eyes were open. Her voice was weak, raw, but there was nothing wrong with her recall. "To compare your driving to a bat out of hell does a grievous injustice to the bat," he responded, careful to keep his voice steady. "How do you feel?"

"Head hurts." In the mirror, he saw her raise one shaky hand to touch the cervical collar, then her temple, then wince. "What happened?"

"That little tin can car of yours lost it on the slick road. You flipped it back there." Turning into the parking lot, he followed the signs to Vanderbilt's ER. "We're almost there. Lie still."

"Don't need hospital," she murmured. "Go home."

"Not until I check you out. A head as hard as yours requires a pretty good blow to be knocked unconscious. We've got to rule out any serious injury." He pulled under the roof overhang that extended twenty-five feet out from the ER entrance, and the incessant ping-ping of ice on metal abruptly stopped. The absence of the sound went a long way to easing the tension that knotted his muscles.

At the back of the truck, he jerked the door open and scooped her once again into his arms. This time, though, she ineffectually brushed at him. "I can walk."

"Yeah, right."

"At least get a wheelchair. This is embarrassing."

It wasn't embarrassing. After six weeks of dreaming about having her in his arms again, it was incredible. She was so warm, so soft, and she felt like every sweet dream he'd ever had. "It's not the first time I've ever carried you. Remember when we moved into the house?"

"But we were married then."

His mouth tightened. So did his nerves. "We're married now, Rebecca," he said harshly. "Or did you forget?"

Instead of answering, she closed her eyes. She was so pale, with shadows under her eyes and lines at the corners of her mouth, that he felt guilty for getting tough with her. He didn't have time to apologize, though, as he carried her through the two sets of automatic doors that led into the emergency room.

"Dr. Wilson, what—"

He interrupted the admitting clerk without slowing his steps. "Which room is open?"

"Number five. I'll page Dr. Petrocelli."

"Do that. And get X-ray down here. I need a cross-table lateral C-spine stat. Also get me an IV administration set. Who's on call for Neuro?"

The clerk practically ran to keep up with him. "Dr. Hassad. Shall I call him?"

Steve scowled as he shouldered open the door. Hassad was a resident with the promise of a bright and profitable future in Neurology ahead of him, but Steve wasn't interested in the future. He wanted the best right now, and at Vanderbilt, that was Art Thomas, the head of the department. "Not yet," he decided. "Let me see how the exam goes and what the films look like. Then, if we need to, we can call Dr. Thomas."

"Dr. Thomas isn't on call," Rebecca said groggily. "Don't you listen?"

"He'll come in for me." He settled her on the bed, then glared at the clerk as he began removing her coat. "What are you waiting for?"

"I—I need the patient's name for her chart."

Rebecca started to answer, but Steve cut her off. "It's Rebecca Wilson." Then, more for her benefit than the clerk's, he stiffly added, "My wife."

The girl made a soft apologetic sound, then left, closing the door behind her. Rebecca found herself foolishly wishing she would come back. The room was so small, and she felt defenseless, and Steve could easily overwhelm her even under the best circumstances. Of all the nights to have a wreck, and of all the people to find her...

Her heavy sigh brought his attention her way. He'd stripped to his shirtsleeves and loosened his tie. "Are you in pain?"

She tried to shake her head, but the cervical collar made it impossible. "Not really. My head hurts."

"It should. You've got a bright purple and red goose egg. My God, Rebecca, when I realized that was your car, I was so—"

She lowered her gaze and looked away, and the flow of words dried up as abruptly as if a faucet had been shut off. The silence between them was heavy and tense, the sort that crawled along her skin and made her want to scream. But what could she say to break it? That she didn't care what he'd thought or felt? That might be the image she wanted to present, but it wasn't true. She cared too damn much for her own good.

In the midst of the silence, a nurse breezed in, greeting them both with smiles and delivering supplies to Steve. She murmured something about returning in just one moment, then breezed out again.

He was the one who finally spoke, his tone as impersonal as if he were speaking to a total stranger.

''The first thing we're going to do is start an IV, then do a neurological exam while we're waiting to get X rays of your neck. Once we're sure there's no injury to the cervical spine, we'll take that collar off, then send you to Radiology for a skull and facial bones series. If everything checks out, you'll be able to go home tonight.''

''Okay.'' It was a stupid response, but the only one she felt capable of making at that moment.

He came to the side of the bed, reaching for her hand—her left hand where she no longer wore his wedding ring. She'd taken it off and hidden it away in a great rush of bitterness the day she'd moved out of his house, but not wearing it didn't make her feel any less connected to him, or less betrayed, or less alone.

For a moment he stared at her bare finger, rubbing his fingertip lightly over her skin. Then, scowling harder, he turned all professional again. Quickly he removed her wristwatch and dropped it in his pocket, then tied a rubber tourniquet around her forearm. She watched him swab the back of her hand, then looked away as he inserted the needle into her vein. Surprised by the pain, Rebecca barely managed to avoid jerking her hand back. ''You don't hurt at all, do you... Except when you want to. Then you're deadly.''

The look he gave her was icy with anger, but before he could respond, Tony Petrocelli came into the room, accompanied by a nurse. Rebecca liked Tony, and would have liked him even more if he would order Steve to leave. But it would take more than a request from the attending physician to make Steve do something he didn't want to do. He was scowling so fiercely that probably nothing less than arrest would accomplish it tonight.

"Well, Rebecca, I've seen you looking better," Tony said cheerfully. "What happened?"

"I've been told I flipped my car." She pretended not to notice the muscle in Steve's jaw twitch because she hadn't answered more simply. *Steve told me...*

"You don't remember?"

"I remember losing control of the car and skidding across the road. I couldn't remember which way to turn the wheel, and I forgot about just tapping the brake. The car went off the road into the grass, and then I was falling, and I hit my head and..." She shrugged, neglecting to mention that she'd lost control because she'd been too upset to pay attention, or that she'd been upset because of the little scene at the party with Steve. No need to make him feel guilty, or to let him know how much power he still held over her.

Tony asked more questions, designed, she supposed, to test her recall. *Do you know your full name? Where are you? What is today's date? Who's on the one-dollar bill? How many months are in a year?*

At the foot of the bed, Steve muttered one question of his own—*Are you married?* One he refused to repeat when Tony asked him to, one she refused to acknowledge.

The exam continued with a look at her eyes, ears, nose and neck, a test of her awareness of sensation, checks of her spine and pelvis, putting her hips, knees and ankles through range-of-motion exercises. The only part she didn't mind was the command to stick out her tongue. Looking straight at Steve, she readily did so.

He wasn't amused.

"You're a lucky woman," Tony said, making notes on her chart. "X-ray will be here in a minute to get your C-spine, then we'll get a skull and facial bones in Radiology. If everything's okay, then you'll be free to go. I'll see you again before you check out."

"Thanks, Tony," she murmured as both he and the nurse left the room. They were replaced almost immediately with two X-ray technologists and an un-wieldy machine. They accomplished what she'd thought no one could—making Steve leave the room.

Closing her eyes, Rebecca breathed deeply. She didn't like herself like this. She was a nice person, and she didn't go around hurting other people. The fact that Steve had hurt her first, and worse, didn't excuse her behavior. She just didn't know how to deal with the hurt. With the other people who'd be-trayed her, removing them from her life had been easy. She'd never missed them. But Steve... He'd meant everything to her. She didn't know how to live without him but didn't know how to forgive him, either.

Once the techs left, Steve returned, standing at the foot of the bed. "I'll take you to the house—"

"No," she said quickly, sharply. "I want to go to my place."

He flinched, but she didn't care. There was no way she was setting foot in the house where they'd lived together, not with things the way they were. That house held too many memories, mostly good, bad only at the end, all of them painful. All she needed was her cozy apartment, her favorite flannel nightshirt and her big comfy bed, and she would be fine.

And Steve. She needed him, even if she couldn't have him.

"What can I do, Rebecca?" he asked, his voice taut with simmering emotion. "If nothing I say matters, what the hell can I do to make things right?"

She stared guiltily at her hands, folded over her middle. She knew too well from her own experience that some things could never be made right. Was their marriage one of them? Maybe, that sly voice whispered, and she felt a stab of pain that had nothing to do with the accident. She'd waited all her life for Steve, had planned the rest of her life around him. Without him she had nothing. Just empty arms and an empty heart.

"Damn it, Rebecca..." He swore hoarsely, but there was no anger to it. Just soul-deep frustration.

Before he could say anything else, one of the X-ray techs returned to claim her for her trip to Radiology. Thankfully, Steve remained behind. She couldn't enjoy the respite, though, because she knew he would be waiting when she came back, knew he would insist on taking her home and would probably insist on staying the night. She wasn't going to escape him so easily.

Truthfully, there was a part of her that didn't want to escape, a part that was hungry for the sight of him, that wanted desperately to be in his arms once more.

By the time the results of the X rays came back—

all normal—Rebecca was exhausted. Tony went over a list of complications to watch for—headache, dizziness, nausea, blurred vision—then discharged her.

Three hours after leaving the party, Rebecca walked—or, rather, was wheeled—out the ER doors. Steve helped her into the truck, then started the half mile to her apartment at the great speed of about eight miles an hour. When they reached the scene of the accident, he stopped at the side of the road and climbed out.

She stared at the overturned vehicle, thinking how much worse the accident could have been. In the mountains that made Grand Springs such a beautiful place, there were countless places where skidding off the roadway might mean a drop of a few feet, like here, or a few thousand feet. She could have been killed. Her problems would have been over.

Steve's would have been just starting.

She watched as he trudged across the icy ground, his head bent against the sleet, his dark hair glistening in the glow of a nearby street lamp. Occasionally he slipped, but for the most part, he was surefooted, confident.

It had been his confidence she'd admired most from the beginning. She'd been a glorified gofer at City Hall in Denver, and he'd been nearing the end of his residency at a local hospital when a friend from work had set them up. She'd been convinced nothing serious could ever come from a blind date until she'd returned home from her first—and last—one. He had been so sure of himself and his place in the world, and so sure of her, while she wasn't sure of anything.

When he opened the door, a blast of frigid air

rushed in. He was shivering as he handed her purse and keys to her. She could feel the chill radiating from him, could actually smell the cold mingled with the fragrance of her favorite aftershave. It was invigorating. Intoxicating.

It was only a few blocks farther to the apartment complex, covered at a snail's pace. When he turned into the parking lot, the truck's rear tires slid. As he drove toward the building at the far end where her apartment was located, at odd moments the truck traveled as far sideways as it did forward. When he pulled into a parking space, the curb stopped their motion when the brakes didn't, and they both gave a sigh of relief.

"Wait," he commanded. He took a bag from the back floorboard, then came around to open her door. She wished she could take herself inside without any help, without needing his arm around her, surely, please, without having to be carried in his arms. But she was exhausted, and the aches the doctor had promised would come had arrived. She was stiff and sore and would certainly be none too steady on a thick layer of solid ice.

They made it safely to the stairs, protected from the weather by the roof. At the landing, she fitted her key in the lock with some difficulty, then gave another deep sigh when she stepped inside. The apartment was warm, lit by lamps on the end tables and above the kitchen sink, and smelled of potpourri and a faint hint of the perfume she'd used before leaving for the party. The television was on, tuned to an all-night movie channel, because without it, the absence of life in the place was impossible to ignore.

Then Steve followed her in and closed the door, and the idea that the apartment could ever be empty of life seemed impossible. Without coming farther than four feet into the room, he filled it with his presence.

She left her purse and keys on the tiny dining table built for two, then carefully shrugged out of her coat, draping it over the back of a chair. She was suddenly nervous, not knowing what to say, where to look, what to do. "I—I appreciate the ride and—and everything," she said lamely. "You'd better go before—"

The look he gave her made her break off. "You wouldn't send your worst enemy out in weather like this. Surely you can loan me your couch for a night."

She'd expected as much. She'd just thought it was worth a try.

He set the bag he carried on the table, then removed his coat and gloves. She recognized the bag. It was one he took to work with him every day, for the lucky days when he had time to stop by the hospital gym. It held gym shorts, a T-shirt with the sleeves ripped out and the toiletries necessary to go from bench-pressing a hundred and fifty pounds to soothing the fears of a five-year-old facing a tonsillectomy.

Moving away from her, he took in two-thirds of the apartment with one long look. "Nice place," he said flatly.

Rebecca flushed. Ninety percent of the complex's residents were college students, and the apartments were exactly what the kids would expect. They were cheaply built and shabbily maintained. Clean, but not much else. It was a lot like their first apartment, just colder, drearier, lonelier.

"No Christmas tree?"

She mutely shook her head, though the answer was obvious.

"Why not? You always loved Christmas."

She started to shrug, but it hurt her head. "I'll get you some blankets and a pillow, then I'm going to bed."

"A hell of a night, wasn't it?"

Her only response was a faint smile as she went into the bedroom. She took a pillow from her bed and blankets, plus a sheet, from the closet, and carried them into the living room, depositing them in a neat pile on the sofa. "If you get hungry, help yourself to whatever you want. The bathroom is through my bedroom. The door's on the left there." She gestured, then combed her fingers through her hair. "I, uh… Good night."

All too aware of his gaze on her, she returned to the bedroom, pushed the door up almost until it clicked, then abruptly sank down on the bed as her legs gave way. She was so tired and sore, both inside and out. More than anything in the world, she wanted to curl up in Steve's arms and let him take care of her, the way he always had. But even though he was in the next room, more than fifteen feet and a partially closed door separated them. Anger, disappointment, bitterness and betrayal stood between them, and might keep them apart forever.

# Chapter 2

Steve stood where he was a long time before finally dropping down on the sofa. It was old and soft, the kind that was great for stretching out on to watch a football game or taking a nap. He was so damn tired that he figured he could fall asleep in suit and tie if he could just sit still for ten minutes, but only a few minutes into the wait, his stomach growled. He hadn't gotten anything to eat at the party—nothing since an early lunch, in fact—and he was starting to regret it.

His refrigerator at home held bottled water, a carton of six-week-old eggs, and a moldy chunk of cheddar. His meals in those weeks had come from the hospital cafeteria, the McDonald's restaurant drive-through or the microwave. Without Rebecca, he saw no point in cooking at home or going to a restaurant for a meal for one. He wasn't sure what she thought about eating alone in a restaurant, but one glance inside her refrigerator showed that she certainly didn't mind cooking for one. There was a pot of chili on the second shelf, the makings for fajitas on the third one, and salad ingredients and fresh vegetables filled the bins.

He dished up a bowl of chili and heated it in the microwave, trying hard not to let the aroma take him back to the countless times he'd helped her prepare the dish in their own kitchen. He wasn't a great cook, but he could chop and sauté under direction with the best of 'em. Helping her in the kitchen had been a simple pleasure that he'd enjoyed a lot. He missed it a lot.

Taking the chili and a cola with him, he settled on the sofa with an old Katherine Hepburn movie on the tube. There had been a time when television had fascinated him. Lately, though, he'd been unable to summon any interest. He used the TV as a noise-maker, something to disguise the fact that he was totally alone.

He suspected Rebecca did the same.

He wondered if she was in bed yet, if she was asleep, if she was in pain. It seemed wrong that she was in the next room while he was confined to this one, seemed incredibly wrong that after giving him the worst scare of his life, she could calmly go off to bed by herself and deny him the satisfaction of simply being with her. Watching her breathe... That was all he wanted to do. Watch her and reassure himself that she was all right. He needed to be with her. But she didn't need him.

After rinsing his dishes, he picked up his bag and

went to her door. For one moment, he stood there, hand raised but not touching the wood. He'd shared a bed with her for more than five years, from their second date until six weeks ago. He'd made love to her, taken showers with her, shared every intimacy known to husband and wife, and yet he felt awkward about walking into her bedroom, even if it was only to reach the bathroom. He felt as if he didn't belong, when with Rebecca was the only place he had ever truly belonged.

His fingers curling into a fist, he pushed the door open. The bedroom was dark, but flickering light shone through the open bathroom door. He tried not to glance at her bed as he walked through, but of course he failed. There wasn't much to see—just shadows and shapes—and only the slow, even sound of her breathing. He knew if he switched on a lamp, or waited until his vision adjusted to the low light, he would find her lying on her back, her pale brown hair falling away from her face, her features so sweetly relaxed that no one would suspect she'd ever had a care in the world.

He knew because for more than five years, he'd watched her sleep. Sometimes he'd simply marveled over her beauty, her gentleness and the fact that she'd chosen him. Sometimes he'd worried whether he could make her happy, had wondered how long a Wentworth—of the old-money, high-society Wentworths—could be satisfied with a man like him. And sometimes he'd just gotten lost in her, so lost that he'd hoped he would never find his way back.

Once the bathroom door was closed, he turned on the light. Like the rest of the apartment, the bathroom was standard issue—functional but cramped. Hot pink and purple towels matched the print shower curtain and provided some color, and a crystal container of potpourri scented the air. A wicker basket on the countertop held her cosmetics, another brushes and combs, and a fat pink candle with three wicks provided the glow he'd noticed from her room.

He changed into gym shorts, brushed his teeth, ran his hand over his beard and was grateful he didn't have to shave tonight. After hanging his suit on a hook on the back of the door, he turned off the light, then returned to the living room.

He fell asleep with the TV turned low and one lamp burning. When he woke up sometime later, both had been turned off. The only illumination came through the sliding doors that led to a tiny balcony, and it was faint.

But not so faint that he couldn't make out the figure standing there, looking out.

The springs creaked as he lifted himself into a sitting position, then pulled the blanket around him. "Are you okay?"

For a moment it seemed that she would ignore him. Then she glanced over her shoulder, too briefly to actually see anything. "I needed water to take some aspirin."

"Head still hurt?"

"Head, shoulder, ribs, hip, abdomen." After another moment of silence, she murmured, "It's still raining."

That was no surprise. It had been raining all night. He wondered if it would be wrong of him to pray for flooding to keep him there through the weekend. He wouldn't wish for power outages, though that was his best chance of ever finding his way back into her bed, but to be trapped, warm, with plenty of food and Rebecca... That might be his idea of heaven.

"What time is it?" he asked.

"A little after four." With a sigh, she turned from the door with purpose. Aware that she intended to retreat once more to her bedroom and shut him out, he spoke before she could take more than a few steps. "Don't go, Rebecca. Stay and talk."

"About what?" Her voice was heavy with the wariness he would see etching her face, if he could see her face.

"I don't care. Anything." He swallowed hard. "I miss the sound of your voice."

She stood still a long time, debating, then reluctantly sank into the easy chair, drawing her feet onto the cushion, tucking her robe around her.

Silence stretched between them while he tried a dozen subjects in his mind, then discarded every one. How had they come to this sad state where he couldn't find anything to talk about with his wife? How had he brought them to this?

"You looked beautiful tonight."

She ducked her head shyly. "Thank you."

Accepting compliments had never come easily to her. Back when he'd first learned about her family, he'd found it oddly disconcerting that one of *those* Wentworths could be so modest. He'd thought she must surely be used to fawning and flattery, to believing she was superior to the rest of the world simply because she was a Wentworth. But he'd been wrong. She'd proven to be one of the most incredibly sincere, modest people he'd ever met. No one would guess to look at her that she came from one of the oldest, wealthiest families in the country.

Especially since she'd been married the last five years to a struggling doctor with college and medical school loans to rival the operating budget of any small nation.

Not wanting to think for even a moment about his insecurities that had contributed so much to their current situation, he forced his mind to a different topic. "What are your plans for Christmas?"

She shrugged. "I don't have any. I've been invited to the Stuarts' house for dinner, but I haven't decided yet."

"So have I," he admitted. Were their friends trying their hands at engineering a reconciliation, or did Colton and Juliette simply not know what the other had done? The latter, he suspected. Juliette was too sensitive to other people's feelings to deliberately create what was sure to be an awkward situation. "Don't turn them down on my account. I'll probably work and let someone with someplace to go have the day off instead."

After another strained silence, she asked, "Will you see your parents over the holidays?" Her voice was too taut for the impersonal tone she was aiming for, and much too taut for talking to the husband she'd sworn to love forever.

"No, they're not coming down from the mountain this time." His father was a biologist, his mother a botanist, both with a passion for the animal and plant life that flourished in the Rockies' higher elevations. They'd spent nearly forty years living in what Steve was convinced was the most isolated place in the country, hours from the nearest town. He'd been born in their log cabin/research facility and had grown up helping them with their projects, anticipating the next three-times-a-year trip into town and waiting for the day he could leave.

That day had come when he was seventeen and starting college. For the first time in his life, he'd had neighbors and classmates. He'd met girls and known he wouldn't have to wait another three or four months to see them again for a few minutes. He'd made up for all the interpersonal relationships he'd missed out on growing up. He'd felt like a convict released to blessed freedom after years in solitary confinement. The world was even better, brighter, louder and filled with more variety than he'd ever dreamed.

And when he'd met Rebecca, his life had been complete. The difficulties and loneliness of his first seventeen years had paid off with the best, brightest future he could hope for. They fell in love, got married. Having babies was the next step before living happily-ever-after, and that was where the dream had fallen apart.

No, that was where he'd *torn* it apart.

"Rebecca—" He guessed his regret was heavy even in those few syllables, because she sharply interrupted him.

"No. Nothing personal tonight. Nothing about... us. I'm not up to it."

"If we never talk about what happened, how are we going to fix it?" he asked gently.

"I tried to talk to you. Do you remember? That morning in the kitchen?"

How could he forget? He'd behaved like a fool. He'd unloaded his childish insecurities and foolish hurts on her, had accused her of not wanting his baby, of deliberately preventing herself from getting pregnant because of who she was, because of who he wasn't, and then he had stormed out. And while he was off indulging his anger, she'd left him.

*She'd left him.* Even six weeks later, those words sounded foreign, impossible. They were the perfect couple, meant to be together forever. They were deeply, passionately, permanently in love. The only thing more impossible than her leaving him was the fact that he'd driven her to it. From the moment they'd met, he'd wanted nothing but her in his life. And he'd wound up with nothing.

"That morning in the kitchen..." He began slowly, with a rueful smile. "You'd think after six weeks, I would know exactly what I want to say, but... There aren't words to express how wrong I was, or how much I regret what I did, or how much I miss you. That morning...I was already hurt and upset, and when I found those birth control pills, I—" Overreacted. Acted like an ass. Struck out. The shock and sense of betrayal had been too much to bear, and so he'd shared it with her by lashing out. It was a human reaction. The *wrong* one.

"I don't want to talk about it tonight," she said coolly, easing to her feet, moving cautiously to avoid aggravating the pain.

When she swayed unsteadily, he threw back the covers and went to her. "How's your vision?" he asked, turning her face toward him even though the light was too dim to make out more than her features.

"Fine. I'm just tired. It's nearly morning, and I need sleep."

Impatiently she brushed at his hand, but he didn't release her immediately. He was standing too close, and his fingers, even his very pores, were too hungry for the touch of her—not the doctor-to-patient touches he'd gotten earlier, but man to woman. Husband to wife. He slid his fingers until his palm extended the length of her jaw, then turned the contact into a tender caress. Her eyes fluttered shut, and a soft sound, a satisfying sort of whimper, escaped her. Continuing the caress, he slowly bent until his mouth was only a breath above hers, until all he had to do to kiss her was think about it and he was there, his lips on hers, so soft, so sweet.

"No!" Slapping his wrist away, she spun too quickly and nearly lost her balance. Steve caught her, steadied her, but she clearly didn't want his help. "Leave me alone," she commanded raggedly. "I don't want— Just leave me alone."

He watched her go, a shadow among shadows. When the bedroom door closed behind her, weariness swept over him, underlaid with loneliness and regret.

And just the slightest bit of hope.

Rebecca awoke the next morning to weak light on her face, aches in her body and the inviting aroma of coffee drifting through the partially opened bedroom door. When she eased her eyes open, she was greeted by a thin colorless sky outside her uncurtained window. Rain mixed with ice coated the glass and the rain continued to fall. It didn't look as if either she or Steve would be going anywhere for a while.

How did she feel about that? She knew she should be upset, and in some ways she was. The only thing worse than being apart from him was being with him with such distance between them.

But she was also grateful. She'd missed him so much. His voice. His stories. His smiles. The simple warm comfort of knowing he was there. She missed rolling over in the middle of the night and touching him, missed the way he'd always sleepily rolled over, too, and pulled her close against his body. She missed everything about him, even his annoying habit of re-organizing her personal spaces when he had a few minutes. She'd loved him in ways she'd never loved anyone.

And he'd betrayed her in ways no one else ever had.

Rolling over, she checked the clock on the night table. When she'd come back to bed early this morning, she'd thought she might sleep through to Wednesday, but the digital clock showed that it was still Tuesday and barely 9:00 a.m. She pulled on her robe and slippers, made a bathroom stop, then, with a deep breath to settle the butterflies in her stomach, went into the living room.

Steve was sitting on the sofa, a blanket pulled over him, with a mug of coffee in hand. There was a movie on TV, but he was paying it little attention, choosing instead to watch her.

Self-consciously she brushed one hand through her hair, even though she'd just combed it in the bathroom, then tugged her robe tighter. "Good morning."

The cautious tone of her greeting made his dark eyes seem even darker. "Morning. How do you feel?"

"A little stiff, that's all."

"How about your head?"

Again she raised her hand, this time gently probing her temple. In the mirror, the knot had been significantly swollen in ugly shades of purple and blue, but considering what the accident had done to her car, she was lucky to have nothing worse. "It's okay," she said dismissively, then shoved her hands into her pockets. "I take it you're not going to work."

"Nope. My schedule's pretty light because of the holidays, so I cancelled the procedures for the next couple days. I also called your boss and told him you wouldn't be in." He gestured toward the chair. "Sit down and I'll get you some coffee."

"I can get—" She broke off as he pushed back the blanket and stood up, heading for the kitchen. He was wearing the same shorts as last night, but during their early-morning conversation, the room had been too dark to see. That wasn't the case this morning. She could see entirely too well—broad shoulders, muscular chest, flat stomach, narrow waist and hips, long, strong legs. He was as perfect physically as any man could hope to be. He was incredible, and just looking at him stirred the need deep inside her for more—to touch him, to press her body against his, to caress him, arouse him, make love with him…

Feeling tense and confused, she sank down in the easy chair. She wasn't supposed to feel any desire for him. She was furious with him, remember? The things he'd said, the way he'd looked at her—they were unforgivable.

And loving him was unforgettable. Wanting him, having him, were damned unforgettable.

He returned with the coffee, doctored the way she liked it, then disappeared into the bedroom. When he returned, he was wearing a T-shirt, intended, she supposed, to put her at ease. But it was too late. Her thoughts had already gone into forbidden territory, and no snug-fitting T-shirt was going to push them back.

"How about some scrambled eggs and toast?"

She nodded. She'd been through enough bad patches in her life to know that she couldn't survive one without food.

Before she'd finished half the coffee, he brought her a plate heaped with eggs and buttered toast spread with peach jam. He returned with his own plate, and they ate in silence. He took the dishes away and washed them in silence, too, then came back to sit across from her.

"Tell me about Carla."

The request was so unexpected that her breath caught in her chest, bringing a sharp pain that had nothing to do with last night's accident. She'd thought he might open with another apology, or keep the conversation general, nonthreatening. But, no, he'd gone straight to one of the two betrayals that had brought them to this point.

When she realized her hands were trembling, she laid the coffee aside and folded them in her lap. She wanted to tell him that Carla was nobody's business but hers, but of course it wasn't true. It was the letter from her that had started the trouble, that had sent Rebecca into a deep sorrow for all she'd lost and had stunned Steve with the secrets she'd been keeping from him. Without Carla between them, he never would have jumped to the wrong conclusions about the birth control pills, never would have made the accusations he'd made, and she never would have left.

But to tell him everything now... It had been impossible five and a half years ago when they'd met, five years ago when they'd married, when she'd been certain he loved her and would never, ever hurt her. Even six weeks ago, when their marriage had been secure and strong, she couldn't answer his questions. How could she do it now, when their relationship was so strained that even small talk was difficult?

But he was waiting patiently, quietly. She searched his face and couldn't find any condemnation ready to heap upon her. There was just curiosity, tenderness, love. But was it enough love?

She took a shallow breath, all the bands around her chest would allow, and started at the beginning. "You know I was never close to my family."

He nodded. How could he not know? He'd never met her parents, though for the last months of his residency in Denver, they'd lived less than ten miles away. No one from her family had been invited to their wedding. No one had sent their best wishes. For all practical purposes, she had no family.

"They gave me everything I could ever want," she said, staring at her hands because she couldn't bear to look at him. "Except attention. Affection. Love.

So I went looking for it elsewhere, and I found it—
the affection, at least—with Devin. I was seventeen
when I got pregnant. On my eighteenth birthday, we
ran off and got married. Of course, my parents didn't
approve of him. He was nobody, his family were no-
bodies. They offered him ten thousand dollars to an-
nul the marriage and get out of my life, and he took
it.''

She remembered the day so clearly, standing in the
shabby apartment that was her home for five wonderful days, not trying to hide her pregnancy for the
first time in six months. Her parents and their lawyer
had stood there, too, so cool, elegant and smug, telling her how they had arranged her life for her. The
marriage was over. Devin was gone. She was going
back to the estate to live practically under lock and
key.

And she hadn't cared—hadn't cared about any of
it, because she still had her baby. She had someone
to love, and that someone would love her, too, just
as soon as she was able.

''I didn't mind that Devin wanted the money more
than me. Though I liked him a great deal, I hadn't
loved him. Once I got pregnant, in fact, I hadn't really needed him at all, because there was still the
baby.'' She broke off for a minute, then forced the
emotion from her voice as she continued. ''She was
born shortly before midnight on a Friday night. They
let me hold her as soon as they cleaned her, and they
told me I could feed her first thing in the morning.
They took her to the nursery and took me to my
room, and I went right off to sleep. When I woke up
the next morning, she was…gone. My parents…''

She broke off and closed her eyes to control the tears filling them. Clasping her hands tighter, she concentrated on deep, calming breaths, on containing the pain that hadn't lessened one bit in the past fifteen years. After a moment, she continued. "They had arranged an adoption. By the time the hospital staff got me settled in my bed that Friday night, she was already being moved to another hospital, where her new...parents were waiting. I never saw or heard of her again, until the day I got that letter."

It had been the letter that had started all their problems. That letter... She'd read it so many times in the last six weeks that it was already showing signs of wear. She carried the photograph it had contained in her wallet, hidden behind a credit card, her secret.

She had gotten home before Steve that day, picked up the mail and carried it into the kitchen where she started dinner. By the time she got around to sorting through it, he was home and helping her by making a salad to go with the baked chicken. She'd taken a break and picked up the plain ivory envelope, obviously a greeting card of some sort, and wondered who would be writing her from Phoenix. Inside had been a pretty card with flowers on the front and a handwritten note and photograph. Hello, the note had begun. *My name is Carla, and I think you're my mother.*

That one line had sent such a shock through Rebecca that she'd dropped both card and photo, and Steve had picked them up. It had been the beginning of the end for them.

Or had it?

He cleared his throat, and finally she risked look-

ing at him. He looked stunned, much as he had that
night. Whose kid? he'd asked as he retrieved the
photo and card. *She looks a lot like you.* And then
he'd read the first line and exploded. Each question
had been more hurtful than the one before.

*Who the hell is this?*

*How could you have a child and not tell me?*

*What kind of woman are you, to give away your
own baby?*

"You can't just give away someone else's baby,"
he said, his voice quiet but underlaid with compas-
sion. Indignation.

"You can if your name is Wentworth and you live
in Colorado."

"But *your* name was Wentworth, too, and she was
*your* baby. The adoption wasn't legal. You could
have fought it."

Numbly she shook her head. "I was eighteen years
old, and my heart—my soul—was broken. I had no
money, no high-powered lawyers, no influence. My
parents were accustomed to getting everything they
ever wanted. Fairness didn't stand in their way. The
law didn't. A helpless, emotionally shattered teenage
girl certainly wouldn't."

He opened his mouth, closed it again and ran his
fingers through his hair. "I'm sorry, Rebecca. I am
so sorry. But...why didn't you tell me?"

"I never told anyone."

"I wasn't just anyone! I was your husband!" he
snapped, then closed his eyes for an instant to regain
his calm. "I *am* your husband. I've confided everything important to you, and you neglected to tell me

about the single most momentous thing that ever happened in your life. Why not?''

Realizing her hands were hurting, she glanced down to see that her knuckles were white, her nails digging into her palms. She straightened her fingers, laid her hands flat on the chair arms, then immediately folded them tightly together again. "It *was* the most momentous thing that ever happened to me. I had a *baby,* a daughter with brown hair like mine, with blue eyes like mine, a tiny little person who was a part of me, who would grow into a beautiful, intelligent, capable human being. And she was taken from me, given away by my own parents as if she were nothing.''

She surged to her feet—too quickly, she discovered, as the bruises across her ribs protested—and went to the sliding door, folding her arms across her chest. It was colder there, and the glass was wet with condensation. The field behind the building was flooded, and the tree branches sagged under the weight of the ice that coated them. Closer, ice glinted wherever water didn't rush. No doubt, the city's drainage system was long past capacity, and when the ice melted, it would only add to the problem. It promised to be a difficult few days for the city, and even longer for the lower elevations having to cope with their runoff.

Steve came to stand on the opposite side of the door, and suddenly she was stricken by the terrible need to feel his arms around her, to feel his breath stirring her hair, to hear his wonderful deep voice saying, It's all right, babe, we'll make it all right. She needed it so badly that she ached with it, and knew if she went to him, he would give her exactly that. But then what? Could they ever make *this* all right? Could she forgive him? Could he forgive her?

Especially when he discovered the other, awful, devastating secret she still kept?

Reluctantly keeping to her side of the door, she sighed. "I couldn't deal with it. When my parents took me home, most days I couldn't get out of bed. I didn't care if I ate once a day or once a week, or if I combed my hair or forgot how to live. I didn't care if I did live."

She was describing the classic symptoms of depression, Steve acknowledged. And how the hell could she not be depressed? Her parents should be shot for what they'd done to her. Who the hell were they to take her husband and baby away from her? To treat her as if she were their property, as if she had no say whatsoever about her own life?

He wished he'd known her then, wished he'd fathered her child instead of the spineless Devin. He would have taken her so far away that all the money in the world wouldn't help her parents find her. He would have protected her and her baby, would have loved them, lived for them, died for them.

"Finally," she went on softly, "my doctor insisted my parents send me to a small, private psychiatric hospital that catered to the rich and famous. They saved my life...but they couldn't teach me how to stop grieving for my daughter. Eventually, I learned to deal with it by ignoring her. By refusing to think about her. By pretending that she never existed." Her voice broke, and her shoulders rounded. Without thinking, he reached for her, pulling her snug against him, wrapping his arms around her. For one moment, she sank against him, limp and trusting him for support, and for that moment, he felt right for the first time in six weeks.

Then she pulled away, and he had to let her go, even though it damn near broke his heart.

"I couldn't tell you, Steve," she murmured, wiping one hand across her eyes. "I tried. I really did, but…it hurt too much. It was so much easier to pretend that it never happened. To pray you would never find out."

But he *had* found out, and had reacted so badly that it had ruined what could have been, should have been, a wonderful moment for her. The daughter she'd been grieving for for fifteen years had found her, had wanted to know about her, had hinted that she wanted to meet, face to face. And instead of having a chance to deal with the surprise, to take in all the possibilities, she'd had to deal with his anger, his accusations.

"I'm so sorry, Rebecca." They were such inadequate words, so trite and insignificant to express his regret. "If I had been prepared…" No, he wouldn't make excuses. Yes, he'd been stunned, and incredibly hurt, but that didn't make it all right for him to hurt her in return. It didn't make losing his temper any more acceptable.

"I never allowed myself to think that she might find me someday. It would have been too painful. Besides, I assumed, since my parents were breaking the law with the adoption, they went all the way, giving fake names and addresses."

"Have you..." Steve hesitated, then went ahead. "Have you been in touch with her?"

Her hand trembled just slightly as she traced an aimless pattern in the condensation on the glass door. "I called the day I moved in here and talked to her— her mother. She didn't know Carla had found me. She was...stunned. Hurt. She asked me not to have anymore contact with Carla until I heard from one of them, until she and her husband had had a chance to talk with her. I—I agreed, and I haven't heard anything from them."

"You haven't been tempted to go to Phoenix, just to see her? Even if you didn't talk to her?"

She shook her head. "I realize that they might discourage her from having anything to do with me until she's grown, and I understand that. They've raised her from birth. In their minds, she's *their* daughter, not mine, and they might not be willing to share her with anyone else. If that's the case, seeing her and knowing I couldn't speak to her or hug her or tell her how very much I've missed her would be too painful."

Though he understood her decision, he didn't share it. If Carla Anderson were *his* daughter, he would need more than a flat, lifeless photograph. He would need to see her walking, talking, smiling, laughing. He would need to study her, to reassure himself that she was safe, well cared for and happy. He would have spent the last six weeks playing shadow to a fifteen-year-old girl, and it wouldn't even begin to make up for the emptiness inside, for all the sorrow and hurt, for the fifteen years lost.

Maybe Rebecca was right. Maybe staying away

and waiting for the Andersons to initiate the next contact was best.

"Did your parents ever fully realize what they'd done to you?"

She shrugged. "They never cared. They got what they wanted, and that's all that mattered to them."

They got it at the cost of their daughter's health and well-being, and at the very high cost of losing her forever. That Rebecca had recovered at all was a testament to her strength and courage. That she remained one of the most generous, loving and giving people he'd ever known was nothing less than a miracle.

Folding her arms across her chest once more, she turned to face him. "No more talk about Carla right now, okay? I'm not up to it."

She wasn't being evasive. She really did look pretty ragged. There was no color in her face except two red spots high on her cheeks, and her blue eyes wore a strained look. He reached out to smooth the lines from her forehead, caught himself, then touched her anyway. For a moment, her eyes closed and she stood utterly unmoving while his fingertips skimmed across her soft skin. When her frown eased, he slid his hand down the side of her face until his palm cupped her jaw.

That was when she wrapped her fingers around his wrist. "Please don't," she whispered, though her plea lacked conviction.

This time he didn't immediately back away. "Don't you miss being touched, Rebecca?" he murmured. "I do. Sometimes I want to feel you against me so badly I could die. I used to think that growing up the way I did, with no kids around, no school, no neighbors, never seeing anyone for months at a time besides my parents, must be the loneliest life in the world. But I was wrong. Living without you, wanting you and knowing I can't have you, loving you and knowing I've made you hate me... This life I've been living the last six weeks is without a doubt the loneliest life in the world.''

Her fingers tightened around his wrist, but she didn't push him away. She didn't draw him nearer, either, but merely held on. "I don't hate you."

"Of course not," he agreed, though he didn't believe her for an instant. "You just can't bear to look at me, touch me, be in the same room with me. Can you imagine how it makes me feel, knowing that I brought you to that? That I made you hate me?''

"I don't hate you," she repeated.

"Then why did you leave me?''

"Because I was hurt, and I thought it would be best for both of us. Because it would save you from having to leave anyway when you found out—'' Abruptly she slipped away, going to the thermostat to turn the heat higher, then taking her coffee cup into the kitchen.

Naturally, he followed her. The galley-style kitchen was small to start with, but with both of them in there, it became downright intimate.

Steve stopped between the refrigerator and the tiny pantry. With his hands on his hips, he literally filled the space. "When I found out what, Rebecca?''

Her gaze darted from side to side, and she looked as if she were seriously debating climbing over the counter and the breakfast bar to flee. Since that exit was obviously impossible—she was stiff and sore, and he would have her cornered before she managed that first big step up—she chose manipulation instead. Her shoulders sagged, and what little color she had in her cheeks drained away. "Please," she said, her voice breathy and weak, her hand trembling as she touched the knot on her temple. "I don't feel good. My head—"

Steve didn't try to contain his grin. "Babe, I've loved you more than life itself since our second date. I know you better than I know myself—in some ways, at least. You're trying to manipulate me, and it's not gonna work. You can't just drop a line like that, then walk off." The grin faded, and his look turned intense. "What other secret do you have that you think would make me leave you?"

The pitiful I-don't-feel-good look was gone, but the seriously pleading look that replaced it was worse, because it was real. "Please, Steve, don't..."

He moved two steps closer, and she retreated an equal distance. "Because it isn't going to happen, Rebecca. I made a commitment to spend the rest of my life with you, to love you until the day I die and throughout eternity. There's nothing you could do that could change my mind about that. I love you. I will always love you. *Always.*"

Tears seeped into her eyes. "I wish I could believe you."

"Why can't you?"

"Because I know, and you don't."

She sounded so certain, but he was equally certain she was wrong. There was nothing that couldn't be forgiven, nothing that could possibly be worth losing her forever. "Have you had an affair?" He was careful to keep any hint of accusation out of his voice. The idea of her making love with another man, caring for another man, very well might kill him, but it wouldn't make him stop loving, wanting, needing her.

"No! How could you even suggest—?"

"Honey, you're the one who's convinced it would make me leave you. I'm just trying to figure out what could be that bad." He leaned against the counter, his arms folded across his chest. "Have you been dealing narcotics acquired with forged prescription pads from my office?"

*"No."*

"Are you paying off my med school loans with money from bank heists all across the state?"

She almost smiled, and he was suddenly hit with the desire to see her really, truly smile—hell, to laugh out loud with pure, sweet pleasure. It had been so long, and she needed to do it even more, he thought, than he needed to hear it.

"Tell me," he demanded. Pleaded.

For so long she remained silent, clearly torn by the need to avoid the answer and the unwelcome acceptance that, if they were going to resolve anything, it had to come out. There could be no more secrets. Finally she moved to stand directly in front of him. Her hands were knotted inside the pockets of her robe, and distress was exquisitely clear on her face. "You haven't asked about the birth control pills."

He swallowed hard. From the very first time they'd made love, they had never used any method of birth control. Getting pregnant, whether before or after their marriage, would have been cause for celebration. They had been *that* sure of their love and each other. That was why finding the birth control pills in her medicine cabinet—the very morning after finding out that she'd given birth to another man's daughter—had thrown him for such a loop. While he'd thought they were diligently trying to get pregnant, she'd been just as diligently taking pills to prevent it from happening. He'd felt like a fool. Rejected. Unwanted.

"You made assumptions about the pills that morning," Rebecca said softly. "Ask me now why I was taking them."

A sick feeling settled in his gut. He wanted to storm from the room, to head outside and down the stairs into the rain and the cold. If he ran far enough, before long he would become numb, inside and out. He wouldn't have to deal with the dread and the fear, wouldn't have to hear her say the words that had surely broken her heart and would now break his. If he ran away, he wouldn't have to face how badly he'd let her down, how he hadn't been there for her when she needed him most.

But he didn't storm from the kitchen, didn't head outside to numb his soul with rain and cold. He stood there and woodenly parroted the question she wanted him to ask. "Why were you taking the pills?"

"Because my periods were so irregular. Of course, you don't try to regulate your periods when you're also trying to get pregnant unless..." Her mouth tightened, and the life went out of her eyes. "Unless you've found out that you *can't* get pregnant. I can't have your baby, Steve. That big family you've always planned on…you'll have to find someone else, because you'll never get it with me.''

## Chapter 3

Steve lay on his back on the sofa, staring at the ceiling but seeing only the grief on Rebecca's face when she'd told her last secret. Immediately afterwards, she'd gone to her room and closed the door. He'd stood where he was for a time—thirty minutes, maybe more—too numb to think or feel anything but sorrow. Pure, raw sorrow.

He'd always wanted kids, and lots of them—six or seven, maybe even more. Part of it came from growing up so damned lonely, and part from loving Rebecca so damned much. Hell, kids were one of the reasons he'd gone into medicine. He'd wanted to help people, sure, and had had a knack for the sciences since he was a kid himself, but he'd wanted a profession that would pay well enough to allow him to have a house full of kids.

He wanted to cry. To shout that it wasn't fair. To

curse God for giving babies to parents who abused them and denying even one to him and Rebecca. It was wrong. Cruel.

Closing his eyes, he tried to envision their future without children, but it seemed too big a mistake. They were meant to have a dozen. They had the desire, the love, the hunger...

Leaving the sofa, he ignored the message unspoken in the closed door and went into the bedroom, anyway. Rebecca was lying in bed, a tissue crumpled in one hand. When she saw him, she immediately turned her back to him. He ignored the message in that, too, and positioned himself where she couldn't ignore him—in her bed, stretched out behind her, his front pressed to her back, his arm tucked securely over her middle. She struggled for a moment, then went still as the most incredible sense of well-being swept over him. Lying in bed with her, holding her— this was good and right, and there was no way in hell he was living without it again. The problem was how to convince her.

He nuzzled her hair back from her ear, making her shiver, and quietly asked, "When did you find out?"

"Two days before Carla's letter arrived."

He thought back to the morning he'd found the pills. That matched the date on the label. "And when were you going to tell me?"

"As soon as I found the courage."

"Courage?" He was crazy about her and always had been. How could she possibly need courage... Then the words she'd said in the living room came whispering back. *Because it would save you from having to leave anyway when you found out—* "Oh, Rebecca," he murmured sadly.

Her response was muted and as stiff as her body against his. "You wanted children more than anything in the world."

"I wanted *you* more than anything. Kids were important, yes, but they were a distant second to you."

She twisted onto her back and stared mutinously at him. "It was all you ever talked about. Getting pregnant, watching your baby grow, feeling him kick inside me, helping deliver him..."

He spread his palm across her flat abdomen. She was so delicate that he could reach from hipbone to hipbone. He'd touched her that way a hundred times before, always imagining her belly rounded and distended, thinking about the wondrous day when, for real, he would hold her and feel their unborn child moving within her. It had been one of his sweetest dreams, and now it would never come true.

"Maybe I did fixate on it too much. After all, it was so damn much fun trying." Feeling her abdominal muscles clench under his palm, he grinned crookedly. "But, babe, you had no right to keep this to yourself. It was *our* news. *We* can't have a baby—"

"No. *I* can't. I have endometriosis. There's nothing wrong with *you*."

His muscles tightened, and his jaw jutted forward. "What did you think I would do, Rebecca? Throw you out on the street and go looking for someone to replace you?"

She didn't have to answer. The guilt in her expression said all he needed to know. He rolled onto his back and stared at the ceiling. "You thought that was all you were to me—a means to have a baby? You thought if I was forced to choose between you and kids, I would take the kids? My God, Rebecca—!"

"They were so important to you," she whispered.

"You were my *life!* I'd spent five and a half years showing you that, and you still had doubts. What did I do wrong? How did I fail so badly that you could think you came second to *anything* in my life?"

She didn't offer an answer. She really didn't need to. He knew where to lay the blame—on the great and powerful Wentworth family. Even with his isolated upbringing, he'd heard of the Wentworths. There had been a time when they'd owned much of the state. There was a town named after them, as well as streets, libraries, museums, parks and buildings. The hospital where he'd interned had had a Wentworth wing, and the name had been prominent at the university.

When he'd first met Rebecca, he'd considered the possibility that she could be one of *those* Wentworths for about ten seconds before dismissing it. She was too real, too down-to-earth and sincere. She lived in an apartment not much better than the one he'd shared with a couple of other residents, and lived on the income from her nine-to-five job like everyone else.

She'd dealt with his curious questions about her family with pat answers that sounded so good at the time that it wasn't until later he'd realized that she'd told him nothing. Finally, when they'd started planning their wedding, he'd insisted on real answers.

Knowing had changed things just a bit. He'd become aware of all sorts of insecurities he hadn't known he had. He wasn't good enough, his blood not blue enough, his bank account not healthy enough, to marry into the Wentworth family. He couldn't give her the life she'd been accustomed to, couldn't offer her luxury or even great comfort, couldn't give her much of anything at all besides love.

Then one evening after work, he'd driven to her parents' house, had parked on the street outside the gate and stared at the mansion rising high above him. He'd felt so damned insignificant—a nobody, like Devin, who'd sold his wife and daughter to the highest bidder—but he'd also felt relieved. The house had reminded him of an ancient castle—cold, sterile, unwelcoming, foreboding. He couldn't imagine Rebecca living there, couldn't imagine all her passion, love and happiness trapped inside those stone walls. He'd known then that all he could give her—love— was truly all she wanted.

But sometimes the occasional doubt surfaced, just as her own doubts still did.

That night outside her parents' house, after a few minutes, a police car had pulled in behind him, lights flashing. One of the Wentworths' security guards had called in a report of suspicious activity. Was anything wrong? the officer had asked. Steve had taken one last look at the mansion, then started his car. No, nothing was wrong. In fact, everything was more right than ever.

The officer had watched with a strange look as he made a U-turn and headed home. To Rebecca.

*More right than ever.* Somehow they had to make

it that way again. Otherwise, life wouldn't be worth living.

Rebecca tried to look at Steve from the corner of her eye to avoid catching his attention or risking looking into his own incredible eyes, but all she could see was a handsome blur. Any time he became still and quiet for more than a few minutes, she could count on one of two things—either he was up to something, or he was asleep. He had a knack for falling asleep anytime or anyplace, which had come in handy during his internship and residency, when the hours were impossible and every minute counted.

But he wasn't asleep this morning, she saw when she finally turned her head to look. He was wide awake, studying the ceiling, lying smack in the middle of her bed, where he belonged...or didn't belong, under the circumstances. She should tell him to go—should probably ask him to leave the apartment. If the roads weren't yet passable, he could easily hike the short distance to the hospital.

Or maybe she should roll over, lay her head on his shoulder and ask him to hold her. Of course, getting that close while lying in bed would probably lead to a lot more than a simple embrace. Even the thought was enough to make her mouth go dry. Steve was an incredible lover—so passionate, so tender and amazing. But making love wouldn't resolve their problems. In fact, it would probably make things worse. How could she bear such intimacy when it wouldn't change anything? When it wouldn't even mean they were able or willing to change?

"You didn't do anything wrong," she said quietly. "It wasn't your failing. It was mine."

"What— Oh." He turned onto his side to face her. "It wasn't your failing, either. It was your parents'. Considering that you were raised by heartless bastards, you turned out pretty damn good."

She smiled faintly. "Considering that you were raised by wolves, you're not bad yourself."

"No, you got it backwards. The *wolves* were raised by *me*—or, at least, I helped. Telling it your way makes people think I'm not civilized."

"My parents are the most 'civilized' people you'll ever meet. Trust me, it's not all it's cracked up to be." There had never been a time when she felt loved by her parents, not even as a small child. She'd lived eighteen years in their home, with orders, expectations, commands and mandates, with great luxury and obscene excess, but never with love, affection or acceptance. She had merely been one more obligation in a world filled with obligations. They had cared how she dressed, how she spoke, how she comported herself. They cared how she'd represented the Wentworth name, but they'd never given a damn about *her*.

And when her own parents didn't love her, how could she ever be one hundred percent sure that someone else did?

"Do you ever miss them?"

She shook her head.

"Do you ever miss me?"

Discomfort stirred in the pit of her stomach. "It's not that easy, Steve."

"What's not easy? It's a simple question with a

simple answer. When I wake up and the sheets where
you should be lying are cold, I miss you. And when
I come home and you're not there. When I walk into
the bathroom and catch a whiff of your perfume.
When the phone rings and it's not you, and when it
doesn't ring and it's still not you. Every minute of
every day I miss you.'' Reaching across the small
space that separated them, he wrapped his fingers
around hers. ''Do you miss me?''

He was right. It was a simple question with a simple answer. ''Yes.'' No explanations, no detailed ac-
counts. Just yes. Always, day or night, asleep or
awake, yes.

The look in his eyes changed from slightly teasing
to most intense. ''Do you love me?''

''Steve—''

''Do you?''

The protective part of her wanted to draw her self-
defenses close, wanted to give him a haughty look
and an icy lie, like last night at the party, but she
couldn't summon the look, couldn't force the lie.
''You know I love you,'' she whispered.

''Then come home with me.''

''I ca—''

''It *is* that easy, Rebecca. We miss each other. We
love each other. Come home with me, where you
belong.''

She tugged her fingers free and scooted up until
the headboard was against her back. ''Sometimes
love isn't enough, Steve,'' she said sadly. ''Sometimes you need more. Like forgiveness. Understanding. Trust.''

He sat up, too, and turned to face her. There was

a weariness in his face that had nothing to do with his late night and everything, she suspected, with the last six weeks, and his eyes were narrowed. "So...I get a big shock, get mad and say a few things, and now you can't forgive me? Is that it? Now you can't trust me?"

"Steve—"

"You lied to me about being married. You lied about having a baby. I had a right to be shocked, Rebecca. I had a right to get angry."

"I never lied to you," she said stiffly.

"You never told me, and a lie of omission, babe, is just as much a lie as an out-and-out untruth. I understand why you did it. I'm not holding it against you. But I make the mistake of having an honest reaction to your lies, and you plan to punish me for—how long? How much do I have to suffer before you'll be satisfied?"

The hostility in his voice sent a chill down her spine. She left the bed and went to stand with the window at her back. Frigid air seeped in around the edges, matching the cold inside her. "'What kind of woman are you, to give away your own baby?'" His own words thrown back at him made him flinch, but she didn't stop. "That's what you call an honest reaction? Without even asking whether what Carla had written was true, you automatically assumed the worst. You claimed to love me more than life itself, and yet you insulted me. You knew me better than anyone else in the world, yet you believed I was a selfish, coldhearted woman who would give away her own child like so much unwanted baggage. Under the circumstances, can you blame me for wondering just how much your 'love' is worth?''

He rose from the bed, too, and took two long, controlled strides toward her. ''You know I didn't mean that! I was angry and hurt!''

''And so you hurt me. What a loving, generous, honorable thing to do.''

He drew back from her scathing words as if she'd slapped him, and she ached as if she had. When she reached toward him, he backed away a half-dozen feet before turning and leaving the room.

Rebecca stood where she was, watching her hand tremble. Her heart was pounding in her ears, and her chest felt tight with panic. She hadn't meant to lose her temper, certainly hadn't meant to hurt him.

When she went after him, she found him standing in the middle of the living room as if he wanted to go somewhere, but didn't know where. She stopped in the doorway. ''I'm sorry, Steve.''

''Sure,'' he said flatly without turning. ''No problem.''

''I didn't mean—''

''Don't worry about it. You're entitled.''

That one innocent word—*entitled*—was enough to make her temper boil. She thought about turning back into the bedroom and slamming and locking the door, or about smacking him, or shaking him until he understood that he wasn't to ever use it again.

Instead, she resorted to an old habit, one started the first time they'd ever fought. She couldn't remember the reason now, clearly something insignificant, but she remembered the resolution—she'd thrown something at him. The action had taken him by such surprise that he'd stopped in midyell, the argument immediately forgotten. They'd made up before the fight was even finished, and a new tradition had been born.

Picking up a pillow from the nearby chair, she flung it across the room, hitting him square in the back.

Slowly he turned. Amazement, anger and amusement warred in his dark eyes as he retrieved the pillow from the floor. When he started in her direction, she backed away, but he was merely returning the pillow to the chair. At least, that was his ruse. Once he'd dropped it, he didn't turn away or back off. "You threw that pillow at me."

"So? It didn't hurt."

"You threw it and *hit* me. I've been physically assaulted by a Wentworth."

"Don't call me that." She smacked him in the chest, maybe with a bit more force than could be fairly described as playful. He didn't seem to notice, though, other than to capture her hand and hold her wrist tightly in his.

"Don't call you what?"

"Wentworth. That's not my name."

He caught her other wrist and held them together against his rib cage. "Rebecca Catherine Wentworth. That's your legal name."

"Rebecca Catherine Wilson," she argued.

With a sly quirk to his mouth, he shook his head. "You don't get my name without taking me, too."

"Then I'll be Rebecca Catherine *Nobody*."

"You couldn't be a nobody if you tried. You're too beautiful. Too sweet. Too incredibly desirable."

Suddenly her palms felt clammy, and his hands seemed hot enough to brand. Had she forgotten how their teasing usually ended? In bed, if it was handy, or on any other piece of furniture that was available, the floor or the ground. Unbearably tempted by the memories, she tried halfheartedly to free her hands while also trying to keep the conversation on a light note. "I—I was a nobody all my life until I met you."

"Oh, yeah, right. You were the crown princess of the Went—" He broke off when she drew back her foot, fully intending to connect with his shin. In her fuzzy house shoes, she didn't know how much damage she could do, but even the threat was enough to make him stop.

Wearing a lazy grin, he backed her against the nearest wall, slid her hands around his waist to clasp in back, then nudged her feet farther apart so he could stand between them. "You've got a mean streak running through you," he murmured as he leaned nearer. "Good thing I'm bigger…and stronger…and know just how to tame you."

…*tame you.* That was her cue to toss her head, to laugh deep in her throat or growl or shriek something about being tamed. But all she could do was stare up at him. Her heart was pounding in her chest, and she was so warm in her flannel shirt and robe that she just might burst into flames or melt into a pool of confused emotions. He was going to kiss her—she'd lived with him long enough to know that—but she was still angry, still hurt, still didn't want him anywhere near her...except right where he was.

Now he was so close that all she saw was his handsome face. All she felt was the need to grab him and hold on tight. All she knew was that she loved him, needed him, wanted him, missed him, couldn't bear living one more day without him even if she couldn't trust or forgive him.

"Ask me to kiss you, Rebecca," he whispered, his lips only a breath from hers.

*...even if she couldn't trust or forgive him.* "It wouldn't mean anything," she whispered back.

"It would mean everything."

She shook her head a few millimeters side to side. "A kiss is just a kiss."

"Nice line, but I think it's been used before. Tell me you want me to kiss you." He was touching her face now, his fingertips gently rubbing her jaw in a way that made her want to arch against him and purr like a satisfied cat. She was rising onto her toes to do just that when he issued his command again. "Tell me, babe."

His fingers slid down her throat, skimmed over her robe, then tugged loose the knot that secured the belt. When her robe fell open, he gave it a little help in sliding off her shoulders, only to catch on her arms. She tried to give her dazed brain the command to unclasp her hands and let the garment drop, but nothing in her body appeared to be working properly, least of all her brain.

"Tell me." This time he was touching her with his mouth, hot little kisses across her face and along her jaw.

"I told you I miss you and love you," she said at last, her voice shaky and insubstantial. "Of course I want—"

Her last words were lost in his kiss as he claimed her mouth. There was nothing sweet and gentle about it, like that kiss he'd given her in the middle of last night. He took her mouth, thrust his tongue inside, gave her passion and raw need. It was hot, greedy, hungry, and it made her weak, made him hard. She was drowning in it, losing whatever bit of control she had, on the verge of losing her very self, when pain shot through her, making her yelp, catching her breath in her chest.

Instantly Steve released her mouth and jerked his hands back from her body. "Are you all right?"

Rebecca closed her eyes while she concentrated on breathing again. "I'm...fine."

"Look at me." When she obeyed, he studied her intently, then stepped back, took her arm and drew her to the bed. "Lie down."

"I'm okay," she protested even as she did as he ordered. Her arms were still trapped in her robe, so she couldn't respond when he sat down beside her and quickly, efficiently unbuttoned her nightshirt. He pulled the two sides apart, gazed at her a moment, then touched her so tenderly that she hardly felt it.

"Jeez, Rebecca...I'm sorry."

Looking down, she caught a glimpse of the bruise that stretched from her left shoulder to right hip, then back across to her left hip. "It's not as bad as it looks. I'm just so pale..."

He gave her a sharp look, then buttoned her shirt again. Carefully he worked her robe back up to her shoulders, then closed it and tied the belt once more. "I shouldn't have touched you. I knew better. I just…"

"Forgot?" She managed a faint smile. "It's not a big deal. It's not really that sore."

"No, you cried out like that because it felt so good."

His tone was heavy with scorn, directed at himself, but it made her smile again. "Well, I do recall a time or two, or two hundred…"

He positioned a pillow beneath her head, then settled beside her once more, holding her hand gently in both of his. "Do you need anything?"

Just him, and a way to live with him. She needed to forget how he'd hurt her, to put that entire awful incident behind her. She wished she could go back six weeks, wave a magic wand and never let it happen.

"No," she replied. "I'm fine."

"Why don't you sleep a while? Your body needs rest."

Her body needed his body, she wanted to protest, but he was already rising from the bed. He hesitated a moment, then bent and brushed a kiss to her forehead. "I'll be in the living room if you need me."

She watched him go, leaving the door open a crack, then sat up to remove her robe. Once she'd settled in bed again, she pulled the covers over her and found they smelled of his brief time in her bed that morning. Holding them to her face, she breathed deeply as his last words echoed in her head.

…*if you need me.* She'd needed him when she'd found out she could never give him the child they wanted so desperately. She'd needed him when she'd gotten the letter from the child whose father had sold his rights to be her father for a lousy few thousand dollars. She'd needed him every minute of every day in the six weeks since then, and he'd let her down.

Why should she believe he would be there for her now?

Or maybe the more important question was... *could* she believe it now?

Time crawled past. Steve tried watching television, but with the volume turned low enough that it wouldn't disturb Rebecca, it was pointless. He tried to read, but her taste ran to fiction, while he rarely had time to devote to any book that wasn't medical in nature. He considered calling the hospital to see how bad things had gotten last night, but what difference would it make? He wasn't leaving Rebecca here alone, not yet. Maybe—please, God—never.

While prowling the small living room for the third time, he found the photo album on the cabinet that held the TV. It was small, meant to hold only one roll of pictures, and was as neatly organized as everything else in Rebecca's life...except their marriage. Returning to the couch with it, he stretched out and opened it.

The memories the first photo brought back were powerful enough to send a wave of grief washing over him. They'd been walking through a wildflower field, holding hands, when his mother had snapped the shot. It was July, over five years ago, and they'd made the trip from Denver to Mountain Aerie, his folks' place, so she could meet them.

In distance it wasn't really so far. It was the journey itself that required patience and time. Research-worthy wilderness demanded isolation, and the Aerie definitely had that. They'd traveled a number of roads, each narrower and more poorly maintained than the one before it. Finally they'd parked at the end of the line, next to his parents' old truck, and hiked the remaining three miles, crossing a steel-cable foot bridge over a rushing stream that delighted Rebecca.

Everything that weekend had delighted Rebecca—his parents, their log cabin, sleeping in the bed where he had slept as a kid. She'd loved the wolves his father studied, fawned over the deer, played with the dogs and cats and llamas. She'd listened intently while his mother explained her current project, had damned near cried while helping his father nurse orphaned wolf pups, had made love with Steve at the top of the mountain and proclaimed the Aerie the most wonderful place on earth.

She had also accepted his proposal of marriage.

She was the embodiment of pure happiness in that first photo. He'd sworn that day that he would never give her cause to lose one bit of that happiness.

He'd broken that vow six weeks ago.

Wearing a T-shirt and loose-fitting cotton pants, she came from the bedroom, glanced at the photograph, then sat in the armchair. Her face was freshly washed, her hair damp around the edges, and she looked much better than she had two hours ago when he'd left her to sleep.

He looked back at the picture for a time before murmuring, "I thought you were so easy."

Drawing her bare feet into the seat, she wrapped her arms around her knees. "Why? Because I made love with you the day after we met?"

"No, not that way. Easy to get along with. Easy to please. To fall in love with. You were so...innocent. Real. Sincere. So full of life. You were everything I'd been looking for in a woman and thought I would never find."

"When I got out of the psychiatric hospital..." Her cheeks turned pink, and her smile filled with self-mocking. "Now there's a novel conversation starter. Ranks right up there with 'When I was in prison...'"

"You've got nothing to be ashamed of. You were a kid, you'd suffered some tremendous losses, and you had no one to help you get through it. You held up incredibly well, considering."

Her smile was slight, and faded as she continued. "When I got out, my parents were there to pick me up—and to give the hospital a fat check for keeping my stay a secret. I walked past them and the limo and down the drive to the street. They were furious. They followed at a speed of about two miles per hour, and they ordered me to get into the car with them, but I refused and, of course, they couldn't make a scene. After all, they were Wentworths. I, on the other hand, could and would make a scene. I'd just been released from a mental hospital. At last my mother said, 'Fine. We'll see how much trouble you want to cause after you've walked all the way home.' And she rolled up the window and they drove away. That was the last time I ever saw them."

Steve wondered what kind of parents would turn their backs on their daughter like that, but the answer came easily. The kind who would buy off her husband, who would steal her baby for someone else to raise. The kind who had never deserved her, who didn't even deserve, in his unbiased opinion, to live.

"I had a little money of my own in the bank—a few thousand dollars. I used it to rent an apartment and to live on while I found a job. I bought second-hand clothes and ate nothing but cereal and macaroni and cheese. During the day I felt so capable and daring. I was finally doing what *I* wanted, living *my* life. I was meeting people, making friends, completely and totally free from my parents for the first time in my life. But at night I cried myself to sleep. I felt so fragile and lost. I thought I might never get over losing my daughter, or trust another man after Devin. But if I did, if I met a man I could love, I promised myself I would love him with all my heart and all my soul."

"And you did." Just as she'd embraced everything about his parents' place wholly and openly.

He resisted the urge to qualify that response, though—to add, Until six weeks ago.

"I did," she agreed, then quietly added, "I do."

She loved him. She just didn't trust him, and she couldn't forgive him. Sometimes he wondered if it might be easier if she'd stopped loving him, too. Then, sooner or later, he would have to quit hoping to make things right. But this way, the hope was always there, always tempting him, always tormenting him, and that kept the pain there, too.

Leaning across the space that separated them, she took the photo album and leisurely flipped through it. "Sometimes I wish that I could live the way your parents do. It seems like the perfect life."

"Sometimes it is. But it can also be very lonely. My idea of heaven when I was a kid was being someplace, anyplace, where there were other kids. I had a few friends in town, but we only went there three or four times a year, and never for long. Mom was nothing if not efficient. She could take care of all the shopping and run all the errands in half a day. I really missed being a kid."

"But you got along with your parents." She held up the album, opened to a photograph of him standing between his mother and father, his arms around their shoulders. They were all wearing big grins, and why shouldn't they have been? Rebecca had agreed to marry him, and he'd just broken the news to his parents.

They would be so sorry to hear that there weren't going to be any grandchildren. But it would break their hearts to know he and Rebecca were separated. Knowing that, and hoping desperately to make things right, he hadn't told them yet. They had adored her from the beginning and had come to love her as if she were their own daughter. They would hate that either she or Steve was hurting and would feel impotent because they couldn't help.

And that was the real reason he wasn't seeing them this Christmas.

"I love my folks, but they weren't much on playing hide-and-seek or baseball or climbing trees—unless, of course, there was some interesting creature in the tree that they wanted a closer look at." He grinned ruefully. "Hell, their idea of a bedtime story

# Get 2 Books FREE!

## MIRA® BOOKS, The Brightest Stars in Fiction, presents

### The Best of the Best™

**Superb collector's editions of the very best novels by the world's best-known authors!**

## FREE BOOKS!
To introduce you to "The Best of the Best" we'll send you 2 books ABSOLUTELY FREE!"

## FREE GIFT!
Get an exciting mystery gift absolutely free!

## BEST BOOKS!
"The Best of the Best" brings you the best books by the world's hottest authors!

2 FREE BOOKS!

▲ To get your 2 free books, affix this peel-off sticker to the reply card and mail it today!

# Get 2

## HOW TO GET YOUR
## 2 FREE BOOKS AND FREE GIFT

1. Peel off the 2 FREE BOOKS seal from the front cover. Place it in the space provided at right. This automatically entitles you to receive two free books and an exciting mystery gift.

2. Send back this card and you'll get 2 "The Best of the Best™" novels. These book have a combined cover price of $11.00 or more in the U.S. and $13.00 or mor in Canada, but they are yours to keep absolutely FREE!

3. There's no catch. You're under no obligation to buy anything. We charge nothing – ZERO – for your first shipment. And you don't have to make any minimum number of purchases – not even one!

4. We call this line "The Best of the Best" because each month you'll receive the best books by the world's hottest authors. These authors show up time and time again on all the major bestseller lists and their books sell out as soon as they h the stores. You'll like the convenience of getting them delivered to your home a our discount prices…and you'll love your subscriber newsletter featuring auth news, horoscopes, recipes, book reviews and much more!

5. We hope that after receiving your free books you'll want to remain a subscriber. But the choice is yours – to continue or cancel, anytime at all! So why not take us up on our invitation, with no risk of any kind. You'll be glad you did!

6. And remember…we'll send you a mystery gift ABSOLUTELY FREE just for giving "The Best of the Best" a try!

**MIRA** ®

Visit us at
www.mirabooks.com

## SPECIAL FREE GIFT!

We'll send you a fabulous mystery gift, absolutely FREE, simply for accepting our no-risk offer!

® and TM are trademarks of Harlequin Enterprises Limited. © 1996 MIRA BOO

was reading me a paper Dad had written on the tagging and tracking of alpha males in various wolf packs that lived in the area.''

''Sweetheart, I'd trade my upbringing for yours anytime.''

That was the first endearment he'd heard from her in a long time. It was casually offered, had probably slipped out without her even noticing, but he didn't care. He would take it any way he could get it.

After a moment, she handed the pictures back. ''It's been a long morning. Would you like some lunch?''

''Such a long morning that it's midafternoon.'' He got to his feet before she could do more than slide hers to the floor. ''I'll get it. You stay there.''

''I'm not an invalid,'' she remarked as he walked past, but she didn't get up to help him in the kitchen.

While the chili heated in the microwave, he found cold drinks in the refrigerator and crackers in the pantry, then carried it all to the coffee table. When he returned for spoons and napkins, Rebecca twisted around to say, ''There's a jar of jalapeños behind the cereal in the pantry.''

He gazed at her across the breakfast bar. ''You don't like jalapeños,'' he said evenly.

''I know. But you do.'' She turned back around, closing the subject. Or so she apparently thought.

As he sat down on the edge of the couch, he remarked, ''Every time I go to the grocery store, I buy a box of fudge ice cream bars.'' Ice cream had been a rare treat up on the mountain, and it was one he didn't care for often now. When he did want it, though, it wasn't the low-fat, reduced-calorie chocolate bars she favored.

She pretended that stirring her chili required her utmost attention as she admitted, "I have two boxes of that caramel popcorn you like in there."

"I've been buying—and using—your shampoo. And I have a bottle of your perfume at home." Suddenly, his throat clogged, his voice grew thick, and his fingers knotted around the handle of his spoon. "Damn it, Rebecca, this is ridiculous. Living without you is killing me, and it's obvious you're no happier. If you would just come back home and give me a chance…"

Circles of color appeared in her cheeks and she still avoided his gaze as she cleared her throat, then politely asked, "Could you pass the crackers, please?"

"I am so damn sorry I let you down. I'm sorry I hurt you. But living apart isn't the answer, and putting our marriage at risk damn sure isn't! Rebecca, please—!"

Carefully she laid her spoon in her dish, pushed it back a few inches, then faced him. Her blue eyes were cool and angry. "You act as if it's a simple decision, as if all I have to do is quit acting like a spoiled princess and do the right thing. Well, I'm sorry to disappoint you, Steve, but I can't turn my emotions on and off so easily. Your saying you're sorry doesn't make everything right again. It helps. It's a start. But it doesn't make the hurt go away. It doesn't mean I can trust you not to let me down again. It doesn't mean I can automatically forgive you and we can go back to exactly the way things were before. Things may *never* be the way they were before. Do you understand that?''

''They can be if you want it enough,'' he insisted stubbornly.

''What I *want* has nothing to do with it!'' she cried. ''I wanted to raise my baby, to have her call *me* Mom instead of some stranger. I wanted someone to love me. I wanted a family, a dozen kids, a wonderful husband, the perfect life. I wanted to cry on your shoulder when I found out I couldn't get pregnant, and I wanted you to make me believe that everything would be all right. I wanted to go back home before I even left. I want to go home now, to be your wife again, to make love with you and live with you and be happy with you again!'' Her voice softened and broke. ''But the truth is, we can't always get what we want. Wanting to forget what happened doesn't mean I can. Wanting to move back in with you doesn't mean things would work out. And wanting to be happy sure doesn't make it so.''

Wearily, she got to her feet. ''I'm not hungry right now. I'm going to my room.''

And he had no choice but to watch her go.

## *Chapter 4*

In a perfect world, Rebecca reflected as she soaked in a hot bath, she would have been born to parents like Steve's. She would have met him instead of Devin when she was seventeen and so hungry for affection that a simple hug seemed the most precious gift in the world, and Carla would have been his daughter—would now be *their* daughter. In a perfect world, getting pregnant would be as easy as breathing, their home would be filled with toys, laughter and sticky-fingered hugs, and *I'm sorry* would be magical words that made any hurt go away.

But she'd never lived in a perfect world. People had envied her for being a Wentworth. They'd thought growing up in a house everyone referred to as *the Mansion* must be an incredible experience, that having money automatically translated to no problems. For the record, while the Mansion was a fabulous monument to the egos, indulgences and excesses of the Wentworths before her, it was a miserable place to call home. And she would take being broke with someone she loved over being rich with people who rarely even noticed her existence any day.

Outside the closed bathroom door, she heard Steve quietly speak her name, and sank deeper into the water. After pouting in her bedroom for a time, she'd sneaked a peek into the living room and saw that he was asleep on the sofa. For moment after moment, she'd stood in the doorway and watched him, simply taking in his familiar, dear features. He was such a handsome man, with his dark hair cut close to his head, his dark brown eyes shadowed by lashes so lush that every woman envied them. He kept his hair so short because it had a tendency to curl, which she thought was adorable and he thought needed taming. How many dreams had she had of a tiny baby with those dark curls? A million, easily.

Carla had pale brown hair in the photo she'd sent, just like Rebecca's. It was impossible to tell what color her eyes were, or whether she was tall or short, slender or plump, an athlete, a bookworm or a brain. It was futile to wonder if she understood why Rebecca had given her up, if she knew that she'd been given no choice, or to hope that she didn't believe she'd been nothing to Rebecca but an unwanted nuisance.

The bathroom door swung open to reveal Steve leaning there, arms across his chest. She didn't panic, though. The bubbles from the aromatherapy gel she'd squirted into the tub covered her as adequately as a robe.

Seeing his mouth move but hearing only distant sounds, she scooted up until her ears were above the waterline. He repeated his words. "I knocked five times. I wasn't sure whether you were mad or had drowned." He glanced at the candles burning on the counter, then sat down on the only seat available. "You probably should have done this hours ago."

"It feels heavenly," she admitted.

"Have any new aches?"

She shook her head. "I feel pretty good. Did I remember to thank you?"

"When you were trying to throw me out into the cold and ice."

"Suggesting that perhaps you should go home while you could still make it isn't trying to throw you out."

"Did you really think I'd go and leave you alone after what you'd been through?"

She shook her head.

"Did you really want me to?"

Another shake of her head.

Sliding to the floor, he leaned against the wall and planted his feet wide apart, his forearms resting on his knees. He was impressive—all soft, dark skin, solid muscle, raw power, brute strength, and yet with the most incredible ability to heal. He looked as if he should be tackling quarterbacks on the football field, or hefting twenty-foot beams on some construction site, but he had the patience, the skill and the control to repair the most delicate of injuries.

She wondered if he could heal *them*.

"There's a new doctor on staff at the hospital. Her name's Melendez, and she came here from Houston.

She…'' For a moment he looked so uncomfortable that Rebecca couldn't help but wonder if he was somehow involved with the woman. Attracted to her? Had an affair with her? Even the possibility seemed ridiculous…but so was the idea that they were separated, and yet here they were.

When he blurted out his next words, though, it eased her suspicions before they even fully formed. ''She's a psychologist, and she did some couples counseling in Houston. Maybe…maybe she could help us.''

Counseling. She'd been through enough of it to last a lifetime—and knew better than most how effective it could be. The staff at the psychiatric hospital had saved her life fifteen years ago. If Dr. Melendez could save her marriage… ''You would be willing to do that?'' she asked noncommittally.

''I'd do anything that would bring you home.''

His words, and the sincerity underlying them, sent a rush of warmth through her. ''I'll think about it.'' She didn't want to unload her problems on a stranger, but if they couldn't resolve the issues themselves— rather, if *she* couldn't resolve *her* issues herself— then Dr. Melendez might be the key.

He raised to his knees and leaned close to her. ''Your bubbles are disappearing, the water's stopped steaming, and now I'm staring. I'd better get out of here before I embarrass us both by staying on my knees and begging for whatever you might be willing to toss my way.''

Scooping the few remaining bubbles into strategic positions, she tried to make light of his remark. ''You've never begged for anything in your life.''

"No. But I'm not too proud to start." Pushing himself to his feet, he gazed down at her. "Give a yell when you're done and I'll give you a back rub."

She smiled crookedly. "I'll think about it." She *loved* his back rubs. He could work miracles on tight muscles and stiff necks. He knew exactly how much pressure to exert and exactly where to exert it, and he was tireless. Magical.

But, as with so many other things in their lives, his back rubs often led to much more intimate activities. All it took to ignite the passion between them was one touch, and they were lost. After all these weeks, for her to lie even seminaked on the bed and let him massage away her stiffness... It was a sure guarantee to create a wholly different kind of stiffness, one that involved pure pleasure and a commitment of the sort that she couldn't make at the moment.

After he left, she opened the drain, then turned on the shower. She scrubbed her hair and her body, then toweled off and pulled on her robe. Carrying a bottle of scented lotion, she went into the bedroom.

"Mind if I take a shower and shave?" Steve asked as he came in from the living room. "I'm starting to feel a little scruffy."

"Sure, go ahead. Want me to toss your clothes in the washer?"

"If you don't mind." He disappeared into the bathroom, then handed out his clothing.

As she took the bundle, Rebecca tried not to think about the fact that he was naked on the other side of the thin door. It wasn't as if she hadn't seen him naked thousands of times—which was why, she suspected, it seemed so significant now. She knew his body as well as her own, knew the contours of his muscles, remembered the exact feel of his ribs underneath her palms, could identify blindfolded the scar on his right arm where an overly playful wolf pup had clawed him. She'd watched the taut brown skin that stretched across his belly ripple when she caressed him, had felt tense muscles relax as she massaged him. She knew exactly how he looked aroused, and unaroused, and at every point in between.

And she missed it all.

The washer and dryer were a stacked set that filled a small closet in the kitchen. She added a few of her own clothes to make a full load and started the washer just as the phone rang. She'd barely gotten out a hello before Juliette launched into conversation.

"Colton just remembered to tell me that you had a wreck on your way home from the party last night. He said Steve called the station from the hospital so none of the officers on duty would worry when they found your car. Are you all right?"

Rebecca curled up on the couch where Steve had been lying, tucking the blanket he'd left behind over her legs. "I'm fine. Just a few bumps and bruises."

"What happened?"

"I found out that inclement weather and my driving don't mix. I skidded off the road and down an embankment and rolled the car. But I'm okay, really."

"And Steve found you?" There was a leading tone to Juliette's voice that made Rebecca smile ruefully. "And he took you to the hospital? And took you home afterward?"

"Yes, he did."

"And—?"

"And he's still here."

After a moment's silence, Juliette said, "Go on. Say something more so I can read your voice."

"There's not much else to say. We've been... talking."

"Does that mean talking as in doing other things, including great sex? Or is that talking as in arguing and not getting along?"

"Maybe it just means *talking*. You know, conversations, questions and answers." Then honesty forced her to admit, "And arguing some. I have a lot to settle."

"Don't you mean you *two* have a lot to settle?"

"No, I had it right the first time. Steve's being pretty flexible. He's apologized, and he says he'll do whatever it takes to fix things."

"He just wants you back," Juliette said quietly. "Anyone can see that."

"I want him back, too, but..."

"But you're afraid."

Though her friend couldn't see, Rebecca nodded. "The things he said, the way he looked at me, the accusations he made... They all hurt terribly, and I'm afraid if I go back to him, either he'll do it all again the next time something catches him off balance, and that'll be too much to bear, or I'll keep throwing it up to him, and eventually that will be too much for *him* to bear. I'm afraid that if he could say those things, then who knows what else he might say. I'm afraid that if I forgive him for this and trust him again, he'll let me down harder next time. I'm afraid of going back to him when I'm still so hurt, and I'm afraid that if I don't go back, I'll lose him." She gave a hollow, empty chuckle. "I'm afraid of everything, Juliette."

There was a moment's interruption on the other end while Juliette talked to Marty. Her voice became softer, sweeter, more motherly. Rebecca wondered if her own voice would have changed like that if she'd been able to speak to Carla at Marty's age. Probably so. Those few precious minutes in the delivery room when she'd held her baby, she had cooed and whispered to her as if adult language had ceased to exist. When the nurse had taken the baby for the supposed trip to the nursery, Rebecca had wept tears of pure joy. For the first time in her life, she'd had someone to love who would love her back. For those few blissful hours, she'd had a reason to live.

"Sorry, Rebecca," Juliette said when she came back on the line. "I won't tell you your fears aren't justified. When someone you trust lets you down, it takes time to heal and to rebuild that trust. Apologies help, but only time is going to take care of the rest. But... Don't get mad at me for this, okay? You aren't the only one who was let down, and Steve isn't the only one with something to apologize for. He never could have disappointed you, or hurt you so badly, if you had been honest with him from the start."

"I would have told him about the birth control pills," Rebecca said defensively.

"When? When the time was right?" Juliette sighed regretfully. "Honey, you'd been with him for more than five years, and you were still waiting to tell him about your daughter. Was the time *ever* going to be right?''

"You don't understand how difficult it was," Rebecca whispered.

"No, honey, I don't, and I'm so sorry you do. But…Steve is your husband. He's the one person who loves you most in the world. More than anyone else, he can help you deal with it. He had a right to know, Rebecca. And if he'd known, the letter from Carla wouldn't have been such a shock. He would have reacted so differently, and then the birth control issue wouldn't have even come up.''

"So you're saying it's all my fault. Gee, thanks. As if my guilt level isn't high enough."

Juliette laughed at her dry tone. "That's not what I'm saying at all. Well…not entirely. Steve shouldn't have jumped to conclusions. But you shouldn't have put him in a position where he had to react to such shocks.''

Rebecca knew she was right. But knowing didn't change the fact that he *hadn't* trusted her to have a good reason for not sharing her greatest secret with him, or for taking the birth control pills. It didn't change the fact that he'd hurt her deeply, or that she couldn't forgive and certainly couldn't forget.

"Where is he now?" Juliette asked.

"He's taking a shower."

"Do yourself and him a favor. Go jump in the shower with him. Then drag him off to bed and work up enough of a sweat that you both need another shower.''

"Sex doesn't resolve anything."

"Sex can resolve a lot of things. For starters, unfulfilled lust can create an awful lot of tension between two people. Get the lust out of the way, and then you can work on the rest of it. Secondly, when two people as much in love as you and Steve are having sex, it's more properly called making love. And, considering the last month and a half you've both had, I'd say the best thing you could do for yourselves and each other is to make a little love."

Rebecca found herself smiling unwillingly. "And thirdly?"

"Um... It's a hell of a lot of fun. And sweet. And precious. Maybe it'll remind you what's at stake, and help you see that hurt feelings and a sense of letdown are sorry reasons to give up the best thing that ever happened in your life. Hurt feelings will heal, and when you count all the times he's been there for you, that one letdown ain't nothin'. It's sure not worth living the rest of your life without him."

The bathroom door opened and steam wafted out. Steve had a towel wrapped around his waist, Rebecca knew without seeing him, and whether it was pink or purple, he looked totally masculine. He would be standing at the sink, humming to himself while he shaved, and when he was done, he would saunter in, naked except for the towel, and ask if she wanted that back rub.

Dragging him off to bed would be the easiest thing in the world. He wanted it. She wanted it. If only she could be sure it wouldn't be wrong.

"Juliette to Rebecca," her friend called. "I take it by your sudden silence that either you've drifted off to sleep or Steve is finished with his shower. I'll let you go, with one last piece of advice. Don't risk your marriage any longer over this. Yell, scream, cry, stamp your feet, throw things. Do whatever you have to do to get it out of your system, but do not tear your marriage apart. You were incredibly lucky to find this guy, but if you hold him at arm's length long enough, some other woman's going to find him, too. And if he thinks he doesn't have a chance with you…''

He wouldn't wait forever. People got lonely. Sooner or later he would have no choice but to put her behind him and find someone else.

And that would kill her.

"Okay, Rebecca, you think about that a while…but not too long. Jump his bones. Steam up the windows. Take his breath away. Remind him and yourself how good the two of you are together. And I'll talk to you Monday, all right?''

"Sure," Rebecca murmured. She hung up, transferred the laundry to the dryer, then went to the bedroom door. Could she follow Juliette's advice? Should she?

She gave a deep sigh of indecision, and the resulting twinge in her ribs decided the matter for her. She could honestly say her aches were less painful this afternoon than they'd been that morning, but they still hurt. She wasn't yet up to anything particularly strenuous, and their lovemaking had *always* been particularly strenuous.

But maybe tomorrow.

Pretending everything was normal, she went into the bedroom. The bathroom door was open, and Steve stood at the sink, razor in hand. He swiped at one last streak of shaving cream, then rinsed his face before catching sight of her in the mirror. Flushing, she forced herself to walk on past, to take underwear from her dresser and a T-shirt and jeans from the closet. As soon as he stepped out of the bathroom, she ducked inside. "Your clothes are in the dryer. If it buzzes before I'm through here, they'll be done."

He caught the door before it closed. "Hey, what about that back rub?"

Her smile was taut. "I don't think so."

"Don't trust me?"

"Don't trust myself."

"I won't seduce you."

"Oh, please... When have you ever had to do more than touch me to seduce me? And how can you give me a back rub without touching me?" Gently removing his hand from the door, she closed it, then locked it for good measure.

She took her time applying lotion, getting dressed, combing her hair. Vanity suggested that she dry and style her hair, add a bit of makeup and spritz herself with perfume. Common sense reminded her that he'd seen her looking worse and wanted her anyway. Besides, any makeup she might choose would definitely clash with the blues and purples of the knot on her forehead.

By the time she left the bathroom, he was dressed once again in shorts and T-shirt, and her own clothes had been meticulously folded and left on her dresser. He'd always been good about that sort of thing. It didn't occur to him to leave clothes in the dryer just because they weren't to be worn immediately.

The man was a surgeon, for heaven's sake, but he picked up dirty clothes and scrubbed toilets with the best of them. By rights, that should cover any number of flaws.

And, as Juliette had so kindly pointed out, in this case, the faults were as much hers as his, probably more so. Which meant the responsibility for fixing things was more hers. She needed to remember that.

When she went into the living room, he was on the couch, a bowl of caramel popcorn in his lap, and was flipping through the channels with the remote. "What do you prefer? A documentary on the mating habits of the silver-tongued gecko? A decades-old repeat of Lawrence Welk? The latest rated-R-for-violence-language-sex blockbuster to hit the airwaves? Or a Cary-Grant-does-comedy festival?"

"Cary Grant," she decided, but he'd already stopped on the channel and put the remote aside.

He watched her cross the room and circle the coffee table to sit at the opposite end of the couch. Acutely aware of his attention, she resisted the urge to toss in a dance step, a beauty-queen wave or some other such nonsense. Instead, she sedately seated herself, propping her bare feet on the coffee table.

"You're truly too cute and too real to be a Wentworth."

His pronouncement made her look at him. "Wentworths tend to be fairly attractive people. They're bred that way."

"And who would they have bred you with, if they'd had a chance?"

She shrugged. "The elder son of somebody like them. Someone with generations of money, class and blue blood. Who lived in the right places, went to the right schools and thought the right way. We would have been incredibly bored with each other, and after producing an heir or two, we would have moved into separate bedrooms and started living more or less separate lives.''

"Take it from me, babe. This separate-lives business sucks.'' He offered her the popcorn, and she took a handful, leaving the peanuts behind since that was his favorite part. "I assume a mountain kid raised with wolves wouldn't be deemed suitable, even if he had become a doctor, would he?''

. She shook her head. "Though it might have been fun to see their faces when they heard the raised-with-wolves part.''

"So being in love isn't important to them.''

"Before me, I doubt any woman in the illustrious history of my family ever loved the man she married. I don't believe my mother and grandmother are capable of loving anyone, but I never figured out if they were born without the ability, or if it's something they lost after years of disappointment and disillusionment. The scary thing is I would have turned out just like them if not for Carla...and you.''

This time it was Steve shaking his head. "You could never be like them. You're way too special.''

Color warming her cheeks, she lowered her gaze. "Thank you.'' For a moment she turned her attention to the television, then glanced at him once more. "Is there really such a thing as a silver-tongued gecko?''

"You got me, babe. My folks studied canines, not reptiles. Whatever the thing was, he was ugly, scaly, and was getting a hell of a lot luckier with his lady than I've been with mine.''

"Be patient," she said quietly, "and this, too, shall pass."

His dark gaze locked with hers. "Will it? Because I can endure anything, Rebecca, if I know we'll be all right in the end."

"I'm doing my best." It wasn't much of a promise, but at the moment, it was all she could offer.

Steve lay on his back, hands clasped under his head, and stared out the sliding glass door. It was the middle of the night, and everything was quiet both inside the apartment and out. He and Rebecca had spent an entire evening without arguing or slipping into dangerous territory. They'd watched movies, fixed dinner together, talked and even laughed. It had been just like old times.

Until she went to bed in the room next door, leaving him to sack out once more on the couch. In all the years they'd been together, that had never happened before. No matter how tired he'd gotten working long shifts at the hospital, or how close to bedtime their rare arguments had come, they had always slept together. Maybe not speaking, but always in the same bed, always touching.

If they got through this, he swore they'd never sleep apart again.

By mid-Wednesday morning, the important streets—the ones from this apartment to their house—would definitely be open. He would be able to leave the apartment, and he intended to take Rebecca with him.

Whether she intended to be taken remained to be seen. But the only way they were going to resolve their differences was together. Living apart was simply out of the question. To work things out, they had to *see* each other, talk to each other. Since they couldn't conjure up an ice storm and an accident every time they needed to be together, her moving back home was the only logical solution. Once she was there, surrounded by mostly good memories, he couldn't help but believe that would make forgiveness come easier.

And once she'd forgiven him, then they could eventually discuss the alternatives for their future. Because the simple—and selfish?—truth was, he still wanted a family. His first choice, of course, would be his and Rebecca's own babies, but if that wasn't possible, then there were viable options. In vitro fertilization, some type of surrogate-mother arrangement or adoption—they were all possibilities for him, at least, but he didn't have a clue how Rebecca felt about any of them. Because they'd always believed they would have babies of their own, the subject had never come up.

*Was* he being selfish? When her heart had been set on having babies of her own, when it had been broken by finding out those babies would never be, was it cruel of him to ask her to love someone else's baby? He honestly didn't know.

If it *was* cruel, then he would beg her forgiveness and resign himself to a lifetime without kids. A big family was one of his dearest dreams, but he'd gotten the others—becoming a doctor and loving and marrying Rebecca. In the dreams-come-true department, two out of three was better than average. He'd been satisfied with that for five years, and he could be for the next fifty-five years.

Even if he desperately wanted more.

From the next room came the creaking of springs, then the shuffle of footsteps. He glanced at the door as Rebecca paused there. "Are you awake?" she whispered.

"Yeah. I think that afternoon nap threw off my internal clock."

"And here I've always envied you for being able to fall asleep any chance you got." She came farther into the chilly room, stopping at the end of the couch. "May I—?"

He slid up until the sofa arm was against his back, leaving one-third of the couch for her. Quickly she slipped under the covers, drawing her knees to her chest, bringing a hint of cold with her.

"I couldn't sleep, either," she said, her voice quiet, hushed, as if she might disturb someone. "You're probably right about the naps. I've been lying in there thinking."

"About what?"

After a moment's hesitation, she answered, "Our first date. Do you remember the people who set it up?"

"James Halliwell and his girlfriend. He was chief resident on my service, and she was…"

"Assistant to the deputy mayor. What did he tell you about me?"

"That you were sweet and had a great personality."

"The kiss of death for a blind date. You must have expected a real dog."

Steve smiled faintly. His schedule had been so full then that he'd rarely met a woman who was neither a doctor, nurse nor patient, and he honestly hadn't cared how she looked. He'd just wanted a date with someone who could talk about things besides illnesses, diagnoses and prognoses. "What did his girlfriend tell you?"

"That you were a doctor. Nothing else mattered, in her opinion."

"And were you impressed by that fact?"

"I was impressed by your dedication, your enthusiasm, your commitment." Though he couldn't see it, he heard the smile that crept into her voice. "To say nothing of your eyes, your face and your body."

"So all those years of chopping firewood, tramping up the mountain with Mom and Dad and wrestling with the wolves paid off."

After a moment's silence, she suddenly spoke. "I knew before dinner was over that evening that I was going to marry you." Then came a sheepish correction. "I was never that confident in my life. I knew that I *wanted* to marry you, presuming that you might possibly want the same thing."

"I wasn't thinking in quite the same terms," he admitted. "But I knew that night that I was going to love you for the rest of my life."

For a time they fell silent. At last, painfully aware of the longing in his voice, he asked, "What happened to us, Rebecca? I would have bet every dime I might ever make that if any couple could make it, it would be us. We were perfect in every way. What the hell happened?"

"*I* happened. My life. My past. My parents. My weaknesses."

"There's nothing weak about you. You're one of the strongest people I know." Shifting on the couch, he moved closer to her, then blindly groped until he found her hand and wrapped his fingers tightly around her. "As easy as it would be to put all the blame on you, I can't. Maybe it was because we *were* so damned perfect. Maybe we didn't allow each other the room to be human—to make human mistakes, to have human responses. It honestly never occurred to me that there could possibly be anything important in your life that I didn't know about, and to hold proof of it in my hands... To see a photograph of your daughter with my own eyes..." He shook his head in dismay.

Rebecca moved, too, scooting closer to him. As if it were the most natural thing in the world, he slid his arm around her shoulders and gently pushed her head to rest against his own shoulder. "Maybe you're right," she murmured. "We had it easy, you know. We met, fell in love, got married and were blissfully happy. We never really argued, never considered calling off the wedding, never had any real problems after we were married. Maybe, because it *had* been so easy, when we were confronted by a serious problem, we didn't know to deal with it."

"And so we're learning the hard way."

"I won't complain about it *too* much, but...did it have to be *so* hard?"

He smiled against her hair, then brushed a very light kiss to her forehead. "Maybe the more you have at stake, the harder the lesson is. Because nothing in this world is more important to me than you, and nothing I've ever been through holds a candle to the misery of the last six weeks. I love you, Rebecca, and I don't want to lose you.''

''I love you, too,'' she whispered, but that was all she said. No promises, no reassurances, no dangling of hope before him. Just a sad *I love you, too.* And, as she'd pointed out Saturday morning, love wasn't always enough.

## Chapter 5

By 6 a.m., thirty-six hours after the bad weather had started, it was slowly clearing up. By nine-thirty, the sun was shining brightly, the constant drip-drip of ice melting could be heard throughout the apartment, and Steve had already been on the phone with the police department dispatcher, checking the conditions of the roads. He would be able to leave soon, Rebecca knew, probably within the hour, and she wasn't sure whether she was dreading or anticipating the moment.

Because she'd decided to go with him.

She didn't belong in this apartment when she had a house she loved across town. When they had enough school loans to keep them company for years to come, they shouldn't be spending money to maintain two separate households. If they weren't living together, how could they possibly learn to live with each other's human mistakes and weaknesses?

Maybe going back home wasn't the answer. But she did know that living apart certainly wasn't the answer. Not until they'd done everything they possibly could to fix what was wrong. If she'd learned anything in these past few weeks, it was that living without Steve was part of the problem, not the solution.

Earlier this morning, in preparation for leaving, he'd changed into the suit he'd worn Monday, tucking the tie into his gym bag, laying the coat with his parka. Now he was in the kitchen, fixing lunch, while she very quietly puttered around the bedroom. She'd chosen one small suitcase and packed only the items she would need right away. Truth was, she could walk out the door without a single thing but the clothes she was wearing, and get along just fine. It wasn't as if she were going someplace new and different.

She was going home.

If Steve didn't object.

He called her for lunch, and she closed the suitcase, setting it on the floor by the door. When she entered the living room, he was setting two plates on the dining table.

"You're moving better," he commented before he returned to the kitchen.

"I feel better. The stiffness is mostly gone." The bruise on her temple was still ugly, but the ones across her torso were already fading.

"You probably weren't driving faster than five or six miles an hour when you lost control. You were lucky. I've seen seat belt bruises that make yours look like little smudges.''

''I *was* lucky,'' she agreed as she sat down. ''Both to be going so slow and to be found so quickly.'' Picking up her fork, she toyed with it a moment before asking, ''Where were you going?''

''To the hospital. I thought I could help out if things got bad. I saw the taillights, thought something seemed odd and went to check it out. When I realized it was you...'' His casual manner faded, and intense emotion crept into his expression. ''It was the worst scare I'd ever gotten.''

''I'm sorry.'' With her free hand, she squeezed his for emphasis. She could imagine how he'd felt. If the situation had been reversed and she'd found him unconscious in the wreckage of his car, she would have full-blown panicked. She wouldn't have been able to help him, or to aid in his rescue at all beyond calling an ambulance. The only thing she could have done was pray.

''It must be an amazing feeling,'' she said quietly, ''to have the ability to help someone who's been injured, to save the life of someone who's dying, to have the knowledge and the skills to heal. I'm very proud of you.''

Steve stared at her. ''That's the first time you've ever told me that.''

''I'm sorry. My only excuse is that this is the first time I've seen you from the patient's perspective.''

He was looking at her as if he might break into a broad grin, or pull her up from the table and into his arms and kiss her soundly. But he didn't do any of it.

The apartment was growing warmer, and the dripping outside increased until it was almost as steady as rainfall. Soon their private weekend would be over, and he would be leaving. Soon...

What if she asked to go with him, and for whatever reason he said no? What if, all the while she'd been thinking of how to make things right, he'd been slowly coming to the decision that there was no right? Could she bear the disappointment? The hurt?

Probably not. But if she didn't ask for fear of being rejected, and he didn't ask for the same reason, could she bear living alone again after spending these past few days with him? Absolutely not.

Summoning her courage, she pushed her nearly empty plate away and spoke. "Steve—"

"Rebecca—"

When they both broke off, he gestured for her to continue. For a long moment she couldn't find the words or the strength or the part of her that could face the risk. While packing, she'd come up with elaborate, eloquent arguments, but now that she needed them, not a word remained, and so she offered the only words that did. "We can't find a way to live together if we're living apart, and I very much want to live together. I want a chance to deal with all this, to try to make things right. I want a chance to make our marriage right. I want...Steve, I want to go home." She swallowed hard, moistened her lips, then added an abrupt afterthought. "Please."

Once again, he stared at her for a long time, leaving her unable to read anything but surprise in his expression. Then he slipped from his chair to kneel in front of her, taking both of her hands in his. "I was prepared to beg you to go with me. My God, of course you can go home with me! That's all I've wanted since the moment you left. Just you, and a reason to hope. Oh, Rebecca…''

And then he kissed her. It was sweet and wicked, generous and greedy, tender and desperate. Though some small demon inside Rebecca was taunting her with the possibility that she'd made the wrong decision, that kiss convinced her that it was the *only* decision. She loved him dearly, and living apart from him was solving nothing. The only way to find out whether the day-to-day intimacy and commitment of their marriage could survive her secrets and his reactions was to *live* through it.

If the answer was no, God help them, *then* they would deal with it, and they would do so with the knowledge that they'd done their best.

Abruptly he released her, swept the dishes from the table and went into the kitchen, where he called the police station to check conditions one last time. The roads were passable, though still slick in spots, he repeated after he hung up. He rinsed the dishes and stacked them in the dishwasher, then came back to claim her hand.

''Let's go home, babe,'' he said quietly.

Though swallowing over the lump in her throat was difficult, she nodded.

The ice that coated the ground seemed out of place with the bright sun and the not-too-uncomfortable temperature. Steve carried his gym bag and her bag over one shoulder and held tightly to her arm as they made their way through flooded areas to the parking lot.

"Do men have some sort of special balance on slick surfaces that women lack?" she teased as he climbed in and started the engine.

"What do you mean?"

"Men always hold on to women on ice to keep them from falling. What keeps the men from falling?"

He carefully backed out, then eased out of the parking lot and into the street. "I can't speak for all of them, of course, but remember, besides wolves, my father also had an interest in mountain goats."

"Really?"

"Really." He grinned at her. "Have you ever seen me fall on ice?"

"No. I've never seen you fall at all."

"Except for you."

His words brought her a small smile and a warmth that had nothing to do with the air blasting from the heater. He *had* fallen for her, fast and hard, and she'd never been appropriately grateful. Now she was.

Driving required most of his attention. Once he turned onto their block, Rebecca let out her breath and was surprised to realize she'd been holding it.

Their neighborhood wasn't fancy. All the houses on the block combined could be bought for not much more than the annual property taxes on the Wentworth estate, but Rebecca loved the area. The houses were older, with front porches, yards and neighbors who'd become friends.

He pulled into the driveway, shut off the engine and looked at her. "The house missed you."

It did look a little forlorn, she thought fancifully, with the blinds drawn and no sign of life. Other than that, it was a perfectly average, fifty-year-old, middle-class house. It was painted a warm, homey shade somewhere between the colors of cinnamon and pumpkin, with ivory trim. In warmer weather there were rockers on the porch and baskets of flowers overflowing from end to end. The backyard was fenced—for the children they'd planned to have someday—and the detached garage straight back, painted to match the house, had been destined for kids, too. A playhouse for youngsters, a place to escape parents and play loud music for teens, an apartment for grown children bringing their children to visit Grandma and Grandpa.

The lump was back in her throat again, and tears welled in her eyes before she hastily blinked them away. "I missed it, too," she murmured as she loosened her seat belt. "I feel as if I've been gone a long time."

"Forever," Steve replied as he got out.

They entered through the side door that opened into the laundry room, then the kitchen. The rooms were chilly, still, somehow empty of life.

"I never figured out how to make it smell the way you did," he said as he turned on light switches behind her. "You know...like home."

She gave him an uneasy smile. "Blueberry-scented candles. That's my secret."

His expression was endearingly solemn as he shook his head. "No, I tried that."

She walked through the family room, where they'd spent weeks stripping layer after layer of paper from the walls, only to discover beautiful old wainscoting underneath, through the living room where they'd torn up scruffy orange-and-brown hi-lo carpet to un-cover heart of pine flooring and into the front hall, where she'd splurged on unglazed Mexican tile and laid it herself. This was home, this place she and Steve had ripped out, redone, stained, painted and salvaged. They'd done it for the children they'd planned to have, but for themselves, too. They'd built a haven for themselves, a place where no one could ever belong quite as perfectly as they did, and she'd missed it.

For a moment she simply stood there. Straight ahead the hall led back to the kitchen and family room. A doorway on the right opened into the small square room they called Steve's study, and the stairs on her left went to the three bedrooms and two baths that still awaited their remodeling magic. All they'd needed, they often joked, was time and money, the two things in shortest supply in their lives.

Hesitantly, she turned toward the stairs, gliding her hand along the banister as she climbed to the top. Still carrying their bags, Steve followed her up. They both were overcome with awkwardness when they reached the second floor.

He set down the bags and slid his hands into his pants pockets. After a long day at work Monday, then hanging on a hook on the bathroom door, his suit was looking pretty rumpled...and the most fabulous custom-tailored suit in existence couldn't look any better. He was extraordinary in looks, in body, in character, in spirit.

"I—I realize we didn't...specify exactly what you meant by...'a chance,'" he said uncomfortably. "I don't want to put any pressure on you. I'll move into one of the guest rooms if... If that's what you want.''

Her gaze remained even in spite of the fact that small creatures were turning somersaults in her stomach. What she wanted was to get as close to him as it was possible for two people to get. It had been six weeks since they'd made love, which was about five and a half weeks too long. She missed that part of their lives very much. And maybe Juliette was right. Maybe the best thing they could do for themselves was make love.

After a moment, Rebecca bent, picked up both bags and went into the master bedroom. She placed them on the bench at the foot of the bed, then slowly turned. Steve was still standing in the hallway, looking awkward. Nervous.

She felt more than a little nervous herself.

The bed was as neatly made as it had been the day she'd left. There was a thin layer of dust on the furniture, but if she knew Steve, he'd worked long hours in the last month and a half to cut down on the time he'd spent there alone.

Idly she wondered if the sheets still smelled of her. Her own sheets—brand new, fresh out of the plastic bag—had lacked his scent. She'd lain awake nights, wishing for some subtle reminder, had even thought about going to the house while he was at work and trading one of her new pillows for his old one. Of course, she hadn't. But she'd wanted to.

''I slept on the sofa most nights.''

She turned to find him standing only a few feet away.

''I couldn't get any rest here. Too many memories.

Too many reminders. So I'd stop and get a burger on the way home, or eat at the hospital before heading home, and I'd stretch out on the sofa with the television on. I'd tell myself I was going to watch just one show, or the news, or a movie, and then I would go to bed. I pretended that falling asleep there was an accident. An accident that kept happening night after night.''

He came a few steps closer, then rubbed his palm across the curved wood of the footboard. They'd found the bed at a flea market, paid practically nothing for it, then put in dozens of hours to strip, sand and stain it. The first thing they'd done after moving it from the garage to the bedroom was make love right there, bathed in the afternoon sunlight.

Rebecca moved forward, laying her hand on the wood next to his. When he glided his palm back across the wood, his hand bumped hers, drew back, then lifted to gently cover hers. "I've missed you, babe," he said quietly. "More than words can say."

"Then show me."

For a moment he stood motionless, then curved his hand tightly around hers and pulled her near. As she stood unsteadily in front of him, he raised his hands to her face, skimming across her skin so lightly she barely felt the touch. "You are so beautiful," he murmured.

She shyly lowered her gaze, then looked up again when he chuckled. "One of these days I'm going to tell you that, and you're going to say, 'Damn straight.'"

Before she could respond, he brought his mouth to hers for a simple kiss—a simple taste. Soft, sweet, tender, innocent—the kiss was all that and more. It was full of promises kept and yet to come, and incredibly erotic despite its innocence. It made her knees weak and her breath uneven, made her blood hot and her heart beat faster, as if they hadn't kissed thousands of times before. As if each time were the first time, or the best time. As if there could never be a last time.

When at last he raised his head, she took in a badly needed breath and immediately longed to be kissed breathless once more. She reached for him, her hands sliding over his shoulders and around his neck. Her fingertips recognized the feel, the shape, the heat of him. Sometimes, she thought, she could pick him blindfolded out of a crowd by nothing more than touch or taste—maybe by nothing more than the way he made her feel. Special. Treasured. Loved.

Though not always trusted.

Frowning, she pushed the thought to the back of her mind. She wished she could forget what had happened, wished she possessed the magic to undo the harsh words he'd spoken—words, as Juliette had pointed out, for which she shared responsibility. But at moments when she least expected it, least needed it, they popped into her head. She suspected it would be a long time before the annoying habit disappeared.

She drew him closer, touched her mouth to his again. At the same time, her fingers moved blindly, confidently, to the buttons down his shirt. She unfastened each one, pulled the garment free of his trousers and pushed it off his shoulders, then guided his hands to the buttons on her own shirt.

He pulled away and held her at a distance when

she would have followed. "Are you sure...? Your ribs...I don't want to hurt you."

Thinking of the ways he'd already hurt her—the ways she'd already hurt him—she smiled faintly. "I'm fine. I'm sure."

For a time his dark gaze searched her face. Then, accepting her answer, he slowly, lazily undid the buttons, taking his sweet time, scattering soft, tantalizing kisses across every bit of skin he exposed. By the time he reached the last button, he was sitting on the edge of the bed and she was leaning heavily against him, her legs unsteady, her body trembling, her skin flushed and hot.

"Beautiful," he murmured as he pushed the fabric aside. His fingers stroked over her, from the pulse pounding in her throat to the swell of her breast to the hard ache of her nipple. When he lowered his head to kiss her there, she gasped and threaded her fingers through his hair, pulling him closer, urging him to suckle harder. Every place he touched her, heat and hunger followed, making her tremble, making her plead wordlessly, helplessly.

Ending the kiss, Steve drew a steadying breath and watched intently as he removed her blouse, sliding it off her shoulders, down her arms. She was so fragile, so pale and incredibly soft. He felt so big, dark and rough in comparison...and so damn lucky. There had been times in the past six weeks when he'd thought he would never see or touch her like this again, times when he'd believed he would never hold her again. Times when he'd known life without her wouldn't be worth living.

But here she stood in front of him, naked to the

waist, head tossed back, eyes closed, body racked
with delicate little shudders. Knowing that he could
touch her breast and make her quake, or stroke between her thighs and draw a raw, ragged cry from
her, gave a tremendous boost to his masculine pride.
Knowing that she could turn the tables and create the
same effect in him kept him humble.

Knowing that this incredible, amazing, beautiful,
capable woman loved him...*that* kept him humble.

Gently he touched the fading bruises that passed
between her breasts, tenderly probing, but her response revealed no pain, just arousal. Then he smiled
tightly. *Just* arousal? There was no such thing as *just*
arousal when he'd thought he would never again be
granted the opportunity to touch her, please her, love
her. It was the sweetest gift he'd ever received.

The snap on her jeans separated with a pop when
he pulled on the fabric, and the zipper glided down.
He slid his hands inside the denim, over satiny skin
and rounded hips, and pushed the jeans away. Bracing herself against him, she stepped out of jeans and
shoes at the same time, kicked them aside, then
moved to sit astride him, settling in with tormenting
slowness.

He wore trousers and briefs. She wore a scrap of
ribbon and lace. That little bit was all that separated
them, but it was too much. Not enough. He wanted
to rip off her panties, to strip off his own clothes,
bury himself deep inside her and get lost in the heat,
the need. At the same time, he wanted to stay like
this, clothing between them, and kiss her, touch her,
stroke her and torment himself. He wanted to test
their limits, wanted to stretch their endurance to the

breaking point and beyond. He wanted to make her mindless with passion, to make himself mad with hunger, and then he wanted the sweetest, purest, deepest satisfaction either of them had ever known.

If he'd made love to her an hour ago, a day ago, even a week ago, he could do that—arouse her until her body hummed with it, let her feed his own need until he begged. But it had been six weeks, forty-five days, and he needed her too desperately, and she was moving against him in the most torturous way, and...

"Oh, babe," he ground out when she wrapped her arms around his neck, rubbing her breasts against his chest.

"Please," he begged when she thrust her hips against his.

When she slid one hand inside his trousers in a mind-numbing caress, he didn't say anything at all. A choked, desperate groan was the best he could manage.

Taking her mouth in a hard, hungry kiss, he rolled back on the bed, lifted her with him, worked free of their clothing. As he kissed her, with one deep thrust, he took her, his tongue in her mouth, her body gloving his. He withdrew almost completely, took her deep again, then did it again and again. He came too quickly, but so did she, and he knew too well this wasn't the end. They were just getting started.

As the shudders subsided, Rebecca raised her head, tossed her hair back and opened her eyes to gaze down at him. Sweat dotted her forehead, and her mouth—her lovely, incredible mouth—glistened from their kisses. For a time she simply looked at him, dazed at first, then serious, then with a womanly smile. Settling her palms on his chest, supporting her weight, she moved—drew back, then pushed forward, let him go, then took him again, deep, hot, tight, within her. They fitted so snugly together, so perfectly, and yet her thrusts were so easy. Smooth. Soothing, with just a faint promise of the torment, the pain—the pleasure—yet to come.

"Like that?" she whispered.

"You know you're killing me."

"Yes, but what a way to die."

He rested his hands on her hips, using his greater strength to subtly alter the rhythm she'd set, to deepen the angle until there was no more for her to take, no more for him to give. She could have resisted, could have insisted on slow and easy, but he knew by the flush spreading down her throat to the curve of her breasts that she wouldn't. He knew her body and its responses so well, knew that gradually she would increase the pace of her thrusts, would take him in deeper, longer, faster strokes. Knew her eyes would glaze over, her breathing grow shallow, her skin become hypersensitive to his slightest touch.

He knew her heart would start racing and her movements would become instinctive. Her skin would grow slick with sweat, and her control would disappear. Before long she'd be making those sweet little helpless sounds, and her body would clench his tightly, spasmodically. And then it would happen—for both of them, because even if he weren't sharing all those sensations, simply watching her peak was enough to bring about his own.

When it started, he was ready, gritting his teeth, trying desperately to endure one more minute of hot, tight sensation before letting it explode through him, explode into her. He heard her cry and recognized it from a thousand times before, and with a great groan, he joined her. He held her tightly, held her still, filling her in a powerful rush of passion, need, satisfaction and pleasure.

Her head falling forward, Rebecca breathed deeply while her body transmitted tiny shudders to his. He raised his hand to her belly and watched her skin ripple in response to his touch. The ripples spread outward as he neared her breast, then, with a husky moan, she shrugged away before bending to kiss him. "I've missed you," she murmured.

"All you had to do was come home. I've been here waiting." Feeling the stiffness pass through her, Steve regretted the answer immediately. It hadn't been such a simple matter as coming home. She'd needed time, a little loneliness, a heartfelt apology and a reason to come back. Now that she *was* back, he intended to never let her go again.

"I'm sorry," he said, sliding both hands to her face. "I didn't mean—"

"I know." With a sleepy sigh, she shifted to lie beside him. It was an incredible feeling after a month and a half of living alone to feel her long, slender body stretched out beside his, her legs tangled with his. He settled in, too, molding to her, holding her close, spreading his hand easily across her flat belly.

For the first time in weeks, he felt relaxed. Satisfied. Grateful. Relieved. Lucky and hopeful as hell. "I love you, Rebecca," he murmured, nuzzling her hair from her ear for a kiss.

He also felt nervous. Insecure. Because she didn't say anything to his declaration. Not *I love you, too.* Not *I know.* Not anything at all. She just snuggled closer, held him tighter and remained silent. And in her silence, words she'd spoken earlier echoed all too clearly in his mind.

*Sometimes love isn't enough.*

But, please, God, not this time. Because love was all he had to offer, and without it—without Rebecca....

Stubbornly he refused to complete the thought and open the door for the accompanying bleakness to wash over him. He was going to make this work. He had to, because he had no choice. The simple fact was he couldn't live without Rebecca.

He *wouldn't* live without her.

Listening to the slow, steady rhythm of Steve's breathing, Rebecca gave up her own pretense at sleep and sighed softly. The lazy, languid weariness that always followed their lovemaking had claimed her body, leaving her feeling so heavy that she might sink through the mattress to the floor below, or was it so light that she might float away if not for Steve's arm anchoring her at his side? She wasn't certain she could feel her fingers or toes except where they touched him, and she knew if she could shut down her mind for half a second, she would fall as deeply and soundly asleep as he was.

But shutting down her mind... That was a problem. It was crowded with doubts and questions. Had she been wrong to come back here? Wrong to make love with Steve? Or had it been the smartest, best thing she could have done? Was he under the mistaken impression that everything was perfectly fine, that he was forgiven, that life would go back to exactly the way it used to be? Could it ever be that way again? Was she justified in her doubts? Or was she punishing him unfairly for problems that were partly her own fault?

She had no answers, only questions. And fears.

And one of her biggest fears was rooted in the way he held her, with his hand covering her abdomen, his fingers splayed from side to side. It was nothing new or different. They'd lain that way countless times. It was sweet, protective, a habit he'd fallen into after they'd begun trying to conceive. The first time he'd made a tender comment about the baby that would soon be growing there. Later he'd made a joke about offering encouragement to the fastest swimmers to help them achieve their goal. Still later, when effort after effort had failed, he'd said nothing at all but simply held her.

Was that all he was doing now—just holding her? Or was he regretting the babies that would never be? And how long would it take for the regret to turn to bitterness? In ten years, twenty or thirty, would he resent that he'd given up the children he so passionately wanted for a woman who'd let him down?

Would he look back on his life with her as a waste
not worth the sacrifice of his children?

As tears filled her eyes, he shifted, bending one
knee over her leg, sliding his hand up to the curve
of her neck. His mouth brushed her forehead, and he
gave a great, satisfied sigh before murmuring, "Love
you, babe."

Even in his sleep, he sounded so sure, so confident.
She only wished she could be, too.

## Chapter 6

Steve knew the instant he awoke Thursday morning that he was alone in bed. Still, just to be sure, he swept his arm across the sheets where Rebecca had lain and found them ice-cold. Throwing back the covers, he sat up and listened, but there were no sounds coming from elsewhere. No lights were on, and no smells gave away her location. He pulled on the sweatshirt and jeans he'd discarded the night before, then went looking for her. She wasn't taking a shower, fixing breakfast or watching television over a cup of coffee. She couldn't have left—his keys were in his pocket, and hers, left behind when she'd moved out, were locked in his desk drawer.

He wandered through the living room, the dining room, the kitchen, then finally found her in the shadows of the family room. She was stretched out on the sofa, her face pressed against the cushions, a dark afghan pulled over her, and she was asleep.

He stood motionless a long time, staring down at her. Last evening had been a little strained, he admitted. She'd obviously felt uncomfortable being back home, and he'd felt a little strange, too. It was as if ghosts from their last arguments still hung in the air, reminding them that she'd been standing right at that cabinet when he'd found out about Carla, that he'd sent her birth control pills skidding across that counter when his world had fallen apart.

But when they'd gone to bed, everything had been all right—hell, better than all right. She'd been wicked, greedy and generous. She'd turned him inside out with her hands, her mouth, her body, and she'd left him exhausted, weak and grateful for it. After the second time—or was it the third?—she'd kissed him good-night and curled up in his arms, and he'd tasted himself in her kiss, had smelled himself on her skin. He'd fallen asleep thinking that he was the luckiest man in the whole damn world.

And then she'd slipped out of their bed to come sleep on the couch alone.

Numbly he rubbed the place in the center of his chest where a cold, empty ache had settled. He'd been foolish enough to think that her moving back home had meant everything was all right, that making love guaranteed it. Now he knew he'd been too optimistic by half. Moving back home only meant she was willing to try—more or less. And making love with him? What had it meant?

He knew what it had meant to him. For the first time in five and a half years, he couldn't swear beyond a doubt that it meant anything at all to her. After all, for the first time in five and a half years, she'd preferred her own company on the couch over his in bed.

He thought about waking her, about going to work and leaving her there, about demanding to know why she'd left him again—even if she hadn't gone far— and about pretending it was no big deal. So she hadn't wanted to sleep with him on her first night home. Hadn't wanted to lie naked beside him. Hadn't wanted his arms around her. Hadn't wanted that skin-to-skin, trusting-him-enough-to-turn-her-back-and-close-her-eyes intimacy. Hadn't wanted anything from him, apparently, but sex.

In the kitchen at the other end of the long room, he nuked a cup of water, then stirred in instant coffee. Returning to her once again, he sat down in the nearest chair and waited for her to awaken. He listened to the clock ticking on the mantle and watched her and wished…. Hell, what did it matter what he wished? If wishes could come true, his and Rebecca's lives would be so different. They would have been spared so much heartache.

It wasn't long after he sat down that she rolled onto her back, then her side, facing him, and not long after that before she opened her eyes. Pushing her hair back from her face, she focused on him almost immediately and smiled. For once, the mere sight of her smile wasn't enough on its own to make him smile, too. "I dreamed I smelled coffee," she murmured, her voice husky and thick.

It took her a moment to realize that he was simply looking at her, and that she wasn't in their bed. She glanced around, then sat up, wrapping the afghan around her. "I must have fallen asleep down here. I just wrapped up in this for a minute and— What's wrong?"

"Gee, I don't know. My wife would rather sleep on the couch than with me. You tell me."

"I'd rather— Oh, please, Steve. I came down here last night to get some aspirin from my purse, which was right there." She pointed to the coffee table where the bag still lay, next to an empty water glass. "I smelled this blanket and wrapped it around me just for a minute and...apparently I fell asleep."

His expression remained stony. "You *smelled* the blanket."

Rising, she approached him with one corner of the afghan extended. "It smells like you. See?"

He drew back from the fuzzy corner, but still caught a whiff of his cologne on the fibers.

"I missed the smell of you," she said solemnly as she stood before him, the blanket wrapped around her like a robe. "On the sheets, in the closet, in the bathroom, on my skin... I missed it."

She looked so serious, and he was suddenly, unbearably aroused. He stood up, grabbed a handful of blanket, yanked her close and gave her a kiss that would have curled her toes if she hadn't been standing on them.

Her voice was shaky—*she* was shaky—when he let her go. She touched her lips with a satisfied smile, then said, "I—I'd better get ready or we'll both be late for work."

"Stay home today."

"Why?"

"You wrecked your car less than three days ago."

"But I'm fine. Yesterday afternoon proved that." She smiled provocatively. "Last night proved it again...and again."

He resisted the smile that tugged at his mouth, but it wasn't easy. "Humor me. Follow doctor's orders for once. Stay home and rest."

The warmth in her eyes cooled. "I'm fine. The bruises are fading. There's no reason for me to stay here." *Here*. Not *home*.

When she started to brush past him, he caught her arm. "Don't, Rebecca."

"Don't what?"

"Don't get angry because I'm worried about you."

"You weren't worried yesterday afternoon when you made love to me, or last night. Or do you only worry once you've gotten what you wanted?"

Steve stared at her. "What *I* wanted? *You're* the one who invited me into the bedroom, the one who said you were fine and wanted to make love. I thought—I asked you—!" Turning away, he dragged his fingers through his hair, then swung back to face her. "Okay. So the sex was for me. It was what *I* wanted. What about you? What did you get out of it? A little exercise to tire you out so you could sleep better on the couch? Damn it, Rebecca, exactly what did you get in exchange for submitting to what *I* wanted?"

Heat flooded her face as she moved away from him. "I've got to get ready for work," she said flatly.

Feeling sick inside, he watched her walk away, but she didn't go far. At the entrance to the hallway, she hesitated, then came back. Her blue eyes were dark with shame, and her voice was heavy with it. "I'm sorry. I shouldn't have— I didn't mean—" Her hands fluttered nervously before she crossed her arms over her chest and tucked her fingers underneath. "I know you worry. I know you tend to be overprotective, and I appreciate it, I do. You're the first person in my life to give a damn about what happens to me, and that means a lot. But I feel fine, and I need to go to work today, and—and what I got out of it was everything I've wanted, everything I've missed for the past six weeks. I got you."

She waited for some response from him, but when moment followed moment and he merely continued to look at her, she turned away again. He could let her go, could resent the things she'd said, could nurse his hurt feelings…and maybe she'd choose to spend tonight back at the apartment. Maybe this time she would never come back.

Or he could behave like an adult. Like a man who wanted more than anything to put his marriage back together and be happy again with his wife.

It was no contest.

As he started after her, he passed a basket filled with beanbag toys. Just as she reached the end of the hallway, a pint-sized pink flamingo grazed her shoulder before falling to the floor. She stopped short, then slowly bent to pick up the toy. When she faced him again, her mouth wasn't smiling, but her eyes were. "When did you take up playing with toys?"

"I had to have something to do while you were gone." He tugged the flamingo from her hand and let its floppy legs dangle over his index finger. "This is Freddie. He and I have had quite a few heart-to-hearts in the last month.''

''And what are Freddie's woes?''

''Same as mine. He's alone.''

''He lives in a basket surrounded by other bean-bags. He's never alone.''

''I live in a town surrounded by other people, but without you, I might as well be buried alive in a cave, because that's damn sure how I feel.''

''Funny, isn't it?'' she said softly, her gaze locked on the beanbag as she gently stroked its hot-pink fur. Steve never would have believed he could be jealous of a four-inch-tall stuffed toy, but in that moment, he was. ''I have more friends here in Grand Springs than in the rest of my life combined. I never had to spend one minute by myself unless I wanted to. But it didn't matter whether I was with one person or fifty or no one at all. Because you weren't there, I felt empty and incomplete.'' Finally she looked at him. ''I'm sorry, Steve. I shouldn't have acted the way I did. I just feel...anxious. We have so much at stake, and I—I can't seem to relax and act normally again.''

He risked touching her, curving his fingers to fit the back of her neck, and drew her closer until their foreheads touched. ''Will it help if I tell you that nothing you could say or do could make me quit loving you?''

Her smile was quick and unsteady, and it faded quickly. ''It would help a lot if I could believe it. I just...''

Wasn't ready to trust him again. Steve hid his disappointment as he gave her a quick kiss, then turned her toward the stairs. "We'd better get moving. My first case is scheduled for nine."

"You're the surgeon. They can't start without you."

"No," he agreed with a chuckle, "but I'd rather not keep them waiting. Besides—" he admired the curve of her long, lean legs and the sway of her hips underneath her flannel nightshirt as she climbed the stairs ahead of him, and wasn't surprised to find himself aroused again before they reached the second floor "—the sooner I get through the day, the sooner I can come back home and be with you."

She paused in the bathroom door. "That's all you want? You're easy to please."

"That's all I've ever wanted," he replied quietly. "You. With me. Forever."

"So how's it going?"

Rebecca gave her tea a stir or two before laying the spoon aside and smiling across the table at Juliette Stuart. "Everything's fine."

"Fine," her friend repeated skeptically. "You got so angry that you *left* your husband and moved out for a month and a half, during which time you refused to acknowledge that he even existed other than to wish he didn't, and then suddenly you spend a few days together, make love a few times, and everything's fine. I don't think so."

"I wasn't angry. I was hurt. There's a big difference."

"Which makes it even less likely that everything is suddenly 'fine.'"

In need of a distraction, Rebecca glanced around

the restaurant. She met Juliette there for lunch every Tuesday, along with their friend Fiona, who owned an antique shop just down the street, so her gaze skimmed over plenty of faces she knew and only a few she didn't. "Fiona must have gotten tied up at the shop. Maybe we should go ahead and order lunch."

"Maybe. And then maybe we should talk about why you felt it necessary to change the subject just now."

Rebecca made a face at Juliette as she signaled their waitress. Then, with a shrug, she admitted, "It's awkward, but we're trying. We never fought before—never let the little annoyances get in the way. But it's easier now to jump to conclusions, to react with suspicion, to be defensive when it's uncalled for. Yesterday morning he got upset because I'd gotten up in the middle of the night and fallen asleep on the couch. I got angry because he wanted me to stay home from work and rest." She shrugged again. "It's tough."

"But your marriage is worth it, and before long, it'll be good again."

Rebecca nodded, though she wasn't totally convinced. Whenever she compared their relationship now to their relationship before the fight, she wanted to weep. She hated being uncomfortable with Steve, hated feeling like a guest in their home, hated the ache whenever she remembered the things he'd said. She missed the easy, warm friendship they'd shared from the start and absolutely detested the doubts and fears that wouldn't leave her alone.

The only place things were totally right between

them was in bed. There they could embrace the intimacy that had always been a part of their everyday lives. There they could talk about loving, needing, wanting, without risk of disappointment. There they were damn near perfect.

Unfortunately, they couldn't live the rest of their lives in bed.

The restaurant door opened, and Fiona Lake swept in along with a blast of frigid air. Her red hair was tousled from the wind that rustled down the street and her cheeks were bright with color from the cold. She whipped off her coat, scarf and gloves, then bent to give Rebecca a tight hug. "I'm so glad you're back with Steve where you belong," she said fervently when she sat down.

Rebecca had no doubt Fiona meant it, but she couldn't help but notice the sadness that touched her hazel eyes. There was someone out there with whom Fiona belonged—most likely her daughter Katy's father—but no one besides Fiona knew anything about him. He was her secret—her pain.

After catching Fiona up on their earlier conversation, Juliette turned the talk to cheerier topics, a favor Rebecca greatly appreciated. By the time they left to return to their various offices, she felt lighter, happier and ever more hopeful. After all, it was Christmas, the time for peace, goodwill, love and miracles. If any season could help her and Steve, it was this one.

When he picked her up shortly after five o'clock, he'd already been home and changed from his suit into jeans and a candy-cane-red sweater. As he said hello to the staff that still remained, she found herself wishing that he would greet her the way he used to—

with a hug, a kiss and a husky, "Hey, babe." He didn't, though he looked as if he wanted to.

After he helped her into the truck, she indulged a forlorn little sigh. She missed the little intimacies enough to make her heart ache, but it hurt even more to know that they both wanted them but were afraid, as often as not, to take them. Afraid of rejection, of being hurt. Afraid of so damn many things.

Steve settled behind the wheel, then gestured toward the back as he pulled out of the parking lot. "I brought your boots and heavy coat."

She glanced back at the sturdy boots and parka, then down at her green tunic and slacks with black pumps. Interesting fashion statement she would be making. "I see. Any particular reason?"

"We're going to get a Christmas tree."

Though he gave the answer confidently, she didn't miss the nervous movement of his gaze as it darted to her, then away, or the clenching of his fingers around the steering wheel. Did he expect her to argue with him? If so, it was one expectation that would go unmet. She wasn't feeling overwhelmingly Christmassy at the moment, but a tree could help. Unpacking and sorting through the ornaments they'd collected over the years could certainly help. And if she was counting on the goodwill of the season to give her hope, well, she had to do her part, too.

"Good," she said, reaching in back for the boots. As she leaned close to him, she swore she heard the faintest of relieved sighs from him.

Every Christmas they'd lived in Grand Springs, they'd cut their tree at a farm a few miles outside of town. Fortunately, the flooding had cleared enough that reaching it was no problem. Picking the tree was, though, and so, as usual, she relied on Steve to pick the perfect one for the corner of the family room opposite the fireplace. Also as usual, she thought, shivering against the cold, he picked the tree farthest from the truck. Not that she could complain, because it was perfect.

"What do you think?" he asked, standing beside her a dozen feet from the tree.

"It's beautiful."

"Someday we'll—" Abruptly his features tightened, and his voice turned gruff. "I'd better start cutting or we'll be out here at midnight."

*Someday we'll buy live trees, and we'll plant them in the backyard—one for each of our kids.* Rebecca knew that was what he'd been about to say, because she'd heard him say it more than a few Christmases before. The first time she'd embraced the suggestion warmly. This time it merely served to emphasize the emptiness inside her.

Standing in the twilight, she watched him fell the tree. When he stood up, he picked up the tree, she took the saw, and together they headed back to the entrance to the lot. There the owner measured the tree and took their money. He secured the fir in a mesh bag, then she settled in the passenger seat while Steve maneuvered it into the back.

With the sweet fragrance filling the truck's interior, they made a silent drive back into town and to their house. She wanted to say something—to tell him that it was all right that he'd almost mentioned the kids they couldn't have, to assure him he didn't have to tiptoe around the subject with her, to let him know that he was allowed to feel cheated or bitter or regretful. She couldn't say a word, though, because it was such a tender subject for them both, and she did want him to tiptoe around it, and if he did feel cheated, bitter or regretful, could resentment be far behind? And if he came to resent her... There wouldn't be much hope left for them.

When they got home, she went upstairs to change into her favorite knit pants and thermal shirt. With the elastic waist and often-washed fabric, they were as comfortable as pajamas and perfect for unpacking boxes of memories and dreams. Padding through the door in thick socks, she came to a stop with a faint gasp. The tree was perfect, as Steve's trees always were, and standing beside it... He looked so endearing, with strings of lights draped around his neck, with his look a mix of little-boy delight tempered by grown-up melancholy. "It's beautiful," she said once more, though it would be more accurate, she thought, to say *you're* rather than *it's.*

The halfhearted smile he gave her tugged at her emotions. He'd always taken such sheer pleasure in Christmas that half her fun had been watching him. She wanted to see him smile for real, wanted him to forget that slip at the tree farm and truly enjoy decorating the tree alone with her, because if he stayed with her, that was how they would do it for the next fifty years.

*If he stayed with her...* And what if he didn't? The possibility set off a flutter of panic in her chest. She breathed deeply until the panic eased, then joined him beside the tree. As naturally as if she did it all the time, she touched his arm. "Can I help?"

"You can start opening those boxes." He gave a jerk of his head to indicate the stacks of boxes near the sofa.

"You've been busy." Normally bringing all this down from the attic was a job they shared. But there wasn't much normal about their lives these days, was there?

She made herself comfortable on the floor and peeled the tape from the first box. They had ornaments dating back to their first Christmas together— inexpensive glass balls in bright colors—as well as purchases made each Christmas since. She carefully unwrapped them, reminiscing over each bit of glass, wood, fabric and clay. She was already surrounded by sweet memories when she unwrapped Steve's gift to her three years ago.

It was a tiny tableau on a base of frosted glass. Great Expectations, it read in gold script around the base, and above stood two figures, one obviously pregnant, the other obviously delighted. Beside them was a tiny crib with a Christmas mobile above that also served as a hanger for the ornament. Steve had brought it home the same day the home-pregnancy kit had given her a definite yes on the test, and they'd hung it front and center on the tree, then made love bathed in Christmas light.

Three days later her period had started, and a test given by her gynecologist had confirmed that the positive result was wrong. Oh, well, they'd said philosophically. Maybe next time.

That was the worst part of knowing for sure. There wouldn't be any *next times*. There wasn't any reason to hope.

Her hand trembling, she held up the ornament, dangling it by its hanger. It swayed, catching the light from the lamps and from the tree, casting prisms of color, sending stabs of pain directly into her heart.

Tears were blurring her vision when a choked sound from across the room caught her attention. She looked up to find Steve watching her. He laid the lights aside, then came to kneel in front of her, gently taking the ornament from her. The pain in his eyes was exquisite. So was the passion in his voice. "I'm so sorry. I forgot—I never should have bought that damn thing. I'm sorry, babe."

"Remember how happy we were?" she whispered. "How excited?"

He shook his head, as if he didn't want to remember.

"We had such plans. Our baby would live the kind of normal life that we never had. He'd play Little League and join the Scouts and go out for football and be a doctor, a lawyer or anything that made him happy. She would wear pretty dresses and ribbons in her hair, or would be a tomboy and climb trees with the best of them, and she would cook better than me or worse than you, and love wolves and one special man, and give us grandchildren to spoil. Such dreams...and I ruined them." Her voice quavered. "I ruined everything."

"You didn't ruin anything, Rebecca," he said fiercely.

She managed a bitter smile and a shrug as she got to her feet. "*I'm* the one who can't have a baby. *I'm* the reason you're being punished. It's all my fault."

She had just reached the kitchen when he spoke

from directly behind her. "I always wanted kids, Rebecca. You know that. But that's not the reason I married you. I married you because I love you. Because I need you in my life. Hell, if all I'd wanted from you was babies, don't you think I would have had you checked out to make sure you could give me those babies *before* I married you?"

With jerky movements, she took a cup from the cabinet and filled it with water. "I was a healthy, normal twenty-eight-year-old woman. You assumed that I could give you children. There was no reason to suspect otherwise."

"I *assumed* I would be spending the rest of my life with you—*you,* Rebecca, not you and six kids. Any kids at all would have been an added bonus. I *assumed* I loved you enough to deal with children if we had them, and to deal with it if we didn't. And I *assumed* that you felt the same about me." His dark eyes narrowed suspiciously. "Apparently, I was wrong."

She was trembling so badly that water sloshed out of the cup before she made it two steps from the sink. She set it down hard, clasped her hands together, then hugged herself tightly. "I loved you more than anything in the world! I still do!"

"And if the situation were reversed? If I couldn't get you pregnant, would you still love me? Would you still want to spend the rest of your life with me? Would you be willing to sacrifice your dreams of having a family to stay with me? Or would you replace me with some guy who could give you all the babies your heart desires?"

"How could you even suggest such a thing?" she

demanded, freeing one hand long enough to smack his shoulder. "I *love* you!"

"But, hypothetically, I can't give you what you want most in your life, while other men can. Are you really going to stick around? You going to settle for less than your dreams?"

"What I want most in my life is you," she said quietly. "To love you. To know that you love me. To wake up in the middle of the night and know you're there. To know that you'll still be there fifty years from now in the middle of the night. I've survived losing a lot of people in my life—my parents, Devin, my daughter. But I can't survive losing you, Steve. You *are* my life."

For a moment he was too overcome to reply. An incredible tenderness had come into his eyes, and he appeared to have trouble speaking. Then, with a great effort, he forced the scowl back into place. "So your love is better than mine. You're more loyal. Nobler. More generous."

She opened her mouth to argue, then closed it again and replayed that last speech in her mind. As much as she wanted children, she wanted Steve more. Loved him more. Needed him more. And, no, she wasn't better, nobler or more generous than he. It was just a simple fact—he was a part of her life, a part of her very self. No one else—no other man, no other lover, certainly no child—could take his place. No one else could make her whole.

Just as no one else could make him whole.

"I—I—" Feeling lightheaded, she gave up trying to speak and pressed her fingers to her mouth instead.

Steve reached out to touch her cheek in the gentlest

of caresses. "If we were blessed with children, Rebecca, whether yours, ours or someone else's, I would be the best damn father I could ever be. But I would rather have one life with you than eternity with all the kids in the world. If you ever trust me on anything, trust me on that."

There had been a time not too long ago when she'd trusted him on everything. If she'd stood in the rain getting drenched while he told her the sun was shining, she would have ignored the wetness and started searching for her sunglasses. Even after all that had happened, there was a part of her that believed him now. And why shouldn't she? He had never lied to her, never steered her wrong. He'd always known exactly what he wanted and had pursued it relentlessly—like becoming a doctor. Like marrying her.

Her chest tight, her eyes glittery with tears, she raised a trembling hand to his face. "I trust you," she whispered. Such sweet words. Freeing words. They made his eyes widen in surprise, then pleasure, then pure, bright joy. They lightened the sorrow that had burdened her the last six weeks. They gave her hope, and his arms when he pulled her tightly against him gave her peace.

His kiss started out tender, innocent, then, in that way she loved so much, quickly turned hot and demanding. By touch, by taste, she could identify the hunger in him, could feel the corresponding hunger in herself.

Too soon he ended the kiss and leaned back, but he didn't release her. "Say it again," he hoarsely commanded.

"I trust you."

Without warning, he scooped her into his arms and started for the hall. "Hey," she exclaimed. "What about the tree?"

"Later, babe. Right now we're going upstairs."

"And what are we going to do there?" she asked innocently.

Finally he gave her the smile she'd been missing earlier. It softened his features and warmed her heart, and it made promises that even she could never doubt. "We're going to make our Christmas wishes come true."

And they did come true, every sweet, loving one of them.

# *Epilogue*

Christmas had always been Steve's favorite holiday. He could honestly say he'd never experienced a disappointing one even once in his thirty-five years, not even at the Aerie, where they'd never had more than three people—and countless animals—to share it with.

But this Christmas, after shaping up to be the worst ever, had been the best. There wasn't a thing he would change about it. He wouldn't even give up one minute of the heartache, because it made the joy so much more...well, joyous.

It was a cold night, and the sky was dark, but their path was well lit by street lamps and Christmas lights. They'd spent the day at Juliette and Colton Stuart's house, surrounded by family and friends. Another half block, and they would be home again. Alone again. Free to make love again. The prospect was enough to make him grin and to send his temperature up a notch or two.

"Steve?" Rebecca squeezed his hand to get his attention. "The other night... Did you mean what you said?"

"I say a lot of things. You've got to narrow it down a bit."

"You said if we were blessed with kids, whether they were mine, ours or someone else's, you would be the best father ever. Did you mean that?"

A small knot formed in his chest, and he rubbed it through his coat with his free hand as he gave a simple, no-arguments reply. "Yes."

"You know...just because I can't have a baby doesn't mean I can't be a mother. We've got a lot of love, and there are kids out there who need it."

"A lot of them," he agreed quietly.

"We don't have to decide right this minute," she said as they turned onto their sidewalk. "But it's something to think about."

Steve stopped walking and drew her into his arms. "I love you, Rebecca," he murmured before bending his head to give her the sort of sweet, innocent, wicked, greedy kiss that was their specialty. He was starting to steam, and she was straining against him as if she might crawl inside him when the fact that they weren't alone finally penetrated. It was an embarrassed cough that made him raise his head, made Rebecca take one small step back.

A girl stood on the sidewalk between them and the porch. She was bundled against the cold, but her head was bare. The porch light glinted off her pale brown hair, and the street lamp showed the nervousness on

her familiar young face. "Ex-excuse me. Are you—
Is this—" She broke off, took a deep breath, then
blurted out, "Are you Rebecca Wilson? Because if
you are, I think you're my mother."

Rebecca stood at the bedroom window, gazing out
into the quiet night. When Steve came in, closing the
door behind him, she smiled faintly but didn't turn
to look at him.

He took up position directly behind her, his arms
holding her snugly, his chin resting on her head. "So
it's a bouncing, fifteen-year-old, hundred-and-ten-
pound girl. What do you think?"

"She's beautiful, isn't she?"

"Very. She looks just like you."

There was a strong resemblance, even more than
the photograph had prepared her for, but she'd never
been as beautiful as her daughter was.

*Her daughter.* Heavens, those words made her
want to dance for joy, to stand utterly immobile with
shock, to drop to her knees in prayer. She'd thought
she would never again see the child who'd brought
her one night of pure peace, who'd taught her about
loving and losing. She'd thought her daughter was
lost to her forever, but she was sleeping down the
hall, not thirty feet away.

Her daughter, asleep in her house. It was a miracle.

"Her par— The Andersons will be here tomorrow
afternoon," Steve said.

She raised her hands to clasp his. "It's okay. You
can call them her parents. They always have been.
They always will be. Were they terribly upset?"

"Their daughter ran away on Christmas Eve to

visit the woman who gave her life—the woman they've always feared would come back someday and steal her away. Yes, they were upset.''

''I'm sorry,'' she replied, and she really was. She could imagine how she would feel in their position. But the Andersons had known of Carla's interest in locating her birth mother, and rather than deal with it, they'd ordered her to forget about it. Unfortunately for them, they hadn't realized how determined a teenage girl with a knack for snooping through personal papers and access to the Internet could be. All it had taken was one yellowed, long-forgotten letter from the Wentworth family attorney, and the rest, according to Carla, was easy.

''She's amazing, isn't she?''

Steve chuckled. ''It's in her genes.''

She looked at him over her shoulder. ''You could love her, couldn't you?''

''In a heartbeat.''

With tears welling, she closed her eyes for a moment. When she thought she could speak in spite of the emotion, she turned in his arms. ''Come to bed with me, Steve.''

His grin was boyishly innocent—and full of promise. ''And what are we going to do there?''

''Celebrate.'' Her hands made short work of his sweater and hers. She needed more time with his jeans because already, with no more encouragement than that, he was hard, straining the denim. But in a matter of seconds, they were naked and in bed, and he was filling her with one long, deep stroke.

''What are we celebrating?'' he asked, bracing himself so he could look down at her.

She looked back at him, her gaze tenderly moving from his dark hair to his dark eyes to the sweet smile that touched his mouth. The tightness around her heart was almost unbearable, and it brought tears to her eyes. "We're celebrating Christmas," she murmured. "Family. And wishes come true."

* * * * *

# Christmas Bonus
## Christine Flynn

Season's Greetings!

We all know there is something magical about the sights, scents and sounds of the holidays. The awed delight in a child's face makes us smile, the music sticks in our heads, and the food... Well, today we splurge. January 2, we diet. There are the familiar stories, too. Comforting old friends such as *The Christmas Carol,* Rudolph, *The Gift of the Magi,* Frosty. And new ones, like those in *36 Hours: The Christmas That Changed Everything.*

I've always loved reading stories that take place this time of year. The spirit of the season so often moves characters to step beyond themselves for the sake of another. Just as that spirit does in reality. I think that's the very best part about the holidays, really. That giving of ourselves. That's what it's all about, anyway. Just like the first Christmas. The one that truly did change everything.

I wish you and your loved ones peace, and joy in whatever holiday you're celebrating.

*Christine Flynn*

# Chapter 1

The cold December rain blurred the Christmas lights beyond Lucas Harding's office window as he drew a dismissing slash through the notation on his desk calendar and tossed his pen aside. The Grand Springs Chamber of Commerce Christmas party would be in full swing by now, but they could spread their holiday cheer without him.

He pushed back his chair, rubbing at the knots in his neck as he drew his six-foot, two-inch frame up to its full, imposing height. A man didn't earn a position as vice president and regional manager of a major public relations firm without understanding that mingling with the business community was the bread and butter of his trade, but he was more into self-defense than socializing this particular Christmas. Lately, it seemed that every time his secretary would reply that he'd be attending a function alone, the hostess would call him wanting to fix him up with a date. The party that had started a half an hour ago wasn't a dinner that required an even number of male and female guests, but feeling about as sociable as scrooge, he'd decided to skip it, anyway.

Snagging a production report he needed to copy, he headed for his office door, wishing the holiday would simply hurry up and be over. He usually thrived on the energy the season created. He'd even looked forward to the big family gathering at his parents' home in San Diego, especially to seeing his little nieces and nephews and watching them get all excited about everything that was going on. The only thing he hadn't cared for was his brothers' teasing about when he was going to add to the brood himself. They'd cut him some slack last year, since it had been the first Christmas since his divorce, but this year his family was playing hardball.

Two days ago, his mom had let it slip that his youngest sister was bringing a girlfriend, with "a great personality who sounded perfect for him," to join them for the holiday.

He'd called back yesterday and, using work as an excuse, told his mom he wouldn't be coming.

He opened his door, looking down at the report as he flipped though the pages. The last thing he needed was his family—or the denizens of Grand Springs—trying to find him a woman. He could find his own, dammit. And what he wanted was a pleasant, articulate female who didn't expect an emotional commitment just because they spent a little time together.

"Shouldn't you be leaving for the party, Mr. Harding?"

Convinced that such a woman didn't exist, Lucas frowned as he glanced up. "Sarah," he muttered, watching his secretary remove her headset and turn from her computer. As usual, her long black hair was rolled and clipped at the back of her head. Neat, wire-rimmed glasses framed her intriguing blue eyes. Her eyes were one of the first things a man noticed about her. Along with the length of her incredible legs, the enticing shape of her mouth and the fact that she possessed the face of an angel.

She was also only twenty-three, which made his thirty-six years feel rather ancient.

"I didn't realize you were still here."

Behind the studious-looking glasses, her glance moved from his loosened tie to her watch. "The party started nearly two hours ago."

"I decided not to go. Did you cancel my flight to San Diego?

"I did. And your rental car." The delicate wings of her eyebrows arched politely. "Would you like me to send flowers to your mother?"

"Flowers?"

"To let her know you're thinking of her even though you're not going home for Christmas. I'm sure she's disappointed that you won't be there."

"Yeah," he muttered, a dutiful enough son to feel slightly guilty about what he'd done. "Flowers would be good."

"You've said before that red roses are her favorite. Shall I send a bouquet or have them made up into a centerpiece?"

The drone of a vacuum cleaner in the hallway

filled the silence as he hesitated. "Which way are you leaning?"

"Toward the centerpiece. If she wants, she can use it on the dinner table Christmas Day for their dinner. It would be reminder that you're there in spirit."

His mom would like that. "Then, a centerpiece it is."

He liked that about Sarah. She made him look good, reminded him to be thoughtful. She'd been his secretary ever since his transfer from San Diego two years ago and he'd come to rely on her for everything from keeping his appointments straight to making sure he remembered client and family birthdays. His family knew how preoccupied he could get, and they would forgive him for forgetting the little touches she supplied. But professionally, he had a certain image to maintain. Sarah had been a godsend helping him maintain it.

She'd even found the condo he'd bought and spared him most of the work with the decorator.

He watched her write send Mrs. H flowers on a yellow sticky note and stick it on her desk calendar to do first thing in the morning. He had no idea how a woman so young had come to possess her sense of style and maturity. He only knew she was the best secretary he'd ever had.

"Why are you still here?" he asked, checking out the computer screen to see what was keeping her so late.

"It's almost year-end. There's a lot to do."

"Unless there's a problem I don't know about, I can't think of anything you need to miss dinner for. That dictation can wait," he added, referring to the tape she'd been transcribing. "Go home, Sarah. It's after eight o'clock."

"There aren't any problems," she assured him, skimming a smile past his chin as she straightened a stack of perfectly straight files. "I'd just really rather work than go home...if you don't mind."

It was her smile that gave her away. The vitality behind it was missing, the spark that inevitably caused a person to smile back when they met her eyes. There had always been a radiance about Sarah that her professionalism couldn't mask. Yet, for the past few weeks, her vibrance had seemed subdued, and her good humor more forced than natural.

Lucas dropped the report on the desk, his lips thinning as he pushed his hands into the pockets of his dress slacks. He didn't know that much about her personal life, but he did know she was engaged to a law student in Denver that she'd been with since before he'd met her. Considering that the guy was so far away and with all the seasonal celebration going on, it was entirely possible that the holidays were getting to her, too. He couldn't imagine any other reason a woman like her would be holing up at the office.

Admitting to himself that he really should put in an appearance at that party, he considered a way to help them both.

"Tell you what. If you don't want to go home and you really want to work, come to Randolph's with me." Randolph's was the restaurant where the function was being held. "As much as I don't want to go, it is good p.r. Especially since a lot of the company's clients will be there. It wouldn't hurt for you to socialize a little with them, either," he told her. "You talk to these people on the phone. It's always good to be able to put a face with a name."

Sarah's immediate reaction was to glance down at the slim gray wool skirt she wore with a black sweater-set and tights.

"It's office attire," he said, fairly well-acquainted with the more obvious workings of the female mind. "You're fine."

The look she gave him was part hesitation, part indulgence. "I was only thinking that I don't look very festive."

"Put on a smile," he muttered, unrolling his shirt-sleeves. "No one will notice."

He turned away to get his coat, leaving Sarah to stifle a groan while she stared at his broad back. Lucas Harding was a big man. Tall, handsome, supremely male. He possessed an aura of command that demanded deference from women and everything from admiration to blatant envy from men. As much as she respected him, it didn't occur to her to tell him she'd really rather stay right where she was.

As messed up as her life was at that moment, the last place she felt like going was to a party. She was alone. She was pregnant. And she didn't know a soul she could confide in who wouldn't chastise, criticize or try to talk her into something she didn't want.

As if on autopilot, she shut down the computer and covered her keyboard. She wouldn't think about her circumstances right now, or the vague sense of panic that accompanied her every waking hour. If Lucas thought she should attend the event, then she'd grin and bear it. She liked Lucas. He was a great boss. A great mentor. He also had a good heart. In the last month alone, he'd paid for paint for the children's safe house and helped install the storm windows himself. And he'd designed the advertising for the animal shelter benefit for free.

Since her fiancé—ex-fiancé, she hastily reminded herself—had proved himself to be an even bigger louse than her deadbeat father, Lucas was also probably the only man on the face of the earth she truly trusted.

The atmosphere at Randolph's was normally one of quiet elegance, all fine crystal, candlelight and spotless table linens. At least, it had been the one and only time Sarah had been there—the night Scott Thompson had proposed to her. Tonight, to her relief, the intimate atmosphere was definitely missing. A Muzak version of "Jingle Bell Rock" underscored the din of conversation and laughter. The twinkling white lights on the Christmas tree by the bar replaced the glow of candles. The only thing intimate was the press of bodies as she and Lucas left their dripping raincoats in the cloak room and he nudged her ahead of him into the noisy crowd.

She'd never accompanied Lucas anywhere in the evening before, but she had to admit there was a certain comfort in being with him tonight. She'd grown to feel secure in her role as his secretary, confident in a way she didn't feel anywhere else. With him, she knew what to say, how to act, what was expected of her. And because she knew what her job entailed, she smiled graciously as one person after another came up to him, grasped his hand in greeting and was introduced to her. She was already acquainted with many of their clients and she'd grown up in Grand Springs, so many of the other names and faces were familiar. Lucas had barely been there two years, yet he seemed to know nearly everyone in the place. Or, at least, everyone in the place knew he was there. She couldn't help but notice that even those he didn't know glanced up as they moved farther into the room, acknowledging him with a nod, a smile or open curiosity.

It had to do with his easy, self-assured bearing, she thought, analytically watching him acknowledge an attractive blonde as he made his way back from the bar a half hour later. And his dynamite smile. He'd been at Myer and Hutchins for over a year before she'd witnessed its full, rather devastating impact. But he'd been in the middle of a hellish divorce when he'd first arrived in Grand Springs so she didn't imagine he'd found a lot back then to feel terribly happy about. She'd never considered it before, but she supposed he'd felt rather the way she felt beneath her own smile now. Numb. Defeated. Drained. The only thing she couldn't imagine him feeling was scared.

"Are you sure you just want tonic?" he asked, edging through to where she'd parked herself against a pillar. "I know I said this was business, but it is after hours. And it is a party."

"Thanks," she replied, accepting what he offered, though she really would have loved a glass of champagne. It wouldn't do the baby any good, though. And that was who she needed to think about. "This really is fine. Did you find the bank president? I know you wanted to talk to him.''

"What I want is his advertising account,'' he corrected. "And no. I missed him. Somebody said he just left and it's raining too hard out there to go after him.''

"It's raining harder than it was when we got here?''

"Definitely. We might as well stick around until it lets up.''

The quality of her smile became a little braver, as if she were bucking herself up for a longer evening than she'd planned. He really did wish she'd relax, loosen up a little and enjoy herself. He doubted anyone else noticed, but beneath her studied composure, she looked decidedly...lost.

Or maybe she was just tired, he told himself. She had looked a little fatigued lately, as if her nights might be as restless as his.

Frowning at the personal direction of his observations, not comfortable at all with the idea that he'd become that attuned to her, he took a swallow of his scotch.

He allowed himself to enjoy the burn long enough to lift his glass over her shoulder. "Heads up,'' he murmured. "Al Brinkmeier's on his way over.''

"Brinkmeier's Bake Shoppes?''

"One and the same. What's his wife's name?''

"Roberta,'' she murmured, recalling the name from the notes she kept about clients in her Rolodex directory.

"I can't tell if she's with him. But he's wearing an elf hat.''

Sarah forced herself not to gape, then not to grin. The effusive man with the expansive middle latched on to Lucas's hand, pumped it like the handle of a tire jack, then did the same with hers while the bell on the tail of his green hat bobbed between his bushy brown eyebrows.

"Hey, Lucas. Hello, there, Sarah. Good to see you both. Listen," he hurried on in his usual jovial manner, "you haven't seen Julie Harrison around have you?"

"Julie Harrison?" Lucas echoed.

"She teaches our boys over at Grand Springs Elementary. She's kind of blond, shorter than you," he said, nodding at Sarah, "and looks like she's about to pop. Deliver, you know?" Slicing his hand downward, he made a mound over his own considerable girth. "My wife's looking for her. Said she thought she looked upset about something and was heading for the door. I guess it's really getting nasty outside and she wants to make sure she can make it home all right."

"I haven't seen anyone like that." Lucas glanced toward Sarah. "Have you?"

Reflected light danced off the small silver studs in Sarah's ears as she shook her head. But before she could offer to help look for the woman herself, a petite brunette in a berry red blazer squeezed between the baker and the group of revelers next to them.

"Oh, Al. There you are. I can't believe this crowd," the woman muttered, adjusting the strap of her shoulder bag with one hand while she balanced a glass of red wine in the other. "Hi," she added, moving a smile between Lucas and Sarah. "I'm Al's wife. Did he ask you about Julie?"

"I did," Al assured her. "I don't think it's going to do any good asking anyone else. She's probably already gone. Give her time to get home, then call her."

"I will. I swear, when I opened the door to check the parking lot, the wind was blowing the rain sideways. The last time I saw that much water was when we had that blackout a couple of years back. Now *there* was a nightmare for you."

Roberta punctuated her emphatic claim by lifting her goblet. As she did, the woman laughing beside her bumped her elbow—which promptly sent her red wine splashing out of her glass and down the front of Sarah's skirt.

Lucas had the feeling the spray nailed his slacks, too. But Sarah definitely caught the worst of it. For a moment she simply stared at the dark oval above the hem of her pale gray skirt while the woman across from her covered her gasp with her hand. Then, with an aplomb he couldn't help but admire, Sarah's dismay melted to sympathy.

"It's all right," she assured the horrified woman. "Really," she added, when Roberta started advancing on her with apologies and her napkin. "It's washable. I just need to get some soda on it before it stains."

"Here." Taking Roberta's napkin, Lucas handed it to Sarah along with his own. "Get what you can before it soaks through. Do you know where the rest rooms are?"

She caught the apology in his deep hazel eyes as

she took what he offered. "Yes. And thanks," she murmured, excusing herself as talk about the mud-slide that had blocked the roads during the last storm escalated around them.

Everyone had a story to tell about the storm a few years ago that had thrown the town into utter chaos. Sarah remembered the night well, herself. She'd been attending a friend's wedding when the lights had gone out and her friend had taken the opportunity to ditch the creep she'd been about to marry. As Sarah worked her way to the bar for a bottle of soda water, then toward the ladies' room, she couldn't help but wish her own problem had such a simple solution. But the mess her life was in wasn't anything she could run away from. No matter what she chose to do, where she went, she would live with the conse-quences of her decisions for the rest of her life.

She wouldn't be running. But she would be leaving Grand Springs.

The thought of how desperately she wanted to stay wasn't something she would consider right now, though. Right now, she insisted to herself, vaguely aware of an icy, wind-driven rain washing the plate glass windows she passed, she was going to get the wine out of her skirt. It was the only thing she could do anything about at the moment.

That. And remain upright.

There was no warning. No one called out for her to get back. No sound could be heard over the con-versations and the music. The window ahead of her simply shattered, popcorn-sized pieces of safety glass bursting into the room like an exploding snowball.

Ice and wind swirled in with rain. The two women

ahead of her screamed as they ducked. Or maybe the
ear-piercing sounds came from the group behind her.
Caught midstep, Sarah ducked herself, trying to keep
her balance as she did, but the floor was already slick
and the soles of her leather flats provided no traction
at all.

She landed hard enough to jar her teeth.

"Somebody get something to cover the window!"

"Anyone hurt back there?"

"Hang on, lady," a harried voice closer to her
insisted. "Are you all right?"

A forest of pant-covered legs materialized around
her, blocking the wind and rain whipping through the
window. Hands came into view, reaching for her as
she sat up and pressed her palm over her stomach.
She didn't know who'd asked the question. She
didn't care. A pain as sharp as a blade had stabbed
through her abdomen the moment she'd hit the floor.

"You okay to get up?"

"Who are you with, dear?"

"She's with me."

Lucas's deep, commanding voice penetrated the
commotion. A heartbeat later, he hunched down beside her, his broad shoulders blocking her view of
everything but his solid presence.

"Does anything feel broken?" He ran his broad
hand from her thigh to her knee to her ankle, his
touch sure, thorough and decidedly impersonal. Seeing her hand resting on her stomach, he gently tested
the fragile bones of her wrist. "Are you okay to
move?"

"Yes. Yes," she repeated, relieved to get her
breath back.

''Then, hold on to me. Let's get you up.''

Nothing hurt. Not really. The pain in her stomach had already eased, then disappeared. If she felt anything at all, it was a disturbing sensation of heat where his hand had skimmed the length of her legs—and where his muscular arm slipped along her back to help her to her feet.

Solid. Strong. Big. The impressions registered over a blend of anxiety and embarrassment as he pulled her to her feet. Tucking her against his side, he moved her through the gathered crowd. She was vaguely conscious of another woman being led past the shimmering Christmas tree and the urgent voices of guests and waiters as the wall of heavy drapes were drawn and tables shoved against them to keep out the cold and the rain.

Mostly, she was aware of the man whose long, hard body burned like a brand from her shoulder to her thigh.

She should have been more disconcerted than she was by that awareness. This was Lucas. Her boss. She shouldn't be thinking about the shift of his powerful muscles against her, or how good it felt to be held so close. But she was too anxious about what her fall might have done to her unborn child to worry about what she should and should not do.

They reached the chairs by the wall. ''Sit down here,'' he coaxed, easing her from beneath his arm. Concern carved his chiseled features as he took the chair beside her. ''Are you all right?''

He reached toward her face as he spoke, his fingertips grazing her temple as he pushed back a strand of hair that had come loose from her clip. The contact was gentle, protective—and far more intimate than he intended.

He pulled back the instant he realized what he was doing, curling his fingers as he dropped his hand to his thigh.

Awkwardness filled the space between them.

"Thank you. For helping me up," she hastily added, intensely conscious of his nearness. Flustered by what he'd done, trying not to be, she motioned beyond them. "What came through the window?"

"I don't think anything did. It was the wind."

"Is everyone okay? All that flying glass…"

"It was safety glass. It crumbles more than breaks. You haven't answered me, Sarah. Are you all right?"

She was holding her stomach. Lucas noticed the way her fingers were splayed low over her belly the second she'd sat down. He'd noticed a few other things about her in the past couple of minutes, too. How perfectly she'd fit against him. How provocative the light scent she wore was close up. How soft her skin felt beneath his fingers. But he was trying to ignore all that—along with the lingering heat that had torn through him at the feel of her long, supple body pressed to his.

"I'm…not sure."

"Do you want to go to the emergency room?"

Sarah was a trouper. She never complained. When other members of his staff went down for the count with an occasional headache or the yearly office cold, she was still in there, plugging away. But right now, she looked as pale as snow, anxious and either worried or in pain.

"Please," she said, just when he'd decided he was taking her whether she wanted to go or not.

# Chapter 2

Lucas leaned against a wall in the crowded emergency waiting room, distractedly listening to the talking head on the television suspended below the acoustic tiles of the ceiling. In the two hours since he'd brought Sarah to Vanderbilt Memorial Hospital, the activity around him had escalated in direct proportion to the intensifying storm. According to the reporter, there were accidents at three major intersections, trees were down, roads were flooded and parts of town were now without power. With the thermometer dropping like the proverbial rock, the freezing temperatures would eventually turn all that rain to ice.

Minutes ago, he'd overheard that even one of the doctors had brought in his injured wife.

Spotting the nurse who'd led Sarah away when they'd first arrived, Lucas shouldered himself from the wall and headed toward her, his raincoat slung over his shoulder and his tie loose. He hadn't been in Grand Springs when the big storm had hit a couple of years ago, but he'd certainly heard stories about it—many of them in the time he'd been waiting for word about his secretary. From what he'd picked up, it sounded to him as if the tempest raging outside was running a close second in intensity.

Keeping the sturdy-looking, gray-haired nurse in sight, he edged behind two police officers in the crowded hallway and skirted a woman frantically gesturing to an orderly. Sarah had told him he didn't have to wait, but he knew she'd need a ride home and it made no sense for her to call a friend out on such a miserable night when he was already there.

"How is Sarah Lewis doing?" he asked, coming up behind the veteran RN in the green scrubs.

The woman turned sharply, her hazel eyes landing in the middle of his chest before jerking to his face. Recognizing him as the man who'd been with her patient, she offered a distracted smile. "She's just fine. So's the baby," she said hurriedly, motioning to a colleague that she'd be right there. "She was more shaken than anything else. The doctor doesn't anticipate any problems, but if she starts cramping or bleeding, call us. Excuse me," she concluded and headed off to intercept the gurney being pushed through the gaping double doors.

The baby?

"Lucas?"

He turned at the sound of his name, confusion etched firmly in his face. Sarah stood behind him with her coat clutched tightly in her crossed arms and a fistful of papers in her hand.

He knew he could be blunt. He also knew when a situation called for tact and diplomacy. He just didn't have any idea why that ability deserted him now. "You're pregnant?"

Her pale cheeks took on the soft blush of a peach. "I am. But I'm not due until summer," she hurried to tell him, as if the delay somehow mitigated the circumstances. "I plan to work for months yet. At least until May," she quickly assured him, sounding guilty for not having mentioned it before, or maybe embarrassed that she was having to mention it at all. "That way you won't need to worry about transitioning anyone in right away. Not that you'll need to worry about that yourself." Her soft tone was insistent, her expression utterly earnest. "I'll train another secretary for you before I have to move. I promise."

The fact that she was babbling about her job instead of her baby was lost on him. All he seemed to hear was that she was leaving. "Your fiancé isn't taking the position with the law firm here?"

She hesitated. "No," she murmured, her voice dropping. "And Scott's not my fiancé anymore."

The squeak of wheels underscored urgent voices as the nurse and paramedics rushed past with the gurney. To keep them both from getting trampled, he took her arm, pulling her with him to the wall.

Beneath his hand, he felt her slender muscles shift as she tightened her grip on her coat.

"I don't want to leave Grand Springs," she continued, her eyes uneasy on his. "I love my job. I really do. But I don't have a better choice. I can start interviewing for a replacement right away, if you'd prefer. That way, you can..."

"Sarah."

"...be sure the person is..."

"Sarah," he repeated, aware of the faint quiver in her voice. She was trying desperately to sound as if she had everything under control, but she wasn't succeeding. He recognized bravado when he saw it. And fear. And to him, she looked frightened and fragile—and desperately in need of a pair of arms.

He reached toward her, taking her coat to keep himself from easing her against his chest. "Don't worry about your job right now," he insisted, forcing himself to focus only on practicalities. "We'll talk about it later. I want to get out of here."

"Of course you do. I'm sorry. Lucas, you really didn't have to wait."

"We've been through that. And I did, so forget it. Okay?"

"Okay," she agreed, letting him help her with her heavy black raincoat. "But my car's still at the office. I hate for you to have to drive all the way back there."

"I'm not going to. I'm not about to dump you at your car and leave you on your own," he informed her, amazed that she'd think he would. "It's nearly midnight, the power is out on your end of town and some of the roads are blocked. My condo is less than a mile away. Then there's the fall you took tonight." Taking her by the shoulders, he turned her around now that he had her coat on her and dropped his hands before he could button it up himself. "I know the nurse said you're fine, but you shouldn't be alone if you start bleeding. You can stay at my place."

His tone was decisive. His expression, intent. Sarah knew the combination well. It was how he became when he was going through ad copy or designs, okaying, dismissing or recommending without hesitation or qualm. She'd always respected the way he so masterfully collected facts, identified problem areas, then bulldozed ahead to fix whatever needed fixing. She even tried to emulate his pragmatic approach. She'd just never encountered his determination on a personal level before.

Had he been anyone else, she would have insisted she was fine and called a cab, assuming she could even get one on such a night. She was actually quite accustomed to taking care of herself. Yet, as he left her by the sliding double doors with instructions to wait while he brought the car under the emergency portico, she realized she hadn't uttered so much as a token protest.

Any other time, she would have wondered at that lack of determination. Right now, with Lucas, it didn't bother her at all. As overwhelmed as she'd felt for the past month, and after struggling through the fear of losing the child complicating her life, there was something terribly appealing about not having to wrestle with decisions herself tonight.

There was also something profoundly compelling about how safe she felt when he returned to tuck her against his side and, shielding her from the worst of the wind, hurried her into his car.

\* \* \*

"I thought for sure the power would be out." Lucas ushered her ahead of him into the kitchen of his spacious condo and closed out the cold air of the garage with the solid thud of the door. "Just in case it does go, I think I'll start a fire. Go on in and get comfortable."

A fire sounded like pure heaven to Sarah. Her shoes were wet from the quick dashes to the car and though they'd given her a blanket in the emergency room, she'd thought she'd freeze waiting on the exam table in the skimpy hospital gown she'd had to put on.

She hadn't been in his condo since before he'd moved into it a year and half ago. Yet, as he took her coat and she moved into the living room, the place felt as familiar to her as her infinitely more modest apartment. She'd picked out the stools at the kitchen counter to go with the antique pine dining set under the bronze oak-leaf chandelier. And she had found the heavy candlesticks on the mantel at an antique shop.

She'd selected pretty much everything in the place. Or, at least, narrowed Lucas's choices to what she and the decorator had felt would go with the pieces he'd okayed. All she'd had to go on was his insistence that he wanted a place that was comfortable without being cute, sophisticated without being cold. With its rich shades of burgundy, accents of cream and daytime views of the majestic mountains and pines, it was a home she would have loved to live in herself, had she been able to afford such luxuries.

She'd had a great time decorating it.

"You hung the picture your sister sent you." She

offered the observation as Lucas crouched in front of the massive fireplace. "It goes well there."

She heard kindling snap as a tongue of flame lapped dry bark. Closing the screen on the stone fireplace, Lucas rose, knees cracking, and glanced toward the family portrait hanging between a potted ficus and a wing-backed chair. Terry, his middle sister, had sent the photograph for his last birthday. She'd called Sarah to find out what color of mat and frame to buy after conversations with her brother had left her clueless as to his decor. It seemed she hadn't been able to get a thing out of him about his thennew home other than that he liked what his secretary and the decorator had done.

Sarah knew she was really going to miss working for him.

"Thanks," he muttered, frowning at the way she had her arms crossed so tightly around herself. "Is something wrong? The nurse said if you started cramping, we should—"

"No. No," she repeated, not sure if she was embarrassed by his frankness or impressed by it. "Everything's…fine."

"Are you sure? I'll get you back there somehow if you think you need to go."

"I'm sure. Really."

His glance slid back to her crossed arms.

"I'm just a little cold," she said.

She couldn't tell if he believed her or not. Still looking skeptical, he motioned her to the sofa.

"You'll be warmer in front of the fire. You should probably be off your feet, anyway," he informed her, handing her a burgundy chenille throw blanket from the wing-backed chair. "I'll get you something hot to drink. Meg left a box of herbal tea last time she was here," he said, referring to his youngest sister. "It's either that or coffee."

The last thing she wanted was caffeine. Aside from having heard it wasn't all that good for the baby, she'd been having a hard enough time sleeping at it was. "The tea would be wonderful."

She would have added that she could get it herself, but he was stripping off his tie and heading for the kitchen even as she spoke. His motions looked automatic as he draped the tie and his jacket over the back of a dining chair and worked loose one more button on his crisp white shirt.

The routine was probably the same one he performed every evening when he came home from the office. Nothing unusual or extraordinary. Yet, there was something enormously compelling to her about watching him shed the business armor, along with the indefinable tension he wore with it. She'd seen him before with his tie loose and his shirtsleeves rolled up, but only at the office and only buried in work. Here, he was allowing her into his personal world.

That world seemed amazingly peaceful to her at the moment. Drawn by it, by him, she sank into a corner of the buttery leather sofa, tucked her icy feet beneath the blanket and watched the fire grow steadily brighter.

She'd actually started to relax for the first time in weeks when he held out a ceramic mug and told her to be careful because the tea was hot. Thanking him, she took it and watched him settle into the wing chair angled three feet away.

"Aren't you having something?" she asked.

"Don't want anything."

"You don't have to wait on me."

"You're pregnant," he said easily. "And you had a scare with that fall. I don't think I'll lose my standing as a chauvinist just for bringing you tea."

Curling her fingers around the heavy mug, she met the smile in his eyes. "If you're a chauvinist, then the sexist little weasel you fired last month from the art department was a raving liberal."

"He interviewed well," he said, toeing off one of his expensive-looking, and damp, loafers. "You didn't pick up on his attitude at first, either.

"So," he continued as the other shoe joined the first, "how far along are you?"

Her glance faltered. "Three months," she replied, finding it easier to concentrate on the steam curling from her mug than the intent hazel eyes watching her so closely.

"I'd thought something wasn't right with you, Sarah. But you never let on that it was something like this."

She gave a faint, one-shouldered shrug. "I tried not to let on that there was anything wrong at all. I always admired the way you were able to keep your job in focus when you first came here," she admitted, thinking of how resolutely he'd plowed ahead when his personal life had fallen apart a couple of years ago. "That's what I tried to do, too. Keep my focus on work, I mean. If it was apparent at all that something was wrong, then I guess I need more practice."

"You don't think of yourself as human?"

"Of course I do. It's just that I used to watch my mom fall apart in the face of any challenge. Everybody knew when her life was a mess." Which had been more often than not while Sarah had been growing up. "I love her a lot, but I don't want to be like that."

"You're not," he informed her flatly. "I doubt anyone else noticed. And you shouldn't use me as an example of anything." Feeling oddly humbled by the knowledge that she had, he watched the graceful motion of her finger as she distractedly traced the rim of her mug. "You're too young to start burying yourself in work. It's nothing but a crutch to avoid facing what's happened to your life, anyway."

The flickering fire caught hints of blue in her thick ebony hair as she lifted her head and glanced at him over the arm of the sofa. A loosened lock curved along one porcelain cheek.

"I know," she murmured.

That's what she'd been trying to do. Avoid thinking about how irrevocably her life had been altered. Lucas understood that all too well.

Hating that she felt such a need, he leaned forward, resting his forearms on his powerful thighs and clasped his hands between them.

"Look, you obviously hadn't wanted to say anything about this before, but now that I know, if you want to talk, I'm willing to listen." A self-deprecating smile touched his mouth. "You had to put up with my moods when I was going through my divorce. I figure I owe you."

To Sarah, there had always been a reserve about

Lucas, a distance a person didn't always notice because of his take-charge manner and charm. That subtle distance was always there, protecting him from getting too close. Or, perhaps, from letting anyone get too close to him. But, that guardedness was missing as he quietly watched her now. If she sensed anything in him at all, it was only a willingness to do what he'd said. To listen.

"Have you told anyone what's going on?" he quietly asked.

She slowly shook her head, drawn by the friendship he was offering.

"I know my friends will tell me I'm crazy if I don't give the baby up or terminate the pregnancy, and my mom will start lecturing about how I've handicapped my future prospects because I have a child. It's just been easier not to say anything to anyone."

"What about your father?"

"I don't have to worry about him," she replied, grateful for once that she didn't have that particular parent to deal with on top of everything else. "He walked out on my mom and my sister and me years ago. I don't even know where he is."

The wind whistled past the windows. Staccato ticking sounds hinted that the rain had now turned to solid sleet. Beyond her, the fire snapped as flames encountered fresh pitch. There was a cozy, intimate feel to the room, but it was Lucas's solid presence that comforted her most.

"What about…what's his name? Scott?"

"He knows."

She took a sip of the aromatic tea. It had been

terribly sweet of Lucas to get it for her, though sweet wasn't a word she had ever associated with him before. Considering the dangerous scowl she glimpsed before contemplating the contents of her mug again, she decided she wasn't inclined to associate it with him at the moment, either.

"Why do I have the feeling he bailed on you?"

"Because he did." She spoke with a simplicity that utterly belied the devastation her ex-fiancé had inflicted on her. "I had the feeling even before I told him I was pregnant that something was wrong. The month before we broke up, he hardly ever called and when he'd return my messages, he was always so vague about when we'd see each other again.

"When I did tell him," she continued, hating that her voice cracked, "he finally admitted he wasn't ready to settle into anything permanent. He said he needed to explore other relationships before he settled down."

"Did he expect you to wait for him?"

"No." He hadn't wanted her at all. "He was already seeing someone else."

She took a breath, slowly blew it out. She needed to stick to the facts. It was easier that way. Safer. "He told me he'd give me the money for an abortion. I handed him back his ring and told him I didn't expect or want anything from him. As far as the baby and I are concerned, he doesn't even exist."

For a moment, Lucas said nothing. He just sat studying her face, his hands clasped and his own thoughts carefully masked.

"Do you know what you're going to do?" he finally asked.

"Keep it. I've always wanted children," she told him, her voice dropping as she admitted a dream she seldom shared. "It's hardly the baby's fault that the timing is lousy. I just wish I knew some way to stay in Grand Springs and keep my job. But I don't think I can raise a child completely on my own."

She shook her head, shoving back the loose strand of hair as the consequences of her decisions descended on her. "Mom will be so disappointed in me for getting pregnant, and my sister... My sister," she repeated, feeling the lump of anxiety grow in her stomach. "Cammy's only sixteen and I'm supposed to be the responsible older sibling. Some example I'm setting for her."

"Maybe you should just think about yourself and your baby right now." Lucas's deep voice held sympathy, and an odd hint of disquiet. "Where is it that you plan to go?"

Picking at a loose thread on the blanket, she pulled a deep breath and slowly blew it out. It was so like him to make her keep her focus. "Salt Lake City. Mom remarried and moved there a few years ago. I'll find an apartment near their house," she told him, wanting to ignore the dull ache burning her chest. "I'm sure I won't be able to find a job until after the baby is born, but I won't leave here until about a month before. That'll give me plenty of time to train a secretary to replace me.

"I'll work with human resources to see who we have in-house," she hurried on, pushing past the sudden constriction in her throat. "If we don't have anyone here that you want to bring in, I'll work with an employment agency." Her voice caught as she lowered her head. She felt betrayed. She felt abandoned. But the thought of having to give up the security of the job she loved only added to the pain of what her ex-fiancé had done. Her position with Lucas had been the one thing she'd felt she could count on. "No matter what," she promised, hating how powerless she was to stop everything from changing, "I'll make sure the new person knows how you like things done before I go."

A single, crystalline tear trailed down her cheek. Lucas saw it despite the way she deliberately ducked her head in an attempt to keep him from seeing it at all. Given the scope of her problems, he couldn't believe she was so concerned about minimizing the inconvenience to him. But then, he couldn't believe how disturbed he was by the thought of not having her in the office to keep track of his life.

Wishing it was only her tears he found so unsettling, he reached into the back pocket of his slacks and pulled out his handkerchief. He'd come to think of this lovely and capable young woman as what his colleagues called an office wife—and the thought of getting used to another secretary held no more appeal than the blind dates he'd pointedly avoided.

"Hey. Here," he muttered, caught off guard by the urge he felt to dry her tears himself when he offered his handkerchief.

"Thank you," she murmured, taking the pristine white square. "I'm not sure why I'm doing this."

"Talking to me?"

"No. Talking to you is easy. I mean this." She swiped at her cheeks, trying to smile, failing miserably. "It's not like it helps."

"Probably not. But it's understandable. You and Scott were together for a long time. I'm sure you miss what you had with him."

"I miss what I *thought* I had," she conceded. She sniffed, took another swipe and wadded the handkerchief into a tight little ball. "I loved the man I thought he was, not the man he turned out to be. And he didn't love me at all."

"You're assuming there is such a thing."

Puzzlement flickered through the depths of her luminous blue eyes as she looked up.

"You're assuming there's such a thing as love," he clarified. "But there isn't. Not the kind people beat themselves up looking for," he announced as casually as he would the fact there was no Santa Claus. "Love is just a word people use to make other feelings sound more noble. Dependence. Desire," he explained, a shrug in his voice. "It's all got to do with who wants what from the other person. Once you get past the myth, you'll be in better shape when the next guy comes along."

A faint frown touched her forehead. With her head tipped as she quietly studied him, she looked very innocent, very vulnerable. She also looked terribly certain. "There isn't going to be a next time."

"That's just hurt talking."

"You're the one who just implied that I should toughen my shell," she reminded him. She'd never realized he was so cynical. It explained a lot about him, though, she supposed; about how dispassionately he viewed relationships, and why he didn't seem interested in one. Yet, she couldn't deny the advantages—and maybe the truth—to his protective way of thinking. "And you're right."

"I'm willing to bet you won't give up that easily. You're young yet," he said, quietly. "Once the hurt is gone, you'll want the same things you wanted out of your relationship with Scott."

"All I ever wanted was stability," she murmured, narrowing all her dreams down to the one thing she'd lacked since she was ten years old. "I've wanted that since the day my father walked out."

Lucas felt himself go still. He'd never considered that she would be searching for something so basic. As young as she was, he'd expected her dreams to lean toward romanticized notions of happily ever after, or whatever it was people expected before time and reality tarnished the fairy tale.

The shadows in her eyes told him the myth had already died for her. They also made him forget to be cautious. He reached toward her, catching her chin when she started to look away, and tipped her face toward him. Beneath his fingers, her skin felt like warm satin.

"That's not an unreasonable thing to want, Sarah."

He thought she might lower her head to break the contact. At the very least, he thought she'd look away. All she did was grip her mug, leaving him to wonder if she even realized how easily she allowed his touch, and why it had felt so necessary to offer the assurance.

His glance fell to the inviting part of her mouth. The soft shade of lipstick she usually wore had worn away, leaving her lips the pale shade of a blush.

The thought of how she would taste, of how her mouth would feel moving beneath his, made his body go as tight as a trip wire.

"It's late." That tightness slipped into his voice, adding an edge that made her blink owlishly back at him. "Things always seem worse when you're tired."

Reaching down, he took the cooling mug from her hands. "The guest room is full of ski equipment and Christmas presents right now. You can have my room and I'll take the sofa."

"I don't want to put you out of your bed," she murmured, feeling oddly bereft of his touch when he pulled away.

He was right. Fatigue did skew the mind. She'd actually hoped he'd put his arms around her. She'd felt so safe in them before. So...sheltered. But this was Lucas. Her boss. The man she'd have to face in the morning, and work with for months. She'd embarrassed herself enough tonight without mistaking his touch for anything more than kindness.

## *Chapter 3*

Sarah's last thought before she fell into an exhausted sleep in Lucas's big bed was that his ex-wife had been nuts to let him go. Her first thoughts when she awoke the next morning were of how incredibly supportive he'd been with her—and that she was going to be sick.

She'd just had her best night's sleep in weeks, but there was clearly no reprieve from the hormonal swing that had her bolting from beneath his heavy comforter and diving for his bathroom. She could have sworn she'd heard that some women went all nine months without suffering anything more than swollen ankles. It seemed she was destined to greet each dawn feeling as if she were on the rolling deck of a storm-tossed ship.

Considering her ashen-faced reflection in Lucas's medicine cabinet mirror five minutes later, she

washed her face and used the toothbrush he'd given
her last night. She needed something in her stomach.
Something plain and dry and devoid of any scent that
might set off another wave of nausea. She also
needed something to wear other than the white
T-shirt he'd given her to sleep in. Her skirt and black
tights hung over the glass shower door, still damp
from when she'd rinsed them out last night. Lucas's
heavy blue robe hung behind the door.

Hoping he wouldn't mind if she borrowed it, she
slipped it on and scraped her long hair back from her
face. The high-tech digital radio alarm on his night-
stand blinked 12:00. Her watch indicated it was
closer to seven o'clock in the morning. The power
had obviously gone out sometime during the night
and come back on again.

Judging from how cold his condo seemed now that
she was thinking about something other than throwing up, she decided it couldn't have been back on for
long. The place was freezing.

The short hallway was dim when she opened the
door, but she could see Lucas standing in front of the
large television in his living room. He was wearing
gray sweatpants and a worn gray sweatshirt that made
his shoulders look a mile wide. The morning news
clearly had his undivided attention.

She stopped beside the sofa, ten feet away. "Morning," she murmured.

He hit the mute button on the remote control in
his hand before he turned. With a night's growth of
beard shadowing the strong line of his jaw and a tuft
of chest hair peeking above the band of his shirt, he
looked supremely, unashamedly male. The quick

glance he slid down her body also made him look vaguely predatory as he tossed the remote control onto the coffee table and walked over to her.

Barefoot, she dug her toes into the soft carpet and tightened his robe around her. She was sure it was just another weird lurch of hormones that made her stomach tighten when she met his eyes.

"I hope you don't mind," she murmured, still too rocky to be as disturbed by the intimacy of the situation as she might have been. "About your robe, I mean. My things are still damp."

"No problem." His glance openly swept her face and narrowed on her pale lips. "You can throw them in the dryer if you want. But there's no hurry." Taking her by the shoulders, he turned her around and steered her toward the kitchen. "It'll be a few hours before we can go anywhere. The flooding in the lower elevations isn't a problem for us, but the roads are closed until the temperature rises and things start to thaw. Take a look."

His hands fell, robbing her of their comforting weight when he motioned toward the window in the dining room and headed behind the breakfast bar. He'd opened the heavy oyster-colored drapes. Beyond the frosted edges of the glass, the gray light of morning blended with the misty gray of evergreens and skeletal aspen coated with a glistening glaze of ice.

The rain had turned into an ice storm.

"What'll it be? Dry toast or crackers?"

Dragging a shaky hand through her hair, she glanced back to where he stood with his hand on an oak cupboard door.

"It shows," he said before she could ask how he knew what she needed. "You'll probably want tea rather than coffee, too. Right?"

"How did you know?"

"I've been around both of my sisters when they were in the first stages of pregnancy. Meg carried crackers with her everywhere she went and Terry...well," he said, looking as if he didn't want to risk mention of anything specific since he didn't know what might send her racing back down the hall, "let's just say no one in their house could have anything but cold cereal in the morning without turning her green." He gave her a hesitant glance. "Would it bother you if I made coffee?"

"No. Please," Sarah insisted, stoically refusing to deny him his morning caffeine. "Go ahead."

He took her at her word and set about filling the glass carafe and measuring grounds and nuking a cup of water for her tea. It had never occurred to her that he would look as comfortable in a kitchen as he did a boardroom, but there was no question that he'd mastered his survival skills.

"So which is it?" he asked, tossing a loaf of bread onto the counter and reaching into the refrigerator for butter and jam for himself. "Crackers or toast."

"Toast," she told him, since he was making it for himself anyway. "May I help?"

"Nothing to do. Just sit down until you feel better."

She'd thought it would feel awkward to be with him this morning. And it did, a little. Yet, he didn't appear to feel at all uncomfortable with her being there wearing his clothes and looking like something the cat had dragged in and abandoned. Taking her cue from him, she settled onto one of the high stools at the beige tiled breakfast counter, and snugged his robe around herself.

If he didn't mind talking about her being pregnant, she figured she might as well take advantage of his knowledge. "Did the morning sickness last very long with your sisters?"

"I don't think so. Seems like it was just the first few months, but it's been a while since we've had a baby in the family. Meg's youngest is three now."

"Four. Joey had a birthday in October," she reminded him, referring to his oldest sister's youngest son. She knew Meg had three boys. Terry had two girls. Lucas's two brothers had three girls and a boy between them. Knowing no relatives other than her mom and her sister and, now, a stepdad, she'd rather envied his big, closely knit family. "You sent him a dinosaur book, remember?"

"He's four?" he repeated, not sounding at all surprised that she was aware of such details. "I can't believe he's getting that big. I'm really going to miss those kids this year," he muttered, handing her his sister's box of herbal tea on his way to the stove. "They're the best part of the holidays.

"That reminds me," he continued, "since I'm not going home, I need to mail the presents I was going to take. Would you take care of that for me?"

"Sure." She didn't so much as blink at the request. It was the sort of thing she handled for him all the time. "I'll take care of it this as soon as we get to the office."

His back was to her. Watching him open the door

of the microwave above the burners, she was conscious of the strong muscles of his back and arms shifting beneath his shirt. He'd picked her up from the floor when she'd fallen as if she weighed no more than air. The word masterful came to mind. And protective. His body had felt hard and honed, his touch confident, certain. Even swamped with embarrassment and fear for her baby, she'd been aware of how very…physical…he was.

Being aware of him now, though, seemed neither sensible nor prudent.

"There's only one problem." He set a blue ceramic mug of steaming water in front of her. "The kids' things aren't wrapped."

"What? Oh," she muttered, jerking her glance from the back of his broad, capable hand. There were little chips of green in his hazel eyes. Odd, she thought, that she'd never noticed them before. "That doesn't matter. If you have paper, I can wrap them now."

"Paper, ribbon and tags. Hang on. I'll get them."

He snagged the toast when it popped up, handed her one and dropped in two more slices of bread. After slathering his own piece with butter and jam, he annihilated it on his way down the hall.

She'd nibbled one corner from her toast and had started on the other when the rustle of paper had her turning on the high stool. Lucas was back with sacks in both hands and tubes of brightly colored paper tucked under one arm.

Shoving aside a brass fruit bowl full of mail, he dumped the lot on the dining table across from her. "Just a couple more," he said, and returned moments later with two more big white bags from Toys 'R Us toy store.

Baffled, she stared through cellophane at the headlights of a bright yellow dump truck with black wheels the size of tea saucers. "How were you going to carry all that on a plane?"

"I usually just box it up and check it as luggage."

"You normally buy this much?"

His broad shoulders lifted in a dismissing shrug as he headed to the toaster to butter the rest of his breakfast. "I could just give them the money, but it wouldn't be as much fun. For them or me."

Taking her tea with her, she slid off the stool and peeked inside the sack by the truck. A high-fashion doll wearing purple eyeshadow and shocking pink lamé stared back at her.

The man was a fraud. He'd told her he hated shopping, which was why he'd come to her this year to buy gifts for his mom and dad and the sister whose name he'd drawn last year, since that was the way they handled presents for the adults in his family. She'd offered to buy for the children, too, but he'd told her not to worry about them, which had left her thinking a family member was covering that base for him. She was obviously wrong. He clearly enjoyed shopping for his nieces and nephews himself.

The thought of the authoritative man she knew wrestling with a decision over a doll in the aisle of a toy store was totally incongruous to her. His remark about kids being the best part of Christmas had caught her off guard, too. But, then, she'd never really allowed herself to think of him outside his role as her boss. She knew he was close to his family in

the same way she knew which restaurants he preferred, how he liked his coffee and that he internal-
ized stress. She worked with him. They spent ten
hours a day together. But discovering his soft spot
for children seemed more revealing to her than anything she'd learned in the long hours they shared at
the office.

He was leaning against the counter by the sink,
watching her and working on his last piece of toast
when her eyes met his.

"You're going to miss not being with them this
year, aren't you?"

"I'm going to miss being with all of my family.
And Mom's chowder," he admitted, casually
crossing his outstretched legs at the ankles. "She always makes clam chowder and corn bread on Christmas Eve. It's almost better than the big meal she puts
together the next day. What about you? What are you
doing for Christmas?"

The question was unremarkable enough. It was the
careful way he watched her that struck her as odd. It
was as if he were measuring her somehow, judging
or weighing what she said and did.

Telling herself he was probably just watching to
see if she was going to turn green again, she contem-
plated her tea.

"I don't know what I'm doing. I'd thought I'd be
spending it with Scott and his family," she told him,
rather wishing she could just crawl into a hole for
the holidays—and come out with the groundhogs
sometime in the spring. "Mom and my sister and my
mom's husband left yesterday to spend it with his
relatives in Chicago."

It seemed she and Lucas were both now officially at loose ends. She was sure he realized that, too. Since the last thing she wanted to do was put him on the spot by asking if he wanted to spend the day with her, she sought to learn whatever else he was willing to share about himself. "What will you miss most about the kids?"

His brow furrowed. "I don't know," he muttered, considering. "I've never really thought about it. Their excitement, I guess. They get a little wired with all the cookies and stuff Mom makes for them, but they try hard to be good, because of the Santa thing. Except for Matt and Jeffrey," he amended, speaking of his ten- and eleven-year-old nephews. "They try not be excited like the little ones because it's not cool for a guy to be too eager. But they haven't lost all their innocence about it yet."

An unavoidable smile touched her mouth as she turned back to his packages. "You should have had kids of your own." She'd never seen this side of Lucas before. She liked it. A lot. "I have the feeling they'd be spoiled rotten, but you're a natural."

For a moment, Lucas said nothing. He just watched Sarah over the rim of his mug as she poked through the pile of gifts he'd admittedly gone a little overboard buying.

His thick terry cloth robe practically swallowed her whole, the sleeves so long that her hands were barely visible. He'd never seen her like this, without makeup, with her hair unrestrained. At work, she always wore it clipped back or up somehow. Now, it tumbled over her shoulders in a fall of ebony silk that fairly begged to be touched—and conjured images that had no place in the improbable idea that had occurred to him in the long hours before dawn.

"I always wanted kids," he admitted, though it wasn't like him to voice what mattered to him most. He knew he'd have to lay his own cards on the table, though, before he could ask to see hers. "My ex just changed her mind about having them."

Her head came up, open interest washing the delicate contours of her face. "Is that why your divorce was so...?"

"Bitter?" he suggested when she suddenly hesitated. "It's okay, Sarah. You put through all the calls from my lawyer. And a few from my ex. I know you're aware it wasn't an amicable parting." He lifted his mug as if to apologize for the imposition, and thank her for her discretion. He'd never once heard any office buzz about his divorce, which meant she'd never said a word to anyone about the emotional merry-go-round he'd been riding when he'd taken over Myer and Hutchins's western operations. He'd appreciated her loyalty far more than he'd ever let on.

"Like I said last night," he continued, "you bore the brunt of my blacker days when I first got here. And about Carol...her decision that she didn't want children was part of the reason we divorced, but it got bitter because there was a lot more wrong with the marriage than there was right."

"I'm sorry." She'd wanted to tell him that a long time ago. At least, tell him she was sorry he was having to deal with so much. But the issue had felt too personal to mention directly. "I really am," she told him, touched that he trusted her enough to confide in her now.

"Ancient history," he muttered, meaning it. Glass bumped wood as he set his mug down and pulled out a Nintendo video game he'd bought for Matt. "But thanks. It's hard to keep a relationship intact when the people in it are operating from totally different agendas. It just all came to a head when I was offered the promotion here."

Distractedly, Sarah reached for the roll of green paper with little red drummers on it. "She didn't want to move?"

"No." He wanted her to know what had happened. Carol had pulled the plug on their marriage, but he wasn't blameless himself. He wanted Sarah to know that, too. "But I was too busy working my way up in the company to see that her interests had taken a different direction from mine. I'd always thought we were working toward a time when we could start our family. That had been the plan since the day we were married," he said, ruthlessly checking the memory of how angry and betrayed he'd felt when he'd realized she'd lost interest in that goal years before she'd bothered to tell him.

"Anyway," he said, his deep voice quiet, "when the promotion came up I thought it was perfect because Grand Springs seems like such a great place to raise kids. She'd known the transfer was coming, but she waited until I'd accepted it to tell me she had no **intention of moving** anywhere. Her friends and family were in La Jolla and that's where she wanted to stay. As for kids, she'd decided she wasn't the maternal type."

In other words, he thought, unable to dodge the thought that kept his defenses locked so securely in place, she hadn't cared at all about their plans, and she hadn't wanted or needed him. They'd outgrown each other, she'd informed him, as if they were nothing more than clothes that had become too small, or gone out of style and lost their appeal.

"All that mattered to her was getting the house, the furniture and our savings so she could go into business with her girlfriend." A muscle in his jaw jumped. "The judge decided she needed the money to earn a living. Since I had a job that paid well, she got nearly everything we had."

A man would have to be a fool to make himself that vulnerable again.

The thought occurred to him without any particular rancor. It was simply a fact, an expensive lesson he'd learned that he had no intention of forgetting. The divorce had cost him a fortune. Yet, the move to Grand Springs had turned out to be worth every penny. The demands of his new position hadn't left him any time to think about how badly he'd wanted what he'd lost.

What he *thought* he'd lost, he reminded himself, thinking of what Sarah had said last night. He didn't regret losing Carol. She'd been a stranger to him when they'd finally parted. He regretted losing the dream he'd thought they'd shared. The home. The children. The growing old together. Coming up to speed with his new position had consumed nearly his every waking hour, and he'd used whatever time was left learning everything he could about the town to make his presence visible in the business community.

Through it all, Sarah had hung in there, buffering him when she could, answering his endless questions, keeping him on top of appointments, dinners and deadlines.

"It sounds as if you really wanted a family, Lucas."

"I did."

"Is work enough for you?"

No, he thought, over the crackle of paper as she unrolled a length and glanced back up at him. It isn't. And, maybe, it didn't have to be.

All he'd admit at the moment, however, was, "I don't know."

He turned away, telling himself as he collected scissors and tape from a drawer in the kitchen that the idea that had taken root in his brain at heaven-only-knew what godawful hour in the morning was pure dumb crazy. As wild as any he'd ever had. But there was a practicality to it, an undeniable logic, that made it impossible for him to ignore.

"Tell me," he murmured, snapping off a piece of tape while she cut paper to size and deftly wrapped the electronic game, "do you think of yourself as a practical person?"

"Practical?" she asked, taking the piece of tape he held out to her.

"You know, sensible. Realistic." As she folded the other end, he held out another two-inch strip. "You've always struck me as being levelheaded. I just wondered if you see yourself that way."

"I suppose so. I've never had the time or the money to be frivolous." A faint frown touched her brow as she finished the box and flipped it over. "I certainly won't now, either," she murmured. "Not with a baby to consider." She held up a spool of ribbon in each hand. "Which do you want?" she asked, wanting, just for a while, not to worry about the direction her life had taken. "Red or green?"

"Red. Listen." An unexpected note of seriousness underscored the deep timbre of his voice. "I've been thinking about everything you said last night...about you having to leave."

It seemed she wasn't going to get her reprieve. The sick, sinking sensation that inevitably knotted her stomach at the thought of moving hit with a vengeance. "I really don't want to go. I told you that. I just don't see how I can stay."

"Because you want to keep your baby."

"Yes," she murmured, focusing on the ribbon she twisted around the end of her finger. "I don't honestly see how I can do both."

"You're like my right arm at the office. You know that?"

"Please don't do this, Lucas. I feel bad enough as it is. I told you I'll find you—"

"I'm not trying to make you feel bad. And I know what you told me," he countered, taking the ribbon from her and setting it aside. "I'm telling you I don't want another secretary." Now that he had her full attention, he considered her cautiously, carefully weighing his words. "Since you don't want to go and I don't want anyone else, I've thought of a way we can help each other out."

Skeptical, she crossed her arms over the knots and waited for him to pull a rabbit out of a hat. "How?"

"I'll marry you."

Sarah felt her whole body go as still as stone.

"It makes perfect sense," he insisted, oblivious to the fact that she wasn't breathing. "If I marry you, you can stay here and keep your baby and your job, which is what you want, and I'll keep you as my secretary, which is what I want."

She sucked in a breath. "Lucas..."

"Just hear me out. Okay?"

"Fine," she murmured and sank to the chair he pulled out.

"There are other benefits, too," he continued, swinging around another chair so he could face her. As he had last night, he leaned forward, his feet planted apart, his elbows resting on his knees. Only now, his knees were six inches from hers, his beautiful hazel eyes were intent on her face and he was talking about making her his wife.

"I have no intention of ever entering a real marriage again," he said flatly. "But this would be my shot at being a dad. And yours for security for yourself and your child. Sharing responsibility for the baby would make your life easier in a lot of ways. Wouldn't it?"

Numb, she thought. She felt numb.

She nodded.

"As for the legalities," he continued, his handsome features intent as he systematically covered his bases, "all I'd ask in return is that you sign a prenuptial agreement to the effect that only what is acquired after the date of the marriage is subject to any claim from you should we divorce. Anything you or I already have remains our own personal property. I'd have to check with my lawyer, but I don't think

I'd have to adopt the baby. Since we'd be married when it's born, my name will go on the birth certificate.'' His brow pinched as he studied her. ''I can't think of anything else on the legal end. Can you?''

She wasn't sure she could think at all. Oddly, at the moment, it was only his request for a prenuptial agreement that made any sense. Considering what he'd been through with his last marriage, she could hardly blame him for wanting to protect himself. It was everything else that left her battling disbelief. ''No, I... No,'' she repeated, wondering at how hard her heart was beating.

''Oh, and there's one more benefit for me.'' A wry smile exposed his dimple. ''With you as my wife, I won't have to worry about finding dates for social functions. You're wonderful with clients.''

She supposed she should thank him. But she simply couldn't believe what she was hearing, much less what he was offering. He was giving her a chance to stay in the town she loved and keep the job she adored instead of going in defeat to her family. He was offering to help her raise her baby.

There was absolutely nothing romantic about the proposal. Not even a hint that there would be any emotional involvement on his part. The man was an absolute cynic where love was concerned and there was no way this side of Hades a woman could mistake his offer for anything but the pragmatic and practical solution it was. Yet, he had a way of looking at her mouth that left her breath shallow and her stomach fluttering.

Certain it was just nerves, she slipped her hand

protectively over her belly. Her child could do far worse than to have Lucas Harding for a father.

''I don't know what to say.''

His glance fell to her hand.

Apparently thinking she was getting queasy again, he moved her tea within reach. ''You don't have to say anything right now. Just think about it and let me know what you decide.''

# Chapter 4

Just think about it, Lucas had said. As if any other
thought could possibly have taken precedence.

Sarah glanced toward Lucas's office as she
smoothed back her restrained hair, brushed a speck
of lint from her navy suit and, files in hand, started
for his closed door. Three steps later, she cut a U and
headed right back to her desk for the mail she'd forgotten.

It wasn't like her to be scattered. Even yesterday
morning after Lucas had hit her with his little prop-
osition, she'd managed to get his packages wrapped
and carry on what had seemed to be a perfectly normal discussion about his moving her into his guest
room and converting the office in his condo into a
nursery.

His amazingly relaxed manner had put her at ease
and kept her there until he'd dropped her off at her

car in the middle of the afternoon. Since the roads were still icy in spots and littered with tree branches the wind had torn from the trees or the weight of ice had broken, he'd followed her to her apartment to make sure she arrived safely home. But from that point on, she'd vacillated between accepting and declining his offer and wondering if he would start questioning his sanity once he'd given the matter a little thought himself.

She was dealing with a hefty dose of confusion and anxiety when she took a deep breath, knocked on his office door and heard him tell her to come in. He'd been holed up in his office on the telephone when she'd arrived late a half hour ago, but the light on his phone had been out for the past five minutes.

He stood behind his desk, a study in concentration and authority in a charcoal suit and burgundy tie. He had one hand clamped behind his neck and his head was bent as he studied a layout. The threads of silver in his dark hair caught the overhead lights.

Seeing her, his hand fell, his glance measuring. "Good morning."

"Morning," she returned, heading for the in-box on the corner of his desk as she did every morning. "I'm sorry I'm late. The roads are still bad in places. Only half of the proofs for the Dairy Association campaign came in. I called art and they're bringing up the rest."

"What about the copy?" he asked, waving off her need to apologize. Half of the people in the office had arrived later than usual. Those were the die-hards. Like them. Presumably, the other half were either stuck in transit or unable to make it at all.

"It's right here. Graphics is the holdup."

"Get on them, will you? Do I still have a meeting with the Grand Springs Auto people at eleven?"

"No one's called to cancel. I'll confirm it and get back to you. You have a nine o'clock with the building manager about renewing the space lease."

"My office or his?"

"His," she replied, referring to an office two floors down.

"Thanks."

"Anything else?"

"I think that about covers it." His hazel eyes slowly shifted from the faint shadows under her eyes to the navy wool covering her slender shape. "How are you feeling this morning?"

Rocky. Nervous. "Fine."

His lips pinched, doubt deepening the masculine creases on either side of his beautifully carved mouth. "Sarah," he said flatly. "You look almost as pale now as you did yesterday morning. Why don't you sit down?"

"Really. I'm okay," she insisted, too nervous to sit, rather wishing she could pace. She glanced toward the open door, her voice dropping in case someone were to walk into her office and overhear. "The nausea is worst when I first wake up. By now, it's usually gone."

Apparently, he decided to take her at her word. Rather than point out that she also looked a little tense, he strode over to the door, closed it with a decisive click and returned to lean against the front of his desk.

With his hands casually braced on either side of

his lean hips, his long legs stretched out and crossed at the ankle, he looked completely, impossibly relaxed. "Have you thought about what I suggested?"

Sitting didn't sound like such a bad idea after all. "Yes," she murmured, sinking into one of the barrel chairs facing him. "I have." She tipped up her chin, eyeing him evenly. "Have you?"

The slash of one dark eyebrow rose fractionally at the challenge. "Me? Of course I have. It was my idea."

"That doesn't mean you thought it through completely."

"I considered the most important aspects. Your needs. My needs."

"What about the gossip here at work?"

He shrugged, clearly unconcerned. "People will talk. We can't stop them. But they'll assume we've been involved since you broke up with your ex-fiancé. Maybe even before that. No one knows you're pregnant. You aren't even far enough along that anyone would suspect," he pointed out, his impersonal perusal moving from her gently rounded breasts to where her hands knotted in her lap. "By the time you do start to show, the assumption will be that the baby is mine."

The thought of how intimate they would have had to be for such a possibility to exist made her breath go shallow. As demanding as he could be at work, she imagined he would be just as demanding a lover. But he would be giving, too. He was so patient when he wanted to be. Thoughtful. Gentle. She'd felt his gentleness herself, and his strength.

Unnerved by the persistent memory of how hard

his body had felt when he'd picked her up from her fall, she pushed herself from the chair. He'd done nothing to make her think he was proposing a physical relationship. He was treating her only as a friend.

"The only thing I'm concerned about," he admitted as she started to pace, "is how comfortable you are with the idea of living with me."

Not, she thought, unable to imagine that he was all that comfortable with the idea himself. But this arrangement was about trade-offs. For him, it was about keeping his secretary and having a son or daughter. For her, it was about providing a future for her child in a way she couldn't possibly do alone.

The maternal side of her, the side shouting down the romantic in her soul, was just grateful for the opportunity. "I'm sure we'll both have some adjusting to do."

He tipped his head, a disarming smile playing at the corners of his mouth. "Is that an acceptance?"

Her heart seemed to be beating a little too fast when he eased himself from the edge of the desk and walked toward her. Towering over her, as strong and solid as an oak, he waited while she swallowed past the knot of nerves in her throat.

"It is," she murmured as the phone began to ring. "And thank you."

She thought he hesitated. But before she could decide if he'd just been attacked by second thoughts, he held out his hand. "No thanks necessary. I'm getting as much out of this as you are. I'll call Andy," he pronounced, speaking of his racquetball buddy, who also happened to be a judge. "Or would you rather have something more elaborate than a ceremony in his chambers? I've had the big wedding before, but maybe you'd…''

''No. No,'' she repeated, refusing to entertain the fantasy. It was terribly sweet that he would consider such a thing for her, though. ''Let's just keep it simple.''

He had the good grace to mask his relief. ''Fine. I'll call him then. We'll work out the other details this afternoon.''

It felt odd to accept a proposal with a handshake. But they weren't lovers. They were friends. And that's all they ever would be, she reminded herself as his strong hand slipped from hers. They also needed to get back to work. He had a meeting in two minutes and she had a telephone to answer.

Outwardly, it was very much like business as usual. For that she was enormously grateful. But the familiarity of the routine only masked the crazy blend of anticipation, apprehension and relief that had replaced the awful anxiety she'd been living with. Thirty-six hours ago, she'd been living in a state of subdued panic, not totally sure how she was going to do what she had to do and sick over the course her future had taken. Now, she was getting married.

''So, Sarah. We finally meet.'' The Honorable Andrew McNeely moved from behind his massive cherry wood desk, shrugging on his black judicial robe. Beneath a slash of thick blond eyebrows, keen brown eyes smiled as he extended his hand from one diaphanous sleeve. ''I kept telling Lucas that anytime he was ready to let you go, I'd be more than happy to hire you. And every time I'd ask if you were sick of him yet, he'd tell me to bug off. I didn't know he'd staked a permanent claim.'' His smile was warm, his grip firm and friendly. "He's only marrying you to keep me from stealing you away from him, you know?''

Beside her, Lucas slanted his friend a droll glance and calmly claimed her hand for himself. "Ignore him," he said easily, lacing his fingers through hers as if holding her hand were nothing at all extraordinary. "He's never been a gracious loser."

"That's true. But I'll concede graciously this time." Looking genuinely happy for his friend, he clapped Lucas on the shoulder. "I'll tell you this, though. She's probably the only woman who's ever been able to keep you on track. It's about time you married her."

Sarah watched the judge give Lucas an approving nod a moment before he motioned them both to the center of the spacious room with its red leather chairs and walls of leather-bound law books. She'd spoken with his honor on the telephone several times before, mostly when he'd call to meet Lucas for lunch or to set up a game. But she'd had no idea she'd been a topic of discussion between the two of them. She was especially surprised to know that Lucas had said enough about her for the man to feel there was actually a personal relationship between them. All she cared about at the moment, however, was that Lucas apparently hadn't shared the details of their agreement with his friend. If people were going to believe that the child she carried was his, they were going to have to believe the marriage was real.

She felt Lucas's fingers squeeze hers almost imperceptibly. The motion, she was sure, was nothing more than a silent request for her to play along, but she clung a little tighter anyway.

"I know you and your staff came in on a Saturday to catch up," Lucas drawled, taking his friend's good-natured ribbing in stride. "So I don't want to take any more of your time than necessary. Shouldn't we get on with this?"

"Hey. It's no problem. We workaholics need to stick together. But I understand your impatience." Andy pronounced with a wink. "Just let me buzz for my clerks. I asked them if they'd be witnesses. Do you have the license?"

"Right here."

Releasing her hand, Lucas took the slim white envelope from the inside pocket of his dark suit jacket. Even with the usual year-end inefficiency of trying to get things done when no one on the staff was in the mood to work over the past couple of days, they'd managed to get their marriage license and make a trip to his attorney's office where she'd signed the prenuptial agreement his lawyer had waiting for her. It had all been very quick. Very businesslike. And totally, completely, without sentiment.

She was getting married.

The thought held a faintly surreal quality as the door to the judge's chambers opened and a sturdy, gray-haired matron with a look of ruthless efficiency about her entered with a studious-looking young man cleaning his wire-rimmed glasses. These were their witnesses. Not family. Not friends. Just two strangers who wouldn't hold up the formalities by asking perfectly understandable questions like *Why didn't you mention that you were seeing each other?* and *Isn't this awfully sudden?*

There would be no music, no flowers, no elaborate cake. No big party with a wedding dinner and dancing. Though the thought of drifting down an aisle in a cloud of white satin had once held enormous appeal, she wasn't going to pretend this marriage was anything but a convenience for them both.

That was why her dress was a simple, calf-length sheath of plum-colored wool jersey. She'd bought it on her way home from work yesterday. So it did happen to be new. She was also wearing her grandmother's old pearl earrings, she had a penny in one black leather pump and she'd borrowed her friend Trisha's pearl hair clip.

The marriage might be a convenience, but it *was* her wedding. It had also already begun.

Andy stood in front of them, speaking to them both as he said that it was his duty to advise them that marriage was a serious responsibility, not to be entered into lightly. He smiled as he spoke, looking from her to the handsome man holding her hands. She wasn't really sure she heard much of what Andy said. She was more aware of the way Lucas's eyes locked on hers when he felt her trembling and the steadiness in his own grip. As if to reassure her, his thumb slowly rubbed her palm. In his glance, she saw the silent request to bear with him just a little longer and this little formality would all be over.

She heard him say, "I do."

"And you, Sarah Elizabeth Lewis, do you take this man to be your lawfully wedded husband? To love, respect and cherish for better or for worse, for richer for poorer, in sickness and health until death do you part?''

''I do,'' she repeated, determined to be as pragmatic as Lucas about their arrangement.

Andy looked to Lucas. ''You have the rings?''

She opened her mouth to say there weren't any. As hectic as the last few days had been, the subject of rings had never come up.

''Yes,'' Lucas murmured, reaching into the pocket of his suit jacket. I have one.''

''Then slip it on her finger and repeat after me,'' Andy instructed. ''With this ring, I thee wed.''

The ring was elegantly simple. There were no stones, no patterns or designs of any sort. It was just a wide gleaming band of platinum that looked like silver satin in the bright overhead lights. It was the sort of thing she would have chosen herself had he asked what she'd wanted. But the thought that Lucas had bought her a ring, much less that he would know her taste, was lost when she heard his deep voice echo the words and he slowly slipped the band on her finger.

She knew it was an act, but he didn't sound like a man who, only yesterday, had made certain she understood the legal agreement that made clear just how completely he intended to protect himself in their relationship. And he didn't look like a man who didn't mean everything he'd just said.

He must have seen the questions in her eyes, but he'd already turned his attention back to his friend.

''You said you wanted quick and simple,'' Andy reminded them. Paper rustled as he lowered the sheet he'd consulted. ''Therefore, by the power vested in me by the State of Colorado, I now pronounce you man and wife. Lucas," he said, looking as if he were trying not to grin in front of his clerks and possibly taint his dignified judicial image, "you may kiss your bride."

Sarah had forgotten about this part of the ceremony. Lucas didn't give her any time to think about it now, either. Seeming to take the idea of kissing her in stride, he cupped his hand at the back of her neck and tipped her chin up with his thumb.

She knew he was only doing what his friend and their witnesses expected him to do. And for her to hesitate would seem awfully strange. So she took a step closer, mirroring his smile and felt her pulse skip as he lowered his head.

His beautifully chiseled mouth felt warm and firm on hers, and far softer than she'd have thought anything that looked so hard could be. His breath brushed her cheek, the freshness of mint mingling with the subtle scents of musk and warm male. The combination knocked her heart against her ribs and snagged her breath in her throat. An instant later, something that felt like liquid fire tingled her breasts and shot straight to her womb.

Her fingers were curled around his biceps when he lifted his head a few unsteady heartbeats later. She didn't remember reaching for him. She didn't know what he saw in her face, either. But whatever it was put a faint frown in his eyes as his thumb slowly crept toward the corner of her mouth.

"Congratulations, you two."

At Andy's comment, Lucas's hand fell and Sarah looked quickly away. She doubted any of the three people reaching out to shake their hands had a clue that the kiss had been nothing more than a show for them. Lucas knew she'd been caught off guard by it, though. The glance he shot her as she thanked Andy's clerks for their time was loaded with as much curiosity as caution.

By the time they left Andy's chambers and the courthouse a few minutes later, she had to admit she was feeling decidedly cautious herself.

*...eye-catching as the shade... their hands high... was... that the tree and gaily... make more than a dozen... them. Lucas knew she'd been caught off guard by it...* *thought... The pleasure he didn't... so the... Andy's characted their hair was shaded with as much... company at caution.*

*By the time she... felt Andy's character and the... company her companions later. She had to admit she was feeling abruptly caught in half.*

# Chapter 5

The leaden sky threatened snow as Sarah walked with Lucas to where he'd left his SUV parked on Main Street. Despite roads still being blocked in parts of town, holiday shoppers laden with stuffed bags and gaily wrapped packages filled the sidewalk. Store windows were painted with festive winter scenes, and the lampposts all sported huge red tinsel bells.

With Lucas beside her, his hands deep in the pockets of his overcoat, Sarah barely noticed any of it.

"Are you all right?" he asked.

"I'm fine." She gave him a little smile, hoping she didn't sound as awkward as she felt. "You just caught me off guard back there. With the ring," she explained. "I wasn't expecting it." With her thumb, she rubbed the back of the wide band, the nervous motion hidden from his quietly assessing gaze. "I'm sorry I didn't get you one. We never talked about how far we were going with…appearances.''

His glance dropped to her mouth, lingering long enough to wreak havoc with her heart rate before he calmly met her eyes. ''I figured we'd need to go as far as necessary to make it look real.''

''Of course. I just…''

''I had to kiss you, Sarah.''

Her heart stumbled. ''I realize that. I just hadn't…I wasn't…I was talking about the ring,'' she concluded lamely.

She'd been thinking about what he'd done, though. She still was. And just the thought of it made her knees a little weak. If he ever got serious and put his heart into a kiss, the effect could be devastating. But his heart, she reminded herself, had nothing to do with her.

''I got it for you because I thought you might want one. Especially once it becomes obvious that you're pregnant.'' The cold breeze tugged at his hair and turned every breath to fog. ''It's up to you whether or not you want to wear it.''

Stopping by the passenger door of his black Lexus SUV, she glanced down at her hand once more. To her, the ring represented his thoughtfulness. To him, it clearly meant nothing.

''Listen,'' he continued, as he noted the time, ''I need to get back to the office. With everyone gone, I'll be able to make some serious headway on that year-end report. I know you want to finish packing your apartment,'' he said, as if to point out that he wasn't the only one with plans that afternoon. ''But we could go to lunch first, if you want.''

The offer brought her head up, and a wry gleam of relief, and understanding, to her eyes. His suggestion had been prompted only by a gentlemanly sense of obligation. She was sure of it. And she was more than willing to let him off the hook.

"You don't want to go to lunch with me, Lucas. I know how preoccupied you get when there's something you want to finish," she explained when he scowled. "You'd spend the whole time in the restaurant wishing you were working."

"Not the whole time," he muttered, unable to totally deny the truth of her conclusion.

"Most of it. I know you. And I know how anxious you are to finish that report. Why don't I just pick up a sandwich at the deli for you? Do you want me to come back with you and help?"

She stood two feet in front of him, her expression expectant as she waited for him to reply. The breeze tugged a strand of her dark hair over her forehead, her cheeks were pink from the cold, and Lucas's only thought at that moment was how tempted he was to lean down and finish what had barely started back in Andy's chambers. He'd suspected that her lips would be soft. He'd even braced himself for the silken feel of her skin when he'd slipped his hand along the side of her throat and tipped her face to his. He just hadn't anticipated the razor-edged jolt of desire that had ripped through him when he'd heard her breath catch.

She'd reached for him. Whether to steady herself or to urge him closer, he didn't know. All he knew for sure was that she wasn't immune to his touch.

That knowledge was incredibly seductive, incredibly dangerous. His heart hadn't been in the vows they'd just taken, but he took the commitment he'd made to her and her child seriously. Sex would only complicate their relationship, and he wasn't about to complicate it any more than they already had.

"There won't be anything for you to do until I've gone over all the department reports. Just give me a couple of hours. Will you be finished packing by then?"

"Pretty much. I need more empty boxes, though. I thought I'd stop at the supermarket and see if they have any I can take."

"Isn't there a tree lot near there?"

"Right next door. Why?"

Puzzled, she'd tilted her head, exposing where he'd cupped the side of her neck.

Her skin had felt so soft, he thought, his fingers curling in his pocket at the remembered feel of it. So, incredibly, impossibly soft.

"I noticed you didn't have one when I picked up some of your things last night. And I didn't put one up because I wasn't planning on being here." Aware that he was rubbing his thumb, he made a fist. "I was just thinking we should get one."

Sarah hadn't realized how stressful the morning had been until she felt the knot of nerves in her stomach slowly began to untangle. This year had been the first since she was twelve years old that she hadn't started hauling out Christmas decorations as soon as the flowers in the Thanksgiving centerpiece died. With all the changes and uncertainty she'd been dealing with, she simply hadn't been able to find the spirit.

The spirit suddenly found her, though. Or, maybe,

it was just the smile in Lucas's eyes that filled her with such a warm little glow.

"I think we probably should, too," she replied, preferring to think it was a delayed reaction to the season. It wouldn't be wise to become too susceptible to his smiles. "At least a little one. I'll pick one up."

The smile died. "How little is 'little'?"

"I don't know. Three feet? Maybe four?"

"My ceiling is ten feet high. It'd look like a sapling."

She eyed him dully. "So how big do you want?" she asked, fully prepared to handle the job as she had so many others for him.

His glance raked the length of her coat. "Bigger than you can handle. Especially in your condition."

"I'm pregnant, Lucas. Not disabled. And I'm stronger than I look."

He knew exactly how strong and supple those slender muscles of hers were. "Come on," he muttered, nudging her toward his car.

"Where are we going?"

"To find us a tree."

"I thought you wanted to go back to the office."

"I'm the boss. I decided to give myself the afternoon off."

"To buy a tree?" she asked, genuinely surprised he'd abandoned his report to come with her.

"Can you think of anything you'd rather do?"

At his question, she looked up, her glance grazing the hard line of his jaw, the firm contours of his mouth, the smile moving back into his hooded eyes. Actually, she could think of something. But the possibility of him holding her, just taking her in his arms and letting her feel the security she'd felt so fleetingly before, didn't appear to be an option.

"No," she admitted, since just being with him had its own brand of appeal. "I can't."

"It looked smaller on the lot."

Sarah stood with her hands on the hips of her toast-colored leggings, her fingers covered by her baggy tan sweater. Lucas was behind the nine-foot monster that had overtaken the far corner of his living room. Beyond the large windows angled to it, dusk had given way to darkness and the distant glow of multi-colored lights from the homes farther down the hill.

Fir boughs rustled as he stepped into view. "I told you it was bigger than you thought."

"The other one you liked wasn't that much shorter."

"Only by two feet," he mumbled. "We won't have enough lights."

"Well, the shape on this one is better," she said in defense. "And you said you wanted a big tree."

That was true enough, Lucas admitted to himself, his attention on the string of lights he was trying to untangle. But *she* was the one who'd said his tree had to be perfect, or as close to it as they could find—which was why they'd hit half the lots on the east side of town before they found the one he'd wrestled inside.

He hadn't pointed out that it was actually *their* tree. All afternoon and evening she'd seemed as determined as he was to keep conversation normal, and away from the little legality they'd tended to barely eight hours ago. There was nothing to discuss now that it was done, anyway. Beyond that, he hadn't wanted to do anything to escalate the subtle tension that had underscored every moment since they'd left the courthouse.

It was there even now, quietly smoldering like a spark under ash, harmless, provided it remained buried. As long as they were working, that faint unease could be ignored. Working with her felt familiar and easy, even if they hadn't worked on this particular project before.

"Isn't this one of the strings we just bought?"

Frowning at the tangle trailing along the floor, he held up a strand of tiny white lights. They'd swung by her apartment and picked up her clothes and her Christmas decorations, since he didn't have any, and bought more trimmings and lights. They'd stopped for a pizza, too, pepperoni and black olive, since she'd been craving it. The remnants were somewhere among the piles of boxed ornaments occupying the coffee table.

"I have no idea," Sarah replied, unable to tell from where she stood opening another box of lights herself. "Why?"

"It's knotted."

"Let me see."

"You don't have your glasses," he muttered. "I can do it. I just need better light."

"I don't need my glasses to do that," she informed him, watching him work at the knot as he moved toward the brass lamp on the end table. "I only wear them at the computer.

"Lucas," she said, patiently, when he ignored her.

''It really would be easier if you'd let me do it. That knot is small and your fingers...aren't.''

''It's the principle.''

''What principle? It's a knot, not a personal obstacle.''

He glanced up. Giving her a blandly level look, he held out the cord.

Matching his expression, she took it.

Thirty seconds later, she held up the string, knot-free, and determinedly bit back a look of triumph.

He should move, Lucas told himself. He should go back to the tree and ignore the way her eyes sparkled with amused tolerance. He should forget how her curvy little body had fit his, and if he had the brains God gave a goat, he'd stop thinking about her lush, lovely mouth.

While he was at it, he should also stop breathing. Her fresh scent wrapped around him, seductive as the arms of a lover as he reached for the lights she held.

''If you say I told you so, I'll fire you.''

She didn't look particularly threatened. But with her smiling at him, he knew he didn't care about what he should do. He knew what he was going to do, though. He'd give her all the time she needed to step away herself, but if she didn't, he was going to put an end to the speculation that had taunted him all afternoon.

Sarah felt the string slip from her hand as Lucas took it—and let it quietly drop to the floor beside him. He wasn't touching her. He wasn't doing anything but watching her as her smile slowly faded and his glance settled on her mouth. Yet, she felt herself being drawn toward him as surely as if he'd curled his fingers around her arms and pulled her to him himself.

She didn't realize she'd reached for him until she felt the strong, steady beat of his heart where her fingers rested against the granite wall of his chest. Something primitive sparked in his eyes at her touch, something feral and thrilling, and quickly banked as he curved his hand over her shoulder and tugged her closer.

His eyes glittered on hers a scant second before he slipped his fingers up through her hair and lowered his head. The warm male scent of him filled her lungs as he brushed his lips over hers once. Then, again. And again.

Each touch was brief, teasing. No more than what they'd shared in the judge's chambers. Only this time, there was an experimental edge to the contact. It was as if he wanted to see what she would do before he pushed any farther, and would go no farther than she would allow.

As his lips grazed hers once more, she let hers part—and felt her knees go weak when his tongue swept inside her mouth.

Sensation flooded her. The velvet softness of his tongue. The heady flavor of him. The strength of his arms as he gathered her closer, supporting her, molding her to him. His heat stole through her body, flowing through her like warm honey, drugging her, stealing her sense, her will. She remembered thinking before that if he ever put his heart into a kiss, the effect could be devastating. Beyond that, she couldn't seem to think at all.

She wants this.

The thought ripped through Lucas, blowing ash from that smoldering spark and fueling hunger like gasoline thrown on open flame. She clung to him, letting him deepen the kiss, allowing his hands to shape the long line of her back, the gentle roundness of her hips. All he'd wanted was to put an end to the curiosity that had distracted him all afternoon. He'd thought that, if he kissed her, he wouldn't have to wonder how she would taste, how she would respond.

She'd come to him as if she trusted him completely.

He eased her closer, urging her arms around his neck and pressing her the length of his body. He'd gotten what he wanted. But it wasn't enough. He now knew that the sweet taste of her was as addictive as a drug, and like a forbidden substance that made a man crave, he needed more. He wanted to know the shape of her breasts, the texture of her nipples, how they would feel growing against his tongue. She trembled at his touch when he grazed one turgid peak, and a kittenish sound vibrated low in her throat when he trailed his lips to her ear. But he wanted to know what she would do at the touch of his hands on her bare skin, and hear her breath catch when he entered her.

The thought of her moving beneath him pumped pure fire through his veins. Digging his fingers into the firm flesh of her hips, he aligned her more intimately with his lower body. As he pulled her closer, he swept the gentle roundness of her belly with this thumbs.

The feel of that soft swell made him go still.

He was breathing hard when sanity hit and he slowly raised his head. His libido had taken over, making mush of his brains and making him all but forget that she was carrying a child. But even if remembering her condition hadn't reminded him to treat her more gently, he didn't trust the demanding need that had caught him in its grip.

He needed a secretary. Not a bed partner. Though the thought of having her in his bed did its best to sabotage his resolve, the practical part of him, the only rational part at the moment, knew the only way to preserve the status quo was to keep his hands to himself.

"I'm sorry, Sarah." Without thinking, he started to smooth her hair, only to catch himself before he could touch her again. "That shouldn't have—"

"Don't. Please." She stepped back, trembling as she unfisted her fingers from his shirt and pressed her hand to the nerves in her stomach. He'd branded her with his touch, all but robbed her of her senses. Yet, the moment he'd been reminded of her pregnancy, his guard had slammed into place as firmly as a wind-blown door. "Let's just say we were both curious and leave it at that."

She turned away, breathing deeply and doing her best to hide her embarrassment. She'd only been intimate with one man in her entire life, and she hadn't dated many others, but she knew she'd never felt the unquestioned abandon she'd experienced in his arms. It had felt as if being close to him were the most natural thing in the world—until he'd frozen. "Shall we get the lights on the tree?"

For several long seconds, she sensed nothing but

a heavy, unnerving stillness behind her. Then, mercifully, she heard the soft tick of glass bulbs bump each other as he picked up the string he'd dropped. "Yeah," he murmured. "Sure."

With her back to him, she reached for another box, judiciously concentrating on opening the tabs. "Do you want to string them or should I?"

She could almost feel his hesitation, and his relief. "You can do the bottom. I'll do the top. I don't want you up on the ladder."

Any other time, she might have told him she was perfectly capable of handling the task. After all, it wasn't as if she were far enough along for her center of gravity to have shifted. Her balance was fine. With the tension shimmering through the room, she let her independent streak slide and settled for telling him that was fine.

She didn't blame him for pulling back from her the way he had. He wanted to be her baby's father, and that made him truly special to her. But as extraordinary and kind as she'd discovered him to be, she couldn't imagine him wanting her when she was carrying another man's child. She couldn't imagine him truly wanting her, period. He'd made it as clear as the crystal icicles on the coffee table that he had no interest in a real relationship.

She'd known that going into their agreement, and she'd accepted his terms when she'd said her vows.

She just hadn't anticipated the strain between them that had him edgy, her uneasy and both of them trying very hard to pretend things were just fine when they obviously weren't.

# Chapter 6

Lucas never realized how much noise he made in the mornings until he tried to leave without waking Sarah. Never before had he thought about the squeak in the front closet door, how loud his footfall was in the hallway or what sort of racket the coffee grinder made. Considering it all as he quietly moved past her closed door, he decided that he didn't need a jacket—his sweater was heavy enough—and that he wouldn't bother with coffee until he got to the office. He had a project he was now behind on because he'd blown yesterday afternoon getting married and buying a tree and he didn't want to lose any more time getting sidetracked by Sarah should she walk in.

He had already planned to work that day, but his conscience made him acknowledge that the year-end report wasn't the real reason he was flying out the door while the sun was still struggling to rise. After

the restless night he'd spent achingly conscious of
Sarah sleeping on the other side of his bedroom wall,
the last thing he needed was to see her looking all
warm and sleepy and touchable. At the office, there
was a professionalism about her attitude and attire
that overshadowed her subtle sensuality. Here,
stripped of those barriers, that sensuality was almost
all he saw.

He needed distance. He figured she did, too. Especially after the way she'd claimed a headache long
before they could finish the tree last night and closed
herself in her room. So he left a note on the kitchen
table that he'd be at the office until around six. Forcing his thoughts to the report, he didn't even think
about it being Christmas Eve—until he walked back
in the door nearly eleven hours later.

His condo had been as dark and quiet as Tut's
tomb when he'd slipped out that morning. When he
opened the door from the garage to the kitchen that
evening, he was greeted by the glow of lights, the
metallic clank of a utensil against a pot and the me-
lodic strains of Amy Grant promising that she'd be
home for Christmas.

It felt odd to walk into his home and find someone
already there. Odd and a little unnerving considering
that this was the one place he'd been able to escape
the stresses of the day. Tonight, though, the stresses
had come with him. All of them having to do with
**Sarah. His next thought** was that whatever she was
cooking smelled absolutely delicious.

She stood at the stove, her cheeks flushed from the
heat and her dark hair pulled back from the delicate

contours of her face with a length of red satin ribbon.
In the black sweater she wore over slim red slacks,
she looked as slender and supple as a willow branch.

She also looked decidedly wary.

"Hi." She offered a small smile, the expression
seeming even more strained than it had last evening.
"You said you'd be back around six, so I planned
dinner for seven. I thought you'd want time to relax
and have a drink...or whatever it is you normally do
when you get home." Looking conspicuously conscious of the fact that she had no idea what his normal routine was, she motioned toward the living
room with her spoon. "There's a fire in the fireplace."

He could see that. On the other side of the large
open space, a fire crackled and blazed in the flagstone
hearth, welcoming him, urging him to warm himself
with its heat. Leaving his briefcase on a counter stool
on his way across the room, he could also see that
she'd set red candles and fir boughs on the mantel,
and finished decorating the tree. In the glow of the
tiny white tree lights and the flickering fire, he
hunched down beside the single gift nestled under the
sweeping branches.

It was for him.

From her.

"How much rum do you put in your eggnog?"

"You bought eggnog?" he asked, his knees cracking as he rose and frowned toward the kitchen.

"You said it was tradition in your family to have
it on Christmas Eve."

She emerged from behind the wall, carrying salt
and pepper shakers to the table she'd already set with

plates and soup bowls and a holly and evergreen centerpiece.

"They do. But I've never cared for the stuff. I usually stick with scotch and water." More interested in the package under the tree than talk of the artery-clogging concoction of eggs and cream the rest of his family consumed by the quart, he picked up the thin gold box and walked over to where Sarah fussed with an already perfectly placed napkin.

It wasn't like her to fidget. But that's what she seemed to be doing in the moments before she noticed what he held and started fiddling with the placement of the plate.

"You got me a present." Thinking she looked as tense as he felt, he lifted the box in his hand. "You didn't have to do that."

He could only see her profile, but he was close enough to catch the faint furrow that came and went from her brow. He was even more conscious of her fresh, powdery scent and how it mingled with the perfume of evergreen and cooking spice. The combination tugged at elemental hungers, tightening his stomach, his body, invading memories the scent of pine always evoked of Christmases past.

The thought of how thoroughly she was invading his life barely registered. "I'm sorry. I don't have anything for you."

"I didn't expect anything," she replied, slipping past him. "And what I got you isn't all that much. It's just something you need."

Glass clinked as she hurriedly snatched up two mugs and a quart of eggnog from the counter and put them away. Curious, unable to imagine what she thought he needed, since he couldn't think of a single thing himself, Lucas fingered the tail of the red bow. The inch-wide red satin looked suspiciously like the length of the rich, shiny ribbon restraining Sarah's gleaming hair.

"May I open it now?"

He wasn't sure what it was, but something about the way she hesitated made him think she rather wished he hadn't found it.

"That's up to you. By the way," she continued, resigning herself to the fact that he had as she opened a cupboard, "one of your brothers called about an hour ago. Mike," she said, identifying his oldest sibling. Mike had sounded surprised that a female had answered Lucas's home phone—until she'd identified herself as his brother's secretary. She'd also told him that she was there decorating a tree for his brother, which was the truth, as far as it went. Mike didn't seem to think her explanation of her presence was at all unusual. That alone told her Lucas's whole family knew how much of his life she took care of for him.

"Your family is all at your parents' house. I told him you were at the office if he wanted to call you there, but he said they'd call back after they finished eating."

Taking down a highball glass, she filled it with ice and set it where the eggnog mugs had been moments ago. Lucas was used to her proficiency. He appreciated, even expected it at the office. But her movements in the moments before she glanced up to see that he'd opened the letter-sized box seemed far more nervous than efficient.

Something was wrong. Something beyond the

knowledge that all they had to do was touch to strike sparks. He just had no idea what it was.

"It's not much," she repeated, pulling his thoughts back to her gift as he unfolded a parchmentlike paper to read what was on it. "But it was the only thing I could think of that you might not buy for yourself."

The certificate was from a local spa, an exclusive place that pampered the rich and the harried. She'd bought him a morning in the men's section.

"They don't allow cell phones or pagers or work of any kind in there," she explained, motioning to what he held. "I only got you a half day instead of a full one because I didn't think you'd take a whole day off just to relax. But you can spend a few hours away from telephones and deadlines while someone rubs the knots out of your neck for you. I figured a couple hours' escape was about all you could take."

She was right. No way would he take off a whole day to do nothing. He'd go out of his mind. "How do you know I have knots in my neck?"

For the first time since he'd come in, she finally met his eyes. When she did, the look she gave him said he had to be kidding. "I work with you, Lucas. A dozen times a week, I walk into your office and you're rubbing your neck or your shoulders. You even do it when you're talking to me about something while you pace. That's not the only place you carry your stress," she quietly informed him, "but I thought you might enjoy a massage more than you would a box of antacids."

Since she was the one who kept the antacids stocked in his desk drawer, he was hardly in a position to deny a need for them. He just hadn't realized how far down he'd let his guard with her. In his business position, it was a matter of pride and survival to mask any potential sign of weakness, vulnerability or stress, and he'd always been careful to keep betraying signs of tension under control around his clients and employees.

Around every employee except Sarah, anyway, he thought, just as the telephone rang.

"I've got it," he murmured, not at all sure how he felt about her knowing him that well. "And thank you."

Still wrestling with the thought, he grabbed the portable phone from the breakfast bar. "Hey, big brother. Merry Christmas to you, too. Sarah said I'd missed your call."

Lucas's deep voice suddenly held a smile. Sarah heard it as she started past him, wanting to give him his privacy, wanting a little for herself. She'd wanted badly to do something special for Lucas, to thank him in some small way for what he was doing for her, and make the evening more pleasant than last night had been. After all, the last thing she wanted was for him to regret marrying her. Then, his brother had called the first time. In less than a minute of seemingly benign conversation, she'd realized Lucas was probably regretting it already.

It was only incidental that she'd blown it with the eggnog, and that her present appeared to hold all the appeal of a root canal.

Lucas called to her just before she rounded the corner to disappear into the hall.

"Pick up the phone in the living room, will you?"

he asked, his hand over the mouthpiece of his receiver. "I need to tell them about you."

Tell them about her? "Now?"

"They already want to know what you're doing here. Mike told them you answered the phone before. Come on, Sarah. It's not like you've never talked to any of them."

"But what are you going to say?"

His eyes remained steady on hers as he dropped his hand from the mouthpiece. "Hang on a minute," he said to whoever was on the other end of the line. "You can say Merry Christmas to my wife. Sarah and I got married yesterday."

Just like that. No hesitation. No preamble. Just straightforward and to the point.

She had no idea why her palms were sweating when she picked up the extension from the end table. Before she could get the phone to her ear, she could hear a quartet of chattering voices. His family members were obviously on extensions of their own.

"Lucas. Dear," she heard his mother say, "I know you've said you don't know what you'd do without her, but I never realized you meant it that way. We didn't even know you were dating!"

"Come on, Mom," a deep male voice cajoled. "She's the only woman he's mentioned more than once in the last two years. That had to tell you something."

"Say 'hello,' Sarah," Lucas murmured.

"Hi," she said, aware of how he deliberately ignored his brother's comment.

Mrs. Harding was the first to welcome her to the family. Lucas's sister, Meg, offered her congratulations in chorus with her brothers'. Moments later, his dad came on the line sputtering about the suddenness of the event, though he didn't sound particularly surprised at Lucas's choice of bride. They were all talking and laughing at once and each of them seemed as pleased for Lucas as had his friend, the judge. But what struck Sarah even beyond their genuine pleasure at Lucas's news, was their easy acceptance of her as his wife.

"Hey, Lucas," Mike said, replacing their father on the line again, "you don't have any excuses now. Mom and Dad will expect a grandchild to be in the works by this time next year, you know?"

"Yeah, bro. You've got some serious catching up to do," his brother Jim teased. "Better make it twins. You're way behind the rest of us. Do twins run in your family, Sarah?"

She knew they were teasing. And she tried to put a smile in her voice so they'd think her a good sport when she told them she was sorry, that she'd never heard of any multiple births and that she'd prefer one at a time anyway. But she felt like a fraud. His family obviously believed Lucas was in love with her, and that the two of them would someday have children of their own.

Her hand stole across the slight swell beneath her sweater, her smile fading. The protective motion caught Lucas's eye as he dryly told his brothers to knock it off before he instructed her to ignore them. There was nothing in his voice to indicate he was at all uncomfortable with the track the conversation had taken. The way he rolled his eyes toward the ceiling even made her think he'd dealt with the subject and the good-natured badgering before. Yet, she could tell from the way he pushed his fingers through his hair and started pacing between her and the dining table a few moments later, that he wasn't as unaffected by his brothers' comments as he wanted her—and them—to think.

Fortunately, the call didn't last much longer. Another round of congratulations from his boisterous family was followed by a round of wishes for a merry Christmas. Then, with the last chorus of goodbyes, there were suddenly no more voices, no more reasons to keep up the pretense, and Sarah realized how very quiet the inside of the condo actually was.

In that echoing silence, she reached toward the end table and hung up the phone.

Lucas returned his to its base on the breakfast bar. "I didn't think we should tell them about the baby just yet."

"No. No," she agreed, protectively crossing her arms. "One surprise tonight was enough."

"There was no sense putting it off. Telling them we're married, I mean."

"No," she murmured again. "It's better that it's out of the way."

A muscle in his jaw bunched as he gave her a tight nod. It jerked again when he headed for the cabinet above the refrigerator to take out a bottle of scotch.

"I guess they must have just finished supper," she said, searching for something, anything, else to talk about.

"I guess so. They always have chowder and corn bread."

"And gingerbread for dessert. I know. That's what I made for you."

The dark slashes of his eyebrows bolted together as he glanced up from pouring his drink. "How did you know what Mom always fixes?"

"You told me. The other morning when we were getting your gifts ready to mail," she reminded him as puzzlement pinched his guarded features. "You told me they always had eggnog in front of the fire while they waited for supper to be ready. Then, after you ate, everyone opened one present."

His glance slid from the uneasiness shadowing her face to the package he'd opened and left on the table. Without a word, he walked over to the pot on the stove and lifted the lid.

She had the feeling he suspected what he would find simmering there even before he saw the creamy blend of potatoes and clams. She'd made chowder for him. And gingerbread. A pan of the golden-brown and spicy cake sat cooling farther down the counter. Next to it sat a bowl and the ingredients for corn bread.

The lid clattered lightly as Lucas slid it back into place. He'd thought she would spend the day getting settled in, fixing up her room, or doing whatever it was she did with her time off. Instead, she'd spent it trying to give him some of what he was missing by not being with his family.

"You didn't need to do all this, Sarah."

His back remained to her, his broad shoulders growing wider beneath his olive green sweater as he drew a breath and pushed his hands into the pockets of his khakis. Sarah tightened her arms around herself, wishing he'd turn around, afraid that he would. Twice now, he'd let her know her efforts weren't necessary.

She had always known what to do in her role as his secretary.

She wasn't at all sure what she was supposed to do as his wife.

"I didn't do it because I felt I had to," she said, her voice as quiet as the tick of the hallway clock. "I'm sorry if I've overstepped myself, Lucas. It's Christmas Eve. I hadn't realized until a while ago that you would have preferred to spend it alone."

He swung around. His eyes, sharp as lasers, fixed on hers. "What are you talking about?"

She kept her tone even and her glance level as she forced herself to hold his penetrating gaze. "Your brother was really surprised that you'd gone to the office. He said you told him you'd planned to work at home today." It had been such an innocuous comment, so innocent for what it had revealed. "Evidently you'd told him you were really looking forward to spending the time here because you're not home that much."

She could have sworn she saw guilt shadow his eyes the instant before he picked up his scotch and moved back around the counter. On the way, he took a swallow, lowering his glass as he stopped three feet away. Up close, he didn't look guilty at all. Just cautious, and a little tired.

"I decided it would be easier to work at the office. Everything I needed for the report was there."

"Please, don't do that," she asked, a hollow sensation growing beneath her breastbone. "I know that everything you needed for that report is accessible by computer. You could have worked here on your laptop just as easily.

"This is hard for me, too," she hurriedly confided, refusing to make him defend himself further. The situation was difficult enough without raising any more barriers. "I know it will take time for us to get used to living together. But we won't get anywhere if we're not honest with each other. I hate that you felt you had to stay away from your home because I was here. But I won't know what to do differently until you tell me what you're comfortable with and what you're not."

"I'm not sure we're ready for that much honesty, Sarah."

His words must have sounded like the slam of a door. She blinked at the finality of his response, then dropped her glance to the floor.

"This is about last night, isn't it?" she said, her tone more statement than question. "That's the reason you stayed away today."

His fingers tightened around his glass. "I mean it, this really isn't a good idea."

"It's better than trying to ignore something that's obviously bothering you," she countered stubbornly. "If this *is* about what happened last night, I want you to know I understand that you don't intend for us to have a physical relationship. I mean, we never really talked about it, but you made that clear enough last night. I know it's the baby you want, not me," she explained, hurriedly, because his method of laying things on the line took all the courage she had. "So it's not like you have to avoid me so I'll get the message.''

It was infinitely easier to watch his thumb slowly rub the side of the crystal tumbler than to witness how he digested her little disclaimer. She'd never before melted at nothing more than a man's touch. She'd never craved the feel of a man's arms around her. She could live without sex. It wasn't like the act itself was that big a deal anyway. At least, not in her experience. What she would have liked was for him to just hold her once in a while, but she wasn't about to mention that. Not when his only response to her so far was nothing but silence.

Lucas slowly reached over and set his glass on the table. Sarah was trying as hard as she could to be reasonable, rational. And she was. They did need to be honest with each other. Yet, beneath her bravado, she looked as lost and alone as she had the night she'd told him no one knew about her baby but him.

The knowledge that she was feeling that isolated because of him, made him feel as low as a snake.

''You're right.'' He spoke quietly, his voice grimly determined. ''I stayed away because of you.''

With a quick blink, she started to turn away. Catching her by the shoulders, he stopped her. ''You're the one who wanted to talk about this,'' he reminded her. ''So we will. I'm *not* comfortable with you here,'' he admitted, because she was right about that, too. ''I'm not comfortable with the way I want you. Or with the way I can't seem to get you out of my head. But there's nothing you can do about that.''

He wasn't sure what he could do about it himself,

for that matter—except tell her what he'd realized while trying not to think about her today.

"I do want your baby," he continued since she'd brought it up. "But I want the whole experience. All of it. I just can't figure out how I can do that and keep my hands off you."

He saw her swallow, the slender cords of her neck convulsing as his hands fell away. Touching her wasn't safe. Not when she was looking at him like that, her blue eyes huge and her lush lips parted as she drew a disbelieving breath.

He'd thought he could be with her without wanting her. He'd thought he could live under the same roof and ignore the way her scent lingered in the room after she'd gone. He'd thought he could think of her only as the woman who kept his life organized and on course. But he'd just spent the day acknowledging how impossible his life was going to be living and working with her when the only way to preserve the status quo was to keep his hands to himself.

"I'm not sure I understand," she said, clearly bewildered by his matter-of-fact admissions. "Are you talking about being my birthing coach?"

"I hadn't thought about that. But, yeah," he murmured, thinking about it now. "I want that, too."

"Too?"

The tension only increased. "I want to feel the baby grow, Sarah. I want to feel it move and see if I can hear its heartbeat."

She hadn't considered that he would want to share that much of the experience. She didn't really consider it now. The thought of his hand splayed over her, his ear pressed to her stomach, made her feel a little lightheaded. Or, maybe, it was the knowledge that he couldn't get her out of his mind that had everything feeling a little unreal.

"You can do that, Lucas." Her heart tripped. "You can do anything you want."

Something dangerous flared in his eyes. "Not without touching you."

"No," she whispered. "Not without touching me."

Tension radiated in waves from his big body as he stepped closer. His eyes steady on hers, he slowly skimmed his hand up, moving her sweater with it so the soft knit caressed her thickening waist and the slight curve of her belly.

The tenderness of the motion stole her breath. The austerity in his taut features weakened her knees.

"There is something more that I want," he told her.

"What's that?"

"I want this baby to be mine."

She would have told him it would be. But he wasn't talking about legalities. She realized that the instant she saw the primitive light in his eyes. His hand snaked around her, catching her at the small of her back. Her heart had scarcely jerked against her ribs before his mouth covered hers.

He hadn't said it was her that he wanted. He wouldn't. But she knew that was what he meant. He could tell her he didn't want to want her, and he could tell her he wanted her child. He could tell her what she did to him and what he wanted to do to her, which he did, quite explicitly when he carried his debilitating kiss to her ear, but he would never say anything to make her think he would ever need her the way she feared she needed him.

Later, she might think about how badly she wanted to mean something to him beyond what she did. For now, swamped in sensation as his tongue mated with hers, her only thought was of the mindless need he was creating in her. The hand at her back slid down, urging her closer. She could feel the length of him press against her stomach. He rocked a little, testing, imagining. The motion drew a moan from deep in his chest. Or, maybe, that yearning sound came from her in the moments before she found herself being swept up and into his arms.

His face was taut with need as he carried her down the hall and lowered her to her feet beside his bed. Except for the slash of light from the hall that fell over them, the room was dark. In that intimate, co-cooning light, he pulled the ribbon from her hair, slowly, as if opening a precious gift, and dropped it to the floor. Gathering the tumbling silk in his hands, he lowered his mouth to hers once more.

She melted into him, trembling. He was so very solid, so very...hard. She had wanted him to hold her, but she'd never let herself imagine that he would hold her the way he was now. It was as if he couldn't get close enough, as if he couldn't get enough of her.

The heat of his body flowed into her, his raw power overwhelming her senses. She'd always known he had the power to dominate, and that's what he was doing now, taking over her heart, her will. There was no thought of protest. She'd always known she trusted Lucas. She'd just had no idea how very deep that trust ran.

He slipped his hand under her sweater, shocking her with the touch of his fingers to her bare skin. Soothing her with the nip of his teeth to her earlobe, he nudged the fabric to the middle of her back, flicked open the catch on her bra and drew back to lift lace and soft knit over her head.

He murmured something faintly guttural at the sight of her. She wasn't a big woman, but her body was changing and she was bigger than she had been, the faint blue veins more visible beneath her pale skin.

Suddenly self-conscious, she started to cover herself.

He caught her arm, hunger tightening his features as he drew it away.

He told her she was beautiful. He made her feel that way, too, as he cupped the weight of her breasts and drugged her with the kiss he carried down her throat to one taut bud.

Floating. She'd never before felt as if her body were suspended in nothing but a sea of sensation, but that was exactly how she felt now. Lucas caused little licks of fire to burn through her, softening her in some places, tensing others. He trailed that fire down her belly with his lips and skimmed away her pants and underwear along with the thought that she'd actually known what making love was all about.

His clothes joined hers and he pressed her back to the bed, guiding her down, promising her he would be careful. She couldn't believe she aroused him the way she so obviously did. And she couldn't believe she'd ever thought she could live without this. But, then, she'd never experienced what she felt with

Lucas before. There was gentleness in his touch as he slowly explored her body, a reverence that nearly brought tears to her eyes when she saw the heat and wonder in his. There was need in his touch, too, deliberately banked, leashed like something savage and wild that he didn't trust around her.

It was the primitive part of him she wanted. The essence of him. The part he never let her see.

She whispered his name. He whispered hers back. She told him he was driving her out of her mind.

Lucas didn't know the exact moment want turned to need. He wasn't even sure what he felt for the woman whose breathless words threatened his tenuous grip on control. He knew only that protectiveness and possession were tangled up with pure physical need.

He moved over her, sucking in his breath at the feel of her silken body wrapping around his. And when he entered her, gritting his teeth against the primal urge to drive himself deep, his only thought was that this woman was his.

# Chapter 7

Sarah stood silently in the doorway of Lucas's guest room, trying to visualize it as a nursery. She'd finished unpacking her boxes days ago and added her books to his shelves, but she hadn't spent a night in the cozy space since the evening Lucas had carried her off to his bed.

Warmth gathered low in her belly at the thought. The past six days had been like a dream. The past six nights had been heaven. He was an amazing lover. Gentle at times. Demanding at others. She hadn't realized how little she'd known about men, or herself, until he'd started working past inhibitions she didn't even know she had. But their physical closeness only made her more aware of the emotional distance he would never allow her to breach.

He'd told her he didn't believe in love. To him the word was a crutch, an excuse, a euphemism for something selfish or self-serving. Less than a week ago, she'd agreed with him. Wanted to, anyway. But she knew love existed. She felt it for her child. She felt it for him. And she was only going to get hurt if she didn't protect herself somehow. They could work together. They could share a bed. But he'd told her up front that he didn't want a real marriage—and that meant he'd never let her into his heart.

"Where do you want to put the crib?"

His hand settled on her shoulder, the weight of it warming the chill she'd just felt sweep through her.

"I was thinking about putting it across from the window."

"Good idea." His magical fingers absently massaged her neck. "Away from drafts."

"Lucas?"

"Yeah?"

"If you don't believe in love, how can you care about a child?"

His hand stopped its delicious movements, only to resume a scant second later. "It's different with kids."

She wasn't sure what was pushing her as she slid from his touch and turned to face him. It could have been concern for her child, a need of her own, or nothing more complicated than a surge of hormones. She was pregnant after all, and she had felt awfully needy the past few days. Not that she'd let on to him. "Can you tell me how?"

"It just is." Suddenly cautious, he studied her face. The jade sweater he wore with faded jeans made his hazel eyes look impossibly green. "Children are innocent. They haven't learned how to take advantage of the fact that you care about them.'' His broad shoulders lifted in a shrug. ''I haven't thought about it that much, but I suppose they're more forgiving, too. More…loyal.''

''They care unconditionally,'' she concluded.

''Exactly.''

''So with them,'' she said, desperate to understand him, ''it's not like adults who hide their agendas.''

Furrows dug into Lucas's forehead. She was echoing his own conclusions, yet he didn't care for the way they sounded coming from her. He didn't care for the topic of the conversation at all. But he had a pretty good idea why she'd brought it up.

''Something like that.'' He reached out, touched her hair and let his glance slide to the slight swell beneath her sweatshirt. ''If you're worrying that I won't care about the baby, you can stop. Kids really need you to be there for them. And I'll be there for this one. In any way I can. I promise you that, Sarah.''

She didn't doubt that he meant exactly what he said. And his promise should have alleviated the anxiety growing steadily inside her. Yet, as he'd spoken of how a child wouldn't deceive, or manipulate or betray, all she'd really heard were all the ways he would never truly trust her.

''Thank you for that,'' she murmured, unable to imagine how he could ever count on her the way she was coming to count on him. He'd said people confused love with dependency. For the life of her, she couldn't see what was wrong with people depending on each other. With sharing. ''I know you'll care about the baby, Lucas.'' She offered him a smile, one that looked a little sadder than she would have liked. Her child was the reason he'd married her, after all. Of course he would care about it. "You'll be a wonderful father."

"I'd settle for being a good one. You look pale," he observed, as much to change the subject as to let her know he was concerned about her. "Are you still feeling sick?"

She shook her head, wishing she could shake off the melancholy that had settled over her. "It didn't last very long this morning. I just need some exercise. If you're going to be here working, I think I'll go for a walk."

He didn't look as if he wanted to let her go. But they had reached a tacit agreement to give each other their space. She was giving him his now by backing off a subject he really didn't want to discuss. He was giving her hers by not questioning her withdrawal. The arrangement would work if she let it, and she fully intended to keep her end of their agreement. She would just never have the closeness with him that she was coming to crave.

It was too late to worry about what their relationship might have been. She'd just have to learn how to settle for 'close enough,' the way Lucas had.

"Don't forget the party tonight."

At Lucas's reminder, she glanced to where he'd remained in the room's doorway as she took her coat from the closet. It was New Year's Eve and they'd been invited by one of their clients to a party at the Mountview Ski Lodge. Many of the more prominent families in town would be there, along with the Irvings and the Parkers—which was why she couldn't get too excited about the evening. The two families had been rivals forever—ever since one of the grandfathers stole the other guy's wife, anyway. The last thing she wanted was to spend the evening among people who could barely be civil to each other.

"Don't worry. I'll get some rest before we go."

She was sure that was the reason for his reminder. The evening was important from a business standpoint and he wouldn't want her turning into a pumpkin before midnight. She'd make sure she held up her end of the deal. After all, he had pointed out that one of the advantages of marrying her was that he no longer had to worry about scraping up dates.

She really did need to do something to get her mind out of the rut it was caught in. Telling him she'd be back in a while, she buttoned her coat to her neck and slipped out the door.

It had been overcast when Sarah left shortly before ten o'clock that morning. By noon, it had started to snow.

By two o'clock, the crystalline flakes had blanketed everything in sight and Sarah had yet to return.

To Lucas, four hours was more than enough time to get a little exercise. The longest walk she'd ever taken before hadn't lasted even two.

He stood at the window in his living room, scanning the tree-lined street below. A few sets of tire tracks meandered down the hill, parallel lines of black in a blanket of white. There was no sign of Sarah, though.

His brow pinched as he drew a deep breath and tried to think of where she would have gone that was

taking her so long. The heady scent of evergreen
from the tree beside him momentarily short-circuiting
the thought. He'd never again breathe that scent without thinking of how charming she'd looked with her
nose wrinkled and her hands on her hips as she'd
tried to decide between the tall skinny tree they
hadn't bought and the tall fat one they had.

He doubted he'd forget, either, all the trouble she'd
gone to for him on Christmas Eve.

Maybe she stopped at the shopping center, he mentally muttered, jerking his thoughts back to where she
might be. Or maybe she'd walked over to a friend's
house. Either was possible. It just seemed to him that
she would have called to tell him that. She'd said
she'd get some rest, too, and that meant she should
be there now, putting up her feet or taking a nap. He
wanted her to enjoy the evening and she wouldn't if
she was tired.

The thick flakes were falling more heavily when
he turned from the window.

There was one other possibility, one that filled him
with a certain unease, but felt far more likely than
the chance that she'd just lost track of time. He'd
known when she left that something was bothering
her. He'd also suspected it had something to do with
him. She'd have mentioned what it was, otherwise.
They could talk about anything. Except how they felt
about each other.

He had the feeling now, though, that when she'd
asked if he could really care about a child, she'd really been asking if he could ever care deeply about
her.

Since she'd been gone, he'd been thinking about that, too.

The admission had him shoving his fingers through his hair as he stared at the artwork for an ad campaign strewn over the dining table. With Myer and Hutchins closed for the New Year holiday, he could have worked at the office uninterrupted. It would certainly have been easier than hauling the oversized boards and files to his condo.

He'd wanted to be home, though. With his wife.

His wife.

It took a moment for the word to sink in. A long, still moment that froze his breath in his lungs and made his whole body to go utterly still.

He'd never before thought of Sarah as his...*wife*. He'd always thought of her only as...Sarah. He'd thought of her as his right arm, the one person he could depend on. He'd thought of her as someone he liked being with and talking to and, lately, constantly, he'd thought of her as the most seductive, incredibly sensual woman he'd ever known. Just knowing that she would slip into his arms and he could carry her off to his bed at the end of the day, made the days painfully long, and the nights exquisite. They came together like lovers who'd been together forever instead of only a week and after they'd made love, she would lie with him in the dark, talking about their plans for their child, sharing their concerns, their hopes.

Sharing. They did share, he realized. Their days. Their nights. Their dreams.

He shoved aside a manila folder, pulling out the portable phone buried under it. He had the feeling he knew where Sarah had gone—the only place she could go where she wouldn't feel like she was on someone else's turf.

He wouldn't think about what he was going to say when he saw her. Right now, he just needed to know she was safe.

Sarah was on her knees, cleaning the bathtub in her old apartment, when she heard the heavy rap on her door. Thirty minutes ago, Lucas had called and told her he was on his way over. She'd been surprised that he'd known where she was, but he hadn't seemed interested in discussing anything on the phone. He'd just said they'd talk when he got there.

Peeling off her yellow rubber gloves, she crossed the empty living room, flipped open the lock and moved back as the door swung in.

Lucas stepped inside, looking very large. Very imposing. Snow clung to his silvering sable hair and the wide shoulders of his heavy jacket. In one hand, he carried a small, not-so-neatly wrapped package. With his other, he closed out the icy breeze. He didn't say a word as the door clicked shut, but his glance swept her face with a thoroughness that made her pulse go thready.

She looked away, wanting badly to hide the yearning she'd yet to escape. "I didn't notice the time until you called," she told him, feeling badly about that. "Or how much it had snowed. I didn't mean for you to have to come after me." She tipped her head, offered an apologetic smile. "How did you know I was here?"

He took a step closer, watching as she set her

gloves on the windowsill beside her. "Instinct, I guess. I had the feeling when you left that you might need to be someplace that felt more like yours than mine for a while."

The frankness of his conclusion was as disquieting as its truth. "Lucas—"

"It's okay," he assured, saving her from explaining what he obviously already understood. "Your life's been pretty much uprooted in the past couple of weeks." His voice dropped. "I was just worried about you."

His last words, quiet as they'd been, seemed to echo between them as he glanced around the room. The place smelled of Lysol disinfectant and lemon oil and was bare of personal possessions. In the past week, everything she owned had been moved to his condo.

"What have you been doing?"

"Cleaning," she told him, wondering at what he'd just admitted. She hadn't expect that he'd be worried. But, then, she'd had expected that he would somehow know her better than she knew herself. When she'd left, she hadn't even realized where she was going—until she'd found herself in the middle of the apartment, wondering why she couldn't simply be happy with everything she had with Lucas instead of wanting more. "I told my landlady I'd have everything done by the tenth so I can get my deposit back."

The physical tasks had helped chase away those nagging thoughts. Work always did.

Wanting to avoid them now, she nodded toward his hand. "What's that?"

His glance fell to the box. "Your Christmas present," he said, holding it out.

He looked a little uncertain as she warily eyed him and took the oddly light, foot-long box. The red and green wrapping paper looked suspiciously like that from a roll they'd used for his nieces and nephews, and while the corners weren't exactly square, he'd tied it with ribbon and stuck on a bow.

The thought of him wrapping the box himself made her chest feel a little tight. It was such a sweet thing for him to do. But, then, it was just like him to do something that made her care for him more and more by the minute.

Unable to imagine what he'd given her, or why, she pulled on the ribbon and untaped the ends.

She was still unable to imagine what the gift was when she lifted the lid and stared down at a thousand tiny little pieces of paper.

When she glanced up, she thought he sounded as guarded as he looked.

"It's the prenuptial agreement you signed," he told her. "Original and copy."

She had no idea what he saw in her face in the moments before she looked back down at the thick confetti of pale blue and white papers. She wasn't even sure what she felt. Shock was somewhere in there, though. Along with confusion and an aching sense of hope.

"Why?" was all she could manage to say.

"Because I'd rather have you as my wife than my secretary. I'd prefer having you as both," he admitted. "For now, anyway. But I wanted you to know which is more important to me."

Taking the box from her, he set it on the windowsill beside them and reached for her hand. The platinum ring on her finger gleamed in the pale light as he looked down at it. "I want to share everything I have with you, Sarah." His thumb slipped over the wide band as he looked up. "We're already sharing everything else."

He sounded as reasonable as he had the morning he'd pointed out how practical their marrying would be. It was the look in his eyes that was so unlike him. He looked pensive, and oddly subdued.

"You want...a real marriage?"

"Yeah," he murmured, lacing his fingers through hers. "I want that very much."

She felt a little weak. He must have sensed that because he slipped their joined hands to the small of her back, drawing her lower body against his while his eyes searched hers.

"I need you, Sarah." He'd needed her all along. He just hadn't realized how much or in how many ways. Andy had known though. And his family. It was as if they'd known how he'd felt about her before he'd even realized it himself. "I think I've been in love with you for a very long time."

She shook her head, fisted her free hand against his heart. Her own leapt wildly in her chest. "You don't believe in love."

"Maybe," he said, his chiseled features beautifully grave, "that's because I'd never really known what it was."

The hope she'd felt broke free, filling her chest with unbearable joy.

"Lucas," she whispered, because it was all she could say.

"Sarah," he whispered back.

"I love you, too."

His devastating smile stole through the somberness. "You do?"

"Oh, yes," she murmured, slipping her hand along the hard line of his jaw. "I do." She fallen in love with him the moment he'd said he was willing to help raise her child. But the seeds of that love had been planted long before that. The respect had always been there, the affection, the trust. "You can't believe how much."

She didn't know if he drew her closer, or if she closed the distance herself. But she'd no more caught the wonderfully possessive gleam in his eyes than his lips were on hers and he was doing what only he could do. Altering her heart rate and her breathing and making her feel as if there were no place she'd rather be than right there in his arms.

His breathing wasn't so even itself when long moments later, he nuzzled her neck, nipped her earlobe. "Do we have to go to that party tonight?"

"Afraid so," she said on a sigh. "We're guests of a client."

"Cancel."

"Too late."

"Then how about we get a room there and spend the weekend? It's not much of a honeymoon, but the ski lodge is nice and it'll do until we can plan something better."

"It's not going to be that romantic," she warned him, shivering as he nipped again. "I have a friend who works registration at the lodge and she said the Irvings and the Parkers will be there.''

He chuckled, his breath warm against her neck. ''You make it sound like the Hatfields and the Mc-Coys.''

''Close enough. There's bound to be friction.''

He lifted his head. Something deliciously wicked carved his handsome features as he drew both her hands up so her arms were looped around his neck. ''In that case, we'll just hole up in our room and rely on room service. I promise,'' he murmured, a scant inch from her lips, ''they could cause an avalanche up there, and we won't notice.''

\* \* \* \* \*

*Find out what happens when
mortal enemies Anne Parker and
Brad Irving are unexpectedly snowbound
together in Doreen Robert's*

*A VERY...PREGNANT NEW YEAR'S,*

*Coming only to
Silhouette Intimate Moments
in December 2000*

*And now for a sneak preview of*

*A VERY...PREGNANT NEW YEAR'S,*

*please turn the page.*

# Chapter 1

"Don't touch me!" Anne Parker pushed long, wispy strands of hair out of her eyes and glared at the boy towering over her. She was doing her very best not to cry. After all, she was seven years old. Only babies cried. But she sure felt like crying.

She'd landed in a pile of mushy snow and her pants were wet. The other kids in the schoolyard were staring at her. They made her feel stupid. Worse than that, it was Bradley Irving she'd run into, and he made her feel even more stupid.

He looked down at her and shoved his hands deep into the pockets of his jacket. "I wasn't going to touch you. You can sit there all afternoon for all I care."

"It's all your fault," she said furiously. "You pushed me down."

Bradley scowled at her. "It was your fault. You ran into me."

She frowned back to show him she wasn't afraid, even though her heart was banging against her ribs. Bradley had yellow hair and dark blue eyes, and looked like the fierce Viking in her history book. Quickly she looked down at her knee. It was bleeding and had bits of dirt in it. And it hurt.

Her parents had warned her to stay away from Bradley Irving. They called him a delinquent. She wasn't exactly sure what that meant, but it sounded a lot like that picture of the Viking.

When Anne asked questions about Bradley, her parents always said the same thing. He was an Irving and all the Irvings were trouble.

Sometimes she found that hard to understand. He had a really nice face, and once she'd seen him smile at another girl. Seeing him like that had made her feel all warm and squishy inside. Still, her parents were always right and they knew best, as her mother was always telling her. After all, Bradley was ten— almost a teenager.

"You'd better get that dirt washed out of there," Bradley said, making her jump. "Or you'll have to get your leg cut off."

His words scared her. Blinking hard, she looked up at him. "You go away, Bradley Irving, and leave me alone. I don't want to talk to you. You're a...a...delinquent!"

His eyes grew darker, and he pushed his chin out, scaring her even more. "And you're a stuck-up spoiled brat."

"I'm not a brat, so there!" Helpless to stop the

tears spurting from her eyes, Anne scrambled to her feet. "I hate you, Bradley Irving."

"Yeah? Well, I hate you, too, Annie Parker. So that makes us even."

He spun around and marched away from her.

Anne watched him go, feeling really bad inside. She didn't really hate him. And she really didn't want him to hate her, either. Confused by feelings she didn't understand, she pulled in her breath to yell her parting shot. "And my name's not Annie. It's Anne—so there!"

The memory of that day haunted Anne throughout her school years. She plagued her mother with endless questions until she'd learned all about the feud between the Irvings and the Parkers. Years ago, Annie May Wilson had left her husband-to-be, Henry Irving, at the alter and had run away to marry John Parker.

Henry Irving had been so angry he'd secretly bought up Parker land and built a spa on it, which made him a wealthy man. The Parkers claimed he'd used a crooked lawyer and had stolen their land. The two families had been fighting over the land ever since.

During the long, hot summer Anne prepared to attend Burke Senior High, and she kept wondering if she'd bump into Brad Irving. The very first week of her freshman year, she saw Brad in the cafeteria, and her heart did a handspring, though she did her best to ignore him.

One day, Anne missed the bus and had to ride her bike to school. Late for class, she flew down the hall and around the corner, and crashed straight into a tall, firm body coming the other way. She went down on her knees with her books scattered around her, and knew in that instant that she'd run into more trouble than she could handle.

"Nice block," Brad drawled in his deep voice, "but I should warn you, you're a little late to make the team this year."

She glared up at him and muttered, "It's not my fault if you're dumb enough to get in my way."

She scrambled to her feet and collected her books, praying he would just disappear. This was the closest she'd been to him since grade school, and even a fourteen-year-old recognized a heartbreaker when she saw one. With that sexy smile, awesome body and dreamy bedroom eyes, it was no wonder the girls hung around him all the time. Not that *she'd* waste her time on him, of course.

"So where's the fire, anyway?"

She lifted her chin. "None of your business."

"I guess you're still a stuck-up brat, Annie Parker."

"I guess you're still a delinquent. I'd rather be stuck-up than a low-down thief."

Sparks danced in his eyes, but his voice was deceptively quiet when he answered. "Is that right? Well, one day I'll make you and your precious family eat those words, Annie Parker."

She snorted. "When hell freezes over."

"Watch me."

She watched him disappear around the corner before yelling after him, "And my name's not Annie. It's Anne."

After that day the years passed swiftly while she

followed a fascination with architecture and earned
her degree in industrial design. She settled in Denver,
and joined a partnership where she began to make a
name for herself designing new office complexes.

The night she drove into Grand Springs to spend
this year's holidays with her family, Brad Irving was
the furthest thing from her mind. It wasn't exactly a
joyful homecoming. Three months earlier, she'd
called off her wedding plans when she'd discovered
that her fiancé had spent the night in her chief brides-
maid's bed.

Devastated by the betrayal, she'd given up her
apartment, as well as her life in Denver, and was
going home to lick her wounds. There were worse
places to make a living than Grand Springs, she'd
decided. The town was growing, she could make
good use of her talents. And it would be good to be
home, at least for a while.

Dan and Carol Parker welcomed their wounded
daughter with open arms and undisguised sympathy.
Her brother, Paul, pointed out how much better off
she was without the jerk, while Sharon and Elise, her
younger sisters, assured her there were plenty more
apples in the orchard.

Anne had no intention of getting involved with another man. Ever. Convinced that all men were scum,
she had no trouble adding Bradley Irving to that list
when her sisters filled her in on the latest gossip.

Brad, who by now had a successful law practice
right there in Grand Springs, was gaining a reputation
as the town's most eligible bachelor. Since his father
had died two years earlier, leaving Brad sole heir to
his estate, this came as no surprise to Anne. He might

be an Irving, but there was no denying Brad was devastating to look at. That combination of money and looks would be enough to draw the women like flies to a garbage can.

According to her sisters, Brad's conquests were numerous and well publicized. That, and the fact that he was almost thirty and still single, only confirmed Anne's opinion of him. Brad Irving was a no-good womanizer with the manners of a barbarian. No better than a Viking savage.

When Anne discovered that her father had arranged to take the family to Mountview Ski Lodge for the New Year weekend celebrations, she did her best to get out of the popular social event. She just wasn't in the mood for partying. The combined efforts of her parents, sisters and brother failed to change her mind, but when James Parker put in his own plea, she found it impossible to refuse her beloved grandfather.

On the night before New Year's Eve, she reluctantly checked into the lodge, determined to make the best of it for the sake of her family.

After settling into her room, she hurried down the wide stairs to join her family in the dining room for dinner. As she rounded the corner of the crowded lobby, she ran smack into someone coming the other way.

With a surprised yelp, she bounced off the man's muscular body and hit the wall hard with her shoulder.

Anne didn't need to look at the man she'd collided with to recognize him. She'd have known that deep, mocking voice anywhere.

"Are you always this clumsy, Annie Parker, or is this just your way of getting my attention?"

Anne gritted her teeth. It seemed she was destined to spend her life crashing into Brad Irving.

# ATTENTION JOAN JOHNSTON FANS!

Silhouette Books is proud to present

# HAWK'S WAY
## BACHELORS

 The first three novels in
the bestselling Hawk's Way series
now in one fabulous collection!

*On Sale December 2000*

## THE RANCHER AND THE RUNAWAY BRIDE
Brawny rancher Adam Phillips has his hands full when
Tate Whitelaw's overprotective, bossy brothers show up with
shotguns in hand!

## THE COWBOY AND THE PRINCESS
Ornery cowboy Faron Whitelaw is caught off-guard
when breathtakingly beautiful Belinda Prescott proves to be
more than a gold digger!

## THE WRANGLER AND THE RICH GIRL
Sparks fly when Texas debutante Candy Baylor makes handsome
horse breeder Garth Whitelaw an offer he can't refuse!

**HAWK'S WAY: Where the Whitelaws of Texas
run free...till passion brands their hearts.**

*"Joan Johnston does contemporary Westerns to perfection."*
*—Publishers Weekly*

*Available at your favorite retail outlet.*

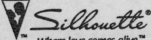

*Where love comes alive*™

Visit Silhouette at www.eHarlequin.com                    PSHWB

If you enjoyed what you just read,
then we've got an offer you can't resist!

## Take 2
## bestselling novels FREE!
## Plus get a FREE surprise gift!

**Clip this page and mail it to The Best of the Best™**

| IN U.S.A. | IN CANADA |
|---|---|
| 3010 Walden Ave. | P.O. Box 609 |
| P.O. Box 1867 | Fort Erie, Ontario |
| Buffalo, N.Y. 14240-1867 | L2A 5X3 |

**YES!** Please send me 2 free Best of the Best™ novels and my free surprise gift. Then send me 4 brand-new novels every month, which I will receive before they're available in stores. In the U.S.A., bill me at the bargain price of $4.24 plus 25¢ delivery per book and applicable sales tax, if any*. In Canada, bill me at the bargain price of $4.74 plus 25¢ delivery per book and applicable taxes**. That's the complete price and a savings of over 15% off the cover prices—what a great deal! I understand that accepting the 2 free books and gift places me under no obligation ever to buy any books. I can always return a shipment and cancel at any time. Even if I never buy another book from The Best of the Best™, the 2 free books and gift are mine to keep forever. So why not take us up on our invitation. You'll be glad you did!

185 MEN C229
385 MEN C23A

| | |
|---|---|
| Name | (PLEASE PRINT) |
| Address | Apt.# |
| City | State/Prov.      Zip/Postal Code |

\* Terms and prices subject to change without notice. Sales tax applicable in N.Y.
\*\* Canadian residents will be charged applicable provincial taxes and GST.
   All orders subject to approval. Offer limited to one per household.
   ® are registered trademarks of Harlequin Enterprises Limited.

BOB00                   ©1998 Harlequin Enterprises Limited

# where love comes alive—online...

## eHARLEQUIN.com

## shop eHarlequin

- ♥ Find all the new Silhouette releases at everyday great discounts.
- ♥ Try before you buy! Read an excerpt from the latest Silhouette novels.
- ♥ Write an online review and share your thoughts with others.

## reading room

- ♥ Read our Internet exclusive daily and weekly online serials, or vote in our interactive novel.
- ♥ Talk to other readers about your favorite novels in our Reading Groups.
- ♥ Take our Choose-a-Book quiz to find the series that matches you!

## authors' alcove

- ♥ Find out interesting tidbits and details about your favorite authors' lives, interests and writing habits.
- ♥ Ever dreamed of being an author? Enter our Writing Round Robin. The Winning Chapter will be published online! Or review our writing guidelines for submitting your novel.

SINTB1

# You're not going to believe this offer!

In October and November 2000, buy any two Harlequin or Silhouette books and save $10.00 off future purchases, or buy any three and save $20.00 off future purchases!

Just fill out this form and attach 2 proofs of purchase (cash register receipts) from October and November 2000 books and Harlequin will send you a coupon booklet worth a total savings of $10.00 off future purchases of Harlequin and Silhouette books in 2001. Send us 3 proofs of purchase and we will send you a coupon booklet worth a total savings of $20.00 off future purchases.

*Saving money has never been this easy.*

## I accept your offer! Please send me a coupon booklet:

Name: _____

Address: _____ City: _____

State/Prov.: _____ Zip/Postal Code: _____

## Optional Survey!

In a typical month, how many Harlequin or Silhouette books would you buy <u>new</u> at retail stores?

☐ Less than 1  ☐ 1  ☐ 2  ☐ 3 to 4  ☐ 5+

Which of the following statements best describes how you <u>buy</u> Harlequin or Silhouette books? Choose one answer only that <u>best</u> describes you.

☐ I am a regular buyer and reader
☐ I am a regular reader but buy only occasionally
☐ I only buy and read for specific times of the year, e.g. vacations
☐ I subscribe through Reader Service but also buy at retail stores
☐ I mainly borrow and buy only occasionally
☐ I am an occasional buyer and reader

Which of the following statements best describes how you <u>choose</u> the Harlequin and Silhouette series books you buy <u>new</u> at retail stores? By "series," we mean books within a particular line, such as *Harlequin PRESENTS* or *Silhouette SPECIAL EDITION*. Choose one answer only that <u>best</u> describes you.

☐ I only buy books from my favorite series
☐ I generally buy books from my favorite series but also buy books from other series on occasion
☐ I buy some books from my favorite series but also buy from many other series regularly
☐ I buy all types of books depending on my mood and what I find interesting and have no favorite series

Please send this form, along with your cash register receipts as proofs of purchase, to:
**In the U.S.:** Harlequin Books, P.O. Box 9057, Buffalo, NY 14269
**In Canada:** Harlequin Books, P.O. Box 622, Fort Erie, Ontario L2A 5X3

(Allow 4-6 weeks for delivery) Offer expires December 31, 2000.          PHQ4002

**Silhouette**

# INTIMATE MOMENTS™

presents a riveting 12-book continuity series:

## a Year of loving dangerously

### *Where passion rules and nothing is what it seems...*

When dishonor threatens a top-secret agency, the brave
men and women of SPEAR are prepared to risk it all as they
put their lives—and their hearts—on the line.

### Available December 2000:

# STRANGERS WHEN WE MARRIED
## by Carla Cassidy

Their courtship was whirlwind, their marriage passionate—and all
too brief. And now that his latest mission had sexy SPEAR agent
Seth Greene sharing a roof with his lovely wife once more, he knew
his greatest challenge lay ahead. For how could he convince his
long-lost bride that their love—their life together—was meant to be?

*Available only from Silhouette Intimate Moments
at your favorite retail outlet.*

**Silhouette®**

*Where love comes alive™*

Visit Silhouette at www.eHarlequin.com          SIMAYOLD7

**#1** *New York Times* **bestselling author**

# NORA ROBERTS

**introduces the loyal and loving, tempestuous and tantalizing Stanislaski family.**

*Coming in November 2000:*

## The Stanislaski Brothers
### Mikhail • Alex

Their immigrant roots and warm, supportive home had made Mikhail and Alex Stanislaski both strong and passionate. And their charm makes them irresistible....

*In February 2001, watch for*
**THE STANISLASKI SISTERS:** *Natasha and Rachel*

*And a brand-new Stanislaski story from Silhouette Special Edition,*
**CONSIDERING KATE**

*Available at your favorite retail outlet.*

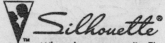

*Where love comes alive*™

Visit Silhouette at www.eHarlequin.com          PSSTANBR2

*Desire*

July 2000
**BACHELOR DOCTOR**
**#1303 by Barbara Boswell**

August 2000
**THE RETURN OF ADAMS CADE**
**#1309 by BJ James**
Men of Belle Terre

September 2000
**SLOW WALTZ ACROSS TEXAS**
**#1315 by Peggy Moreland**
Texas Grooms

October 2000
**THE DAKOTA MAN**
**#1321 by Joan Hohl**

November 2000
**HER PERFECT MAN**
**#1328 by Mary Lynn Baxter**

December 2000
**IRRESISTIBLE YOU**
**#1333 by Barbara Boswell**

**MAN OF THE MONTH**

# MAN OF THE MONTH

For twenty years Silhouette has been giving
you the ultimate in romantic reads. Come join
some of your favorite authors in helping us to
celebrate our anniversary with the most rugged,
sexy and lovable heroes ever!

*Available at your favorite retail outlet.*

Silhouette®

*Where love comes alive*™

Visit Silhouette at www.eHarlequin.com          SDMOM00-3